SUSAN ELIZABETH PHILLIPS

HONEY MOON

POCKET BOOKS

New York   London   Toronto   Sydney   Tokyo   Singapore

An *Original* Publication of POCKET BOOKS

POCKET BOOKS, a division of Simon & Schuster Inc.
1230 Avenue of the Americas, New York, NY 10020

Copyright © 1993 by Susan Elizabeth Phillips

ISBN: 0-671-73593-4

First Pocket Books printing June 1993

13 12 11 10 9 8 7 6 5 4

POCKET and colophon are registered trademarks of Simon & Schuster Inc.

Cover art by Ben Perini

Printed in the U.S.A.

Books by Susan Elizabeth Phillips

Fancy Pants*
Glitter Baby
Honey Moon*
Hot Shot*
Risen Glory

*Published by POCKET BOOKS

In memory of my father

A great roller coaster makes you
find God when you ride it.

—Anonymous

The
Lift Hill

1980–1982

1

All that spring Honey prayed to Walt Disney. From her bedroom in the rear of the rusty old trailer that sat in a clump of pines behind the third hill of the Black Thunder roller coaster, she prayed to God and Walt and sometimes even Jesus in hopes that one of those powerful heavenly figures would help her out. With her arms resting on the bent track that held the room's only window, she gazed out through the sagging screen at the patch of night sky just visible over the tops of the pines.

"Mr. Disney, it's Honey again. I know that the Silver Lake Amusement Park doesn't look like much right now with the water level down so far you can see all the stumps and with the *Bobby Lee* sitting on the bottom of the lake right at the end of the dock. Maybe we haven't had more than a hundred people through the park in the past week, but that doesn't mean things have to stay this way."

Ever since the Paxawatchie County *Democrat* had printed the rumor that the Walt Disney people were thinking about buying the Silver Lake Amusement Park as a location for a South Carolina version of Disney World, Honey hadn't been able to think of anything else. She was sixteen years old, and she knew that praying to Mr. Disney was a childish thing to do (not to mention questionable theology for a Southern Baptist), but circumstances had made her desperate.

Now she ticked off the advantages she wanted Mr. Disney to consider. "We're only an hour from the interstate. And with some good directional signs, everybody on their way to Myrtle Beach would be sure to stop here with their kids. If you don't count the mosquitoes and the humidity, the climate is good. The lake could be real pretty if your employees made the Purlex Paint Company stop dumping their toxics in it. And those people who are carrying on your business now that you're dead could buy it real cheap. Could you use your influence with them? Could you somehow make them understand that the Silver Lake Amusement Park is just what they're looking for?"

Her aunt's thin, listless voice interrupted Honey's combination of prayer and sales presentation. "Who're you talkin' to, Honey? You don't have a boy in that bedroom, do you?"

"Yeah, Sophie," Honey replied with a grin. "I got about a dozen in here. And one of 'em is gettin' ready to show me his dingdong."

"Oh, my, Honey. I don't think you should talk like that. It's not nice."

"Sorry." Honey knew she shouldn't bait Sophie, but she liked it when her aunt fussed over her. It didn't happen very often, and nothing ever came of it, but when Sophie fussed, Honey could almost pretend she was her real mother instead of her aunt.

A burst of laughter sounded from the next room as the *Tonight Show* audience responded to one of Johnny's jokes about peanuts and President Carter. Sophie always had the television on. She said it kept her from missing Uncle Earl's voice.

Earl Booker had died a year and a half ago, leaving Sophie the owner of the Silver Lake Amusement Park. She hadn't exactly been a ball of fire when he was alive, but it was even worse now that he was dead, and Honey was pretty much in charge of things. As she drew back from the window, she knew it wouldn't be much longer before Sophie fell asleep. She never lasted much past midnight even though she hardly ever got out of bed before noon.

Honey propped herself up against the pillows. The trailer was hot and airless. Despite the fact that she was wearing only an orange Budweiser T-shirt and a pair of underpants, she couldn't get comfortable. They used to have a window air conditioner, but it had broken down two summers ago just like everything else, and they couldn't afford to replace it.

Honey glanced at the dial on the clock sitting next to the bed she shared with Sophie's daughter, Chantal, and felt a twinge of alarm. Her cousin should have been home by now. It was Monday night, the park was closed, and there wasn't anything to do. Chantal was central to Honey's backup plan if Mr. Disney's employees didn't buy the park, and Honey couldn't afford to misplace her cousin, not even for an evening.

Swinging her feet down off the bed onto the cracked linoleum, she reached for the pair of faded red shorts she'd worn that day. She was small-boned, barely five feet tall, and the shorts were hand-me-downs from Chantal. They were too big for her hips and hung in baggy folds that made her toothpick legs seem even skinnier than they were. But vanity was one of the few faults Honey didn't possess, so she paid no attention.

Although Honey couldn't see it herself, she in fact had some cause for vanity. She had thickly lashed light blue eyes topped by dark slashes of brow. Her heart-shaped face held small cheekbones dusted with freckles and a pert little excuse for a nose. But she hadn't quite grown into her mouth, which was wide and framed by full lips that always reminded her of a big old sucker fish. For as long as she could remember, she had hated the way she looked, and not just because people had mistaken her for a boy until her small breasts had poked through, but because no one wanted to take a person seriously who looked so much like a child. Since Honey very much needed to be taken seriously, she had done her best to disguise every one of her physical assets with a perpetually hostile scowl and a generally belligerent attitude.

After slipping on a pair of flattened blue rubber flip-flops that had long ago conformed to the bottoms of her feet, she shoved her hands through her short, chewed hair. She performed this action not to straighten it but to scratch a mosquito bite on her scalp. Her hair was light brown, exactly the same color as her name. It liked to curl, but she seldom gave it the opportunity. Instead, she cut it whenever it got in her way, using whatever reasonably sharp implement happened to be handy: a pocketknife, a pair of pinking shears, and, on one unfortunate occasion, a fish scaler.

She closed the door behind her as she slipped out into a short, narrow hallway carpeted with an indoor-outdoor remnant patterned in brown and gold lozenges that also covered the uneven floor in the combination living and eating area. Just as she had predicted, Sophie had fallen asleep on an old couch upholstered in a worn tan fabric printed with faded tavern signs, American eagles, and thirteen-star flags. The perm Chantal had given her mother hadn't turned out too well, and Sophie's thin salt-and-pepper hair looked dry and vaguely electrified. She was overweight, and her knit top outlined breasts that had fallen like water balloons to opposite sides of her body.

Honey regarded her aunt with a familiar combination of exasperation and love. Sophie Moon Booker was the one who should have been worrying about her daughter's whereabouts, not Honey. She was the one who should have been thinking about how they were going to pay all those bills that were piling up and how they were going to keep their family together without falling into the peckerhead welfare system. But Honey knew that getting mad at Sophie was just like getting mad at Sophie's daughter, Chantal. It didn't do any good.

"I'm going out for a while."

Sophie snorted in her sleep.

The night air was heavy with humidity as Honey jumped down off the crumbling concrete step. The trailer's exterior was a particularly jarring shade of robin's-egg blue, improved only by the dulling film of age. Her flip-flops sank into the sand, and grit settled between her toes. As she moved away from the trailer, she sniffed. The June night smelled like pine, creosote, and the disinfectant they used in the toilets. All of those smells were overlaid by the distant, musty scent of Silver Lake.

As she passed beneath a series of weathered Southern yellow-pine support columns, she shoved her hands in the pockets of her shorts and told herself that this time she would keep going. This time she wouldn't stop and look. Looking made her think, and thinking made her feel like the inside of a week-old bait bucket. She moved doggedly ahead for another minute, but then she stopped anyway. Turning back the way she had come, she craned her neck and let her gaze move along the sweeping length of Black Thunder.

The roller coaster's massive wooden frame stood silhouetted against the night sky like the skeleton of a prehistoric dinosaur. Her eyes traveled up the steep incline of Black Thunder's mountainous lift hill and down that heart-stopping sixty-degree drop. She traced the slopes of the next two hills with their chilling dips all the way to the final spiral that twisted down in a nightmare whirlpool over Silver Lake itself. Her heart ached with an awful combination of yearning and bitterness as she took in the three hills and the steeply banked death spiral. Everything had begun to go wrong for them the summer Black Thunder had stopped running.

Even though the Silver Lake Amusement Park was small and old-fashioned compared to places like Busch Gardens and Six Flags over Georgia, it had something none of the others could claim. It had the last great wooden roller coaster in the South, a coaster some enthusiasts considered more thrilling than the legendary Coney Island Cyclone. Since it was built in the late 1920s, people had come from all over the country to ride Black Thunder. For legions of roller-coaster enthusiasts, the trip to Silver Lake had been a religious pilgrimage.

After a dozen rides on the legendary wooden coaster, they would visit the park's other more mundane attractions, including spending two dollars a person to take a cruise up and down Silver Lake on the paddle wheeler *Robert E. Lee*. But the *Bobby Lee* had fallen victim to disaster just like Black Thunder.

Almost two years ago, on Labor Day 1978, a wheel assembly had snapped off Black Thunder's rear car, separating it from the other cars and sending it hurtling over the side. Luckily no one had been hurt, but the State of South

Carolina had closed down the roller coaster that same day, and none of the banks would finance the expensive renovation the state required before the ride could be reopened. Without its famous attraction, the Silver Lake Amusement Park had been dying a slow and painful death.

Honey walked farther into the park. On her right a bug-encrusted light bulb illuminated the deserted interior of the Dodgem Hall, where the battered fiberglass cars sat in a sleeping herd waiting for the park to open at ten the next morning. She passed through Kiddieland, with its miniature motorcycles and fire trucks sitting motionless on their endless circular tracks. Further on, the Scrambler and Tilt-a-Whirl rested from their labors. She paused in front of the House of Horror, where a Day-Glo mural of a decapitated body gushing phosphorescent blood from its severed neck stretched over the entryway.

"Chantal?"

There was no answer.

Removing the flashlight from its hook behind the ticket booth, she walked purposefully up the ramp into the House of Horror. In the daytime the ramp vibrated and a loudspeaker emitted hollow groans and shrill screams, but now everything was quiet. She entered the Passageway of Death and shone her light on the seven-foot hooded executioner with his bloody ax.

"Chantal, you in here?"

She heard only silence. Brushing through the artificial cobwebs, she passed the chopping block on her way to the Rat Den. Once inside, she shone her flashlight around the small room. Scores of glowing red eyes looked back at her from the one hundred and six snarling gray rats that lurked in the rafters and hung from invisible wires over her head.

Honey regarded them with satisfaction. The Rat Den was the best part of the House of Horror, because the animals were real. They had been stuffed by a New Jersey taxidermist in 1952 for the spook house at Palisades Park in Fort Lee. In the late sixties her Uncle Earl had bought them thirdhand from a North Carolina man whose park near Forest City had gone bust.

"Chantal?" She called out her cousin's name one more time, and when she got no response left the House of Horror through the back fire exit. Dodging power cables, she cut behind the Roundup and headed for the midway.

Only a few of the colored light bulbs strung through the sagging pennants that zigzagged over the midway were still working. The hanky-panks were boarded up for the night: the milk-bottle pitch and the fish tank, the Crazy Ball game, and the Iron Claw with its glass case full of combs, dice, and Dukes of Hazzard key chains. The stale smell of popcorn, pizza, and rancid oil from the funnel cakes clung to everything.

It was the smell of Honey's rapidly vanishing childhood, and she breathed it deeply into her lungs. If the Disney people took over, the smell would disappear forever, right along with the hanky-panks, Kiddieland, and the House of Horror. She clasped her arms over her small chest and hugged herself, a habit she had developed over the years because no one else would do it.

Since her mother had died when she was six, this was the only home she'd known, and she loved it with all her heart. Writing the Disney people had been the worst thing she'd ever had to do. She had been forced to suppress all of her softer emotions in a desperate attempt to find the money she needed to keep her family together, the money that would keep them out of the welfare system and allow them to buy a small house in a clean neighborhood where they could maybe have some nice furniture and a garden. But as she stood in the middle of the deserted midway, she wished that she were old enough and smart enough to make things turn out differently. Because most of all, she couldn't bear the idea that she was losing Black Thunder, and if the coaster had still been running, nothing in the world could have made her give up this park.

The eerie night quiet and the smell of old popcorn brought back the memory of a small child huddled in the corner of the trailer, scabby knees drawn up to her chin, light blue eyes large and stunned. An angry voice from the past echoed in her mind.

"Get her out of here, Sophie! Goddamnit, she's givin' me the willies. She's hardly moved since she you brung her here last night. All she's done is sit in that corner and stare." She heard the crash of her Uncle Earl's meaty fist on the kitchen table, Sophie's monotonous whine.

"Where am I gonna put her, Earl?"

"I don't give a shit where you put her. It's not my fault your sister went and got herself drowned. Those Alabama welfare people had no right to make you go get her. I want to eat my lunch in goddamn peace without her spookin' me!"

Sophie came over to the corner of the trailer's living area and poked the sole of Honey's cheap canvas sneaker with the toe of her own red espadrille. "You stop actin' like that, Honey. You go on outside and find Chantal. You haven't seen the park yet. She'll show it to you."

"I want my mama," Honey whispered.

"Goddamnit! Get her out of here, Sophie!"

"Now see what you done," Sophie sighed. "You got your Uncle Earl all mad." She grasped Honey's upper arm and tugged on it. "Come on. Let's go get you some cotton candy."

She took Honey from the trailer and led her through the pines and out into the scorching sun of a Carolina afternoon. Honey moved like a tiny robot. She didn't want any cotton candy. Sophie'd made her eat some Captain Crunch that morning, and she'd thrown up.

Sophie dropped her arm. Honey already sensed that her aunt didn't like to touch people, not like Honey's mother, Carolann. Carolann was always picking Honey up and cuddling her and calling her sweetie pie, even when she was tired from working all day at the dry cleaners in Montgomery.

"I want my mama," Honey whispered as they stepped through the grass into a colonnade of great wooden posts.

"Your mama's dead. She's not—"

The rest of Sophie's reply was drowned out as a monster screamed above Honey's head.

Honey screamed then, too. All the grief and fear that had been building up inside her since her mother had died and she was snatched away from everything familiar were released by the terror of that unexpected noise. Again and again she screamed.

She had a vague idea what a roller coaster was, but she had never ridden one, never seen one this size, and it didn't occur to her to connect the sound with the ride. She heard only a monster, the monster that hides in the closet and skulks under the bed and carries off little girls' mothers in fearsome fiery jaws.

The piercing screams spilled from her mouth. After being nearly catatonic for the six days since her mother had died, she couldn't stop, not even when Sophie began to shake her arm.

"Quit that! Quit that screamin', you hear?"

But Honey couldn't quit. Instead, she fought against Sophie until she broke away. Then she began running beneath the tracks, arms flailing, her small lungs heaving as over and over she screamed her sorrow and fear. When she came to a dip in the track too low for her to pass beneath, she grasped one of the wooden posts. Splinters dug into her arms as she held onto the thing she feared most in the confused belief that it couldn't devour her if she clasped it tightly enough.

She wasn't aware of the passage of time, only the sound of her screams, the sporadic roar of the monster as it rushed overhead, the rough splinters of the post digging into the baby-soft skin of her arms, and the fact that she wasn't ever going to see her mother again.

"Goddamnit, stop that noise!"

While Sophie stood helplessly watching, Uncle Earl came up behind them and dragged her off the post with a bellow. "What's wrong with her? What the hell is wrong with her now?"

"I don't know," Sophie whined. "She started doin' that when she heard Black Thunder. I think she's afraid of it."

"Well, that's just too goddamn bad. We're not coddling her, goddamnit."

He snatched Honey up by the waist and pulled her out from beneath the coaster. Walking with great loping strides, he carried her through the clusters of people visiting the park that day and up the ramp into the station house where Black Thunder loaded its riders.

A train sat empty, ready for its next group of passengers. Ignoring the protests of the people waiting in line, he pushed her beneath the lap bar in the first car. Her shrill screams echoed hollowly beneath the wooden roof. She struggled desperately to get out, but her uncle held her fast with one hairy arm.

"Earl, whatcha doin'?" Chester, the old man who ran Black Thunder, rushed up to him.

"She's goin' on a ride."

"She's too little, Earl. You know she's not tall enough for this coaster."

"That's too damn bad. Strap her in. And no goddamn brakes."

"But, Earl . . ."

"Do what I say, or pick up your paycheck."

She was vaguely aware of the loud objections of several of the adults waiting in line, but then the train began to move, and she realized that she was being delivered into the very stomach of the beast that had taken her mother.

"No!" she screamed. "No! *Mama!*"

Her fingers barely met at the tips as she clutched the lap bar in a death grip. Sobs ripped through her. "Mama . . . Mama . . ."

The structure creaked and groaned as the train crawled up the great lift hill that had helped create the legend of Black Thunder. It moved with sadistic slowness, giving her child's mind time to conjure ghastly visions of terrifying horror. She was six years old and alone in the universe with the beast of death. Utterly defenseless, she wasn't big enough, strong enough, old enough to protect herself, and there was no adult left on earth who would do it for her.

Fear clogged her throat and her tiny heart throbbed in her chest as the car climbed inexorably to the top of the great lift hill. Higher than the tallest mountain in the world. Beyond the comfort of clouds. Above the hot sky to a dark place where only devils lurked.

Her last scream ripped from her throat as the car cleared the top, and she had one glimpse of the terrifying descent before she was thrown into the stomach of the beast to be gobbled up and gnawed apart through the darkest night of her child's soul only to . . .

Rise again.

And then pitch back into hell.

And rise again.

She was plunged into hell and resurrected three times before she was hurled out over the lake and down into the devil's spiral. She slammed against the side of the car as she catapulted in a deadly whirlpool straight down into the water, only to level out at the last second, barely two feet above the surface, and be shot back to higher ground. The coaster slowed and gently delivered her to the station.

She was no longer crying.

The cars came to a stop. Her Uncle Earl had disappeared, but Chester, the ride operator, rushed up to lift her out. She shook her head, her eyes still tragic, her tiny face chalky.

"Again," she whispered.

She was too young to articulate the feelings the coaster had given her. She knew only that she had to experience them again—the sense that there was a force greater than herself, a force that could punish but would also rescue. The sense that somehow that force had allowed her to touch her mother.

She rode Black Thunder a dozen times that day and on through the rest of her childhood whenever she needed to experience hope in the protection of a higher power. The coaster confronted her with all the terrors of human existence, but then carried her safely to the other side.

Life with the Booker family gradually settled into a routine. Her Uncle Earl never liked her, but he put up with her because she became a much bigger help to him than either his wife or daughter. Sophie was as kind as it was possible for someone entirely self-absorbed to be. She made few demands other than to insist that Honey and Chantal go to Sunday school at least once a month.

But the great wooden coaster had taught Honey more

about God than the Baptist Church, and the coaster's theology was easier to understand. For someone who was small for her age, orphaned, and female to boot, she drew courage from the knowledge that a higher power existed, something strong and eternal that would watch over her.

A sound coming from inside the arcade jolted Honey back to the present. She reprimanded herself for getting distracted from her purpose. Before long, she was going to be as bad as her cousin. Walking forward, she stuck her head into the arcade. "Hey, Buck, have you seen Chantal?"

Buck Ochs looked up from the pinball machine he was trying to fix because she had told him that if he didn't get at least a few of the machines running she was going to kick his big old ugly butt right back to Georgia. His beer gut pushed against the buttons of his dirty plaid shirt as he shifted his weight and gave her his doltish grin.

"Chantal who?"

He laughed uproariously at his wit. She wished she could fire him right there on the spot, but she had lost too many men already because she couldn't always meet her payroll on time, and she knew she couldn't afford to lose another. Besides, Buck wasn't malicious, just stupid. He also had a disgusting habit of scratching himself right where he shouldn't when females were present.

"You're a real joker, aren't you, Buck? Has Chantal been around?"

"Naw, Honey. It's just been me, myself, and me."

"Well, let's see if one of you can get a couple of those damned machines working before morning."

With a quelling look, she left the arcade and continued to the end of the midway. The Bullpen, a run-down wooden building where the unmarried male employees bunked, sat in the trees behind the picnic grove. Only Buck and two others lived there now. She could see yellow light seeping from the windows, but she didn't go closer because she couldn't imagine Chantal visiting either Cliff or Rusty. Chantal wasn't one to sit and talk to people.

The uneasiness that had been growing inside her ever since she had realized how late it was settled deeper into her stomach. This was no time for Chantal to disappear. Something was definitely wrong. And Honey was afraid she knew exactly what it was.

She turned in a circle, taking in the dilapidated trailers, the midway, the rides. Dominating it all were the great hills of Black Thunder, stripped now of all their power to hurl a frightened young girl to a place where she could once again find hope in something eternal to protect her. Hesitating for only a moment, she began to head down the overgrown concrete walk that led to Silver Lake.

The night was deep and still. As the old pines closed over her head, shutting out the moonlight, the calliope sounds of "Dixie" began to drift through her memory.

Ladies and gentlemen. Children of all ages. Take a step back in time to those grand old days when cotton was king. Join us for a ride on the paddle wheeler Robert E. Lee *and see beautiful Silver Lake, the largest lake in Paxawatchie County, South Carolina. . . .*

The pines ended at a dilapidated dock. She stopped walking and shivered. At the end of the dock rose the ghostly hulk of the *Bobby Lee.*

The *Robert E. Lee* sat right where it had been anchored when it had sunk in a winter storm a few months after the Black Thunder disaster. Now its bottom rested in the polluted muddy ooze of Silver Lake fifteen feet down. All of its lower deck was underwater, along with the once-proud paddle wheel that had churned at its stern. Only the upper deck and pilothouse rose above the lake's surface. The *Bobby Lee* sat at the end of the dock, useless and half submerged, a phantom ship in the eerie moonlight.

Honey shivered again and crossed her arms over her chest. Watery moonlight etched ghostly fingers over the dying lake, and her nostrils twitched at the musty scent of decaying vegetation, dead fish, and rotting wood. She wasn't a chicken, but she didn't like being around the *Bobby Lee* at night. She curled her toes in her flip-flops so they wouldn't make any noise as she took first one and then another step along the dock. Some of the boards were broken, and she could see the stagnant waters of the lake below. She slid forward another step and stopped, opening her mouth to call out Chantal's name. But creepy-crawlies were strangling her voice box and nothing came out. She wished she'd stopped at the Bullpen and asked Cliff or Rusty to come with her.

Her cowardice made her angry. She was having a hard enough time as it was getting them to follow her orders. Men like that didn't respect women bosses, especially when they were only sixteen. If any of them ever found out she was afraid of something as foolish as an old dead boat, they'd never listen to her again.

A flutter of wings burst from behind her as an owl swooped out over the lake from the trees. She sucked in her breath. Just then, she heard the distant sound of a moan.

She didn't have any patience with superstition, but the menacing shape of the dead ship looming at the end of the dock had her spooked, and for a fraction of a second she thought the sound might be coming from a vampire or a succubus or some kind of zombie. Then the moon skidded out from beneath a wisp of cloud and common sense reasserted itself. She knew exactly what she had heard, and it didn't have anything to do with zombies.

She tore down the dock, her flip-flops spanking her heels as she sidestepped the rotted boards and dodged a pile of rope. The boat had sunk five feet from the end of the dock, and the upper deck railing, broken like a gap-toothed smile, loomed ahead of her above the water level. She raced toward the piece of plywood that served as a makeshift ramp and dashed up its incline. It sprang beneath her ninety pounds like a trampoline.

The bottoms of her feet stung as she landed hard on the upper deck. She clutched a piece of the railing to balance herself and then ran toward the staircase. It descended into the murky water. Even in the darkness, she could see the white belly of a dead fish floating near the submerged stair treads. Throwing her leg over the peeling wooden railing, she raced up the section of staircase that still rose above the surface of the water to the pilothouse.

A man and woman were sprawled near its door, their

bodies intertwined. They were too caught up in each other to hear the noise of Honey's approach.

"Let her go, you peckerhead!" Honey shouted as she reached the top.

The figures sprang apart. A bat flew out from the broken window of the pilothouse.

"Honey!" Chantal exclaimed. Her blouse was open, her nipples silver dollars in the moonlight.

The young man she was with sprang to his feet, jerking up the zipper of the cutoffs he wore with a University of South Carolina T-shirt that had "Gamecocks" written across the front. For a moment he looked dazed and disoriented, and then he took in Honey's chewed hair, tiny stature, and the hostile scowl that made her look more like an ill-tempered ten-year-old boy than a young girl.

"You go on, y'hear?" he said belligerently. "Y'all got no business here."

Chantal rose from the deck and lifted her hand to close the front of her blouse. The movement was slow and lazy, just like all her movements were. The boy draped his arm around her shoulders.

The familiar way he embraced Chantal, as if she belonged to him instead of to Honey, ignited her already simmering temper. Chantal was hers, along with Aunt Sophie and the ruins of the Silver Lake Amusement Park! Using her index finger as a weapon, she pointed down to the deck by her side. "You get over here, Chantal Booker. I mean it. You get over here right now."

Chantal stared at her sandals for a moment and then took a reluctant step forward.

The college boy grabbed her arm. "Wait a minute. Who is she? What's she doin' here, Chantal?"

"My cousin Honey," Chantal replied. "She runs things, I guess."

Once again Honey punched her finger toward the deck. "You bet I run things. Now you get over here this minute."

Chantal attempted to move forward, but the boy wouldn't release her. He curled his other hand over her arm. "Aw, she's just a kid. You don't have to listen to her." He gestured

17

toward the shore. "You go on back where you came from, little girl."

Honey's eyes narrowed into slits. "Listen to me, college boy. If you know what's good for you, you'll pack that undersized pecker of yours right back in your dirty underwear and get off this boat before you make me mad."

He shook his head incredulously. "I think I might just throw you right over the side of this boat, baby face, and let the fish eat you."

"I wouldn't try it." Honey took a threatening step, her small chin jutted forward. She despised it when people made fun of the way she looked. "Maybe I better tell you that I got out of reform school just last week for knifing a man who was a lot bigger than you are. They would have give me the electric chair, but I was underage."

"Is that so? Well, I don't happen to believe you."

Chantal signed. "Honey, you gonna tell Mama?"

Honey ignored her and concentrated on the boy. "How old did Chantal tell you she was?"

"None of your beeswax."

"Did she tell you she was eighteen?"

He glanced at Chantal, and for the first time he looked uncertain.

"I might of known," Honey said with disgust. "That girl's only fifteen years old. Didn't they teach you anything about statutory rape at the University of South Carolina?"

The boy released Chantal as if she were radioactive. "Is that true, Chantal? You sure look older than fifteen."

Honey spoke before Chantal had the chance. "She matured early."

"Now, Honey . . ." Chantal protested.

He began easing away. "Maybe we better call it a night, Chantal." He sauntered toward the staircase. "I had a real good time. Maybe I'll see you again sometime, all right?"

"Sure, Chris. I'd like that."

He fled down the stairs. They could hear the *sprong* of the plywood plank and then a thump as he landed on the dock. Both girls watched him disappear into the pines.

Chantal sighed, eased down onto the deck, and leaned

back against the pilothouse. "You got any cigarettes on you?"

Honey pulled out a crushed pack of Salems and handed it over as she lowered herself next to her cousin. Chantal slipped the matches out from under the cellophane and lit the cigarette. She took a deep, easy drag. "Why'd you go and tell him I was only fifteen?"

"I didn't want to have to fight him."

"Honey, you weren't gonna fight him. You didn't even come up to his chin. And you know that I'm eighteen—two years older'n you are."

"I might have fought him." Honey took the cigarettes back but, after a moment's hesitation, decided not to light one. She'd been trying for months to learn how to smoke, but she just couldn't get the hang of it.

"And all that stuff about reform school and knifing a man. Nobody believes you."

"Some do."

"I don't think it's good to tell so many lies."

"It goes along with being a woman in the business world. Otherwise people take advantage of you."

Chantal's legs stretched bare and shapely from beneath her white shorts as she crossed her ankles. Honey studied her cousin's sandaled feet and polished toenails. She considered Chantal the prettiest woman she'd ever seen. It was hard to believe she was the daughter of Earl and Sophie Booker, neither of whom had ever won any prizes for good looks. Chantal had a cloud of curly dark hair, exotic eyes that tilted up at the corners, a small red mouth, and a soft, feminine figure. With her dark hair and olive skin, she looked like a Latin spitfire, a misleading impression since Chantal didn't have much more spirit than an old hound dog on a hot day in August. Honey loved her anyway.

Cigarette smoke ribboned from Chantal's top lip into her nostrils as she French-inhaled. "I'd give just about anything to be married to a movie star. I mean it, Honey. I'd give just about anything to be Mrs. Burt Reynolds."

In Honey's opinion, Burt Reynolds was about twenty years too old for Chantal, but she knew she could never convince her cousin of that fact so she played her trump card right off the top. "Mr. Burt Reynolds is a southern boy. Southern boys like to marry virgins."

"I'm still sort of a virgin."

"Thanks to me."

"I wasn't gonna let Chris go all the way."

"Chantal, you might not of been able to stop him once he got worked up. You know you're not real good at saying no to people."

"You gonna tell Mama?"

"A lot of good that'd do. She'd just change the channel and go back to sleep. This is the third time I've caught you with one of those college boys. They come sniffin' around you just like you're sending out some kind of radio signal or something. And what about that boy you were with in the House of Horror last month? When I found you, he had his hand right inside your shorts."

"It feels good when boys do that. And he was real nice."

Honey snorted in disgust. There was no talking to Chantal. She was sweet, but she wasn't too bright. Not that Honey had room to criticize. At least Chantal had made it through high school, which was more than Honey had been able to do.

Honey hadn't quit school because she was dumb—she was a voracious reader and she'd always been smart as a whip. She'd quit because she had better things to do than spend her time with a bunch of ignorant peckerhead girls who told everybody she was a lesbian just because they were afraid of her.

The memory still made her feel like crawling away somewhere and hiding. Honey wasn't pretty like the other girls. She didn't wear cute clothes or have a bubbly personality, but that didn't mean she was a lesbian, did it? The question bothered her because she wasn't absolutely sure of the answer. She certainly couldn't imagine letting a boy touch her under her shorts like Chantal did.

Chantal's voice interrupted the silence that had fallen between them. "Do you ever think about your mama?"

"Not so much anymore." Honey picked at a piece of

splintered wood on the deck. "But since you brought up the subject, it wouldn't do you any harm to think about what happened to my mama when she was even younger than you. She let a college boy come sniffin' around her, and it ruined her life."

"I don't follow you. If your mama hadn't slept with that college boy, you wouldn't of been born. Then where would you be?"

"That's not the point. The point is—college boys only want one thing from girls like you and my mama. They only want sex. And after they get it, they disappear. Do you want to end up all by yourself with a baby to take care of and nothing except the welfare system to support you?"

"Chris said I was prettier than any of the sorority girls he knows."

It was no use. Chantal always managed to get sidetracked when Honey was trying to make a point. At times like this, Honey despaired over Chantal. How could her cousin ever manage life if Honey weren't around to look after her? Even though Chantal was older, Honey had been taking care of her for years, trying to teach her right from wrong and how to get along in the world. Knowing about those things seemed to come naturally to Honey, but Chantal was a lot like Sophie. She didn't have much interest in anything that required effort.

"Honey, how come you don't fix yourself up a little bit so you could have some boyfriends, too?"

Honey leapt to her feet. "I'm not a damn lesbian, if that's what you're tryin' to say!"

"I'm not sayin' that at all." Chantal gazed thoughtfully at the smoke curling from the end of her cigarette. "I guess if you was a lesbian, I would of been the first one to know about it. We been sleepin' in the same bed ever since you came to live with us, and you never tried anything with me."

Vaguely mollified, Honey resumed her seat. "Did you practice your baton today?"

"Maybe . . . I don't remember."

"You didn't, did you?"

"Baton twirling is hard, Honey."

"It's not hard. You've just got to practice, that's all. You know I'm planning to put flames on it next week."

"Why'd you have to pick something hard like baton twirling?"

"You can't sing. You don't play any musical instrument or tap-dance. It was the only thing I could think of."

"I just don't see why it's so important for me to win the Miss Paxawatchie County Beauty Pageant. Not if the Walt Disney people are gonna buy the park."

"We don't know that, Chantal. It's just a rumor. I wrote them another letter, but we haven't heard anything, and we can't just sit back and wait."

"You didn't make me enter the contest last year. Why do I have to do it this year?"

"Because last year's prize was a hundred dollars and a beauty make-over at Dundee's Department Store. This year it's an all-expense-paid overnight trip to Charleston to audition for *The Dash Coogan Show.*"

"That's another thing, Honey," Chantal complained. "I think you got unrealistic expectations about all of this. I don't know anything about being on TV. I been thinking more along the lines of being a hairdresser. I like hair."

"You don't have to know anything about being on TV. They want a fresh face. I've explained it to you about a hundred times."

Honey reached into her pocket and pulled out the well-worn pamphlet that gave all the information about this year's Miss Paxawatchie County Beauty Pageant. She turned to the back page. The moonlight wasn't bright enough for her to read the small print, but she had studied it so many times she knew it by heart.

The winner of the Miss Paxawatchie County title will receive an all-expense-paid overnight trip to Charleston, compliments of the pageant's sponsor, Dundee's Department Store. While in Charleston, she will audition for *The Dash Coogan Show,* a much-anticipated new fall network television program that will be filmed in California.

The producers of *The Dash Coogan Show* are auditioning Southern lovelies in seven cities in search of an actress to play the part of Celeste, Mr. Coogan's daughter. She must be between eighteen and twenty-one years old, beautiful, and have a strong regional accent. In addition to visiting Charleston, the producers will also be auditioning actresses in Atlanta, New Orleans, Birmingham, Dallas, Houston, and San Antonio.

Honey frowned. That part bothered her. Those TV people were visiting three cities in Texas, but only one in the southern states. It didn't take much brain power to figure out that they would prefer a Texan, which she supposed wasn't surprising since Dash Coogan was the king of the cowboy movie stars, but she still didn't like it. As she gazed back down at the pamphlet, she comforted herself with the knowledge that there couldn't be a single woman in all of Texas who was prettier than Chantal Booker.

The final choices from the seven-city talent search will be flown to Los Angeles for a personal screen test with Mr. Coogan. Moviegoers will remember Dash Coogan for his many roles as the star of over 20 westerns including *Lariat* and *Alamo Sunset,* his most famous. This will be his first television show. All of us are hoping that our own Miss Paxawatchie County will be portraying his daughter.

Chantal interrupted her thoughts. "See, the thing of it is—I want to *marry* a movie star. Not *be* one."

Honey ignored her. "Right now what you want doesn't mean spit. We're pretty close to being desperate, and that means we have to make our own opportunities. Idleness is the beginning of a long slide into the welfare system, and that's where we're going to end up if we don't force things to happen." She hugged her knees, and her voice dropped nearly to a whisper. "I got this feeling way down deep in my stomach, Chantal. I can hardly explain it, but I just got this strong feeling that those TV people are going to take one look at you and they're going to make you a star."

Chantal's sigh was so prolonged it seemed to come from her toes. "Sometimes you make my head spin, Honey. You must take after that college boy who was your daddy because you sure don't take after any of us."

"We have to keep our family together," Honey said fiercely. "Sophie's useless, and I'm too young to get a decent job. You're our only hope, Chantal. Ever since you started modeling at Dundee's Department Store, it's been evident that you're the best chance this family's got. If the Disney people won't buy this park, we have to have another plan to fall back on. The three of us are a family. We can't let anything happen to our family."

But Chantal had gotten distracted by the night sky and dreams of marrying a movie star, and she wasn't listening.

2

"And our new Miss Paxawatchie County, 1980, is . . . Chantal Booker!"

Honey leapt to her feet with a bloodcurdling yell that rose above the applause of the audience. The loudspeaker blared out "Give My Regards to Broadway" and Laura Liskey, last year's Miss Paxawatchie County, placed the crown on Chantal's head. Chantal gave her vague smile. The crown slipped to the side, but she didn't notice.

Honey jumped up and down, clapping and hollering. This miserable week was having a happy ending after all. Chantal had won the title, despite the fact that her baton twirling was the worst talent routine anyone had seen since three years ago when Mary Ellen Ballinger had tap-danced to "Jesus Christ Superstar." Chantal had dropped the baton on every double reverse and left out half of her grand finale, but she had looked so pretty that nobody cared. And she had done better than Honey had expected during the question and answer part. When she had been asked about her plans for the future, she had dutifully announced that she wanted to be either a speech and hearing therapist or a missionary, just as Honey had told her to. Honey didn't suffer a single pang of conscience over insisting on the lie. It was a lot better than having Chantal announce to the world that what she really wanted out of life was to marry Burt Reynolds.

As Honey applauded, she breathed a silent prayer of thanksgiving that she had been smart enough to abandon the fire baton. Chantal would have done more damage to Paxawatchie County with those flames than William Tecumseh Sherman's entire army.

Ten minutes later, as she made her way through the crowd to the backstage area of the high school auditorium, she determinedly ignored the clusters of families gathered everywhere beaming at the girls in their filmy dresses: plump mothers and balding fathers, aunts and uncles, grandmothers and grandfathers. She never looked at families if she could avoid it. *Never.* Some things hurt too much to be borne.

She spotted Shep Watley, the county sheriff, with his daughter Amelia. Just the sight of him crimped the edges of her excitement over Chantal's victory. Yesterday Shep had nailed a foreclosure sign on the front gates, closing the park down forever and making her so scared about today that she hadn't been able to sleep. Now that Chantal had won the contest, Honey told herself it didn't matter about the foreclosure or the fact that the Disney people hadn't answered any of her letters. When those television casting agents saw Chantal, they were going to fall in love with her just as the judges had. Chantal would start making lots of money, and they'd be able to buy back the park.

Here her imagination faltered. If Chantal was going to be a movie star in California, how could they all be together again at the park?

Worrying was getting to be a bad habit with her lately, and she did her best to shake it off. Her heart swelled with pride as she saw Chantal talking with Miss Monica Waring, the pageant director. Chantal looked so beautiful standing there in the white gown she'd worn to her senior prom, with the rhinestone crown perched in her inky black curls, nodding and smiling at whatever Miss Waring was telling her. The television people wouldn't be able to resist her.

"That's fine, Miss Waring," Chantal was saying as Honey approached. "I don't mind the change at all."

"You're a darling girl for being so understanding." Monica Waring, the thin, stylish woman who was both the pageant director and the executive in charge of public relations for Dundee's Department Store, looked so relieved by Chantal's response that Honey immediately grew suspicious.

"What's this?" Honey stepped forward, her instincts twitching like a rabbit's nose at the hint of danger.

Chantal's eyes shifted nervously between the two women as she reluctantly introduced them. "Miss Waring, this is my cousin, Honey Moon."

Monica Waring looked startled, as people generally did when they heard her name for the first time. "What an unusual name."

According to Sophie, when Honey was born, the nurse had told Carolann that she had a little baby girl sweet as honey, and Carolann had decided right then that she liked the name. It wasn't until the birth certificate had arrived and Honey's mother saw the whole thing in print for the first time that she realized she might have made a mistake.

Since Honey didn't want anybody to think that her mother was stupid, she gave her usual response. "It's a family name. Oldest daughter to oldest daughter. One Honey Moon after another all the way back to the Revolutionary War."

"I see." If Monica Waring thought it was unusual that so many generations of childbearing women had never changed their last name, she gave no indication. Turning to Chantal, she patted her arm. "Congratulations again, dear. And I'll take care of the changes on Monday."

"What changes would those be?" Honey asked before Miss Waring could walk away.

"Uh—Jimmy McCully and his friends are waving at me," Chantal said nervously. "I'd better go say hi to them." Before Honey could stop her, she slipped away.

Miss Waring glanced past Honey. "I've explained our little mix-up to Chantal, but I did want to speak with Mrs. Booker personally."

"My Aunt Sophie isn't here. She's suffering from—uh—gall bladder, and what with the pain and everything, she has to stay at home. I'm sort of *in loco parentis,* if you know what I mean."

Miss Waring's skillfully penciled eyebrows shot up. "Aren't you a little young to be *in loco parentis?*"

"Nineteen on my last birthday," Honey replied.

Miss Waring looked skeptical but didn't press the issue. "I was explaining to Chantal that we've had to make a slight change in the prize for the winner. We're still offering the overnight trip to Charleston, but instead of the television show audition we're hiring a limousine to take the winner and a guest of her choice on a city tour followed by a marvelous dinner at a four-star restaurant. And of course Chantal will have the customary make-over at Dundee's Department Store."

The backstage area was hot from the press of people, but Honey felt cold chills racing through her bloodstream. "No! The first prize is an audition for *The Dash Coogan Show!*"

"I'm afraid that's no longer possible. Through no fault of Dundee's, I might add. Apparently the casting people have had to move up their schedule—although I do think they could have notified me earlier than yesterday afternoon. Instead of coming to Charleston next Wednesday as scheduled, they're going to be in Los Angeles holding final auditions for the girls they've already picked."

"They're not coming to Charleston? They can't do that! How are they going to see Chantal?"

"I'm sorry, but they're not going to see Chantal. They found enough girls in Texas to call off the search."

"But you don't understand, Miss Waring. I know they would choose Chantal for the part if they just had a chance to see her."

"I'm afraid I'm not as confident as you. Chantal is quite beautiful, but the competition for the part has been enormous."

Honey immediately leapt to her cousin's defense. "Are you blaming her just because she dropped the baton? That was all my idea. She's a natural actress. I should have let her do that Quality of Mercy speech from *The Merchant of Venice* like she wanted, but, no, I had to make her twirl that stupid baton. Chantal's extremely talented. Katharine and Audrey Hepburn are her idols." She knew she was sounding frantic, but she couldn't help herself. Her fear was growing by the second. This contest was the last hope they had for a decent future, and she wouldn't let them snatch it away.

"I've spoken to the casting director several times. They've seen hundreds of girls just to weed out the final group they're auditioning in Los Angeles, and the chance of Chantal having actually been the one chosen is quite slim."

Honey set her jaw and tilted up on her toes until she was nearly on the same eye level as the pageant director. "You listen to me, Miss Waring, and you listen real good. I got the contest brochure right here in my pocket. It says in black and white that the winner of Miss Paxawatchie County gets to audition for *The Dash Coogan Show,* and I intend to hold you to that. I'm giving you until Monday afternoon to make sure Chantal gets her audition. Otherwise, I'm going to get me a lawyer, and that lawyer's going to sue you. Then he's going to sue Dundee's Department Store. And then he's going to sue every Paxawatchie County official who even came within a mile of this pageant."

"Honey—"

"I'll be at the store at four o'clock on Monday afternoon." She pointed her finger at Monica Waring's chest. "Unless you've got some positive news for me, that'll be the last time you see me without the meanest sonovabitch the courts of South Carolina have ever seen walking right by my side."

Honey's bravado collapsed on the ride home. She didn't

have the money to hire a lawyer. How could anyone at the store take her threat seriously?

But there was no place in her life for negative thinking, so she spent all day Sunday and most of Monday trying to convince herself that her bluff would work. Nothing made people more nervous than the threat of a lawsuit, and Dundee's Department Store wasn't going to want bad publicity. But no matter how much she tried to encourage herself, she felt as if her dreams for their future were sinking right along with the *Bobby Lee*.

Monday afternoon arrived. Despite her mental bravado, Honey was nearly sick with nervousness by the time she located Monica Waring's office on the third floor of Dundee's. As she stood in the doorway and peered in, she saw a small room dominated by a steel desk covered with neat stacks of paper. Promotional posters and store ads were lined up on a cork bulletin board that hung opposite the office's single window.

Honey cleared her throat, and the pageant director glanced up from her desk, which faced the door.

"Well, look who's arrived," she said, slipping off a pair of glasses with large black plastic frames and rising from her chair.

There was a smugness in her voice that Honey didn't like at all. The pageant director came around to the front of her desk. Leaning one hip against the edge, she crossed her arms.

"You're not nineteen, Honey," she said, obviously seeing no need to beat around the bush. "You're a sixteen-year-old high-school dropout with a reputation as a troublemaker. As a minor, you have no legal authority over your cousin."

Honey told herself that facing down Miss Waring shouldn't be any harder than facing down Uncle Earl when he had a few belts of whiskey in him. She walked over to the room's only window and, acting as if she didn't have a care in the world, gazed down at the drive-in lane of the First Carolina Bank across the street.

"You sure have been busy digging into my personal life,

Miss Waring," she drawled. "While you were doing that digging did you happen to discover that Chantal's mother, my aunt, Mrs. Sophie Moon Booker, is suffering from extreme craziness brought on by her sorrow over the death of her husband, Earl T. Booker?" Slowly, she turned back to the pageant director. "And did you also happen to find out that I've been running the family ever since he died? And that Mrs. Booker—who hasn't been a minor for a good twenty-five years—pretty much does whatever I tell her, up to and including slapping this candy-ass department store with the biggest lawsuit it's ever seen?"

To Honey's amazement and delight, that speech pretty much took the wind out of Monica Waring's sails. She hemmed and hawed around for a while longer, but Honey could tell it was mainly bluster. Obviously, she had been instructed by her superiors to protect the good name of Dundee's at any cost. She asked a secretary to bring Honey a Coke, then excused herself and bustled off down the hallway. Half an hour later, she returned with several pieces of paper stapled together.

"The producers of *The Dash Coogan Show* have very graciously agreed to give Chantal a short audition in Los Angeles with the other girls on Thursday," she said stiffly. "I've written down the address of the studio and have also included the information they sent me several months ago about the program. Chantal and her chaperon need to be in Los Angeles by eight o'clock Thursday morning."

"How's she supposed to get there?"

"I'm afraid that's your problem," she replied coldly as she passed the material she was holding over to Honey. "The pageant isn't responsible for transportation. I think you'll have to agree that we have been more than reasonable about this entire situation. Please wish Chantal good luck from all of us."

Honey took the papers as if she were doing Miss Waring a favor and sauntered out of the office. But once she reached the hallway, her bravado collapsed. She didn't have nearly enough money for plane tickets. How was she going to get Chantal to Los Angeles?

As she stepped onto the escalator, she tried to take courage from the lesson of Black Thunder. There was always hope.

"I think you have finally lost what's left of your mind, Honey Jane Moon," Chantal said. "That truck couldn't make it to the state line, let alone all the way to California."

The battered old pickup that stood near Sophie's trailer was the only vehicle left in the park. The body had once been red, but it had been patched with gray putty so many times that little of its original paint job remained. Because Honey was worried about exactly the same thing, she turned on Chantal.

"You're never gonna get anywhere in life if you keep being such a negative thinker. You've got to have a positive attitude toward the challenges life throws at you. Besides, Buck just put in a new alternator. Now load that suitcase in the back while I try one more time to talk to Sophie."

"But Honey, I don't want to go to California."

Honey ignored the whine in her cousin's voice. "That's just too bad, 'cause you're going. Get in that truck and wait for me."

Sophie was lying on the couch watching her Monday evening television shows. Honey knelt on the floor and touched her aunt's hand, running a gentle finger over the swollen knuckles. She knew that Sophie didn't like being touched, but sometimes she couldn't help herself.

"Sophie, you've got to change your mind and come with us. I don't want to leave you here by yourself. Besides, when those TV people offer Chantal that part on *The Dash Coogan Show,* they're gonna want to talk to her mama."

Sophie's eyes remained focused on the flickering screen. "I'm afraid I'm too tired to go anywhere, Honey. Besides, Cinnamon and Shade are getting married this week."

Honey could barely contain her frustration. "This is real life, Sophie, not a soap opera. We have to make plans for our future. The bank owns the park now, and you're not going to be able to go on living here much longer."

Sophie's lids formed saggy canopies over her small eyes as

she looked at Honey for the first time. Honey automatically searched her face for some small sign of affection, but, as usual, she saw nothing there except disinterest and weariness. "The bank didn't say anything about me moving out, so I think I'll just stay right where I am."

She attempted one final plea. "We need you, Sophie. You know how Chantal is. What if some boy tries to get fresh with her?"

"You'll take care of him," Sophie said wearily. "You'll take care of everything. You always do."

By early Wednesday afternoon, Honey was sick with fatigue. Her eyes were as dry as the Oklahoma prairie that stretched endlessly on both sides of the road, and her head had begun rolling forward without warning. A horn blared and her eyes snapped open. She jerked the wheel just before she slid over the double yellow line.

They had been on the road since Monday evening, but they hadn't even made it to Oklahoma City. They'd lost the muffler near Birmingham, sprung a leak in a water hose just past Shreveport, and had the same tire patched twice. Honey didn't believe in negative thinking, but her emergency cash supply was dwindling more rapidly than she had imagined it could, and she knew she couldn't drive much longer without sleep.

On the other side of the cab, Chantal slept like a baby, her cheeks flushed from the heat, strands of black hair whipping out the open window.

"Chantal, wake up."

Chantal's mouth puckered like an infant's in search of a nipple. Her breasts flattened under her white tank top as she stretched. "What's wrong?"

"You're going to have to drive for a while. I've got to get some sleep."

"Driving makes me nervous, Honey. Just pull off at one of the roadside stops and take a nap."

"We have to keep going or we'll never make it to Los Angeles by eight o'clock tomorrow morning. We're already way behind schedule."

"I don't want to drive, Honey. It makes me too nervous."

Honey considered pressing the issue and then decided against it. The last time she had made Chantal drive, her cousin had complained so much that Honey couldn't sleep anyway. Once again the truck wove toward the yellow line. She shook her head, trying to clear it, and then slammed on the brakes as she spotted the hitchhiker.

"Honey, what are you doing?"

"Never you mind."

She pulled over to the side and climbed out of the truck, leaving the motor running so she wouldn't have to go through all the work of starting it up again. She stepped over a torn rubber boot as she made her way down the shoulder of the interstate. The hitchhiker walked toward her carrying an old gray duffel bag.

She had no intention of endangering Chantal by picking up a pervert, so she studied him carefully. He was in his early twenties, a pleasant-faced boy with shaggy brown hair, a scraggly mustache, and sleepy eyes. His chin was a little weak, but she decided that she couldn't fault him for something that might be more of a reflection of his ancestors than his character.

She noted the fatigue pants he was wearing with his T-shirt and asked hopefully, "Are you military?"

"Naw. Not me."

Her eyes narrowed. "A college boy?"

"I spent a semester at Iowa State, but I flunked out."

She gave a small, approving nod. "Where are you on your way to?"

"Albuquerque, I guess."

He looked harmless, but so did all those serial killers she read about in Chantal's *National Enquirer*. "Did you ever drive a pickup?"

"Sure. Tractors, too. My folks are farmers. They got a place not far from Dubuque."

"My name's Honey Jane Moon."

He blinked his eyes. "Kind of a funny name."

"Yeah? Well, I didn't happen to choose it, so I'd appreciate it if you kept your opinions to yourself."

"Okay by me. I'm Gordon Delaweese."

She knew she had to make up her mind, and she couldn't afford a mistake. "You go to church, Gordon?"

"Naw. Not any more. I used to be Methodist, though."

Methodist wasn't as good as Baptist, but it would have to do. She shoved her thumb in the pocket of her jeans and glared at him, letting him see right off who was boss. "Me and my cousin Chantal are on our way to California so Chantal can get a part in a TV show. We're driving straight through and we've got to be there by eight o'clock tomorrow morning or we're going to miss what's looking like our last chance at self-respect. You try anything funny and I'll kick your ass right out of that truck. You understand me?"

Gordon nodded in a vague way that made her think he might not be any brighter than Chantal. She led him to the truck and when they got there told him he was driving.

He looked down at her and scratched his chest. "How old are you, anyway?"

"Almost twenty. And I just got out of prison last week for shooting a man in the head, so if you know what's good for you, you won't give me any trouble."

He didn't say anything after that, just tossed his duffel bag behind the seat and blinked a few times when he saw Chantal. Honey climbed in on the passenger side, putting Chantal in the middle. He worked the truck into gear and chugged out onto the highway. Honey was asleep within seconds.

Several hours later something woke her up, and when she saw the way Gordon Delaweese and Chantal Booker were making eyes at each other, she realized that she had made a big mistake.

"You sure are pretty," Gordon said, his skin taking on a rosy flush beneath his tan as he gazed over at Chantal.

Her elbow was propped up on the back of the seat and she was leaning toward him like a cottonwood in the wind. "I admire a man with a mustache."

"You do? I was thinking about shaving it off."

"Oh, no, don't. It makes you look just like Mr. Burt Reynolds."

Honey's eyelids sprang the rest of the way open.

Chantal's voice was breathless with admiration. "I think it's exciting how you're hitchhiking all over the country just so you can experience life."

"I figure you've got to see everything if you're going to be an artist," Gordon replied. He pulled into the left lane to pass an old clunker that was making nearly as much noise as their pickup.

"I never met a painter before."

Honey didn't like the soft, mushy quality in Chantal's voice. They didn't need any more complications. Why did her cousin have to fall for every boy she met? She decided the time had come to interrupt. "That's not true, Chantal. What about that man who came to the park to paint the mural over the House of Horror?"

"That's not real art," Chantal scoffed. "Gordon's a real artist."

Honey liked the mural over the House of Horror, but her tastes in art tended to be more catholic than most people's. Gordon sent another prurient glance in Chantal's direction, and Honey made up her mind to bring him down to size. "How many pictures have you painted, Gordon?"

"I don't know."

"More than a hundred?"

"Not that many."

"More than fifty?"

"Probably not."

Honey snorted. "I don't see how you can call yourself a painter if you haven't even painted fifty pictures."

"It's quality that counts," Chantal said. "Not how many."

"Since when did you turn into such a big art authority, Chantal Booker? I know for a fact that the only paintings you ever pay any attention to are ones of naked people."

"Don't let Honey hurt your feelings, Gordon. She gets moods sometimes."

Honey wanted to order him to pull over to the shoulder of

the road right that minute and get his weak chin out of her truck, but she knew that she needed him if she wanted to arrive in Los Angeles in time for that audition, so she held her tongue.

She wasn't anxious to take over the driving quite yet, but she couldn't stand watching the two of them drooling over each other so she pulled out the papers that Monica Waring had given her. They contained handwritten directions to the studio, as well as a short summary of *The Dash Coogan Show*. She studied it.

> Rollicking laugh-a-minute humor results as ex-rodeo rider Dash Jones (Dash Coogan) marries beautiful East Coast socialite Eleanor Chadwick (Liz Castleberry) and they discover that love is funnier the second time around. He has a yen for country life, while she favors fancy cocktail parties. To complicate matters, his beautiful teenage daughter Celeste (to be cast) and Eleanor's almost-grown son Blake (Eric Dillon) form an attraction for each other. All of them discover that love is funnier the second time around.

Honey found herself wondering who wrote stuff like "rollicking laugh-a-minute humor." *The Dash Coogan Show* didn't sound all that funny to her, but since she couldn't afford to be critical, she told herself that Mr. Coogan wouldn't be part of something that was garbage.

She had never been enamored of movie stars, not like Chantal, but she had always cherished a secret admiration for Dash Coogan. Ever since she was a kid, she had watched his movies. Now that she thought about it, however, she realized it had been a long time since he'd made a new one. Cowboy movies didn't seem to be too popular anymore.

A sliver of excitement crept through her. She wasn't one to be impressed by movie stars, but wouldn't it be something if she actually got the chance to meet ol' Dash Coogan when she went to Hollywood? Now wouldn't that be something.

3

Honey shoved Chantal's best sundress through the partially opened door of the Shell station's rest room. "Hurry up, Chantal. It's almost eleven o'clock. The auditions started three hours ago."

Honey's old Myrtle Beach Fun in the Sun T-shirt was stuck to her chest with nervous sweat. She rubbed her damp palms on her shorts and nervously watched the traffic go by.

"Chantal, hurry up!" Her stomach was pumping bile. What if the auditions were already over? The truck had broken down on the San Bernardino Freeway, and then Chantal and Gordon had had a lover's quarrel right there on the shoulder of the road. Honey had begun to feel as if she were stuck in one of those nightmares where she was trying to get someplace but couldn't make it. "If you don't hurry up, Chantal, we're going to miss the audition."

"I feel like I'm getting ready to start my period," Chantal whined from the other side of the door.

"I'm sure they've got rest rooms where we're going."

"What if they don't have one of those Tampax machines? Then what am I going to do?"

"I'll go out and buy you some damned Tampax! Chantal, if you don't come out here right this minute . . ."

The door opened and Chantal came through, looking as fresh and pretty in her white sundress as if she'd just stepped out of a magazine ad for Tide laundry detergent. "You don't have to shout."

"I'm sorry. I'm just edgy." Honey grabbed her arm and dragged her toward the truck.

Gordon had followed Honey's orders and kept the pickup running. Honey pushed him out of the way and climbed behind the wheel herself. She peeled out of the parking lot and turned into the traffic, ignoring a light that was more red than yellow. She had never been in a city larger than Charleston, and the noise and bustle of Los Angeles was terrifying, but she didn't have time to give in to her fears. Another thirty minutes passed before she found the studio off one of Burbank's cross streets. She had expected something glamorous, but the high concrete walls made the place look like a prison. More time passed before the guard finally cleared them and they were permitted to drive inside.

Following the guard's instructions, Honey drove down a narrow street, then turned left toward another building with concrete walls and a few small windows near the entrance. As she climbed out of the truck, she was sweating so bad she looked like she'd just gotten out of the shower. She had hoped to get rid of Gordon back at the Shell station, but he wouldn't leave Chantal. He wasn't exactly an appetizing sight with his stubbly jaw and dirty clothes, and she told him he had to wait in the truck. Like her cousin, he was starting to get into the habit of following her orders, and he agreed.

The woman stationed inside the entrance told them that auditions were still going on, but that the last girl had already been called. For several terrifying moments, Honey was afraid the woman would tell them they were too late, but instead she directed them to a shabby waiting room with gray walls, mismatched furniture, and a litter of discarded magazines and diet-soda cans left behind by its former occupants.

As they walked into the empty room, Chantal began to make a whimpery noise at Honey's side. "I'm scared, Honey. Let's go. I don't want to do this."

In desperation Honey turned Chantal toward a smudged mirror hanging on the wall. "Look at yourself, Chantal Booker. Half the movie stars in Hollywood don't look as good as you. Now put your shoulders back and your chin up. Who knows? Burt Reynolds might walk through that door at any minute."

"But I can't do this, Honey. I'm too scared. Besides, since I met Gordon Delaweese, I don't think about Burt Reynolds so much anymore."

"You haven't even known Gordon for twenty-four hours, and you've been in love with Burt for two years. I don't think you should give up on him so fast. Now I don't want to hear another word, Chantal. Our whole damn future is resting on what happens here today."

The door opened behind her and a man's voice intruded on their privacy. "Tell her that I need to see Ross, will you?"

Honey automatically girded herself to do battle with whatever new enemy might have appeared to contest their right to be here. Setting her teeth, she spun around.

And her heart dropped through a gaping hole in the bottom of her stomach.

As he walked into the room, she felt as if she'd been hit by an eighteen-wheeler that had lost its brakes on a downhill curve. He was the handsomest young man she had ever seen: in his early twenties, tall and slender, dark brown hair falling in disarray over his forehead. His nose and jaw were strong and sunbrowned, just as a man's should be. Beneath thickly slashed eyebrows, his eyes were the same bright turquoise as the painted saddles on the park's carousel horses, and they speared right into her deepest female parts. In that moment, as she gazed into the depths of those turquoise eyes that seemed to burn right through her skin, womanhood paid her an unwelcome visit.

Her physical shortcomings gaped in her mind like festering wounds— her freckled little-boy's face, her mutilated hair and sucker-fish mouth. Her shorts were smeared with carburetor grease, she had spilled Orange Crush on her T-shirt, and her old blue rubber flip-flops had a piece missing from the heel. She agonized over her lack of height, her lack of breasts, her lack of any single redeeming feminine attribute.

He regarded Honey and Chantal steadily, not seeming to find it at all strange to be confronted with two speechless females. She tried and failed to manage the simple syllables of "hello." She waited for Chantal to step in—Chantal who was always so forward with boys—but her cousin had slipped behind her. When Chantal finally did speak, she addressed her remark to Honey and not to the gorgeous stranger.

"It's Jared Fairhaven," she whispered, sliding even farther behind Honey.

How did Chantal know who he was? "H—Hi, Mr. Fairhaven," Honey finally managed, her voice not much more than a little girl's quiver, certainly nothing at all like the profane bray she used to keep the employees at the park in line.

His eyes took in all the parts of Chantal that weren't hidden behind Honey's smaller body. He didn't smile— somehow his thin, hard mouth didn't seem to be made for that—but Honey's insides still twisted like a piece of hand laundry.

"My name is Eric Dillon. Jared Fairhaven is the part I used to play on *Destiny*."

Honey vaguely recalled that *Destiny* was one of Sophie's soap operas. She felt a pang as she saw the way he was gazing at her cousin. But then what did she expect? Did she really think he would notice her when Chantal was around?

Men were about the only thing that Chantal was good at, and Honey couldn't understand why she kept hovering behind her instead of stepping forward and taking over the conversation like she usually did. Unable to endure the indignity of appearing not only ugly but stupid, she swallowed hard.

"I'm Honey Jane Moon. This here's my cousin, Chantal Booker. We're from Paxawatchie County, South Carolina, and we're here to get Chantal a part on *The Dash Coogan Show*."

"Is that so?" His voice was deep-pitched and rich. He walked forward, ignoring Honey as he took in every inch of Chantal. "Hi there, Chantal Booker." He spoke in a soft, silky way that sent a shiver up Honey's spine.

To Honey's absolute and utter amazement, Chantal began pulling her toward the doorway. "Come on, Honey. We're gettin' out of here right now."

Honey tried to resist, but Chantal was determined. Sweet,

lazy Chantal who didn't have the gumption of a gnat was dragging her across the carpet!

Honey grabbed on to the soft-drink machine. "What's wrong with you? We're not going anywhere."

"Yes, we are. I'm not doing this. We're leavin' right now."

The waiting room door opened, and a frazzled-looking young woman with a clipboard appeared. When she saw Eric Dillon, she looked momentarily disconcerted, and then she turned to Chantal. "We're ready to see you now, Miss Booker."

This new arrival was one obstacle too many for Chantal to cope with and her momentary rebellion collapsed. She released Honey's arm and her bottom lip began to quiver. "Please, don't make me do this."

Honey was pricked with guilt, but she steeled herself against Chantal's distress. "You have to. We don't have anything else left."

"But . . ."

Eric Dillon stepped forward and took Chantal's arm. "Come on, I'll go in with you."

Honey thought she saw Chantal recoil from his touch, but she decided it was her imagination because Chantal had never recoiled from a man in her life. Chantal's shoulders slumped in resignation as she permitted Eric Dillon to lead her from the waiting room.

The door closed. She pressed the flat of her hand over her heart to keep it from jumping right out of her chest. Their entire future was riding on what happened now, but she was completely disoriented from her meeting with Eric Dillon. If only she were beautiful he might have noticed her. But who could blame him for ignoring an ugly little redneck girl who looked like a boy anyway.

She walked restlessly over to the room's single window to look out on the parking lot. She heard the sound of an ambulance in the distance. Her palms were damp. She counted her breaths for a few minutes to calm herself, then looked out. There wasn't much to see; some shrubbery, a few delivery trucks passing by.

The door opened and Chantal reappeared, this time alone. "They said I wasn't the right type."

Honey blinked.

Not even five minutes had passed.

They had driven all the way across the United States of America and these people hadn't even spent five minutes with Chantal.

All of her dreams crumbled like old yellow paper. She thought of the carefully hoarded money she had spent to get here. She thought of her hopes, her plans. The world spun around her, dangerous and out of her control. She was losing her home; she had no way to keep their family together. And they hadn't even given Chantal five minutes.

"No!"

She raced out through the door Chantal had just entered and ran into the hallway. Nobody was going to push her around like this! Not after all she'd been through. Somebody was going to pay!

Chantal called out her name, but Honey had spotted a set of metal doors with a glowing red light bulb above them at the end of the hallway, and her cousin's voice sounded a thousand miles away. Her heart pumping, Honey raced toward the doors. She shoved against them with all her strength and burst through into the studio.

"You sons of bitches!"

A half dozen heads turned in her direction. They were gathered in the rear of the studio behind pieces of equipment, a blur of male and female faces. A few of them were standing, others sat on folding chairs around a table littered with coffee cups and fast-food containers. Eric Dillon leaned against the wall and smoked a cigarette, but not even his magnetism was a powerful enough force to make her forget the horrible injustice that had been done her.

A women, tall and stern, shot up from her chair. "Now just a minute, young lady," she said, advancing on Honey. "You have no business in here."

"My cousin and me traveled all the way from South Carolina, you rotten sons of bitches," Honey shouted, pushing a folding chair out of the way to get to them. "We blew out three tires, used up most of our money, and you didn't even spend five minutes with her!"

"Call security." The woman tossed the command over her shoulder.

Honey turned her rage on the woman. "Chantal's pretty and she's sweet, and you treated her like she was a stinking pile of dog shit . . . "

The woman snapped her fingers. "Richard, get her out of here!"

"You think just because you're some big Hollywood hotshot, you can treat her like dirt. Well you're the one who's dirt, you hear me? You and all those peckerheads sitting over there."

Several more people had risen to their feet. She turned on them, her eyes hot and burning, her throat clogged.

"You're all going to burn in hell. You're going to burn in the fires of everlasting hell, and—"

"Richard!" The woman's voice barked with command.

An overweight red-haired man with glasses had come forward, and now he grabbed Honey's arm. "You're leaving."

"Like hell." Drawing back her foot, she kicked him hard in the shin, then sucked in her breath as pain shot from her unprotected toes through her foot.

The man took advantage of her distraction to push her toward the door. "This is a private meeting. You can't come barging in here like this."

She struggled against him, trying futilely to escape from the bite of his fingers. "Let me go, you ignorant peckerhead! I killed a man! I killed three of them!"

"Did you call security?" This was a new voice, and it belonged to a man in a shirt and tie with silver hair and an air of authority.

"I called them, Ross," someone else replied. "They're on their way."

She was dragged past Eric Dillon. He looked at her with blank eyes. The man named Richard almost had her to the door. He was soft and flabby and wouldn't have presented much of a challenge to anyone with reasonable strength. But she was so little. If only she were bigger, stronger, more of a *man!* Then she'd show him. She'd show them all!

She punched him with her fists, blasting all of them with every curse she knew. They were so smug and self-righteous, these rich people with families waiting for them at home, beds to sleep in at night.

"Let her go."

The voice came from behind her. It was rough and tired, with a drawl that stretched from here to forever.

The stern-faced woman sucked in her breath indignantly. "Not until she's out of here."

Again the tired voice spoke. "I said to let her go."

The silver-haired man named Ross intervened. "I don't think that's wise."

"I don't care whether it's wise or not. Richard, get your hands off her."

Miraculously, Honey found herself free.

"Come here, honey," that rough, tired voice said.

How did he know her name? She turned toward her rescuer.

Creases like gullies bracketed his mouth, and a tan line from a hatband divided his forehead—pale skin above the line, sun-weathered skin below. He was lean and spare, and she didn't have to see him walk to know that he'd be bowlegged. Her first thought was that he should be on a billboard somewhere with a Stetson on his head and a Marlboro stuck in his mouth, except his face was a little too beat-up for billboards. His short, wiry hair was a combination of dusty blond, brown, and auburn. He looked like he was in his early forties, but his hazel eyes were a million years old.

"How'd you know my name?" she asked.

"I don't."

"You called me Honey."

"Is that your name?"

His eyes were kind, and so she nodded. "Honey Jane Moon."

"How about that."

She waited for him to make a crack about her name, but

he stood quietly, not asking anything of her, just letting her take him in. She liked his clothes: an old denim work shirt, nondescript pants, boots, everything comfortable and well-worn.

"Do you feel like coming over here and talking to me a little bit?" he said after a while. "It'll give you a chance to catch your breath."

She was starting to feel dizzy from yelling so much. Her stomach was upset, and her toes were hurting. "I guess that'd be okay."

As he led her toward a couple of chairs set up in front of some sort of light blue paper, she ignored the low conversation in the background.

"How about you sit right here, Honey," he said. "If you don't mind, I'm gonna ask these fellas to turn the cameras on while you and me talk."

The man named Ross stepped forward. "I don't see any need for this."

Honey's rescuer just looked at him with a cold, dead stare. "We've been doing it your way for weeks, Ross," he said in a hard voice. "I just ran out of patience."

Honey looked at the cameras suspiciously. "Why do you want to turn those cameras on? Are you trying to get me in trouble with the police?"

He chuckled. "The police would be more likely to come after me than you, little girl."

"Is that so? Why?"

"How about I ask the questions for a while?" He inclined his head toward the chair, not making her sit, but giving her a choice about it. She looked deeply into his eyes, but she couldn't see anything there that made her afraid, and so she sat.

It was a wise decision, because her legs wouldn't have held her up much longer.

"You mind telling me how old you are?"

He'd hit her with a stumper right off the top. She studied him, trying to position herself by reading his intent, but his face was closed up tighter than a Ziploc bag. "Sixteen," she finally volunteered, somewhat to her surprise.

"You look like you're about twelve or thirteen."

"I look like a boy, too, but I'm not."

"I don't think you look like a boy."

"You don't?"

"Nope. In fact, I think you're kind of a cute little thing."

Before she could ask him if he was being a male chauvinist pig patronizer, he hit her with another question.

"Where're you from?"

"Paxawatchie County, South Carolina. The Silver Lake Amusement Park. It's the home of the Black Thunder Roller Coaster. You might have heard of it. It's the most famous roller coaster in the South. Some say the whole country."

"I don't believe I knew that."

"Technically speaking, I guess maybe I'm not from the park any longer. The sheriff closed us down last week."

"I'm sorry to hear it."

His sympathy seemed so genuine that she began to tell him a little bit about what had happened. Because he was so undemanding and he always seemed to give her the choice not to answer his gentle questions, she found herself forgetting about the other people in the room, forgetting about the lights and cameras. Crossing her legs in her lap, she rubbed her sore toes and told him everything. She spoke of Uncle Earl's death, the *Bobby Lee*, and Mr. Disney's betrayal. The only thing she didn't tell him about was Sophie's mental condition, because she didn't want him to know she had a crazy person in her family.

After a while her toes stopped aching so bad, but when she began describing their trip across the country, her insides twisted up again. "Did you see my cousin?" she asked him.

He nodded.

"How could y'all only spend five minutes with her? How could anybody treat her like that? Don't you think she's beautiful?"

"Yeah, she's real pretty, all right. I can see why you're so proud of her."

"You bet I'm proud of her. She's pretty and sweet, and she came in here even though she was half scared to death."

"She looked like she was more than half scared, Honey.

She wouldn't even sit in front of the camera. Not everybody is cut out for a career in television."

"She could do it," Honey said stubbornly. "People can do anything they set their minds to."

"You've been going through life with your fists swinging for a long time, haven't you?"

"I do what I have to."

"Doesn't sound like you've had anybody looking after you."

"I look after myself. And I look after my family. I'm going to find us a house somewhere. A place where we can all be together. And we won't be on welfare, either."

"That's good. Nobody likes taking handouts."

"I think keeping your family together's the most important thing in the world."

Quiet fell between them. In the shadows beyond the lights, she saw an occasional movement. It was creepy having them watch her like this, not saying anything, just sitting there like a bunch of vultures.

"You ever cry, Honey?"

"Me? Hell, no."

"Why is that?"

"What good does crying do?"

"I'll bet you cried when you were a little kid."

"Only right after my mother died. From then on, whenever things got tough, I rode Black Thunder. I guess that's one of the best things about a roller coaster."

"How's that?"

She wasn't going to say that she felt close to God on the coaster, so she simply said, "A coaster gives you hope. You can pretty much ride a good one through the worst tragedy life throws at you. You can even ride it through somebody dying, I guess."

A noise distracted her. Beyond the cameras, she saw Eric Dillon slap the metal doors with the flat of one hand and stalk out.

The man sitting next to her shifted his weight. "I'm going to ask you to do something for me, Honey, and I don't think it'll be too hard. The way I look at it, these people here owe you a favor. You came all this way to see them, the least they can do is put you and your cousin up at a fine hotel for a few nights. You'll have plenty to eat and people to wait on you, and they'll pay for everything."

She eyed him suspiciously. "These people here don't think I'm any better than a maggot on spoiled meat. Why would they pay for me and Chantal to stay in some fancy hotel?"

"Because I'm gonna tell them they have to."

His absolute certainty filled her with a combination of envy and adoration. Someday she wanted to be powerful like him, to have people do exactly what she said. She thought over his offer and couldn't see any obvious hitch. Besides, she didn't think she could manage the drive back to South Carolina without some decent food and a night's sleep. Not to mention the fact that she'd just about run out of money.

"All right. I'll stay. But only until I decide I'm ready to go."

He nodded and everybody began to move at once. There was a whispered conference in the back of the studio, and then the frazzled-looking assistant who had originally taken Chantal to her audition came forward. After introducing herself as Maria, she told Honey she would help her get settled in a hotel. Maria pointed out some of the other people in the studio. The stern-faced woman was the casting director and Maria's boss. The man in the suit and tie with the silver hair was Ross Bachardy, one of the producers.

Maria led her to the studio doors. At the last minute, Honey turned back to address the man who had rescued her. "I'm not ignorant, you know. I recognized you the moment I set eyes on you. I know exactly who you are."

Dash Coogan nodded. "I figured you did."

As the doors swung closed on Maria and Honey, Ross Bachardy slapped down his clipboard and shot up from the chair. "We need to talk, Dash. Let's go to my office."

Dash tapped his pockets until he came up with an

unopened pack of peppermint LifeSavers. He pulled on the red strip and then peeled away the coin of silver foil as he followed Ross out of the studio through a side door. They crossed a parking lot and entered a low stucco building that contained the production offices and editing rooms. Positioned at the end of a narrow hallway, Ross Bachardy's cluttered office was decorated with framed citations as well as autographed photos of the actors he had worked with over his twenty years as a television producer. A Lucite ice bucket half full of jelly beans sat on his desk.

"You were way out of line, Dash."

Dash slipped a LifeSaver in his mouth. "Seems to me that since this show is going right down the toilet, you shouldn't worry so much about the formalities."

"It isn't going down the toilet."

"I may not be a mental giant, Ross, but I can read, and that pilot script you told me was going to be so wonderful is the sorriest piece of horse crap I've ever seen. The relationship between my character and Eleanor is just plain silly. Why would the two of them ever get married? And that's not the only problem. Wet toilet paper is more interesting than that daughter, Celeste. It's amazing that people who call themselves writers could actually produce something like that."

"We're working with a preliminary draft," Ross said defensively. "Things are always a little rough at the beginning. The new version will be a big improvement."

Ross's reassurances sounded hollow even to his own ears. He walked over to a small bar and pulled out a bottle of Canadian Club. He wasn't much of a drinker, and certainly not this early in the day, but the strain of getting his troubled television series on the air had stretched his nerves to the breaking point. He had already splashed some into a glass before he remembered who he was with, and he hurriedly set down the tumbler.

"Oh, Christ. I'm sorry, Dash. I wasn't thinking."

Dash studied the bottle of whiskey for a few seconds, then tucked the LifeSavers into his shirt pocket. "You can drink around me. I've been sober for almost six years; I won't grab it away from you."

Ross took a sip, but he was clearly uncomfortable. Dash Coogan's old struggles with the bottle were as well known as his three marriages and his more recent battle with the Internal Revenue Service.

One of the technicians stuck his head in the office. "What do you want me to do with this videotape? The one of Mr. Coogan and the kid."

Dash was nearest the door, and he took the cassette. "You can give it to me."

The technician disappeared. Dash looked down at the cassette. "This is where your story lies," he said quietly. "Right here. Her and me."

"That's ridiculous. It would be an entirely different show if we used that kid."

"That's for sure. It might not be the piece of crap it is right now." He tossed the cassette on Ross's desk. "This little girl is what we've been looking for, the element that's been missing from the beginning. She's the catalyst that'll make this show work."

"Celeste is eighteen, for chrissake, and she's supposed to be beautiful. I don't care how old your girl says she is, she doesn't look more than twelve, and she sure as hell isn't beautiful."

"She may not be beautiful, but you can't fault her for personality."

"Her romance with Eric Dillon's character forms a major story line. She's hardly leading lady material for Dillon."

Coogan's lip curled at the mention of the young actor's name. He had made no secret of his antipathy toward Dillon, and Ross regretted introducing the subject.

"That's another point you and I happen to differ on," Dash said. "Instead of hiring somebody reliable, you had to find yourself a pretty boy with a talent for throwing temper tantrums and causing trouble."

For the first time since they'd entered his office, Ross felt as if he were on solid ground. "That pretty boy is the best young actor this town has seen in years. *Destiny* was the network's lowest-rated soap opera until he joined the cast, and within six months, it went to number one."

"Yeah, I watched it a couple of times. All he did was walk around with his shirt off."

"And he's going to have his shirt off on this show, too. We'd be fools not to take advantage of his sex appeal. But don't get that mixed up with his talent. He's intense, he's driven, and he's barely tapped the edges of what he can do."

"If he's so talented, he should be able to handle a more challenging story line than a romance with one of those Texas lingerie models you're trying to hire to play my daughter."

"The concept of the show—"

"The concept doesn't work. That cornball plot about a second marriage isn't cutting it because the audience is never going to understand why the stuck-up city lady and the cowboy got married in the first place. And nobody in the world will believe any of those beauty queens you brought in to audition is really my daughter. You know as well as I do that I'm no Lawrence Olivier. I play myself on the screen. It's what people expect. Those girls and I don't fit together."

"Dash, we didn't even have the kid read any lines. Look, if you're serious about this, I'll have her come back tomorrow and the two of you can do that opening scene between Dash and Celeste. Than you'll see how ridiculous this whole idea is."

"You still don't get it, do you, Ross? We're not reading that opening scene together. It's a piece of crap. That little girl isn't going to be playing Celeste. She's going to play herself. She's going to play Honey."

"It upsets the whole concept of the show!"

"The concept stinks."

"She came out of nowhere, and we don't know a damned thing about her."

"We know that she's part kid and part field commander. We know that she's years younger than her real age and a few decades older, both at the same time."

"She's not an actress, for chrissake."

"She may not be, but you look me in the eye and tell me you didn't feel some kind of excitement when you watched her talk to me."

Ross held out a hand, palm open, in a gesture of appeasement. "All right, she's quite a character, I'll give you that. And I'll even go so far as to admit that the two of you together had some interesting moments. But that's not what *The Dash Coogan Show* is about. You and Liz are supposed to be newlyweds with nearly grown children. Look, Dash, we both know the pilot script isn't what we hoped it would be, but the writing will improve. And even without a great opening script, the show's going to work because people will tune in to see you. America loves you. You're the best, Dash. You always have been, and nothing's going to change that."

"Yeah. That's right. Nobody plays Dash Coogan like I do. Now how about you stop grin-fuckin' this ol' boy and let those high-priced writers of yours see that videotape? Judging by their track records, they aren't half as stupid as they seem. Give them forty-eight hours to come up with a new concept."

"We can't change the concept of the show at this late date!"

"Why not? We don't start filming for six more weeks. The sets and locations don't have to change. Just give it a try. And tell them to forget the laugh track while they're at it."

"The show's a comedy, for chrissake!"

"Then let's make it funny."

"It *is* funny," Ross said defensively. "A lot of people think it's pretty goddamn funny."

Dash spoke with a core of sadness in his voice. "It's not funny, and it's not honest. How about asking the writers to try to make it at least a little bit honest this time?"

Ross gazed after Dash as he walked out of his office. The actor had a reputation for doing his job but ignoring the details. He had never heard of Dash Coogan worrying about a script.

Ross picked up his drink and took a long, thoughtful sip.

Maybe it wasn't so strange that Dash was taking more of an interest in this project than in others. The ravages of a hard life had stamped themselves on the actor's face, camouflaging the fact that he was barely forty years old. He was also the last of a proud breed of movie cowboys that had been given life in the early 1900s with William S. Hart and Tom Mix. A breed that had blazed into glory with Coop and the Duke in the fifties and then grown cynical with the times in the Eastwood spaghetti westerns of the seventies. Now Dash Coogan was an anachronism. The last of America's movie cowboy heroes was trapped in the eighties trying to fit on a screen much too small to contain a legend.

No wonder he was running scared.

4

Eric Dillon was the stuff of female fantasy. Dark, sullen, and gorgeous, he was Heathcliff gone supersonic and blasted through time into the nuclear age. People stared at him as he followed the two stuntmen through the crowd that jammed the Auto Plant, L.A.'s hot new night spot. The stuntmen were blond, with flashing smiles and party-animal demeanors, while Eric was grim and aloof. He wore a sports coat over a torn black T-shirt and faded jeans. His hair was brushed back from his forehead, and his turquoise eyes narrowly observed the world with a cynicism much too genuine for someone so young.

A hostess wearing a hard hat and short bib overalls that showed both breast and leg led them toward a table. He could tell by the way she looked at him that she recognized him, but she didn't say anything until he was seated.

"*Destiny's* my favorite soap, and I think you're the greatest, Eric."

"Thanks." He wondered why he'd let Scotty and Tom talk him into coming with them tonight. He hated meat markets like this, and he wasn't overly fond of either one of the stuntmen.

"I'm going to UCLA during the day," the hostess said, "and I schedule all my classes so I don't miss it."

"No kidding." His eyes flicked to the dancers on the floor. He'd heard it a dozen times before. Sometimes he wondered why UCLA even bothered to hold classes between one and two in the afternoon.

"I can't believe you're leaving *Destiny*," she pouted, her face girlish and surprisingly innocent beneath its veneer of professionally applied makeup. "It's going to ruin everything."

"The show's got a great cast. You won't even miss me." The cast was mediocre at best, made up of a bunch of has-beens and wanna-bes most of whom didn't even have enough respect for their profession to learn their lines.

The hostess was looking for an excuse to linger. He turned away from her and made a meaningless remark to Tom. Despite the girl's revealing outfit, there was a dewy freshness about her that attracted him, but as he lit a cigarette, he knew he wouldn't do anything about it. He never got involved with the innocents. Although he was only twenty-three himself, he had learned long ago that he hurt defenseless creatures with eager eyes and soft hearts, and so he stayed away from them.

As the hostess left, a waitress popped up at his elbow. "Hey, Mr. Dillon. I can't believe I got you at my table. I had Sylvester Stallone last week."

"How 'bout that."

"So how was he?" Scotty asked. The stuntmen collected movie-star gossip like other people collected stamps. He'd been trying to get work on a Stallone picture for months.

"Oh, he was real nice. And he left me a fifty-dollar tip."

Scotty laughed and shook his big blond head in admiration. "He can afford it, I guess. That Sly is some guy."

Eric ordered a beer. He cared too much about his body to

abuse it, and he never had more than two drinks when he went out. He didn't do drugs, either. He refused to turn into a burned-out zombie like so many other people in the business. Cigarettes were his only vice, and he was going to kick that habit as soon as things settled down.

For the next couple of hours, he tried to have a good time. Most of the girls in the place wanted to meet him, but he put up his invisible No Trespassing sign so that only the most aggressive bothered him. A guy with blow-dried hair offered him some coke that he guaranteed was pure, but Eric told him to fuck off.

He and Tom were shooting a game of pool in an alcove lined with metal lockers and time clocks when a busty blond in a sparkly blue dress came up to him. He saw right away that she was his kind of woman—stacked and gorgeous, four or five years older than he was, with good makeup and experienced eyes. One of the indestructibles. As she approached the pool table, he remembered why he had let Scotty and Tom talk him into coming along with them tonight. He wanted to get laid.

"Hi." She let her gaze travel from a dark lock of hair that had tumbled over his forehead all the way down to the crotch of his jeans. "My name's Cindy. I'm a big fan of yours."

He stuck his cigarette in the corner of his mouth and squinted at her through the smoke. "Is that so?"

"A *big* fan. My friends dared me to get your autograph."

He chalked his pool cue. "And you're not the kind of girl who's going to turn down a dare, are you?"

"No way."

He set down the pool cue and took the thick black marking pen she held out, then waited for her to pass over a piece of paper for the autograph. Instead, she sauntered closer toward him and slipped down the strap on her blue dress, exposing her shoulder for his signature.

He lightly scraped the clip of the pen over the flesh she had revealed. "If I'm going to autograph skin, how about I autograph something more interesting than a shoulder?"

"Maybe I'm shy."

"Why don't I believe that?"

Without bothering to raise the strap on her dress, she propped one hip up on the edge of the pool table and picked up his glass of 7-Up. She took a sip and then made a face when she realized it wasn't alcoholic.

"This girl I know said she slept with you."

"Could be." He flicked his cigarette to the floor and ground it out.

"You sleep with a lot of girls?"

"It's better than watching TV." He let his gaze drop to her breast. "So, do you want your autograph or not?"

The ice clicked in the tumbler as she set it back down. "Sure. Why not?" Grinning, she flipped over onto her stomach and offered him her buttocks. "Is this worth your time?"

Scotty and Tom snickered.

Eric hesitated for only a moment before he passed over his pool cue. Hell, if she didn't care, neither did he. "Definitely worth it."

Pushing her skirt up, he revealed a transparent pair of light blue panties. With one hand he slipped them down to the top of her thighs and uncapped the pen. The pool players at the next table caught sight of what was happening and stopped to watch. In bold script, he autographed her buttocks—"Eric" on the right side, "Dillon" on the left.

"Too bad you don't have a middle name," Scotty said with a leer.

Eric picked up his drink and took a sip. She didn't move, and he continued to gaze down at her. Condensation dripped from the glass onto her skin, trickling down over the rounded slope and into the valley. Her flesh pebbled with the sudden cold, and he could feel himself getting hard.

He slapped her lightly on the rear and hooked her panties with his index finger to pull them back up. "What do you say we get out of here, Cindy?"

Handing his glass over to Tom, he tossed Scotty a couple of twenties and headed toward the exit. It didn't occur to him to turn around and see if she was following. They always did.

"Let me come with you, Eric. Please."

"Get real, runt."

"But, Eric, I want to go with you. It's boring here."

"You'll miss Sesame Street.*"*

"I haven't watched Sesame Street *since I was a kid, you jerk."*

"When was that, Jase? Two weeks ago?"

"You think you're tough just because you're fifteen and I'm only ten. Come on, Eric. Please, Eric. Please."

Eric's eyes flew open. His pillow was soaked with sweat and his heart was thudding against his ribs. He gasped for air.

Jason. Oh, God, Jase, I'm sorry.

The sheet was clammy around his chest. At least he'd awakened before the dream got bad, before he heard that awful scream.

He sat up in bed, flicked on the light, and fumbled for his cigarettes. The woman beside him stirred.

"Eric?"

For a moment he couldn't remember who she was. And then it came back to him. The chick with the autographed ass. Dropping his feet over the side of the bed, he lit his cigarette with trembling hands and drew the smoke deep into his lungs. "Get out of here."

"What?"

"I said get out."

"It's three o'clock in the morning."

"You've got a car."

"But, Eric—"

"Get the fuck out!"

She jumped from the bed and snatched up her clothes. After scrambling into them, she walked over to the door. "You're a real asshole, you know that? And you're not even a good lay."

As the door slammed behind her, he sagged back down

into the pillows. Taking another drag on his cigarette, he stared up at the ceiling. If Jase were still alive, he'd be seventeen now. Eric tried to imagine a teenaged version of his half brother, with his chubby short-legged body, round face, and scholar's eyeglasses. Clumsy, nerdy, tender-hearted Jase, who had thought the sun rose and set on his big brother. God, how he'd loved that kid. More than he'd ever loved anybody.

The voices came back to him. The voices that were never far away.

"You're going to take Dad's car, aren't you?"

"Nib out, nerd-face."

"You shouldn't do it, Eric. If he finds out, he'll never let you get your license."

"He won't find out. Not unless somebody tells him."

"Take me with you and I won't tell. I promise."

"You won't tell anyway. 'Cause if you do, I'll beat the shit out of you."

"Liar. You always say you will, but you never do."

Eric squeezed his eyes shut. He remembered grabbing Jase in a good-natured headlock and giving him a Dutch rub, being careful not to hurt him—always so careful not to really hurt him—just to toughen him up a little. His stepmother, Elaine, who was Jason's mother, protected him too much. It made Eric worry about the little rodent. Jason was the kind of kid other kids automatically picked on, and they didn't know when to stop, not like Eric did. Sometimes Eric wanted to beat the shit out of all of them for picking on Jase, but he never did because he knew he'd only make it worse for his half brother.

"All right, runt. But if I take you with me tonight, you've got to promise me you won't bug me for the next two months."

"I promise. Promise, Eric."

And so he'd taken him. He'd let Jason climb into the passenger seat of his dad's Porsche 911, the car that was forbidden to him because he was only fifteen. The car that was too powerful for an inexperienced driver to handle.

He'd peeled from the driveway of their fashionable home

in the Philadelphia suburbs, a fifteen-year-old without a care in the world out for a joyride. His father was in Manhattan for the night on business and his stepmother was playing bridge with her friends. He hadn't worried about either of them finding out. He hadn't worried about the sleet that was beginning to fall. He hadn't worried about dying. At fifteen he was immortal.

But a nerdy pest of a little brother proved to be far more fragile.

Eric lost control of the car on a curve in a road that ran alongside the Schuylkill River. The Porsche spun like a top as it was tossed against a concrete abutment. Eric—too cool to wear a seat belt—was thrown free at the moment of impact, but law-abiding Jason had been trapped. He had died quickly, but not quickly enough. Not before Eric had heard him scream.

Tears trickled from the corners of Eric's eyes and slid down into his ears. *Jase, I'm sorry. I wish it had been me, Jase. I wish it had been me instead of you.*

Liz Castleberry's wardrobe fitting had taken longer than she'd planned. As a result, she was glancing down at her watch as she stepped into the hallway outside the studio's costume shop instead of watching where she was going. Just as she cleared the doorway, she found herself bumping against something solid.

She let out a soft exclamation. "Oh, excuse me. I'm sorry. I—" Her apology faded as she lifted her eyes and saw the man standing before her.

"Lizzie?"

His slow, deep drawl wrapped around her, drawing her back into the past. Hollywood wasn't as small a town as outsiders thought, and it had been over seventeen years since they had spoken. As she lifted her eyes, she experienced the dizzying sensation of being shot back through time to 1962 when she had arrived in Hollywood with a beautiful face and a spanking new degree from Vassar. Because she had been caught with her guard down, the words that slipped from her mouth were unexpected.

"Hello, Randy."

He chuckled. "It's been a long time since anybody in Hollywood has called me that. Nobody else remembers."

Each of them took a moment to study the other. Little was left of the Randolph Dashwell Coogan of those days, the wild young rodeo rider from Oklahoma who had been working as a stuntman when they met and had been so dangerously attractive to a well-bred young woman from Connecticut. His wiry blond-brown hair was shorter than it had been then. Although his body was still tall and spare, the passage of time had engraved unforgiving lines on the hard planes of his face.

His eyes weren't as critical as hers and they warmed with admiration. "You look beautiful, Liz. Those green eyes are as pretty as ever. I was real happy when Ross told me you were going to play Eleanor. It'll be great working together after all these years."

She lifted one dramatically curved eyebrow. "Did you read the same script I read?"

"Piece of crap, isn't it? But something interesting happened yesterday. We may see a few changes."

"I'm not going to hold my breath."

"Why did you take the job?"

"Tactless question, darling. I'm of a certain age, as they say. Work isn't as easy to find as it used to be, and my tastes are as expensive as ever."

"As I remember you're just about the same age I am."

"Just about the same age as Jimmy Caan and Nick Nolte, too. But while all of you forty-year-olds can still make screen whoopie with cute little ingenues, I'm reduced to playing a mother."

She said the last word with such distaste that Dash laughed. "You don't look much like any mother I ever saw."

Liz smiled. Despite her grumbling about her age and the career problems it was causing, she wasn't entirely displeased with being forty. Her long hair was the same rich shade of mahogany it had always been, and the green eyes that had first made her famous were still luminous. She hadn't put on weight, and her skin was only beginning to crease gently at the corners of her eyes. Being forty had its advantages. She was old enough to know exactly what she wanted out of life—enough money to maintain her Malibu beach house, buy the beautiful clothes she loved, and contribute generously to her favorite charity, the Humane Society. Her golden retriever, Mitzi, provided daytime fellowship and an assortment of discreet attractive men offered nighttime thrills. She truly enjoyed her life, which was more than many of her friends could say.

"How is your family?" she inquired.

"Which one?"

Once again, she smiled. There had always been something wonderfully self-effacing about Dash. "Take your pick."

"Well, you might have read that my last wife, Barbara, and I split a couple of years ago. She's doing real well for herself, though. Married a Denver banker. We still get together every once in a while. And Marietta started a chain of aerobics studios in San Diego. She always did have a good head for business."

"I seem to remember reading about that. She kept you in and out of the courtroom for years, didn't she?"

"I didn't mind the courtroom so much as the way she sicced the IRS on me six months ago. Those bastards don't have any sense of humor."

Seventeen years had passed since she had fallen in love with him, and she was no longer fooled by that easy cowboy charm. Dash Coogan was a complex man. She remembered him as a gentle, giving lover, generous to a fault with his money but unable to share anything of himself. Like the western heroes he played, he was a loner, a man who put up so many subtle barriers against intimacy that it was impossible to truly know him.

"My kids are doing real good," he went on. "Josh is in his junior year at the University of Oklahoma and Meredith's going to be a freshman at Oral Roberts."

"And Wanda?" After all these years there was still a slight sting to her voice. She and Dash had spent several weeks in bed together before he'd gotten around to mentioning the fact that he had a wife and two children tucked away in Tulsa. She thought too much of herself to be involved with another woman's husband, and that had been the end of the affair. But Dash Coogan wasn't the easiest man to get over, and it had taken her months to put her life back in order, something for which she had never quite forgiven him.

"Wanda's doing fine. She never changes."

Liz wondered if Wife Number Four was looming on the horizon. She also wondered what he would do if the show wasn't a success. Everyone knew that Dash had only agreed to do the show because he'd struck a deal with the IRS to pay off his debt. If he'd had a choice, she had no doubt that he would have stayed on his ranch with his horses.

A younger version of herself might have asked some of these questions, but the more mature Liz had learned to appreciate a life without messy personal entanglements, and so she made a play of looking at her watch. "Oh, dear. I'm late for my appointment with my masseuse, and my cellulite simply *hates* it when that happens."

He chuckled. "You and the second Mrs. Coogan would get along fine. Both of you enjoy all that fitness stuff, and you're both a lot smarter than you like to pretend. Of course, Marietta's degree came from the school of hard knocks, and yours came from Harvard or one of those places, didn't it?"

"Vassar, darling." Laughing, she gave him a brief wave.

He grinned and disappeared into the costume shop.

Several hours later, as Liz carried a glass of iced herbal tea and a small endive salad out onto the deck of her beach house, she found that she was still thinking about Dash. Mitzi, her golden retriever, trailed after her and plunked down across her feet. As Liz took a sip of her tea, she considered how much there was about Dash to admire.

He had fought a fierce battle with alcoholism and come out the winner. But he didn't seem to have taken his recovery for granted, and over the years she had heard stories of the ways in which he had helped other alcoholics.

The hero's white hat would have fit him perfectly, she decided, if it weren't for his womanizing.

In many ways he was an improbable Lothario, and if rumor were to be believed, he hadn't changed that much over the years. There had never been anything lecherous about his behavior. Quite the opposite. She remembered that he had always been shy around women, never directly seeking them out or trying to draw their attention. As much as she might want to rewrite her personal history, she knew that she had been the aggressor, setting her sights on the young stunt rider the moment they had been introduced on the set of her first picture. She had been drawn as so many women would be over the years by his overwhelming masculinity, made even more irresistible by a quiet, old-fashioned courtesy and deep sense of reserve.

No, Dash's flaw hadn't been lechery; it had been spinelessness. He couldn't seem to say no to an attractive woman, not even when he was wearing a wedding ring.

The afternoon was hot and breezy, and the faint sound of music came from the house next door. Liz glanced over to see Lilly Isabella sitting beneath an umbrella on her deck with several friends.

Lilly looked over and waved, her silvery-blond hair glistening in the sunlight. "Hi, Liz. Is the music too loud?"

"Not at all," Liz called back. "Enjoy yourselves."

Lilly was the twenty-year-old daughter of Guy Isabella, one of Liz's leading men in the seventies. He had bought the house several years ago, but his beautiful young daughter spent more time there than he did. Occasionally Liz invited the girl over, but she had grown selfish with her solitude and she didn't enjoy being around young people very much. All that desperate self-centeredness was too wearing.

As she sipped her tea, she reminded herself that she would be spending lots of time with young people for the next few months—the unknown actress Ross chose to play that silly part of Celeste, and Eric Dillon, of course. It pricked her vanity to be playing the mother of a twenty-three-year-old, even though Dillon's character was only supposed to be eighteen on the show. But more than that, she was worried about working with someone reputed to be difficult. Her hairdresser had been on the set of *Destiny* for a while, and Liz had heard stories that Dillon had a reputation for being surly and demanding.

He was also wildly talented. Her intuition about these things seldom failed her, and she had no doubt that he would one day be a big star. Those cruel good looks combined with a burning intensity that couldn't be taught in any acting class were going to catapult Eric Dillon to the very pinnacle. The question remained, would he be able to handle his fame or would he burn out as so many others had before him?

Eric had slept poorly, and he didn't get up until one in the afternoon. His head was aching and he felt like shit. Throwing his bare legs over the side of the bed, he reached for his cigarettes. A cigarette, a glass of high-protein breakfast drink, and then he'd work out for a couple of hours.

His clothes were strewn on the floor from the night before, and he thought about how much he liked sex. When he was in bed with a chick, he didn't have to think about anything —not who he was with, not anything. Life was reduced to the simple task of getting off. Once he'd heard a guy say he'd fucked some chick's brains out. Eric didn't think like that. He thought about fucking his own brains out.

As he got up, he spotted some black smudges soiling the bottom sheet. Puzzled, he made a closer inspection. It looked like writing, like script letters: ƆIЯƎ. His mouth curled as he remembered Cindy and her autographed ass. Just like a rubber stamp.

He pulled on a jock and a pair of running shorts, then walked out into the living room. The house was a small Benedict Canyon ranch, a perfect bachelor's quarters with its few pieces of comfortable furniture and big-screen television. He went into the kitchen and snatched a container of high-protein drink from the shelf. After dumping a couple of scoops into the blender, he added some milk and hit the button. But the night dreams were still too near, and the sound filled the small kitchen like the whine of a siren. It drilled into his brain, bringing back the chilling memory of the siren on the ambulance that had carried Jason's broken body away. He jabbed at the blender to turn it off, then stared at the foamy contents.

"Your stepmother feels— You have to understand, Eric, that with Jason gone . . . You have to understand how difficult it is for Elaine to have you around."

Two weeks after Jason's funeral, Eric had looked into his father's drawn, handsome face and known that Lawrence Dillon couldn't stand to have him around, either. Since his own mother had died when he was a baby, it wasn't too hard for him to figure out what was going to happen to him.

He had ended up at an exclusive private school near Princeton where he had broken every rule and been kicked out after six months. His father sent him to two more schools before he managed to graduate, and then only because he had discovered the school's drama department and learned that he could forget who he was when he slipped into another person's body. He'd even spent a couple of years in college, but he'd missed so many classes going into the city for casting calls that he'd eventually flunked out.

Two years ago one of the *Destiny* casting agents had spotted him in an Off-off Broadway play and signed him to portray a character who was scheduled to die after six weeks. But viewer response had been so strong that his character had become a regular. Recently, he had attracted the interest of the Coogan show producers.

His agent wanted him to be a star, but Eric wanted to be an actor. He loved acting. Slipping inside another person's skin took away the pain. And sometimes, for a few moments, a look, a couple of lines of dialogue, he was good, really good.

He drank the protein mix straight from the blender, then lit a cigarette while he wandered back out into the living room. As he passed the couch, he caught a glimpse of his face in the oval wall mirror. For a moment he stared at his reflection, wishing it were ordinary, wishing he were a regular guy with a funny nose and crooked teeth.

He turned away from the face he hated, but he couldn't turn away from what was inside himself. And he hated that even more.

5

As far as Honey was concerned, the Beverly Hills Hotel was a chunk of pink-stucco heaven right on earth. The moment she stepped into the small, flower-bedecked lobby, she decided that this was the place all good people should go the second they died.

The Iranian lady at the front desk explained how everything in the hotel worked, and she wasn't the slightest bit condescending, although it had to be pretty obvious to her that neither Honey nor Chantal had ever stayed at any place nicer than a ten-unit motel.

Honey loved the wallpaper printed with fat banana fronds, the louvered doors, and the private patio that opened off their spacious, homey room. With the exception of a couple of snooty peckerhead waiters in the Polo Lounge, she decided that the folks who ran the place were just about the nicest people on earth, not stuck-up at all. The maids and bell boys said hi to her even though they must have suspected that Gordon Delaweese was sneaking into their room and sleeping on the couch.

Gordon looked up as she came out of the dressing room on Saturday afternoon. It was their second day in the hotel, and she had just changed into a bright red tank suit that one of the maids had gotten for her so she could go swimming. Gordon and Chantal were curled up on the couch watching *Wheel of Fortune* and trying to guess the puzzle.

"Hey, Honey, why don't we order up some more food

from room service?" he said, speaking through a mouthful of potato chips. "Those hamburgers sure were good."

"We just ate lunch an hour ago." Honey couldn't keep the disgust out of her voice. "When did you say you were leaving, Gordon? I know there's a lot of true life out there you still need to observe if you want to be a painter."

"I can't think of a better place for Gordon to observe real life than here at the Beverly Hills Hotel," Chantal commented, taking a sip of her Diet Pepsi. "This is a once in a lifetime opportunity for him."

Honey debated starting an argument, but every time she pressed the idea of Gordon leaving, Chantal began to cry. "I'm finished in the dressing room, Chantal. You can go change into your bathing suit now."

"I guess I'm too tired to swim. I think I'll stay here and watch TV."

"You said you'd come swimming with me! Come on, Chantal. It'll be fun."

"I'm feeling a little headachy. You go on."

"And leave the two of you alone in this hotel room? Do you think I'm crazy?"

"Some like it hot!" Gordon cried out, pointing to the television screen.

Chantal gazed at him with admiration. "Gordon, you are *so* smart. He's guessed every puzzle, Honey. Every single one."

Honey looked at the two of them curled up on that couch in the middle of the afternoon just like a couple of pieces of white trash. This would probably be their last day at the Beverly Hills Hotel, and she had been looking forward to swimming in that great big pool ever since she got here.

Inspiration seized her. Walking over to the small chest by the bed, she began opening the drawers. When she found what she wanted, she snatched it up and carried it over to Chantal.

"You put your hand right square in the middle of this Holy Bible and swear you won't do anything with Gordon Delaweese that you're not supposed to."

Chantal immediately looked guilty, which told Honey

everything she needed to know. "I want you to swear, Chantal Booker."

Chantal reluctantly swore. For good measure Honey made Gordon Delaweese swear, too, even though she wasn't sure exactly where his theology lay. As she left the room, she was relieved to see that both of them looked miserable.

The pool at the Beverly Hills Hotel was a wondrous place, bigger than most people's houses and inhabited by the most interesting group of human beings Honey had ever seen. As she stepped through the gate, she observed the women with thin, dark, oiled bodies and glimmering gold jewelry stretched out on the white lounges. Some of the men wore tiny bikinis and looked like Tarzan. One had straight white-blond hair that hung past his shoulders—either a WWF wrestler or a Norwegian. Some of the poolside loungers looked like ordinary rich men—paunchy bellies, thin slicked-back hair, and funny little canvas slippers.

Still, Honey felt sorry for them. None of them knew how to have real fun in a swimming pool. Occasionally, one of the men did a neat dive off the low board or swam a few slow laps. And a couple of women with diamonds in their ears squatted down in the water while they talked to each other, but they didn't even get their shoulders wet, let alone their hair.

What fun was it to be rich if you couldn't enjoy a swimming pool? Kicking off her flip-flops, she raced toward the water and, giving her best rebel yell, did a cannonball right into the deep end. The splash she sent up was one of her best. When she surfaced, she saw that everybody had turned to look at her. She called over to the people closest to her, a darkly tanned man and woman, both of whom had telephones pressed to their ears.

"Y'all should come in. The water's real nice."

They averted their eyes and went back to their phone conversations.

She dove beneath the water and swam along the bottom. The tank suit was too big and the nylon ballooned around her rear. She surfaced to catch her breath, then again dove for the bottom. As the peaceful underwater world engulfed her, she once again tried to sort out what was happening. Why had Dash Coogan wanted to videotape her? He had said he wasn't trying to get her into trouble with the police, but what if he'd been lying?

She came to the surface and flipped over onto her back. Water filled her ears and her chopped hair floated unevenly around her head. She thought about Eric Dillon and wondered if she would ever see him again. He was the handsomest man she had ever met. It was funny, though. When she'd casually mentioned his name, Chantal had gotten this strange look on her face and told Honey that Eric Dillon was scary. Honey had never heard Chantal say such a thing about a person in her life, and she figured her cousin must have gotten the real Eric Dillon mixed up with that character he played on the soap opera.

Half an hour later she was climbing out of the pool to do another cannonball off the diving board when she saw Ross Bachardy coming toward her. She nodded politely at the producer, but inside she felt like crying. She'd known their time in paradise had to come to an end, but she'd been hoping for one more day. She walked over to her lounge chair, retrieved her towel, and tucked it high into her armpits.

"Hello, Honey. Your cousin told me you were out here. Are you enjoying your stay?"

"It's about the best place I've ever been in my life."

"That's good. I'm glad you like it. Could we sit over here and talk?" He gestured toward a table tucked into the greenery.

She thought it was nice of him to show up personally to kick them out, but she wished he'd just get it over with. "It's your nickel." She followed him over to the table and pulled out a chair with her foot so she didn't lose the beach towel anchored under her arms. He looked hot in his taffy-colored sports coat, and she couldn't help feeling a little sorry for him.

"It's a shame you didn't bring your trunks along so you could take a swim. The water's real nice."

He smiled. "Maybe another time." A waiter appeared.

The producer ordered some kind of foreign beer for himself and an Orange Crush for her. Then he hit her with his bombshell.

"Honey, we want to cast you as the daughter in *The Dash Coogan Show*."

She thought she must have pool water in her ears. "Beg your pardon?"

"We want you to play Dash Coogan's daughter."

She gaped at him. "You want *me* to play Celeste?"

"Not exactly. We're making some changes in the show, and we've gotten rid of that character. All of us liked that videotape you and Dash made together, and it gave us a few ideas that we're quite excited about. The details aren't worked out yet, but we think we have something special."

"You want me?"

"We certainly do. You'll be playing Janie, Dash's thirteen-year-old daughter. Dash and Eleanor won't be newlyweds anymore." He began to outline a story line for her, but she couldn't seem to take it in and eventually she interrupted in a voice that had a funny little squeak to it.

"No offense, Mr. Bachardy, but that's the craziest idea I've ever heard. I can't be an actress. I'm not the slightest bit pretty. Did you look close at my mouth—like a big old sucker fish? It's Chantal you should be casting in that part, not me."

"Why don't you let me be the judge of that."

Something he'd said earlier suddenly hit her. "Thirteen? But I'm sixteen years old."

"You're small, Honey. You can easily pass for thirteen."

Normally she wouldn't have swallowed such an insult, but she was too stunned to be offended.

Ross went on, giving her more details about the show and then talking about contracts and agents. Honey felt as if her head was spinning right off her neck, just like that poor little girl in *The Exorcist*. The breeze raised goose bumps on her skin as she realized how fiercely she wanted all this to be true. She was smart and ambitious. This was her chance to make something of herself instead of expending all of her energy trying to prod Chantal. But a TV star? Not even in her wildest imagination could she have conjured up something like that.

Ross began to talk about salary, and the amounts he mentioned were so astronomical she could barely comprehend them. Her mind raced. This would change everything for them.

He pulled a small notebook from his suit-coat pocket. "You're a minor, so before we can go any farther with this, I'll need to meet with your legal guardian."

Honey fumbled with her glass of Orange Crush.

"You do have a guardian?"

"Of course I do. My Aunt Sophie. Mrs. Earl T. Booker."

"I'll need her phone number so I can call her to arrange for a meeting. Thursday at the latest. We'll fly her out at our expense, of course."

She tried to imagine Sophie getting on a plane, but she couldn't even imagine her getting up off the couch. "She's been sick lately. Uh—female trouble. I don't think she'll come to California. She's afraid to fly. Plus the female trouble."

He looked disturbed. "That's going to be a problem, but you'll have to get an agent to represent you anyway and he can take care of it. I'll give you a list of some of the better ones. We begin filming in six weeks, so you'll need to get it taken care of right away." The lines around his mouth grew deeper. "I have to tell you, Honey, that I think it was unwise of you to have come all the way to California without an adult."

"I came with an adult," Honey reminded him. "Chantal's eighteen."

He wasn't impressed.

After she returned to the room, she stumbled all over herself explaining what had happened, and Chantal and Gordon started whooping and hollering so much that before long they were all rolling around on the floor and acting crazy. When she settled down, she remembered what Mr. Bachardy had said about getting an agent and she pulled out the list of the names he had given her. She began to reach for the telephone, and then her eyes narrowed. She might be a redneck girl from South Carolina, and she certainly didn't know anything about agents or Hollywood, but she wasn't born yesterday either. Why should she trust Mr. Bachardy to give her a name? Wasn't that a little bit like trusting the fox to guard the chickens?

She considered the problem while she changed from her bathing suit back into her shorts. She didn't know anybody in Hollywood, so who could she turn to for advice? And then she smiled and picked up the phone.

The Beverly Hills Hotel prided itself on handling every emergency, even helping one of its guests find an agent, and by noon the next day the concierge had helped Honey hire Arthur Lockwood, an aggressive young lawyer who worked for one of the better-known talent agencies and promised to fly to South Carolina to meet with Aunt Sophie.

That night as Honey drifted off to sleep, she could hear the distant roar of Black Thunder in her ears. She smiled against her pillow. *There's always hope.*

6

THE DASH COOGAN SHOW
Episode One

EXTERIOR. TEXAS DIRT ROAD—LATE AFTERNOON. AS THEME MUSIC/CREDITS ROLL . . .

A battered pickup truck shudders to a stop, steam rising from the hood. CLOSE ON worn pair of cowboy boots emerging from cab. Boot kicks tire then walks around side to back and pulls out saddle. A second pair of boots emerges from the cab, this one small. Together, they begin walking down the flat Texas road, their heels kicking up puffs of dust. Smaller pair occasionally takes two steps to keep up with larger pair. As theme music ends, we hear voices:

JANIE'S VOICE

Promise me you'll try this time, Pop. Promise me you won't quit after two days like last time. We need a home, a place to settle down.

Both pairs of boots stop in front of a picket fence gate with peeling white paint.

DASH'S VOICE

Nobody likes a nagging woman, Janie. When you gonna learn that?

JANIE'S VOICE

I'm not a woman. I'm thirteen.

DASH'S VOICE

You're a thorn in my side is what you are.

JANIE'S VOICE

Do you really mean that?

DASH'S VOICE
(softening)

Naw.

ANGLE TO DASH. CLOSE on his rodeo champion belt buckle. WIDER ANGLE to Dash and Janie. They look hot, thirsty, and tired.

EXTERIOR. FRONT YARD OF PDQ RANCH.

Dash opens gate. They begin moving up sidewalk to dilapidated ranch house.

DASH

I'm a rodeo rider, Janie. Not a ranch manager. And this spread isn't even respectable. It's a *dude* ranch. I still plan on tanning your hide for forging my name on that job application.

JANIE

You used to be a rodeo rider, Pop, but you're not anymore. You heard what the doc said. No more broncs unless you want to spend the rest of your life in a wheelchair.

DASH

At least I'd have something underneath me that moved.

JANIE

What about that cocktail waitress in El Paso?

DASH

Janie?

JANIE

Yeah, Pop?

DASH

Remind me to tan your hide.

EXTERIOR. PDQ RANCH HOUSE FRONT PORCH

ELEANOR CHADWICK steps out looking harried. She is beautiful, perfectly coiffed, and too stylishly dressed for her surroundings. She speaks to someone still in the house.

ELEANOR

I don't care if we *do* have a horse foaling. Dusty can call an obstetrician. I'm going into Goose Creek and see if there's anyone in that godforsaken town who knows how to give a cucumber/Grand Marnier facial.

She spots Dash and Janie.

Oh, Lord, what now?

Dash and Janie stop at the bottom of the stairs. Dash sets down saddle. He and Eleanor take each other in. He is a handsome man, and she can't help admiring him. On the other hand, she hates everything about the West, including cowboys.

ELEANOR
My, my. If it isn't Wyatt Earp and Billy the Kidette.

Eleanor's sarcasm doesn't go over well with Dash. Although he has a weakness for beautiful women, her patronizing attitude sets his teeth on edge. Janie knows her father too well and quickly intercedes.

JANIE
Howdy, ma'am. My name's Janie Jones. This here is my pop, Mr. Dash Jones. He's your new ranch manager.

DASH
I'll do my own talking, Jane Marie.

ELEANOR
(taking in Dash)
They certain do grow them big out here in the West. It must be from smoking all that sagebrush. You're late, by the way. You were supposed to be here yesterday. If you're going to work for me, you'll have to be more reliable.

DASH
(resting one boot on the step)
Well, you see ma'am, that's just it. I'm not going to be working for you. I just remembered that I got a better offer from this fellow who runs a rattlesnake ranch right off the interstate. All he wants me to do is hand-feed those critters. The way I figure it, the company'd be more polite.

ELEANOR
(indignantly)
Of all the gall. You're fired, do you hear me? I wouldn't have you working for me if you were the last ranch manager in Texas.

DASH

That's just fine with me, ma'am, because from
the looks of this place, you won't be in business
much longer.

Janie's eyes dart from her father to Eleanor and back
again. Realizing she has to do something, she clutches her
stomach and falls down on porch, groaning loudly.
Eleanor looks alarmed and runs to her side, fussing over
her.

ELEANOR

What's wrong? What's wrong with her?

DASH

(impervious to Janie's dramatic groans)
I'd watch yourself there, ma'am. When she gets
like this, she has a tendency to upchuck, and I
don't think the color scheme would coordinate
with those nice clothes of yours.

Janie's groans intensify. Eleanor becomes more alarmed.
She continues to fuss over Janie.

ELEANOR

Do something, will you! What kind of a father
are you to let your child suffer like this?

DASH

It's probably just another busted appendix. She
gets them all the time. I wouldn't trouble yourself.

With that, Dash picks Janie up and throws her over his
shoulder.

ANGLE TO SIDE OF HOUSE WITH BARN IN BACK-
GROUND

BLAKE CHADWICK comes running toward the house. A
handsome and charming young man, he's dressed in
jeans and a work shirt, both obviously new. But even

though he's a city slicker, Blake likes the PDQ Ranch, and he wants to make a go of it.

Janie's screams stop as she spots Blake. She stares at him open-mouthed. He's the handsomest man she's ever seen, and at the age of thirteen, she falls in love for the first time.

> BLAKE
> Mom, Dusty says the foal's not turned right. We're going to lose both the foal and the mare if that vet doesn't get here soon. And the trail party that left this morning should have been back hours ago. I'm going to have to go after them.

> ELEANOR
> That's impossible! You don't know the trails, and you'll get lost yourself. Where is that vet? How could he do something like this? If your father weren't already dead, I'd kill him for leaving me this awful ranch in his will. I swear, I'll sell it to the first person who makes me a decent offer. If it weren't for this horrid place, I could be lunching at the Russian Tea Room right now with Cissy and Pat and Caroline!

Pushing up the sleeves of her expensive suit, Eleanor sets off purposefully toward the barn, her head high, her spiked heels sinking deeply into the dirt.

Dash stares after her. Janie, still upside down over her father's shoulder, stares at Blake. Blake notices them and walks toward Dash, his hand extended.

> BLAKE
> Hi, there. I'm Blake Chadwick. Welcome to the PDQ.

> DASH
> Dash Jones.

BLAKE

The new ranch manager! Am I ever glad to see you.

DASH

Ex-ranch manager. I'm afraid your ma and me didn't hit it off too well.

JANIE
(still upside down)
Could I say something?

DASH

No.

Dash stares thoughtfully toward the barn.

Your ma doesn't look like she knows too much about horses.

BLAKE
(fondly)
She's not too crazy about any animal that can't be made into a coat. She tries, but this has been hard on her.

A beautiful buxom female appears in the background near the barn. She is dressed in jeans and a tight gingham blouse and calls out Blake's name.

BLAKE

I'll be there in a minute, Dusty.

BLAKE turns back to Dash, who has picked up the saddle with his other arm.

Are you sure you won't change your mind, Mr. Jones? We could really use some help.

DASH

I'm afraid not, son.

BLAKE
(with resignation)
Yeah, you look like a man with good sense.

Blake heads toward the barn without having acknowledged Janie's presence.

Dash stares after Blake and slowly lowers Janie to the
ground. Reluctantly, he puts down the saddle.

                    DASH
    Janie?

                    JANIE
    Yeah, Pop?

                    DASH
    Remind me to tan your hide.

Grimly, he sets off toward the barn.

"And cut," the director called out. "Print it. Good work,
everybody. Let's break for lunch."

It was the last week of July and their final day of shooting
the pilot episode. They hadn't been filming the show in
order, and they were just now doing the opening scenes. It
was a confusing way to go about things as far as Honey was
concerned, but then no one had asked her opinion. They
didn't ask her about anything, in fact. They just told her
what to do.

She gazed around her at the set for the PDQ ranch. They
were filming all the exteriors at a former chicken ranch
near the Tajunga Wash, an area in the San Gabriel Mountains north of Pasadena. The rugged slopes of the San Gabriels were covered by chaparral at the lower elevations,
giving way to pine and fir as the peaks rose. Just that
morning she had glimpsed desert bighorn sheep as well
as a golden eagle soaring on the thermal updrafts. Most
half-hour television shows were videotaped, she had
learned, but since so much of *The Dash Coogan Show*
took place outside, it was being filmed, instead, like a
movie.

"Good job, Honey." Jack Swackhammer, the director,
patted her on top of her head just as if she were some damn
poodle dog. He was young and skinny, and he hopped

around a lot. All week he had looked as if he was getting ready to have a nervous breakdown.

As he walked over to talk to his assistant, Honey looked after him with disgust. Everybody was treating her as if she were really thirteen. She shouldn't have been surprised, she supposed, considering the fact that those stupid writers kept taking her into their conference room and raping her mind.

The first time the writers had called her in, they'd been so nice, explaining the new concept for the show and asking her opinion about everything under the sun. Since there was nothing she enjoyed more than talking, she'd been pulled in like a fool. She had sat there sucking on the can of Orange Crush they'd offered her and talked, talked, talked—too stupid to figure out that all of her opinions would become Janie's opinions, that her feelings would become Janie's.

They had stuck her need for a home in the script, right along with all her secret feelings about Eric Dillon, although how they'd figured that out, she had no idea, since she certainly hadn't come out and told them. Maybe it wouldn't have been quite so humiliating if they had made Janie a mature, self-sufficient sixteen-year-old like herself, but instead they had turned her into a puny little thirteen-year-old retard. She still got indignant whenever she thought about it.

As the director ended his conversation with his assistant, she approached him. "Mr. Swackhammer—"

"Please, Honey. Call me Jack. We're all family here."

But they weren't her family. What should have been the most exciting time of her life was being ruined because Sophie refused to leave the park to come to California and Gordon Delaweese spent all his time at the new apartment she and Chantal had moved into. With Chantal paying so much attention to Gordon and with Sophie still in South Carolina, Honey was feeling all jangly, as if she didn't belong anywhere.

Working on the television show wasn't like she'd imagined it, either. After having been so nice to her the day they had met, Dash Coogan had gradually changed. He'd been real helpful to her at first, but then it seemed the friendlier she got, the more he backed off. Now he barely spoke to her unless they were on-camera together. And the only time Eric Dillon had sought her out was to ask her if Chantal would be coming around.

The director looked back down at his clipboard. She remembered her most pressing grievance. "I've got to talk to you about this haircut."

"Shoot."

"It's embarrassing."

"What do you mean?"

"It looks like somebody put a dog's dish on top of my head and cut right around it." The sides were cut high over her ears and the back formed a straight line two inches above her nape. Her bangs fell long and fine past her eyebrows, making the whole thing look off balance.

"It's great, Honey. Perfect for the part."

"I'm going to be seventeen in December. What kind of haircut is this for a girl who's almost seventeen?"

"Janie's thirteen. You have to get used to thinking younger."

"That's another thing. I saw that press kit you sent out, and it gives my *real* age as thirteen."

"That was Ross's idea. Audiences don't like it when they find out kid actors are lots older than the part they're playing. You're small, and you're an unknown. Ross wants to keep you away from the press for a while until you get your bearings, so it doesn't really make much difference, now, does it?"

Not to him, maybe. But it certainly did to her.

"Jacko! Honey! You're doing great, sweetheart. Just great."

One of the older network executives, a nervous-looking man in his late fifties, popped a little white pill in his mouth as he came up to them. She stepped back before he could chuck her under the chin as he'd done that morning.

"I think we've got a hit in the making here," he said with too much heartiness. Even without his eyelid twitching, she would have known that he didn't believe a word he was saying. The network was nervous because they said the new concept for *The Dash Coogan Show* wasn't really situation comedy but it wasn't quite drama either, and they were worried about confusing the audience.

Honey didn't see what the big deal was. The show was funny in some parts, sad in other parts, and pretty sentimental a lot of the time. What was so hard to understand about that? The American people might be getting ready to vote another Republican into the White House, but that didn't mean they were stupid about everything.

He smiled at her, displaying teeth too big and white to be real. "You've got star written all over you, sweetheart. She's the real thing, isn't she, Jacko?"

"Uh— Thanks, Mr. Evans."

"Call me Jeffrey, sweetheart. And I mean it. Really. You're going to be another Gary Coleman."

He started raving about all her natural talent and carrying on like she was the second coming. Her stomach began to feel queasy. She told herself it was from spending so much time upside down over Mr. Coogan's shoulder, but it was really because she didn't believe him. All of them knew that she didn't understand the first thing about acting. She was nothing more than a little redneck girl from South Carolina who had jumped into water that was way over her head.

The executive excused himself to corner Ross. Honey was getting ready to argue some more with Jack about her haircut when Eric Dillon appeared from behind them.

"Jack, I need to talk to you."

Honey hadn't heard him coming, and, at the sound of his voice, an achy sense of longing came over her. She was painfully conscious of her scruffy jeans and dog-dish hair. She wished she were beautiful and sophisticated like Liz Castleberry.

As Eric closed in on the director, his eyes darkened with an intensity that sent a shiver through Honey. "I'm not happy with the pacing, Jack. You're rushing me through lines where I need to take my time. I'm not driving a race car here."

Honey looked at him with admiration. Eric was a real actor, not a pretend one like herself. He studied with an acting coach, and he talked about things like sensory awareness. She, on the other hand, just did what people told her.

Jack glanced uncomfortably toward Honey. "Why don't we take this up in private, Eric? Tell you what. Give me five minutes, and then meet me in the production trailer."

Eric gave a curt nod. Jack walked off, and she tried to think of something intelligent to say before Eric left her side, too, but her tongue was paralyzed. The worst part of the way the writers had raped her mind was the fact they she had to act like a lovestruck ninny in all their scenes together. As a result, she had no idea how to act when they weren't on camera.

He pulled a cigarette from his shirt pocket and stared off into space as he lit it.

She stared off into space, too. "You—uh— You're real serious about acting, aren't you, Eric?"

"Yeah," he muttered, not bothering to look at her. "I'm real serious."

"I heard you talking about that sensory awareness stuff with Liz. Maybe sometime you could explain it to me."

"Yeah, maybe." He took off for the production trailer.

Feeling discouraged, she watched him go. As her spirits dipped lower, she told herself she was acting like a spoiled brat. In less than a month, she would have earned more money than the Silver Lake Amusement Park had made in gate receipts for the entire winter. She didn't have any reason to be unhappy. Still, she couldn't shake off the uneasy feeling that nothing was going right.

It was eight o'clock that evening before shooting was finished and Honey had climbed out of her costume jeans and into her own jeans. By the time she reached the apartment she shared with Chantal and parked the racy little fire-engine-red Trans Am her agent's secretary had helped her buy, she was so tired she could barely keep her eyes open.

The building was the nicest place Honey had ever lived—a vine-covered white stucco quadrangle with a red-tiled roof and a small courtyard in the center. The apartment itself boasted comfortable furniture, a little patio, and museum posters on the walls. It had everything she could want except Sophie. And one thing she didn't want—Gordon Delaweese.

As soon as she unlocked the front door and stepped into the foyer, she knew something was wrong. Usually when she came home, Gordon and Chantal were propped up in front of the television eating Hungry Man dinners, but now everything was dark.

A twinge of alarm shot through her. She flipped on the overhead light and dashed through the kitchen into the living room. Snack wrappers and ashtrays littered the coffee table. She rushed upstairs. Her heart pounding in her throat, she pushed open Chantal's bedroom door.

The two of them were lying naked in each other's arms, sound asleep. All the blood rushed from Honey's head. Her hand shook as she flipped on the overhead light. Chantal stirred and then blinked. Abruptly, she sat upright, pulling the sheet up over her breasts.

"Honey!"

"You Judas," she whispered.

Gordon struggled awake. A few strands of dark hair hung like ravelings at the center of his bony chest. He looked uneasily back and forth between the two women.

Honey shoved the words out through a small tight space in her throat. "You swore on the Holy Bible. How could you do this?"

"It's not what you think."

"I'm not blind, Chantal. I know what I see."

Chantal pushed her dark curls back from her face. Her red mouth grew soft and pouty. "You made it so hard on us, Honey. Maybe if you hadn't forced us to swear on the Bible, me and Gordon could have just done what came naturally and waited for the rest. But after you made us swear . . ."

"What are you talking about? What do you mean 'waited for the rest'?"

Chantal bit at her lip nervously. "Me and Gordon. We got married this afternoon."

"You did what?"

"It's not a sin now. We're married, so we can do whatever we want."

Honey stared at the two of them huddled in the bed, and she felt as if her whole life had just fallen apart around her. They were pressed together, already excluding her. Chantal, the person she loved most in the world, now loved somebody else more.

Chantal bit at her bottom lip. "Me and Gordon getting married doesn't make any difference, don't you see? Since you got the part on the TV show, we don't have to depend on me anymore. Now you're the one who can do great things, Honey. I can just be a regular person. Maybe learn how to do hair. I don't have to be anybody special."

Honey's jaw set into a hard line. "You Judas! I won't ever forgive you for this!"

She raced out of the room and down the steps. When she reached the front door, she threw it open and ran out into the night. She heard a roaring in her ears, the sound of Black Thunder hurling her through time and space. But Black Thunder was too far away for her to feel reassured that everything would be all right again.

She stayed in the courtyard by the fountain until she was shivering, as much from emotion as from the chill air. Then she went back inside and, sealing herself in her bedroom, called Sophie.

"Sophie, it's me."

"Who?"

Honey wanted to scream at her aunt, but she knew it wouldn't do any good. "Sophie, you can't put off coming to California any longer. I need you. Chantal married Gordon Delaweese, that boy I told you about. You got to come out and help me."

"Chantal got married?"

"This afternoon."

"I missed my baby's wedding?"

"I don't think it was much of a wedding. Now write this

down. I'm going to send you some airplane tickets for next week through that Federal Express mail. You're going to fly to L.A."

"I don't think so, Honey. The bank said I could live in the trailer for a while."

"Sophie, you can't stay there. It's not safe."

"It's safe. They hired Buck to stay around as caretaker and keep an eye on things."

"Buck can hardly keep an eye on himself, let alone you."

"I don't know why you're always so nasty about Buck. He gets my groceries and watches my soaps with me and everything."

Honey refused to let herself get sidetracked. "Listen to me, Sophie. Chantal just got married to a boy she hardly even knows. I need your help."

There was a long silence, and then the sound of Sophie's weary voice, no stronger than a sigh. "You don't need me, Honey. You'll take care of everything. Just like always."

7

Honey curled into Dash's lap. His shoulder was warm and solid against her cheek. She could feel the bite of his belt buckle at her waist and breathed in his particular scent. It was crisp and piney, overlaid with the hint of spearmint LifeSavers.

"I'm too old for cuddling," she whispered, cuddling closer.

His arm enfolded her more tightly, and his voice was husky with tenderness. "You're not too old until I say you're too old. I love you, Janie."

Silence fell between them, tender and good. His jaw rested on the top of her head, sheltering her. His arms and chest were a warm, snug harbor in a world that had grown too dangerous. The camera pulled back for a wider angle. Honey closed her eyes, savoring every second. If only he were her dad, instead of Janie's. She had just celebrated her seventeenth birthday, and she knew she was too old to be taking pleasure in something so childish, but she couldn't help it. She had never had a father, but she had dreamed about it, and she wanted to stay in Dash Coogan's arms for the next thousand years.

He picked up her hand and enfolded it in his much larger one. "My sweet little Jane Marie."

"And cut! Print it. That looked good."

Dash dropped her hand. He stirred beneath her, and she rose reluctantly. As he stood, the big front-porch rocker they had been sitting in banged against the wall of the ranch house. Her body had been so warm seconds ago, but now her skin felt cold. He began to walk away, just as he always did when they were done, as if being in her presence for more than five minutes would contaminate him.

She rushed to the edge of the porch and spoke to his back as he walked down the steps. "I think that was a real good scene, don't you, Dash?

"It seemed to go okay."

"Better than okay." She hurried after him, jumping over a tangle of electrical cables on the way. "You were terrific. Really. I think you're a terrific actor. Maybe the best in the world. I think—"

"Sorry, Honey. I can't talk now. I've got things to do."

"But Dash—"

He picked up his stride, and before she knew it, he had left her behind. Lowering her head, she dragged her heels as she began walking toward the motor home they had given her to use when they were on location. Maybe her mind was playing tricks on her. Maybe her memory of that first day when he had treated her so kindly was a delusion. If only she knew what she had done to make him stop liking her.

From the very beginning she'd been just as friendly as she knew how to be. She'd run off all the time to get him coffee and donuts. She'd given him her chair. She'd told him how much she admired him and offered him back rubs. She entertained him with witty conversation during breaks and brought him newspapers. She'd even begged him to let her wash his shirt one day when he'd spilled coffee on it. Why had he turned on her?

When they were acting in a scene together, it seemed as if she really were his daughter and he truly did love her. Sometimes he looked at her so tenderly she felt as if a whole pitcher of warm wine was speeding through her blood veins. But then the camera stopped and the wine turned to ice water because she knew he'd do his best to get away from her.

She paused for a moment in the shade of one of the big sycamore trees, ignoring the fact that she had to finish her history assignment before her tutor arrived. They had asked her to go back to school, something she didn't mind too much even though the tutor they had given her was old and boring. Sitting down on the rope swing that hung from the branches, a prop they used from time to time, she pushed herself gently back and forth.

It was January now, and *The Dash Coogan Show* had turned into the biggest hit of the fall season. Reaching into the pocket of her flannel shirt, she pulled out a Xerox of an article that had just appeared in one of the most important news magazines in the country. Everyone had been given a copy that morning, but this was the first chance she'd had to look at it. She scanned it, but then slowed down as she came to the end.

The Dash Coogan Show has captured America's imagination in large part because of its superior acting. Liz Castleberry's intelligence shines through the stereotype of Eleanor, giving the spoiled socialite a delightfully ironic edge. Eric Dillon, an actor many critics thought to dismiss as another Hollywood hunk, plays her son Blake with the intensity and brooding melancholy of a young man still trying to discover his place in the world, adding layers of nuance to a character who would have been merely a piece of beefcake in the hands of someone less talented.

But most of all, America has fallen in love with the two leading characters. Dash Coogan has been looking for this part all his life, and he slips into the persona of the broken-down rodeo rider without a single misstep. And thirteen-year-old Honey Jane Moon as the feisty little girl who wants to settle down in a real home is the most winning child star in years. She's spunky without being precious, and so real it's hard to believe she's delivering a performance. The relationship between father and daughter as portrayed by Coogan and Moon is the way love between a parent and child should be—full of sharp edges, bristling with conflict, but deep and abiding.

She stared at the page, absorbing the painful irony of the final sentence. Not once since she was six years old had she known a deep and abiding love.

She sniffed and resolutely stuffed the article back in her pocket for Chantal to put in her shoe box along with the others. Some day when she got the time, her cousin planned to paste all of them in a scrapbook. There were a lot of articles in Chantal's shoe box, despite the fact that Ross wouldn't let any of the reporters who were clamoring to interview her get close. He said he wanted to shield her from public scrutiny until she grew more accustomed to the business, but she suspected his real reason for keeping her away from reporters was that he didn't trust her not to go on one of her talking jags and say things he didn't want made public, such as how old she really was.

She jumped up from the swing, and her heart started a rickety-rack clattering in her chest as she spotted Eric Dillon walking toward his trailer. He was wearing a pair of stone-washed jeans so tight that the outline of the wallet in his back pocket was visible, along with a black T-shirt that had the sleeves cut out.

He turned slightly and her mouth went cotton dry as she took in the clean lines of his profile. Her eyes traced the height of his forehead, the lean straight nose, that thin, strong mouth with its sharply chiseled bow. She loved his mouth and spent a lot of her spare time daydreaming about what it would be like to kiss it. But the only way that would happen was if the writers made it happen, and right now that didn't seem too likely.

Sometimes it gave her chills the way the writers kept calling her into that conference room and making her talk. In her old life, God had been in charge, but now that she had met the show's five writers, she understood real power.

"Eric!" His name spilled from her lips with embarrassing eagerness.

He turned toward her and she glimpsed something scary in his face, but then she decided it was only annoyance. People were after him all the time. Some of the crew members complained because Eric was sort of temperamental, but she couldn't find it in her heart to hold it against him. Not with all the pressures of stardom bearing down on him. She rushed toward him, telling herself to act casual, but he started walking away, so she had to move even faster.

"Would you like to run some lines, Eric? I've been working on those sensory-awareness exercises I heard you telling Liz about. We're filming the scene by the corral this afternoon. It's an important scene, and we need to be ready for it."

He began walking. "Sorry, kid. Not right now."

It was the dog-dish haircut. How could he ever think of her as a seventeen-year-old woman when she looked like somebody's little brother? She found herself moving faster, occasionally taking two steps to keep up.

"How about half an hour? Would half an hour be good for you?"

"I'm afraid not. I've got some business to attend to." He mounted the steps to his motor home and opened the door.

"But Eric—"

"Sorry, Honey. No time."

The door shut. As she stared at its unyielding surface, she realized that she'd done it again. Even though she kept telling herself to act mature and sophisticated, she ended up acting just like Janie.

She glanced around, hoping no one had witnessed what a fool she'd made of herself, but the only person nearby was Liz Castleberry, and she didn't seem to be paying attention. Honey slipped her hands back into her jeans pockets so she looked as if she were just wandering around with nothing particular on her mind.

On location, the four leading actors each had a small motor home. Liz's motor home was parked next to Eric's. She was sitting in a lawn chair near the door with Mitzi, her golden retriever, sprawled at her side. She had a sweater tossed over her shoulders and was studying her script through a pair of large sunglasses with clear pink rims.

From the beginning Honey had liked Liz's dog a lot better than she liked Liz. Liz was too glamorous for her to be comfortable in her presence. More than anyone else on the show, she acted like a real movie star, and since the first days of filming, Honey had been steering a wide berth around her. It hadn't been difficult to do. All the show's stars tended to keep to themselves.

Mitzi rose and trotted forward, her tail wagging. Honey was feeling bruised from her encounter with Eric and she wanted to be alone for a while, but it was hard to ignore a dog with a yen to play, especially one the size of Mitzi. She reached down and stroked the dog's large, handsome head. "Hi, girl."

Mitzi began circling her and nuzzling her knees, the rhythm of her tail moving from adagio to allegro. Honey sank down and pushed her fingers into the dog's soft, butterscotch fur. Leaning forward, she rested her cheek against Mitzi's neck, not minding the musty scent of dog breath. Mitzi's tongue scraped her cheek. Even though Mitzi was only a dog, Honey appreciated the affection.

It was getting harder all the time for her to blame other people for not wanting to be with her. There were so many things wrong with her. She was ugly and bossy. Other than the fact that she could cook and she was a good driver, she didn't have any particular talents. When she thought about it, she realized that there wasn't much to like, let alone love.

"Bad day?

Honey's head shot up at the sound of Liz's quiet voice. "Hell, no. I'm having a great day. A *great* one."

Releasing Mitzi, she sat back on her heels, taking in the actress's billowy chestnut hair and flawless skin and wishing she could look like her. Honey was beginning to think that she was the only ugly person in all of Southern California.

Liz slipped her sunglasses on top of her head. Her eyes were as green as Silver Lake before the water had gone bad. She nodded her head toward Eric's trailer. "You're way out of your league, kiddo. Be careful with that one."

Honey leaped to her feet. "I don't have the slightest idea what you're talking about. And I don't appreciate other people nibbing into my business."

Liz shrugged and pulled her glasses back down over her eyes.

Honey spun around and began to stomp away only to run into Lisa Harper, the actress who was playing Dusty. When she realized that Lisa was heading for Eric's trailer, she intercepted her.

"I wouldn't bother him if I were you, Lisa. Eric's got some business to attend to, and he doesn't want to be interrupted." She tried to conceal her resentment at the way Lisa's breasts stretched out the front of her purple knit top.

"You're a stitch, Honey." Lisa laughed. *"I'm* Eric's business." She climbed the steps to his trailer and disappeared inside.

An hour later she reappeared. Her purple knit top had been replaced with one of Eric's cropped-off T-shirts.

The conference room was dim, with only weak threads of late afternoon light seeping through the closed draperies. Honey sat before them like a sinner on judgment day called to the presence of the Almighty. Except there was only one of Him, and there were five of them.

A woman with burgundy fingernails gestured toward the can of Orange Crush they had set out for her. "Help yourself, Honey," she said quietly.

The man at the center of the table lit a cigarette and

leaned back in his chair. "You can start whenever you're ready."

Honey gazed stubbornly down at the floor. "I don't have anything to say."

"Look at us when you talk, please."

"I'm not saying anything. I mean it this time. I don't have a single thing on my mind."

Someone flicked a lighter. A chair creaked softly.

One of the men tapped a pencil on his notepad. "Why don't you tell us about Eric?"

"There's nothing to tell."

"We hear things."

She stiffened in her chair. "I'm not talking about him anymore."

"Don't hold out on us, Honey. That's not a good idea."

Honey's hand clamped tighter around the soda pop can. "Why should I tell you anything? I don't even know why I'm here. I don't like you people!"

Unmoved by her rebellion, they picked up their notepads. "Anytime you're ready."

And because she had no one else to talk to, she told the writers everything. . . .

EXTERIOR. THE LANDING OUTSIDE BLAKE'S APARTMENT
OVER THE GARAGE—NIGHT.

Janie stands on the landing looking at the door of Blake's apartment. Nervously, she tucks her T-shirt into her pants and then tries to tidy her hair with her fingers, only to realize the task is hopeless and mess it up again. Finally, she loses her nerve and begins to go back down the stairs, then changes her mind and returns. Summoning her courage, she knocks on the door. When there is no answer, she knocks again.

JANIE
Blake? Blake, are you there?

BLAKE'S VOICE
What do you want, Janie?

JANIE

You—uh— You said you'd help me with my
arithmetic homework one of these nights. The—
uh—the fractions. Oh, man, those fractions are
really hard.

Blake slowly opens the door. He is dressed in jeans, his
chest bare. Janie stares at him and gulps.

BLAKE

I'm sorry, Janie, but tonight's not a real good
night for me.

JANIE
(disappointed)
Oh . . . Well, maybe . . . You want to play
some cards instead?

BLAKE

Not tonight, kid.

JANIE

How about some TV? The Cowboys are playing
tonight.

DUSTY'S VOICE
(coming from inside the apartment)
Blake? Is something wrong?

Janie's face falls as she absorbs what is taking place.

BLAKE
(gives Janie a sympathetic smile)
Maybe some other time.

As he turns to go back inside, Janie's heartbreak changes
to anger.

JANIE

You toad sucker! Dusty's in there. I heard her
voice. You got Dusty in your apartment!

BLAKE

Now, Janie . . .

JANIE
(furiously)

Does your mama know about this? Because if your mama knew, she'd kill you! I'm gonna tell her! I'm going right down there and pound on her door and tell her that her only son is a low-life, scum-suckin' womanizer!

Dusty appears behind Blake's shoulder. She is wearing Blake's robe and her hair is rumpled.

DUSTY
(not unkindly)

Hey, Janie. What're you doin' here?

JANIE

And you! You should be ashamed of yourself! All this time I thought you were a nice person! Now it turns out you're nothing but a—a—*slut!*

BLAKE
(coldly)

I think you'd better calm down, Janie.

JANIE
(hysterically)

I *am* calm. I am completely calm.

BLAKE
(steps out on landing and shuts door)

Janie, you can't talk to Dusty like that. There are things you don't understand. You're still a kid, and—

JANIE

I'm not a kid! Don't ever say I'm a kid! I'm almost fourteen and I'm—

Janie bursts into tears . . .

Silence fell over the set as they all waited.

Dry-eyed and furious, Honey rounded on the cameras. "This is stupid! I'm not doing this!"

"Cut!"

Eric slammed his hand down on the railing. "Aw, for chrissake. This is the ninth take."

The director stepped forward. Although the landing to Blake's apartment was supposed to be above the garage, the set rose just a few feet off the studio floor. While one of the wardrobe assistants handed Eric a shirt, the director gazed up at Honey.

"Do you need makeup to get the crystals?"

Honey had been working on the show for six months, long enough to know that he was talking about menthol crystals that could be blown into her eyes to make them tear. She shook her head, imagining Eric's disgust. Real actors didn't need menthol crystals. Not if they had prepared properly. Not if they'd done their sensory-awareness exercises. But doing this scene was like pulling at an open wound, and all she wanted was to get out of here.

Eric clenched his teeth. "For God's sake use the crystals. We don't have the time to wait for you to do it right."

His callousness destroyed the last vestige of her self-control. "Janie's not some damn crybaby! And she sure as hell wouldn't waste her time crying over a damn peckerhead like Blake!"

Lisa stuck her head out the door. "Are we going to take a break? Because I have to pee."

"No!" Eric shouted. "No goddamn break. It's six o'clock. If Honey doesn't get it right this time, I'm walking. I've got things to do."

"And everybody here knows exactly what kind of things!" Honey shouted.

"That's it. I'm out of here. I don't have to take this shit."

Eric vaulted over the railing to the studio floor. He worked out daily and there was no reason for him to be breathing so hard, but the panic that gripped him couldn't be cured by physical conditioning. From the beginning, he had hated working with her. He couldn't stand the way she looked at him, the way she followed him around. If he'd known about her in the beginning, he would never have signed the contract to do the show. Even his growing fame wasn't worth being forced to stare into those big, needy eyes, that face that begged for his attention.

"Hold it, everybody," the director exclaimed. "Things are getting a little out of control here. One more take, Eric. If Honey doesn't get it this time, we'll start fresh tomorrow. Come on, Eric, cut me some slack. It's late and everybody's nerves are shot. Makeup, get the menthol crystals."

Eric ground his teeth. He wanted to tell all of them to go to hell, but if he walked out now, he'd have to work with the little pest first thing tomorrow morning, and he had enough trouble sleeping as it was. Sometimes in his nightmares her voice was starting to get mixed up with Jason's.

Begrudgingly, he threw off his shirt and climbed back up the three steps. She stared at him, hurt and adoration making her light blue eyes huge. They wanted to suck him in, eat him up. He tried to distance himself from her by studying her face objectively. She was going to be a knock-out one of these days, when she stopped looking like a kid.

His small flash of objectivity faded, and all he could see was someone who reminded him far too much of his pain in the ass little brother.

He set his jaw and spoke in a nasty snarl, hoping to make her hate him. "Next time do your homework first. You're getting paid to be a professional. Start acting like one."

She sucked in her breath as if he'd hit her. Her eyes grew luminous with misery, and her bottom lip sagged with vulnerability. He felt the impact of her hurt in his own gut.

The director spoke up. "Let's take it from Janie's close-up. Positions, everybody."

The makeup man blew the crystals in her eyes, and they began to tear.

"Quiet, please. We're rolling. Marker. Action."

The camera came in for a close-up. One fat drop rolled over her bottom lashes and trickled down her cheek, but her expression remained mutinous.

Eric told himself that it was Blake who had to touch her. Blake. Not himself.

Stepping forward, he put his arms around her and pulled her to his chest. Her head didn't even reach his chin. She was just about Jason's height, and like his half brother, she only wanted his attention.

The squeal of brakes shrieked in his mind, the sound of a scream.

"Cut. Print it. Good. We can all go home."

"Asshole!" Honey shoved hard against his chest and ran from the set.

He stood at the top of the landing looking after her, his eyes dark and tormented.

Take me with you, Eric. Please.

8

Despite her determination to keep her head up, by lunchtime the next day Honey was in desperate need of a quiet place where she could go to lick her wounds. Everybody who hadn't been on the set the day before had heard about her fight with Eric, and she knew all of them were whispering behind her back. They were shooting on location today, but she rejected her motor home as a place to escape because her tutor was waiting there with a trigonometry lesson. Instead, she slipped behind the catering wagon to an outcrop of man-made rock. But as she stepped into the cool shadows, she realized that even here she couldn't be alone.

Thirty feet away, Dash Coogan leaned against one of the boulders with his hat pulled low over his eyes and one knee drawn up. She knew she should leave, but despite Dash's coolness toward her, she was enveloped with the sensation of having stumbled into a safe, secure place. If only she could crawl into his lap like Janie did. Knowing how impossible that was, she sank down in a shady spot about twelve feet away from him, drew up her knees, and dug the heels of her cowboy boots into the dirt. Maybe if she sat here for a little bit without talking, he wouldn't mind.

A minute ticked by, each second lasting forever. She tried to hold back, but the words spilled out anyway. "I hate people who don't have anything better to do than gossip about other people."

He didn't respond, even though he had to have heard about what had happened.

She told herself to keep quiet. She already knew that Dash didn't like talky women, but she was going to burst if she couldn't confide in someone other than that pack of jackal writers who took her deepest secrets and spread them out for all of America to see. And who better to confide in than this man who was sort of the closest thing she had to a father?

"Eric's a real peckerhead, if you ask me. Everybody thinks I've got a crush on him, but what kind of idiot would I be to have a crush on a conceited jerk like that?"

Coogan tilted up his hat with his thumb and stared at the horizon in the distance.

She waited for him to give her some advice like adults were supposed to give teenagers. Like a father might give his daughter.

She prodded him. "I guess I'm not stupid enough to think that somebody like him would look twice at a girl who looks like me."

Her muscles tense, she waited for him to respond. If only he would tell her there wasn't anything wrong with the way she looked. If only he'd tell her she was a late bloomer, just like he always told Janie.

But as silence ticked away between them, she decided she shouldn't expect him to read her mind.

"I know I'm not exactly pretty, but do you think—" She picked at a small hole on the knee of her jeans. "Do you think I might be—You know. Maybe a late bloomer?"

He turned to her with cold, dead eyes. "I came back here to be alone. I'd appreciate it if you'd take off."

She sprang to her feet. Why had she ever thought for a moment that he'd understand? That he cared enough about her to try to make her feel better? When was she ever going to admit that he didn't give a damn about her? Cocooned in her misery, she looked for a way to punch right back at him, to hurt him as he'd just hurt her.

Sucking in her breath, she glared at him, her voice crackling with hostility. "Who wants to be with you anyway, you old drunk?"

He didn't even flinch. He just sat there looking out toward the San Gabriels. The brim of his hat shaded his eyes so she couldn't see their expression, but his voice was as flat as the Oklahoma prairie.

"Then how about you leave this old drunk alone."

All her hurt turned to venom. Never again would she confess her true feelings to any of them. Beneath a black scowl that camouflaged her broken heart, she spun away from him and stalked back to her motor home.

Behind the outcrop of man-made rocks, Dash Coogan had sweated through his shirt. He squeezed his eyes shut, trying to block out the craving that had hit him so hard he felt as if his skin were being stripped from his bones. That little girl would never know how close her taunt had hit on the truth. He needed a drink.

With a trembling hand, he reached for the roll of LifeSavers he kept in his shirt pocket. These past few years, he'd begun to take his recovery for granted, but lately he'd realized that his complacency was a big mistake. As he shoved two of the spearmint candies into his mouth, he reminded himself that he'd long ago given up blaming his alcoholism on other people, and he wouldn't do it now. But it was an undeniable fact that every time that little girl came running after him expecting him to be her pa in real life, the urge to drink hit him like a slap in his face. He hadn't even been a decent parent to his real children, and he sure as hell couldn't be a parent to her.

Those first few days when they'd begun reading through the scripts and talking about the show, he'd been friendly, but it hadn't taken him long to see that he was making a big mistake. She followed him everywhere, not giving him an inch of breathing space. He had realized right then that he had to keep his distance. He had too many empty spaces inside himself to be able to fill up hers.

He knew how badly he was hurting her, but he told himself that she was a strong little cuss, just as he'd been when he was a kid, and she'd survive his rejection the same way he'd survived being shuttled from one foster home to another the whole time he was growing up. Maybe she'd even be stronger for it. She'd be better off learning right now that she shouldn't expect so much from other people, that she should stop wearing every one of her feelings right out in the open where anybody who came along could stomp all over them.

But damn, there was something about her that tore at his guts, and that, more than anything else, was the reason he had to stay away from her. Because when he felt vulnerable, he wanted to drink, and nothing on earth, not even that feisty little kid, was going to make him ruin six hard-earned years of sobriety.

Honey saw the house in early March, right before the show went on its four-month break, or hiatus, as all of them called it. They moved in a few weeks later, and she wandered outside the first evening just before the sun set to gaze at the whitewashed brick exterior. A network of bougainvillea vines climbed the walls and curled around the charcoal shutters that framed the mullioned windows. The small copper roof over the entrance had long ago formed the chalky-green patina of respectability. The shrubbery was well established and a small rose garden formed a crescent at the side. She had never imagined she would live in such a beautiful house. It was everything she had always dreamed of.

"Of course it's too close to Wilshire to be really fashionable," the realtor had told her. "But Beverly Hills is Beverly Hills."

Honey didn't care about what was fashionable. She didn't even care about living in Beverly Hills. The house was cozy and pretty, the perfect place for a family to live. Maybe things would start to get better for her now. She hugged herself, trying to take comfort in the house and forget everything else that was going wrong in her life: the conflicts on the set, the way people were talking behind her back. One of the directors had complained to Ross because she'd shown up late a few times and kept the cast waiting. But it hadn't been all the cast. Just Dash Coogan. And she had kept him waiting twice because she was sick of the way he ignored her, especially since the press had started treating him like Mr. Father of the Year.

The sound of a car pulling into the driveway distracted her. She turned to see her agent getting out of his BMW. Arthur Lockwood walked toward her, his wiry red hair and beard looking darker than normal in the fading light. She respected him, but the fact that he had two college degrees intimidated her, and she couldn't really warm up to his beard.

"Are you all settled?" he asked.

"We're getting there. One of the salesladies from this ritzy furniture store is arranging the furniture."

"It's a nice house."

"Let me show you the grapefruit tree." She led him toward the side, where he admired the tree, and then they entered the screened-in porch through the back door. The furniture saleslady hadn't gotten this far yet, so there was only an old folding chair, which Arthur declined. Honey looked out over the small backyard. She was going to string a hammock between two of the trees and buy a barbecue grill just like on all those TV commercials.

Arthur jiggled the change in the pocket of his chinos. "Honey, hiatus starts in a couple of weeks, and you won't have to report back to work until the end of July. It's not too late for you to accept the offer from TriStar."

The early evening air suddenly developed a chill. "I don't want to do any movies, Arthur. I already told you that. I want to finish up my high school courses during the break so I can graduate before we start filming again."

"You're working with a tutor. Another few months won't make any difference."

"It will to me."

"You're making a mistake. Even though the Coogan show is a huge hit now, it won't last forever, and you need to start planning for the future. You're a natural talent, Honey. The TriStar part will really showcase you."

"A fourteen-year-old girl dying of cancer. Just the thing to cheer America's heart."

"It's a great script."

"She's a rich girl, Arthur. I couldn't convince anybody in the world that I'm a rich girl." Playing a character other than Janie Jones scared her. No matter what the critics said, she knew she wasn't a real actress. All she did was play herself.

"You sell yourself short, Honey. You have real talent, and you'd be wonderful in this part."

"Forget it." She could imagine Eric's contemptuous reaction if he ever saw her trying to play a fourteen-year-old rich girl dying from cancer.

Just the thought of Eric made her ache. Unless they were doing a scene together, he acted as if she didn't exist. And Dash hadn't spoken to her off camera since that day three weeks ago when she'd tried to talk to him behind the rock. The only person who never seemed to avoid her was Liz Castleberry, and Honey figured that was just because of Mitzi. Liz's dog had become the closest thing Honey had to a best friend. She gazed out at her backyard, loneliness creeping all the way through her.

"You need a chance to stretch yourself," her agent said.

"I thought you worked for *me*, Arthur. I told you I don't want to do any movies, and I meant it."

His face tightened, and she knew he was angry with her, but she didn't care. He bossed her around too much, and sometimes she had to remind him who was in charge.

When he finally left, she went inside. She found Chantal in the living room, lying on their new gold and white brocade sectional couch and reading a magazine. Gordon sat across from her fiddling with his pocketknife.

"This room looks real pretty, Chantal. That saleslady did

a good job." Thick white carpet stretched from one wall to the next. In addition to the couch the room held fancy French chairs and amoeba-shaped glass tabletops sitting on thin brass legs. One of those tables held the remnants of a Hungry Man dinner.

"The plants come tomorrow."

"Plants'll be nice." Chantal stretched and set down her magazine. "Honey, me and Gordon have been talking. We think we might be takin' off in a couple of days."

Honey froze. "What do you mean?"

Chantal looked nervous. "Gordon, you tell her."

Gordon pocketed his knife. "We're thinking about driving around the country, Honey. Seeing more of America. Sort of making a life for ourselves."

Honey's heart slammed against her ribs.

"Gordon's got his career to think about," Chantal went on. "He needs inspiration if he's going to be a painter."

Honey tried to stem her panic. "Are both of you crazy? I just bought this house. I bought it for all of us. You can't take off now."

Chantal wouldn't look at her. "Gordon says Beverly Hills is suffocating him."

"We just moved in today!" Honey shouted. "How could it be suffocating him?"

"I knew you wouldn't understand. You always yell at people. You never try to understand." With a small, choked sob, Chantal fled from the room.

Honey spun on Gordon. "Just what the hell do you think you're doing, you stupid fool?"

Gordon stuck out his weak chin. "Don't call me that! I guess Chantal and me can take off if we want to."

"And how do you plan to support yourselves?"

"We'll find jobs. We've already talked about it. We're going to work our way around the country."

"*You* can work, maybe, but don't fool yourself about Chantal. Selling Ferris wheel tickets is the hardest thing she ever did, and she messed up the cash box so many times that she would have gotten fired if she hadn't been family."

"She might do hair. She's talked about it."

"She talked about marrying Burt Reynolds, too, but she didn't do that, either."

Gordon shoved his hands in his pockets, his frustration evident. "I can't keep going on like this. I've got to start painting."

"Then start!" Honey said desperately.

"I don't think I'm going to be able to paint here. This house. This neighborhood. Everything's too—"

"Just try it," she pleaded. "If it doesn't work out, we can always move." The idea of moving made her sick. They weren't even unpacked, and she loved this house, but she wasn't going to let him take Chantal away.

"I don't know. I—"

"What do you need? I'll buy you anything you need."

"I don't like taking your money all the time. I'm a man. I should—"

"I'll pay you two thousand dollars a month to stay right here."

Gordon stared at her.

"Two thousand dollars a month for as long as you stay. I'm already paying for the house and all the food. That's two thousand dollars just for spending money."

Gordon's breath made a soft, hissing sound. His face looked pinched, and when he spoke, his voice was soft and hoarse. "What gives you the right to try to run our lives like this?"

"I care about Chantal, that's all. I want to take care of her."

"I'm her husband. I'll take care of her."

But there wasn't much conviction left in his voice, and Honey knew that she had won.

The hiatus began. While Gordon and Chantal lay around the house eating the meals Honey cooked and watching television, Honey finished her high-school courses with straight As, except for physical science, which she hated. In June, the three of them flew to South Carolina to see Sophie. The park was even more depressing than she remembered. The rides had been sold off, and the *Bobby Lee* had finally broken apart during a storm and sunk to the bottom of Silver Lake. Once again, Honey tried to talk her aunt into coming to L.A., but Sophie refused.

"This is my home, Honey. I don't want to live anyplace else."

"It's not safe, Sophie."

"Sure it is. Buck's here."

Honey drove into town the next day to meet with the lawyer she'd hired last December to negotiate the purchase of the park. By late afternoon, she had signed the final papers. The acquisition was going to wipe her out financially for a while, and she wouldn't be able to reopen the park, but at least she had it back.

"Honey, I asked you to walk past Dash and over to the window on the last line." Janice Stein, the show's only female director, pointed toward the correct position.

Hiatus was over. It was August, and they were in the studio working on their second show for the '81–'82 season. Honey had been in a foul mood ever since shooting had resumed. Dash hadn't acted as if he were the tiniest bit glad to see her again, and Eric had barely returned her greeting. Only Liz Castleberry, the Queen of the Bitches, had stopped to chat, and she was the last person Honey had wanted to talk to.

She splayed her hand on her hip and glared at Janice, who was standing in the middle of the ranch house living room set. "I don't want to move until I say, 'Calm down, Pop.' It'll work better there."

"That's too late," Janice said. "You should already be at the window by then."

"I don't want to do it that way."

"I'm the director, Honey."

Narrowing her eyes, Honey spoke in her snottiest voice. "And I'm an actress trying to do a decent job. If you don't like my work, maybe you should find another show to direct."

She flounced past Dash, who was standing next to the window with his script in one hand and a coffee cup in the other, and walked off the set. Last year she had been intimidated by all of them, but this year would be different. She was tired of people pushing her around, tired of listening to Gordon's endless complaints about living in Beverly Hills, tired of Chantal's pouting. Nobody liked her anyway, so what difference did it make how she behaved?

She turned down the corridor that led to the dressing rooms and saw Eric at the end. Just the sight of him made her knees go weak. He had spent the summer filming his first feature role in a movie, and he looked so handsome it was hard for her to keep from staring.

Melanie Osborne, an attractive redhead who was one of the new assistant directors, was talking with him. They were standing just close enough for Honey to be certain the conversation wasn't about business. Melanie leaned toward him in a confident, sexy way that made Honey's toes curl with envy.

Eric looked up and saw her coming. He patted Melanie on the cheek and disappeared down the hallway into his dressing room.

Honey's mood grew uglier.

Melanie walked toward her, a friendly smile on her face. "Hi, Honey. I just overheard Ross say that he needs you as soon as you're free."

"Then he can come find me."

"Yes, ma'am," Melanie muttered as Honey swept past.

Honey stopped and spun around. "What did you say?"

"I didn't say anything."

Honey took in Melanie's long, wavy hair and generous breasts. Last week they'd cut her own hair in another dog's dish style. "You'd better watch yourself. I don't like smartasses."

"I apologize," Melanie said coldly. "I didn't mean to offend you."

"Well, you did."

"I'll try my best to avoid repeating the mistake."

"Try your best to stay out of my way."

Melanie clenched her teeth and began to move on, but something evil had taken possession of Honey. She wanted to punish Melanie for being pretty and feminine and for knowing how to talk to Eric. She wanted to punish Melanie for exchanging jokes with Dash and being popular with the crew and for having polished red fingernails the shape of almonds.

"Get me some coffee first," she snapped. "Bring it to my dressing room. And hurry it up."

Melanie stared at her for a moment. "What?"

"You heard me."

When the redhead didn't move, Honey planted her hand on her hip. "Well?"

"Go to hell."

Ross came around the corner just in time to hear the assistant director's words. He stopped in his tracks. Melanie spun around, saw who had approached, and paled.

Honey leapt forward. "Did you hear what she said?"

"What's your name?" Ross barked.

The assistant director looked sick. "Uh—Melanie Osborne."

"Well, Melanie Osborne, you've just joined the ranks of the unemployed. Pack up and get out."

"But—"

"Honey's a star," he said quietly. "Nobody talks to her like that."

Melanie turned back to Honey, waiting for her to say something, but it was as if a cadre of devils had speared her lips shut with their pitchforks. Her conscience screamed at her to set things right, but her pride was too strong.

As it became apparent that Honey wasn't going to speak, Melanie's eyes grew bitter. "Thanks for nothing." Straightening her spine, she turned and walked away.

"I'm sorry about that, Honey," Ross said, running one hand through his long, silver hair. "I'll make certain she doesn't work around here again."

A chill slithered along Honey's spine as she absorbed the awesome power of celebrity. He wasn't even going to ask her what had happened. She was important; Melanie wasn't. Nothing else mattered.

He began talking about a press conference for the new

season and the publicist who would accompany her on one of the few interviews he was permitting. Honey barely listened. She had done something terrible, but acknowledging that she was wrong stuck in her throat like a great lump of unchewed bread. She began the slow process of justifying her actions. She was hardly ever wrong about anything, she told herself. Maybe she wasn't wrong about this. Maybe Melanie was a troublemaker. She probably would have gotten herself fired anyway. But no matter how much she rationalized, she couldn't make the sick feeling inside her go away.

Ross left and she rushed toward her dressing room so she could be alone for a few minutes to think things over. But before she could get inside, she saw Liz Castleberry leaning in the open doorway of her own dressing room across the corridor. It was obvious from the disapproving expression on her face that her costar had heard everything.

"A word of advice, kiddo," she said quietly. "Don't screw people over. It'll come back to haunt you."

Honey felt as if she were being attacked from all sides, and she bristled. "Now isn't that funny. I can't seem to remember asking for your advice."

"Maybe you should."

"I suppose you're going to run to Ross."

"You're the one who should do that."

"Don't hold your breath."

"You're making a mistake," Liz replied. "I hope you figure that out before it's too late."

"Go to Ross," Honey said viciously. "But if Melanie shows up on this set, I'm walking!"

She went into her dressing room and slammed the door.

Melanie had a lot of friends on the set, and it didn't take long for word of her firing to spread. By the end of the week, Honey had become a pariah. The crew members only addressed her when they had to, and in retaliation Honey grew more demanding. She complained about her lines, her hair. She didn't like the lighting or the blocking.

The thought kept skittering through her mind that if she behaved badly enough, they'd have to pay attention to her, but Dash stopped talking to her completely, and Eric looked at her as if she were a slug leaving a slimy trail on the sidewalk of his life. Hatred joined the other complex feelings she held for him.

The following week, Arthur took her out to dinner. He'd heard about what had happened with Melanie, and he started giving her a big lecture about getting a reputation in the business for being difficult.

Instead of asking him to help her set things right, as she knew she should, she cut him off with a long recitation of all the slights she had suffered since her first day on the set. Then she told him that he could either take her side or she'd find another agent. He immediately backed off.

When she left the restaurant, she had the awful feeling that a devil had taken over her body. An internal voice whispered that she was turning into a spoiled Hollywood brat, just like a lot of the kid stars she had read about. She tried to repress it. Nobody understood her, and that was their problem, not hers. She told herself she should feel proud of the fact that she'd put her agent in his place, but as she got into her car, she was shaking, and she knew it wasn't pride she felt, but fear. Wasn't anybody going to stop her?

The next day she dropped by to see the writers. Not to talk to them. Hell, no, she wasn't going to talk to them. Just to sort of say hi.

9

The house sat all alone at the end of one of the murderously twisting narrow roads that wound through Topanga Canyon. The road had no guardrail, and the darkness, combined with a late November drizzle, made even as fearless a driver as Honey jumpy. She tried to work up some enthusiasm for her new house as it came into view around the final hairpin turn, but she hated its sweeping roof and stark contemporary lines as much as she hated its location.

Topanga Canyon was a far cry from Beverly Hills and the pretty little house she had loved so much. Every leftover hippie in Southern California lived here, along with packs of wild dogs that bred with the coyotes. But after seven months in Beverly Hills, Gordon still hadn't been able to paint, and so they had moved.

Honey was drooping with fatigue as she pulled into the drive. When they had lived in Beverly Hills, it had only taken her half an hour to get back and forth from the studio. Now she had to get up at five to be at work in time for a seven A.M. call, and at night, she rarely got home before eight.

Her stomach rumbled as she walked into the house. She wished that Chantal and Gordon would have dinner ready, but neither of them was good in the kitchen, and they usually waited till she came home to cook. She had hired four different housekeepers to take care of the cooking and cleaning, but they kept quitting.

She dragged herself into the great room that stretched across the back of the house, and as her eyes fell on Sophie and her new husband, the old adage about being careful what you wish for because you just might get it sprang into her mind.

"Mama's not feeling well," Chantal said, looking up from the issue of *Cosmo* she was thumbing through.

"Another one of my headaches." Sophie sighed from the couch. "And my throat is real scratchy. Buck, honey, could you turn down that TV?"

Buck Ochs, the amusement park's former handyman and Sophie's new spouse, was sprawled in the big recliner Honey had bought them for a wedding present, where he was eating Cheez Doodles and watching a swimsuit show on ESPN. He obediently reached for the remote control and pointed it toward the big-screen TV Honey had bought for them.

"Look at the busts on that one, Gordon. Man-oh-man."

Unlike Sophie, Buck had been more than willing to leave the decaying amusement park for the riches of LaLa Land, and the two of them had shown up on Honey's doorstep early in the fall, right after their marriage.

"Honey, would you mind going out and buying me some lozenges?" Sophie's voice rose weakly from the couch. "My throat's so dry I can barely swallow."

Buck zapped the volume back up. "Aw, Sophie, Honey can get those lozenges later. Right now what I'd like is a good steak dinner. How 'bout it, Honey?"

The expensive white furniture was grimy with stains. An overturned beer can lay on the rug. Honey was exhausted and heartsick, and she exploded.

"You're all pigs! Look at you, lolling around like white trash, not contributing one single thing to society. I'm sick of this. I'm sick of all of you!"

Buck tore his attention away from the television and looked around at the others, his expression befuddled. "Now what's wrong with her?"

Chantal slapped down her *Cosmo* and got up in a huff. "I don't appreciate being talked to like that, Honey. Thanks to you, I've lost my appetite for dinner."

Gordon unwound from the floor where he had been sitting with his eyes shut doing what he called his "mind painting." "I haven't lost my appetite. What's to eat, Honey?"

She opened her mouth to deliver a stinging retort, but then she checked it. No matter what, they were the only family she had. With a weary sigh, she went into the kitchen and began dinner.

In the three months since she had gotten Melanie fired, Honey's relationship with the crew and her coworkers had steadily deteriorated. One part of her couldn't blame them for hating her. How could anybody like somebody who was so horrible? But the other part of her—the scared part— couldn't back down.

The Monday after her unpleasant weekend with her

family, they began filming an episode in which Janie, jealous of Dusty's relationship with Blake, tries to get her fired. At the climax Dash was to rescue Janie from the roof of the barn while Dusty and Blake watched.

Dash ignored her as usual all week. Honey bided her time until the afternoon they were to shoot the final scene. She watched from her perch on top of the roof as Dash worked out the movements of the rigorous climb from the ground to the hayloft and then over two levels of roof. After almost an hour, they were finally ready to do the scene for real.

The cameras rolled. She waited until Dash had completed the climb. As he pulled himself up onto the top level of the barn roof, she stood and looked at the camera.

"I forgot my line."

"Cut! Give Junie her line." Jack Swackhammer was in charge of this episode. As the director who had been with them the longest, he had also had more than his share of run-ins with her. Honey hated him.

"Honey, this is a tough scene on Dash," he said. "Try to get it right the next time."

"Sure, Jack," she replied sweetly.

Dash gave her a warning glare.

During the next take, she managed to slip as she stood. On the following take, she flubbed her line. Then she didn't hit her mark. Dash had sweated through his shirt from the exertion and they had to stop while he changed. They began again, but once more she failed to hit her mark.

One hour later, after she had slipped again and ruined the shot for the fifth time, Dash exploded and walked off the set.

Jack immediately went to Ross to complain about Honey's increasingly disruptive behavior, but *The Dash Coogan Show* was a ratings giant, and Ross wouldn't risk antagonizing the actress that the newspapers were calling the most popular "child" star on television. Before the episode was over, Honey had gotten Jack Swackhammer fired.

When she heard the news, she felt sick. Why couldn't somebody care enough about her to make her stop?

* * *

The writers sat around the conference table and stared at the door Honey had just stamped out of and slammed shut. For several moments everything was silent, and then one of the women put down her yellow pad. "We can't let this go on any longer."

The man sitting to her left cleared his throat. "We said we wouldn't interfere."

"That's right," another agreed. "We promised to function as impartial observers."

"As writers we report reality; we don't alter it."

The woman shook her head. "I don't care what we promised. She's self-destructing, and we have to do something."

EXTERIOR. FRONT PORCH OF RANCH HOUSE—DAY.

Eleanor, dressed in a mud-spattered white designer suit, is filthy and furious. Dash is grim. Janie stands by the porch rocker looking guilty.

DASH
Is this true, Janie? Did you deliberately set that booby trap?

JANIE
(desperately)
It was a mistake, Pop. Miz Chadwick wasn't supposed to fall into the trap. Old Man Winters was. I had to do something! She was getting ready to sell him the ranch.

ELEANOR
(wipes a clump of something organic from her cheek)
That does it! I finally get a buyer for this miserable place, and what does your little hellion of a daughter do? She tries to kill him!

JANIE
I wasn't actually trying to kill him, Miz Chadwick.

Just slow him up until Pop got back from town. I'm
really sorry you fell into the trap instead.

ELEANOR

I'm afraid sorry isn't good enough this time. I've
overlooked a lot from your daughter, Mr. Jones.
but I'm not going to overlook this. I know you
think I'm spoiled and frivolous and possessed
of half a dozen other qualities of which you rugged cowboy types disapprove. But I will tell you
this. Never once have I not been a parent to my
son.

JANIE
(jumping forward)
Your son is a low-life, stinkin' womanizer who
should be struck right off the face of this earth!

DASH

That's enough Janie. If you're finished, Miz
Chadwick.

ELEANOR

I'm not finished. Not by a long shot. Never once
have I let my son harm other people, Mr. Jones.
Never once have I failed to point out to him the
difference between right and wrong. Perhaps
basic qualities of decency aren't fashionable
here in Texas, but I can assure you, they are
respected in the rest of this country.

DASH
(coldly)
When I need advice on how to raise my daughter, I'll ask for it.

ELEANOR

By that time, it may very well be too late.

Eleanor snatches up her purse and exits into the ranch
house.

JANIE
(smugly)
You sure told her, Pop.

DASH
Yeah, I told her, all right. And now I'm gonna tell
you. Miss Jane Marie Jones, your days as a
carefree child untouched by human hand are
about to come to an abrupt end.

He snatches up Janie by the waist and carries her
purposefully across the porch and down the steps toward
the barn.

"Cut it. Print it." The director looked down at his clip
board. "Janie and Dash, I need you back in fifteen minutes.
Liz, you're off till after lunch."

Before Dash could set her down, Honey began to struggle.
"You don't have to suffocate me, you clumsy sonovabitch!"

Dash dropped her like a rabid dog.

Liz came through the doorway back onto the porch,
wiping her face with a tissue. "Honey, you stepped on my
lines again. Give me a little space to work, all right?"

Liz's request had been mildly uttered, but Honey blew up.
"Why don't you both go straight to hell!" She stomped away
from them. As she passed one of the cameras, she slapped it
with all her force and launched her final verbal rocket.

"Fuckers!"

"Charming," Liz drawled.

The crew members looked away. Dash slowly shook his
head and mounted the porch steps toward Liz. "My biggest
regret is the fact that those fool writers chickened out and I
don't get to whale her butt this afternoon."

"Do it anyway."

"Yeah, right."

Liz spoke quietly. "I'm serious, Dash."

He scowled and pulled a pack of LifeSavers from his shirt
pocket. She scrupulously avoided personal entanglements
on the set, but the situation with Honey had grown so
impossible that Liz felt she could no longer ignore it.

She walked over to the far side of the porch out of earshot of the crew, hesitating for a moment before she spoke. "Honey's completely out of control."

"You're not telling me anything. She kept us waiting almost an hour this morning."

"Ross is useless, and the network's even worse. They're all so afraid she'll walk out on the show that they let her get away with murder. I'm really worried about her. For some perverse reason, I happen to be fond of the little monster."

"Well, believe me when I tell you the feeling isn't mutual. She doesn't make much secret of the fact that she hates your guts." Dash sank down into the rocker near where she was standing. "Every time I do a scene with that kid, I feel like she's going to stick a knife right through my back the minute it's turned. You'd think she'd show a little gratitude. If it weren't for me, she wouldn't even have a career."

"From the tone of this new script, the writers seem to be sending you a message to do something about her." Liz stopped trying to clean herself up and held the towel loosely in her hand. "You know what Honey wants from you. Everybody on the set knows it. Would it kill you to give it to her?"

His voice was flat. "I don't know what you're talking about."

"From the beginning, she's looked at you like you were God Almighty. She wants some attention, Dash. She wants you to care about her."

"I'm an actor, not a baby-sitter."

"But she's hurting. God knows how long she's been on her own. You've met that parasitic family of hers. It's obvious that she's raised herself."

"I was on my own when I was a kid, and I did all right."

"Sure you did," she said sarcastically. Anyone with three ex-wives, two children he hardly ever saw, and a long history of fighting the bottle could hardly brag about how well adjusted he was.

He got up from the chair. "If you're so worried about her, why don't *you* play mother hen?"

"Because she'd spit in my face. I'm more the wicked

stepmother type than a fairy godmother. This is a dangerous business for a young girl who doesn't have anyone watching out for her. She's looking for a father, Dash. She needs someone to put the reins on her." She tried to lighten the tension between them with a small smile. "Who better to do that than an old cowboy?"

"You're crazy," he said, turning away from her. "I don't know a damned thing about kids."

"You've got two of them. You must know something."

"Their mother has raised them. All I do is write the checks."

"And that's the way you like to keep it, isn't it? Just writing the checks." The words had slipped out of their own volition, and she wanted to bite off her tongue.

Dash turned back to her, his eyes narrowed. "Why don't you just come out and say whatever it is you've got on your mind."

She took a deep breath. "All right. I think Honey's identity has gotten all tangled up with Janie's. Maybe the writers are to blame, I don't know, but for whatever reason, the more you distance yourself from her, the more she resents it and the worse she behaves. I think you're the only person who can help her."

"I don't have the slightest intention of helping her. It's not my problem."

His coldness unearthed a fragment of old pain that Liz hadn't even known still existed. She was suddenly twenty-two again and in love with a stunt rider from Oklahoma who she had just learned was a married man.

"Honey's too needy for you, isn't she? That first month we filmed, she ran after you like a little puppy dog practically begging for some attention, and the more she begged, the colder you got. She was too needy, and you don't like needy women, do you, Dash?"

He gave her a dead, hard stare. "You don't know anything about me, so why don't you just mind your own goddamn business?"

Liz was silently berating herself for ever having begun this conversation. This show had enough problems without adding a conflict between Dash and herself. She shrugged and smiled brittlely. "But of course, darling. Why don't I do just that."

Without another word, she walked off the porch and headed for her motor home.

Dash stormed over to the catering wagon and got himself a cup of coffee. It burned his tongue as he swallowed, but he kept drinking it anyway. He was furiously angry with Liz. Where did she get the gall to act as if that little monster from hell was his responsibility? He had only one responsibility, and that was to keep himself sober, something that hadn't been requiring much effort on his part until Honey had stomped into his life.

He swallowed the last of his coffee and tossed away the cup. Ross was the person who should be keeping Honey in line, not himself. And from now on Miss Liz Castleberry could just mind her own goddamn business.

They called him for the next scene, a simple one in which he had to carry Honey across the yard and into the barn. The scene that followed in the barn would be trickier— what television people called the MOS, when the moral lesson for the episode was delivered. MOS stood for "Moral of Show," but all of them referred to it as the "Moment of Shit."

"Where's Honey?" the assistant director asked. "We're ready to shoot."

"I heard Jack Swackhammer took out a contract on her," one of the camera men said. "Maybe the hit man finally delivered."

"We should be so lucky," the AD murmured.

For ten more minutes, Dash cooled his heels while his temper burned. Someone located Honey with the horses, and one of the camera operators suggested that she spent so much time with the animals because they were the only ones who could stand being with her since they didn't have to worry about getting fired.

Bruce Rand was directing that week's episode. He had

been responsible for some of the best episodes of *M.A.S.H.*, and Ross had brought him in because he had a reputation for tact. But after working with Honey all week, even he was starting to show wear around the edges.

When she finally ambled onto the set, Bruce looked relieved and began blocking out the scene. "Dash, carry Janie from the bottom of the porch steps across the yard toward the barn. Janie, give the line about being opposed to violence when you reach the corner of the porch, then start to struggle when he ignores you."

He finished the blocking and called for a rehearsal. Dash and Honey climbed the porch steps to the open front door. The assistant director, whose job it was to maintain continuity from one shot to the next, looked down at her notes.

"You had her under your left arm, Dash. And Honey, you need your hat."

Several more minutes passed while one of the wardrobe people ran back over to the corral to retrieve the navy blue cap she had been wearing. When it was on her head with the bill turned up, Dash tucked her under his left arm and they walked through it.

They returned to the porch, but as Dash turned to pick her up, he saw something he didn't like in those light blue eyes of hers, a subtle air of calculation. He remembered the episode in November when she'd been stuck on the roof of the barn and had deliberately blown her lines so he had to keep climbing up after her. His back had bothered him for a week afterward.

"No tricks, Honey," he warned. "This is an easy scene. Let's get it over with."

"You just worry about yourself, old man," she sneered. "I'll take care of me."

He didn't like it when she called him that, and his anger settled in deeper. No matter what the mirror said, he was only forty-one. Not that damned old.

"Quiet, please," Bruce called.

Dash walked to the bottom of the porch steps and picked Honey up under his left arm

"Stand by now. We're rolling. Marker. Action."

"No, Pop," Janie screamed, as he began to walk. "What are you doing? I said I was sorry."

He reached the corner of the porch.

"Don't forget you're opposed to unnecessary violence," she shrieked. "You can't turn your back on your principles."

She was giving it one hundred percent, just like always, and he had to clutch her more tightly as she struggled.

"No, Pop! Don't do this! I'm too old for this . . . "

She started to kick, and her knee caught him in the small of his back. He grunted and his arm tightened around her waist as he continued to move purposefully toward the barn. Without warning, she jabbed the sharp point of her elbow in his ribs. He gripped her even tighter, warning her without words that she was going too far.

Her teeth sank into the flesh of his arm.

"God damn it!" With a sharp exclamation of pain, he dropped her to the ground.

"Ow . . . " Her hat flew off, and she looked up at him, outrage stamped all over her small, furious face. "You dropped me, you fucker!"

Fireworks went off inside his brain. She was ruining his life, and he'd had enough. Reaching down, he snatched her up by the seat of her jeans and the collar of her shirt.

"Hey!" She cried out in a combination of surprise and indignation as she left the ground.

"You messed with me one too many times, little girl," he said, hauling her off to the barn, this time in earnest.

Her struggles before were merely a rehearsal for what she did now. He pinned her against his side, not giving a damn whether he hurt her or not.

Honey felt the painful pressure of hard muscles clamping her ribs and cutting off her breath. Apprehension ate away at her anger as she grew conscious of the fact that he was in deadly earnest. She'd been looking for her limits, and she'd finally found them.

The faces of the crew members flew by. She called out to them. "Help! Bruce, help! Ross! Somebody call Ross!"

No one moved.

And then she saw Eric standing on the side smoking a cigarette. "Eric, stop him!"

He took a drag and looked away.

"No! Put me down!"

He was carrying her into the barn. To her relief she spotted half a dozen crew members working there, adjusting the lights for the next scene. He couldn't do anything horrible to her with so many people standing around.

"Get out of here!" Dash barked. "Now!"

"No!" she screamed. "No, don't leave."

They scampered away like rats from a burning building. The last one out closed the barn door.

With a rough curse Dash sprawled down on a stack of hay bales that had been arranged for the next scene and threw her over his knees.

She'd read the script and she knew what happened next. He lifted his hand to spank her only to find out that he didn't have the heart. Then he told her a story about her mother, she started to cry, and everything was all right again.

The flat of his hand slammed down hard on her bottom. She screamed in surprise.

He hit her again, and her scream changed into a yelp of pain.

The next one hurt even worse.

And then he stopped. The flat of his hand cupped her bottom. "Here's the way it's going to be. From now on you've got one person to answer to, and that's me. If I'm happy, you don't have anything to worry about. But if I'm not happy, then you'd better start saying your prayers." He lifted his hand and slapped it down smartly on her rear. "And believe me. Right now, I'm not happy."

"You can't do this," she gasped.

He smacked her again. "Who says?"

Tears stung her eyes. "I'm a star! I'll quit the show!" *Smack.* "Good."

"I'll sue you!" *Smack.* "Ouch!"

"You'll have to stand in line." *Smack.*

Her face was hot with pain and mortification, and her nose had started to run. A tear plopped down onto the floor of the barn and made a small dark stain on the wood. Her muscles screamed with tension as she waited for the next blow, but his hand had fallen still—as still as his voice.

"Now what I'm going to do is this. I'm going to start calling people in here that you've insulted. One by one, I'm going to call them in and hold you down and let each one of them take a whack at you."

A sob erupted from her throat. "This isn't the way it's supposed to be! This isn't the way it is in the script."

"Life isn't a script, little girl. You have to take responsibility for yourself."

"Please." The word slipped from her lips, small and lonely. "Please don't do this."

"Why shouldn't I?"

She tried to take a breath, but it hurt. "Because."

"I'm afraid you're going to have to do better than that."

Her bottom was burning and his big hand cupping over it seemed to hold in the heat and make it worse. But worse than the pain in her body was the pain in her heart. "Because . . ." she gasped. "Because I don't want to be like this."

He was quiet for a moment. "Are you crying?"

"Me? Hell, no. I—I never cry." Her voice broke.

He lifted his hand from her bottom. She scrambled up, pushing herself off his lap and trying to get to her feet. But the scattered hay on the barn floor was slippery and she lost her balance so that she sprawled awkwardly on the bale next to him. She immediately turned her back so he couldn't see her tear-smeared cheeks.

Everything was quiet for a moment. Her bottom burned, and she clenched her hands together to keep from rubbing it. "I—I didn't mean to hurt anybody," she said softly. "I just wanted people to like me."

"You sure have a strange way of going about it."

"Everybody hates me."

"You're a mean-tempered little bitch. Why shouldn't they?"

"I'm not a b-bitch! I'm a decent person. I'm a good Baptist with a-a strong moral code."

"Uh-huh," he replied skeptically.

She hunched her shoulder so she could use the sleeve of her T-shirt to catch her tears before he saw them drip off her jaw. "You're not—You're not really going to call all those people in here and—and let them take a whack at me, are you?"

"Since you're such a fine Baptist, you shouldn't mind a little public repentance."

She tried to stiffen her spine, but her misery was cramping her insides and keeping her bent forward. How had her life come to this? All she'd wanted was for them to like her, especially this man who held her in such contempt. There were too many tears to hold them back, and a few of them dripped onto her jeans. "I—I can't apologize. I can't embarrass myself like that."

"You've embarrassed yourself every other way. I don't see what difference it'd make."

She thought of Eric seeing her like this. "Please. Please, don't do it."

His boots shifted in the straw. There was a long silence. She hiccupped on a sob.

"I guess I could hold off for a while. Until I see if you've decided to mend your ways."

Her misery didn't ease. "You—you shouldn't have hit me. Do you know how old I am?"

"Well, Janie's thirteen, but I know you're older than that."

"She's sup—supposed to be fourteen this season, but the writers haven't changed her."

"Television time passes slow."

The tears kept leaking out like a faucet with an old washer, and her voice sounded all mushy. "Except on the s—soaps. My Aunt Sophie watched one show where a baby was born. Three—three years later, that baby was a pregnant teenager."

"The way I remember it, you're around sixteen."

Another sob squeezed through the narrow passageway in

her throat. "I'm eighteen. Eighteen years, o—one month and two weeks."

"I guess I hadn't realized. In a way that kind of makes it worse, doesn't it? Somebody who's eighteen should act more like a woman and less like a kid who has to be turned over somebody's knee."

Her voice broke. "I don't th—think I'm ever going to be a woman. I'm—I'm going to be caught in this kid's body forever."

"There's nothing wrong with your body. It's your mind that needs to grow up."

She crumpled forward, her arms squeezed between her chest and her legs, her body shivering. Self-hatred consumed her. She couldn't stand being herself anymore.

The brush of his fingers against her spine was so light that at first she didn't realize he was touching her. And then his hand opened and settled over the center of her back. The storehouse of emotions that she had locked away for so many years broke free. The feelings of abandonment, the loneliness, the need for love that was like an unmelting cone of ice at the center of her heart.

She twisted around and threw herself against his chest. Her arms wrapped around his neck, and she buried her face in his shirt collar. She could feel him stiffen and knew he hadn't meant to let her into his arms—nobody ever wanted her in their arms—but she couldn't help herself. She just took possession.

"I'm everything you said," she whispered into his shirt collar. "I'm hateful and selfish and a mean-tempered bitch."

"People change their ways all the time."

"You—you really think I should apologize, don't you?"

He held her awkwardly, neither pushing her away nor embracing her. "Let's just say I think you've reached a crossroads. You might not realize it now, but later on you'll look back at this moment and you'll know that you were forced to make a decision that affected how you were going to live the rest of your life."

She was quiet, pressing her cheek against his shoulder and thinking about what he had said. She'd gotten two people fired and insulted nearly everyone on the show. It was a lot to make up for.

Her breath caught on a small hiccup. "This is the real MOS, isn't it, Dash?"

There was a moment of silence.

"I guess it is, at that," he replied.

10

When she emerged from the barn, she found that the shooting schedule had been mysteriously rearranged while she was inside, and instead of filming her scenes with Dash, they were shooting a scene with Blake and Eleanor. Everyone was unnaturally busy, and nobody would meet her eyes, but she saw by their smug expressions that they all knew exactly what had happened inside. The sons of bitches had probably pressed their ears right up to the barn door.

Her eyes narrowed and her lips tightened. She wasn't going to let anybody laugh at her. She'd take care of all of them. She'd—

"I wouldn't advise it," Dash said softly at her side.

She looked up at him, eyes shadowed by the brim of his hat, mouth set in a firm line. She waited for the familiar resentment to bubble up inside of her, but she felt a peculiar sense of peace instead. Someone had finally drawn a line in the sand and told her she couldn't cross it.

"I suggest you make yourself an appointment to see Ross before you leave today. There are a few people you need to get un-fired."

She didn't really believe he'd hold her down and let everybody take a whack at her, but she wasn't going to take a chance, and she nodded.

"And don't even think about whining to anyone from the

network about what happened today. It's between you and me."

A small spark of spirit returned to her. "For your information, I didn't have any intention of whining to anybody."

The corner of his mouth twitched. "Good. You might have more brains than I've been giving you credit for." He touched the brim of his hat with his thumb and began to walk away.

She watched him for several seconds. Her shoulders drooped. By tomorrow, he wouldn't even speak to her. It would be just like always.

His steps slowed and then halted. He turned back to her, studying her for a moment before he spoke. "I know you like horses. If you want to drive out to my ranch some weekend, I'll show you a few I've got."

Her heart swelled in her chest until it seemed to fill every space. "Really?"

He nodded and once again began to walk toward his motor home.

"When?" She took several quick steps after him.

"Well . . . "

"This weekend? Would Saturday be all right? I mean, Saturday's good for me, and if it's good for you . . . "

He stuck his thumb in the pocket of his jeans and looked as if he regretted his invitation.

Please, she prayed. *Please don't take it back.*

"Well—This weekend isn't real good for me, but I guess next Saturday would be okay."

"That's great!" She could feel her grin stretching like Silly Putty over her face. "Next Saturday'd be just great."

"All right then. Let's make it around noon."

"Noon. Oh, that's great. Noon'll be fine."

Her heart floated like a baby's bath toy. It continued to float right through the rest of the day, allowing her to ignore the crew members' smirks and the satisfaction in Liz's eyes. Despite the blow to her pride, she was surprised at how good it felt not being bad any longer.

That evening she cornered Ross in his office and asked

him to rehire Melanie and Jack. He agreed with alacrity, and before she left the studio, she called both of them and apologized. Neither of them forced her to grovel, which made her feel even worse than she had before.

The next week dragged on forever as she waited for Saturday and her visit to the ranch. She bent over backward trying to be nice to everybody, and although most of the crew continued to keep her at a distance, a few of them began to warm up to her.

On Saturday she drove down a narrow dirt road in the rugged mountains north of Malibu and caught her first glimpse of Dash Coogan's ranch. It was tucked neatly into the hills amidst chaparral, oaks, and sycamore. A pair of red-tailed hawks circled in the sky overhead.

She pulled over to the side. The clock on the Trans Am's dash read 10:38 and she wasn't due at the ranch until noon. She flipped down the visor and studied her reflection, trying to decide if the lipstick she'd put on looked silly with her dog's dish haircut. It did. But then, everything looked silly with the haircut, so what difference did it make?

The clock read 10:40.

What if he had forgotten? Her palms were sweating, and she wiped them on her jeans. She tried to tell herself that he wouldn't forget something so important. Their day together was going to be everything she had dreamed about. He would show her around the place. They'd talk about horses, go riding, stop and talk some more. Maybe his housekeeper would have packed a picnic lunch. They'd spread a blanket next to a creek and share a few secrets. He'd smile at her just like he smiled at Janie and—

She pressed her eyes shut. She was getting too old for this kind of childish fantasy. She should be daydreaming about sex, instead. But whenever she did that, she imagined herself making love with Eric Dillon and that got her excited and upset all at the same time. Still, daydreaming about Dash Coogan treating her like Dash Jones treated his daughter Janie wasn't any better.

The clock read 10:43. One hour and seventeen minutes to go.

The hell with it. She turned the key in the ignition and pulled out on the road. She would just pretend she'd gotten the time mixed up.

The ranch house was a rambling one-story stone-and-cypress structure with green shutters at the windows and a front door painted charcoal gray. Considering the fact that Dash was a star, the place was relatively modest, probably the reason the IRS hadn't made him sell it. She got out of the Trans Am and walked up the steps to the front door. As she pushed the bell, she lectured herself about mature behavior. If she didn't want people to treat her as if she were fourteen, she shouldn't act that way. She needed to develop the gift of restraint. And she had to stop wearing her heart on her sleeve all the time.

She pushed the bell again. There were no signs of life. Her nervousness took a quantum leap into full anxiety, and she leaned on the bell. He couldn't have forgotten. This was too important. He—

The door swung open.

He had obviously just gotten out of bed. He wore only a pair of khaki pants, and he hadn't shaved. The wiry strands of his hair lay flat on one side of his head and stuck out on the other as if a herd of cattle had run a stampede right through it. Above all, he didn't look happy.

"You're early."

She swallowed hard. "Am I?"

"I said noon."

"Did you?"

"Yeah."

She didn't know what to do. "Do you want me to go for a walk or something?"

"As a matter of fact, I'd appreciate it."

"Dash?" A woman's voice called out from inside the house.

A look of displeasure came over his face. There was something familiar about the low husky tones of that female voice. Honey bit down on her lip. It was none of her business.

"Dash?" the woman called out again. "Where's your coffeepot?"

Honey's mouth gaped in outrage. *"Dusty!"*

Lisa Harper's familiar blond head appeared behind his shoulder. "Honey, is that you?"

"It's me all right," she replied through clenched teeth.

Lisa's eyes widened in baby-blue innocence. "Oops."

"She's sleeping with *you,* too?" Honey exclaimed, glaring at Dash.

"How about you go take that walk now?" he replied.

She ignored him and glared at Lisa. "You certainly do spread your favors around."

"Comparison shopping," Lisa replied sweetly. "And just between the two of us, the old cowboy leaves Eric Dillon way back at the starter's gate."

"I think that's just about enough," Dash said. "Honey, if one word of this gets to those writers, your butt is going to become public property. Do you hear me?"

"Yeah, I hear you," Honey replied sullenly.

Lisa, who was always looking for ways to expand Dusty's role, grinned at Honey behind Dash's back, obviously hoping she'd talk her head off.

"I'll go take that walk now," Honey said, before he could order her to leave. She fled down the walk, barely breathing until she heard the front door close behind her.

Later, as she stood over by the paddock admiring three of Dash's horses and breathing in the tang of eucalyptus overlaid with the faint scent of manure, she heard Lisa drive away. Envy gnawed at her as she thought of Lisa and Dash, Lisa and Eric—Lisa, who knew all the secrets of womanhood that were still mysteries to her.

Not long after, Dash appeared wearing a long-sleeved plaid shirt with a pair of jeans and worn cowboy boots. Beneath his Stetson, the sides of his hair were still damp from his shower. He extended one of the two mugs of coffee he carried toward her. After she took it, he put a foot up on the fence rail and gazed out at the horses.

She put a foot up, too.

"I'm sorry," she finally said. She was beginning to discover that it was less work to apologize than to defend herself when she was wrong. "I knew I wasn't supposed to show up until noon."

He sipped his coffee from the white ceramic mug. "I figured you did."

That was all. He didn't give her any big lectures or say anything more about it. Instead, he pointed toward the animals in the paddock.

"Those two are quarter horses, and the other's an Arabian. I'm boarding them for friends."

"They're not yours?"

"I wish they were, but I was forced to sell mine off."

"The IRS?"

"Yep."

"Scum suckers."

"You got that right."

"We were audited once, right before Uncle Earl died. Sometimes I think that's what killed him. Nobody except serial killers should have to deal with the IRS. It ended up that I had to handle most of it."

"How old were you?"

"Fourteen. But I was always good in math."

"There's a lot more than math involved when you're up against the IRS."

"I'm smart about people. That helps."

He shook his head and chuckled. "I've got to tell you, Honey, that in all my life I can't ever remember meeting anybody—male or female—who was a worse judge of character than you are."

She bristled. "That's a terrible thing to say. And it's not true."

"It's true all right. The most competent people on the crew are the ones you give the most trouble to, and it's not just the crew, either. You only seem to attach yourself to people with character faults a mile wide. The best people are the ones you turn your back on."

"Like who?" she inquired indignantly.

"Well, Liz for one. She's smart and she's got integrity. She also liked you right from the beginning, although I have no idea why."

"That's ridiculous. Liz Castleberry is the queen of the bitches. And she hates my guts. It seems to me that all you've proved is that I'm a better judge of character than you are."

He snorted.

Honey pressed her point. "I'll give you a perfect example of how vindictive she is. Last week I got back to my trailer and I found a package from her. There was a note with it that said she was sorry she'd missed my birthday, and she hoped I'd like her present even though it was late."

"That doesn't sound too vindictive to me."

"That's what I thought until I opened the present. You'll never guess what was inside."

"A hand grenade?"

"A *dress.*"

"Imagine that. You should take her to court."

"No. Listen. Not just any dress, but this frilly little yellow thing with a ruffle. And these stupid-looking shoes. And *pearls.*"

"Pearls? Well, now."

"Don't you see? She was making fun of me."

"I'm having a little trouble following you here, Honey."

"It looked like something a Barbie doll would wear, not a person like me. If I put an outfit like that on, everybody would fall on the floor laughing. It was so—"

"Feminine?"

"Yes. Exactly. Silly. You know. Frivolous."

"Instead of being made out of barbed wire and razor blades."

"That's not funny."

"So what did you do?"

"I bundled it right back up and returned it to her."

For the first time he looked irritated. "Now why did you have to go and do that? I thought we decided that you were going to mend you manners."

"I didn't *throw* it at her."

"That's a relief."

"I merely said that I appreciated the gesture, but I didn't feel right accepting a gift from her because I hadn't bought her a birthday present."

"And *then* you threw it at her."

She grinned at him. "I'm a reformed character, Dash. Emily Post would have been proud of me."

He smiled, then reached out, and for a moment she thought he was going to rumple her hair, just like he rumpled Jane Marie's. But his arm fell back to his side, and he walked over to talk to the stable hand who worked for him.

He picked out one of the quarter horses for her, a gentle mare since she wasn't an experienced rider, while he took the spirited Arabian. As they headed out into the hills, the sun felt warm on her head, and she couldn't remember the last time she had felt so happy. Dash sat in the saddle with the easy slouch of a man who was more at home on a horse than he was on the ground. They rode in companionable silence for some time before the compulsion to talk became too much for her.

"It's beautiful out here. How much of the land is yours?"

"All of it used to be mine, but the IRS took a lot of it. Pretty soon it'll be part of the Santa Monica National Recreation Area." He pointed off to a steep-walled canyon on their right. "That was the northern boundary of my property, and that creek up ahead marked the western edge. It dries up in the summer, but it's real pretty now."

"You've still got a lot left."

"It's all relative, I guess. I don't think a man can ever own too much land."

"Did you grow up on a ranch?"

"I grew up just about everywhere."

"Did your family move around a lot?"

"Not exactly."

"What do you mean?"

"I didn't mean anything."

"You moved around by yourself?" she asked.

"Just what I said."

"You didn't say anything."

"That's right."

He gazed out at the line of trees that grew near the creek bed. She studied his profile, taking in the deep-set eyes and strong nose, the high cheekbones and square jaw. He looked like a national monument.

Still staring into the distance, he finally spoke. "I'm a private man, Honey. I don't like the idea of my personal life being broadcast to the world."

She looked down at her hands where they rested on the pommel. "You think I'll talk to the writers, don't you?"

"You've been known to do it."

"I don't have to talk to them. It's just that things get bottled up inside me and I don't have anybody else to tell."

"What you do is up to you, but my business is my own."

"Like you and Lisa."

"Like that."

"Lisa's just praying I'll tell the writers that I found the two of you in a compromising situation."

"Lisa's ambitious."

She sighed. "I won't say anything."

"We'll see."

His lack of faith made her angry. Just because she'd told the writers a few things in the past didn't mean she was a blabbermouth. "Do you love her?" she asked.

"Hell, no, I don't love her."

"Then why—"

"Jesus, Honey, there's such a thing in this world as recreational sex." He looked away, and she wondered if she had actually managed to embarrass him.

"I understand that. I just thought—"

"You thought I was too *old*. Is that it? I'll have you know I'm only forty-one."

"That old?"

His head snapped around and she grinned at him. His irritation faded. She looked out over the rugged landscape. Her mare whinnied and tossed its head. "I promise you right now, Dash, that anything you tell me stays with me."

"I appreciate your sincerity, but—"

"But you don't think I can keep my word. I guess I deserve that. The thing is—if occassionally I had someone else to talk to, I wouldn't have to go spilling my guts to the writers all the time."

"This is starting to sound a lot like blackmail."

"I guess you can take it however you like."

Dash released a long, put-upon sigh. "See, from my viewpoint, you're a pretty big talker, and I'm a man with a definite attachment to silence."

"It must have been hard being married to all those women."

"They were mutes compared to you."

"Those writers sure are going to be interested to hear about you and Lisa."

"Honey?"

"Yeah?"

"Remind me to tan your hide."

"You already did. And don't think I've forgotten it."

It was nearly three when they got back to the barn. They cooled off the horses and then handed them over to the stable hand. Dash led her to her Trans Am, which was parked at the side of the house near a heating-oil tank that was partially camouflaged by a hedge of hydrangeas. Honey didn't want the afternoon to be over. She hated the idea of going home to her family's unending complaints. Her stomach rumbled, and she was struck with inspiration.

"Do you ever get hungry for homemade biscuits, Dash? The kind that are so thick and fluffy that when you split them open a big puff of steam comes out. And the butter melts in this golden yellow puddle right in the middle. Then you pour some warm maple syrup—"

"I knew you were ornery, Honey, but I didn't think you were sadistic." He came to a stop near the trunk of the car.

"I guess I never told you what a good cook I am. That's exactly the way my biscuits turn out."

He was clearly dubious. "You don't exactly look like the domesticated type."

"See. That just goes to prove what a poor judge of character you are. I've been cooking for my family for years.

My Aunt Sophie was always too tired to fix meals, and by the time I was ten, I started to develop this allergy to TV dinners, so I began experimenting, and before long, I became an excellent cook. No fancy stuff. Just plain home cooking."

She pulled the car keys from the pocket of her jeans and jiggled them casually in the palm of her hand. "Gosh, now that I've got my mind on biscuits, I think I'll go on home and make up a batch. Thanks a lot for inviting me, Dash. I had a real good time."

He stuck his thumb in the pocket of his jeans and looked down at the ground. She jingled her car keys. He poked at a rock with the toe of his boot. She passed her keys from her right hand to her left.

"I guess if you wanted to check out my kitchen pantry and see if you can find what you need, I wouldn't object."

She widened her eyes. "Are you sure? I don't want to wear out my welcome."

He grunted and headed toward the ranch house.

Grinning, she fell into step behind him.

The kitchen was old-fashioned and roomy, with oak cupboards and toasted-almond paint. She hummed as she gathered up the biscuit ingredients and dug a pound of bacon from the freezer. As she began measuring the flour into a speckled stoneware mixing bowl, she could hear a Sooners basketball game on television in the family room. Although she would have enjoyed Dash's company while she cooked, it was still nice being alone in his kitchen.

Forty-five minutes later, she called him in to take a chair at the antique oak table that sat in the kitchen's small bay. Uncle Earl hadn't liked talk with his meals, so she didn't have any trouble keeping quiet as she flipped back a clean blue tea towel to reveal a bowl full of steaming golden-brown biscuits. He took two of them and speared a half dozen bacon slices onto his plate.

As he broke open the first biscuit, the steam rose up, just as she'd described. She handed him the butter and a pitcher of syrup she had warmed. It wasn't pure maple, but it was all she'd been able to find. The pat of butter soaked into the biscuit and the syrup sluiced down over the sides. She served herself.

"Good," he murmured as he polished off the first one and began his attack on the second.

She took a sip from the fresh coffee she had brewed. It was a little strong for her, but she knew he liked it that way. As he finished his second biscuit, she surreptitiously pushed the basket forward so he could take another.

She wasn't a big eater and she was satisfied with one biscuit and her coffee. He ate a fourth.

"Good," he murmured for the second time.

His enjoyment of her food filled her with pride. She might not be pretty or flirtatious or know how to talk to men, but she definitely knew how to feed them.

He ate nine strips of bacon and half a dozen biscuits before he finally stopped. Looking over at her, he grinned. "You are one fine cook, little girl."

"You should try my fried chicken. Real golden crispy on the outside, but on the inside it's moist and—"

"Stop! You ever heard of cholesterol, Honey?"

"Sure. That's what Lisa uses to bleach her hair."

"I think that's Clairol."

"My mistake." She smiled innocently.

While he was eating, she had been thinking about something he had said earlier. As he stirred a heaping teaspoon of sugar into his coffee, she decided to ask him about it. "Name one person with a weak character that I've attached myself to."

"Pardon?"

"Earlier. You said the strongest people are the ones I turn my back on. You said I only attach myself to weak characters. Name one."

"Did I say that?"

"You said it. Who were you talking about?"

"Well . . ." He stirred his coffee. "How about Eric Dillon for starters?"

"I haven't *attached myself* to Eric Dillon. As a matter of fact, I hate his guts."

"Sure you do."

"He's rude and stuck on himself."

"You got that right."

"But he's very talented." She felt a perverse need to leap to his defense.

"You're right about that, too."

"I'd have to be crazy to care about Eric Dillon. There isn't any way in the world somebody like him would ever look twice at somebody like me—a runty little redneck girl with a big old sucker-fish mouth."

"What's this thing you've got about your mouth?"

"Just look at it." She puckered.

Amusement flickered in his eyes as he studied her lips. "Honey, a lot of males would consider a mouth like yours sexy. If it wasn't moving so much, that is."

She glared at him. "Just try to name someone other than Eric Dillon. I happen to know you won't be able to because I see right through people. I admire strength."

"Is that so?"

"Yes, that is so."

"Then why, Miss Great Judge of Human Nature, have you been so all-fired determined to attach yourself to me?"

She could see that he'd meant to say it as a joke, but it didn't come out that way. As soon as he spoke, his face stiffened and the warmth that had been growing between them dissolved.

Abruptly, he pushed his coffee cup away and stood. "I think it's about time you go on. I've got some things I have to do this afternoon."

She rose and followed him out through the kitchen and across the comfortable family room that stretched along the back of the ranch house. It was decorated with leather furniture and framed posters from his old movies. He led her toward the front door, his boots clicking on the terracotta tiles, the air heavy with tension.

She couldn't stand for their day to end like this. Reaching out, she touched his arm and spoke in a voice so gentle that it hardly seemed to belong to her. "You're just about the strongest person I know, Dash. I mean that."

He turned to face her, his eyes weary and defeated. "I remember one day when you called me a worn-out old drunk."

Shame filled her. "I apologize for that. It's like Satan has taken over my mouth this past year."

"You didn't do much more than speak the truth."

"Don't say that. It makes me feel even worse."

He rested his hand on his hip, stared down at the floor for a moment, and then looked back up at her. "Honey, I'm an alcoholic. Every day is a struggle for me, and a lot of the time I'm not sure it's worth it. The bottle isn't my only problem, either. I'm hard on women. My own kids hate my guts. I've got a hot temper and I don't care much about anybody except myself."

"I don't believe that."

"You'd better believe it," he said harshly. "I'm a selfish son of a bitch, and I don't have any intention of changing at this point in my life."

He stalked from the house, and she couldn't do anything more than follow after him to her car. Their beautiful day together had been ruined, and somehow, it was all her fault.

11

Monday morning Honey arrived on the set with three dozen Rice Krispies squares and a chocolate sheet cake. The crew was surprised, but delighted.

"Clever, darling," Liz Castleberry drawled as she licked a dab of frosting from her bottom lip. "Bribery by chocolate."

"I'm not trying to bribe anybody," Honey countered, not at all happy that the Queen of the Bitches had seen through her so clearly.

She waited two days, and then she brought in several

dozen homemade chocolate-chip cookies. Adding baking to her already exhausting work day had left her so weary that she kept falling asleep between scenes, but the crew members began to smile at her, so she decided it was worth the sacrifice. Dash chatted casually with her during the day, but he didn't invite her out to the ranch or mention the possibility of taking her riding again. She blamed herself.

February slipped by. The writers began sending her frantic notes to meet with them, but she tore them up. Maybe if she proved to Dash that she could keep her mouth shut, he'd invite her back. But as the weeks passed and he didn't make an overture, she began to despair. They would go on hiatus soon, and then she wouldn't see him for four months.

After spending the weekend with her family, listening to Sophie whine and Buck burp beer, she arrived at work on a Monday in mid-March to begin shooting the last show of the season.

Connie Evans, who did her makeup, studied her critically in the mirror. "Those circles under your eyes are getting worse, Honey. It's a good thing the season's over or I'd have to start using industrial-strength concealer on you."

As Connie dabbed away at the shadows, Honey picked up the manila envelope printed with her name that lay on the makeup table. She was supposed to receive her script for the week by messenger no later than Saturday afternoon, but more frequently, she didn't see it until she arrived at work on Monday. She wondered what the writers had in store for her this week. Since she continued to ignore their increasingly strident demands to come and talk to them, she hoped they hadn't decided to get even with her by making Janie fall into a beehive or something like that.

The last few scripts had spotlighted Blake. In one of them, he had a steamy romance with an older woman who was a friend of Eleanor's. The script had taken full advantage of Eric's dark sexuality, and Honey had gotten so upset watching it that she'd turned off the TV.

As Connie dabbed her with makeup, Honey drew the

current week's script from the envelope and stared down at the title. "Janie's Daydream." That didn't sound too bad.

Ten minutes later, she leapt up from her chair and raced out to find Ross.

Liz, wrapped in a pale pink terry-cloth robe, was emerging from her own dressing room when Honey came barreling down the hall. Liz took one look at Honey's face and lunged for her as she flew by. With a hard yank, Liz pulled her into her dressing room and shut the door with her hip.

"What do you think you're doing?" Honey snatched her arm away.

"Giving you a minute to calm down."

Honey's hands clenched into fists at her side. "I don't need to calm down. I'm perfectly calm. Now get out of my way."

Liz leaned against the jamb. "I'm not moving. Pour a cup of coffee, sit down on that sofa, and get yourself under control."

"I don't want coffee. I want—"

"Now!"

Even in a bathrobe, the Queen of the Bitches looked forbidding, and Honey hesitated. Maybe she did need a few minutes to get herself together. Stepping over Mitzi, who was sprawled on the floor, she filled one of the floral china cups Liz kept next to her stainless-steel German coffeemaker.

Liz edged away from the door and gestured toward her own copy of the script lying open on her dressing table. "Be grateful that it's a family show and you don't have to do the scene nude."

Honey's stomach did a flip-flop. "How do you know what I'm upset about?"

"It doesn't take a mind reader, darling."

She stared down into her coffee cup. "I'm not kissing him. I mean it. I'm not going to do it."

"Half the women in America would be glad to stand in for you."

"Everybody's going to think I've been talking to the

writers again, and I haven't. I haven't talked to them in weeks."

"It's just a kiss, Honey. It's perfectly believable that Janie would be having daydreams about kissing Blake."

"But nobody's going to think it's *Janie's* daydream. They're all going to think it's *mine.*"

"Isn't it?"

She jumped up, sloshing her coffee into the saucer. "No! I can't stand him. He's conceited and arrogant and mean."

"He's a lot more than that." Liz sat down on the dressing-table stool and began pulling on a pair of sheer pearl-gray nylons. "Forgive the theatrics, darling, but Eric Dillon is a walking danger zone." She shuddered delicately. "I just hope I'm not around when he finally explodes."

Honey placed her untasted coffee on the table. "I've got to wear a nightgown and a wig and dance around with him under a tree. What a stupid daydream. It's so embarrassing I can't even stand to think about it."

"It's a long dress, not a nightgown. And the wig will probably be beautiful. You'd look silly kissing Blake in those jeans with that awful hair. If you ask me, you're going to look a hundred times better than you usually do."

"Thanks a lot."

Liz drew the panty hose to her waist. Beneath them, Honey could glimpse a skimpy pair of black lace panties.

"With all those marvelous displays of temperament, I could never understand why you didn't throw one of your hissy fits over something important. That horrid haircut, for example."

"I'm not talking about my hair," Honey retorted. "I'm talking about kissing Eric Dillon. I'm going to Ross right now, and I'm—"

"If you throw one of your famous fits, you'll undo all those delicious high-calorie bribes you've been baking. Besides, we start shooting in half an hour, so it's a little late to get a script change. And, anyway, what would you say? Spending a morning dancing around outside and kissing Eric Dillon hardly qualifies as hazardous duty."

"But . . ."

"You've never kissed a man, have you, Honey?"

She drew herself up to her full five feet and one inch. "I'm eighteen years old. I kissed my first man when I was fifteen."

"Was he the one you knifed or the one you shot in the head?" Liz drawled.

"I might have lied about that, but I'm not lying about the kissing. I've had a few romances." She searched her mind for some details that would convince her. "There was this one boy. His name was Chris, and he went to the University of South Carolina. He had this T-shirt with Gamecocks written on it."

"I don't believe you."

"I don't happen to care."

Liz slipped off her robe and reached for the dress she was wearing in the first scene. Honey stared at her bra. It was nothing more than two black lace scallop shells.

"Eric will do all the work, Honey. God knows he has enough experience. Janie's not supposed to know anything about lovemaking, anyway."

"It's not lovemaking! It's only a kiss."

"Exactly. I checked the shooting schedule. Since it's an exterior, they're not filming the scene until Friday. You'll have all week to get yourself together. Now calm down and treat it like any other piece of business."

Honey held Liz's gaze for a few moments and then dropped her eyes. Absentmindedly, she stroked Mitzi's head. "I don't understand why you're trying to help me. You do it all the time, don't you?"

"I try."

"That's what Dash said. But I can't understand why."

"Women should help each other, Honey."

Honey looked up at Liz and smiled. It was nice to hear herself classified as a woman. Giving Mitzi a final pat, she rose and made her way to the door. "Thanks," she said, just before she let herself out.

That afternoon, Liz caught Dash alone. "You'd better keep an eye on your young charge, cowboy. She's a bit upset about this week's show, and you know as well as I do that when Honey gets upset, anything can happen."

"Honey's not my responsibility!"

"Once you smacked her, you made her yours for life."

"Damn it, Liz . . ."

"Ta-ta, darling." She wiggled her fingers and walked away, leaving a cloud of expensive fragrance behind.

Dash swore softly under his breath. He didn't want Honey in his private life, but it was getting harder and harder to keep her out. If only he hadn't gotten soft in the head that day he'd blistered her butt. He should never have invited her to his ranch. Not that he'd had a bad time. In fact, he'd had a damn good time with her, and he hadn't once thought about taking a drink.

She was surprisingly easy to be with for a female. Of course, she wasn't much of a female, which had been the major reason he had enjoyed their day together. No hidden sexual agenda had been percolating beneath the surface, and there had been something relaxing about being with someone who pretty much said whatever was on her mind. Besides, in a funny way, Honey saw a lot of things the same way he did. The IRS, for example.

As Honey came toward him and they took their places for the next scene, he realized that he liked Honey more than he liked his own daughter. Not that he didn't love Meredith, because he did, but even when she was a child he hadn't felt close to her. When she'd turned fifteen she'd gotten religion, and after that there'd been no stopping her. Just last week Wanda had called him with the news that Meredith had decided to drop out of Oral Roberts because the place was getting too liberal for her. As far as his son, Josh, was concerned, things weren't any better. Josh had always been pretty much a mama's boy, something a little more attention from his father might have prevented.

A light meter popped up in front of his face. Honey yawned next to him. Even wearing makeup she looked tired.

"Did you get any of those cookies I brought in last week?" she asked. "The ones with M & Ms in them?"

"I had a couple."

"I didn't think they were as good as those frosted brownies. What did you think?"

"Honey, are you doing any sleeping when you get home, or do you just stay up all night and bake cookies?"

"I sleep."

"Not enough. Look at you. You're getting all run down." He knew he should stop right there, but she looked so small and worn-out that his heart took possession of his brain. "Starting right now, your baking days are over, little girl."

Her eyes shot open in outrage. "What?"

"You heard me. People are going to have to start liking you for your sweet personality and not for your cookies. The next time you bring anything to eat on the set, I'm pitching it right in the garbage."

"You urc not! This isn't any of your business!"

"It is if you want to come out to the ranch on Saturday and go riding."

Right before his eyes, he watched the war going on inside her, the battle between her desire to be with him and her independent nature. Her jaw set in that stubborn line he'd grown all too familiar with.

"You're manipulating me. You think you can go hot or cold on me whenever you feel like it, without the slightest regard for my feelings."

"I told you the kind of man I am, Honey."

"I just want to be your friend. Is that so terrible?"

"Not if that was all you wanted. But you make me nervous." He looked out beyond the cameras to the rear of the studio and decided to say what was on his mind. "You want a lot from people, Honey. I get this feeling that you'd suck out my last drop of blood if I let you. To be honest, I don't have any to spare."

"That's an awful thing to say. You make me sound like a vampire."

He didn't reply. Just gave her some time to sort out her options.

"All right," she said sullenly. "If I can come out to the ranch, I won't bake anymore."

A queer glow of pleasure warmed his insides at the idea

that she enjoyed being with him enough to compromise her pride. She was a great kid when she wasn't being a pain in the ass. "One more thing," he added. "You also have to get through this week with a little dignity. I'm specifically talking about Friday's shooting schedule."

Honey glared over at Liz, who was flirting with a new cameraman. "Somebody has a big mouth."

"You should be glad that particular somebody is watching out for you."

They were interrupted before she could reply, which was probably just as well.

Friday crept toward her like smog. When it finally arrived, she refused to look in the mirror as they fussed with her makeup and zipped her into a white lace dress that sloped down off her shoulders and brushed the floor. They fastened a lavender lace choker around her neck, then set the wig on top of her head. It was long and honey-colored, just like her real hair.

"Perfect," Evelyn, her newest hairdresser, said, standing back to admire Honey.

Connie, who had just finished her makeup, concurred. "Go on, Honey. Stop being a chicken. Take a look."

Honey braced herself and turned toward the mirror. She looked . . .

"Holy shit," she whispered softly under her breath.

"My sentiments exactly," Evelyn replied dryly.

Honey had been afraid she'd look like a boy in drag, but instead, the delicate young woman who stared back at her was a vision of femininity. There was a blurry, dreamlike quality about her features—from the light blue luminosity of her eyes to her soft pink mouth, which didn't look like it belonged on a sucker fish at all but on someone beautiful. Her hair curled softly around her face and fell in waves over the tops of her shoulders, just like a story-book princess.

The AD stuck his head in the trailer. "Show time, Honey. We need you on—Wow!"

Evelyn and Connie laughed, then escorted Honey from the trailer. She squinted slightly in the sunlight. The women walked on each side of her, picking up the hem of her dress to keep it off the grass and giving her last-minute instructions.

"Don't sit down, Honey. And don't eat anything."

"Stop licking your lips. I'll have to powder you again."

Eric was already on the set. Honey avoided looking at him. She felt excited and scared at the same time. It was one thing to have to kiss Eric Dillon when she looked like a horse's rear end. It was quite another when she looked like Sleeping Beauty. She pressed her hand to the pocket in the side seam of the dress and was reassured to feel the tiny tube of Binaca breath spray she had slipped there.

Eric adjusted the lavender sash at his waist. He was dressed like Prince Charming in a white shirt with billowy sleeves, tight-fitting purple trousers, and calf-hugging black leather boots. The costume was constrictive, but as he leaned down to wipe a smudge off his boots, he decided he'd worn worse.

At the sound of female laughter, he looked up. Honey was coming toward him, but several seconds passed before his brain registered what he was seeing. His mouth set in a grim line. He should have known. For two seasons he'd been looking at those tiny features and that incredible mouth, but he still hadn't realized quite how pretty she could be.

She drew closer and lifted her head. Light blue eyes, dewy and star-filled, drank him in, begging him to find her beautiful. His stomach clenched. If he wasn't very careful today, she would go off in another love spin.

"What do you think, Eric?" she asked softly. "How do I look?"

He shrugged, his face blank of any expression. "Okay, I guess. The wig's a little weird, though."

Her bubble burst.

Jack Swackhammer, who was directing his first episode since Honey had gotten him fired, stepped into the shade beneath the oak tree. "Honey, we're going to begin with you in the swing." He motioned her toward the rope swing, which had been embellished with corny purple satin ribbons and puffy lavender tulle bows.

Honey did as he asked, and they began blocking out the

first shot. Since there was no dialogue in the scene, all she had to do was let Eric push her, but she was so tense she felt as if she would break apart if he even touched her.

"We're laying in an orchestral track on top of the video—lots of strings and schmaltz," Jack said. "Ray'll play it for you while we're shooting to get you in the mood."

She wanted to die from embarrassment when one of the speakers began emitting a romantic orchestral score.

"Will you relax?" Eric grumbled from behind her as the cameras rolled and he began to push.

Her insides cramped as she realized that she knew how to be Janie but she didn't have the faintest idea how to be Janie's fantasy of herself. "I am relaxed," she hissed, finding it easier to talk to him since she didn't have to face him.

"Your back is like a board," Eric complained.

She had never felt more awkward, more at a loss. She knew exactly who she was when she was dressed in jeans with her dog's dish haircut, but who was the creature in the fairy-tale gown?

"You worry about yourself, and I'll worry about me," she retorted, the skin beneath her lace dress hot with embarrassment.

He gave the swing a hard push. "It's going to be a long afternoon if you don't take it easy."

"It's going to be a long one anyway, because I have to work with you."

"Cut! We don't look like we're having a good time," Jack drawled from his position next to the first camera. "And we seem to have forgotten that some of our viewers can read lips."

Because she was embarrassed and unsure of herself, she took refuge in hostility. Lifting her head, she spoke directly to the camera. "This is bullshit."

The swing jerked to a stop.

Jack ran his hands through his thinning hair. "Let's settle down and try it again."

But the next take didn't go any better, nor did the one after that. She simply couldn't relax, and Eric wasn't helping. Instead of acting romantic, he behaved as if he hated her guts, which he probably did, but he didn't have to be so obvious about it. She tried to remember if he had eaten any of her cookies.

At Jack's orders, Ray, the sound man, turned off the music. The director looked at his watch. They were already behind schedule, and it was all her fault. This time she wasn't causing trouble on purpose, but nobody would believe that.

"How about a break?" she suggested, jumping up from the swing as Jack approached them both.

The director shook his head. "Honey, I understand that you've never done anything like this before, and you're bound to feel awkward—"

"I don't feel the slightest bit awkward. I'm as comfortable as I can be."

He apparently decided it was a waste of time to argue with her because he turned on Eric. "We've done at least ten shows together, and this is the first time I've seen you do half-assed work. You're holding out. What's going on here?"

To Honey's surprise, Eric didn't try to defend himself. He stared down at a bare spot in the grass as if he were trying to make up his mind about something. Probably whether or not he could kiss her without throwing up.

When he looked up, his mouth had thinned into a grim line. "All right," he said slowly. "You're right. Give us a chance to improvise a little . . . work it through. Just start to roll and then leave us alone for a while."

"We're on a tight schedule," Jack replied. And then he threw up his hands in frustration. "Go ahead. It can't be any worse. Okay with you, Honey?"

She nodded stiffly. Anything was better than what they had been doing.

There was a sudden purposefulness about Eric, as if he'd made some sort of decision. "Have sound crank up the music a little so the two of us can talk without everybody on the crew listening in."

Jack nodded and returned to his position behind the

camera. Connie scampered over and touched up their makeup. Within moments, the lush sound of strings filled the set.

Honey's stomach clenched. The Binaca! She'd forgotten to spray her mouth. What if her breath was bad?

"We're rolling," Jack said, speaking just loudly enough to be heard over the music. "Marker. Action."

She turned to Eric for direction and saw that he was studying her. He looked deeply unhappy. And then, as she watched, he seemed to go inside himself. She had observed him do this when he was getting ready for a difficult scene, but she had never been standing quite so close. It was eerie. An absolute stillness came over him, a blankness of expression, as if he were emptying himself out.

And then his chest began to rise and fall in gentle rhythm. A transformation came over him, subtle at first but gradually becoming more visible. He seemed to come into focus before her eyes in a new form. The ice chips melted in those turquoise eyes and the furrows eased from his forehead. Her bones turned to gelatin as the hard lines around his mouth softened. Before her eyes, he became young and sweet. He reminded her of someone, but for a moment she couldn't think who it was. And then she knew.

He looked like all of her daydreams of him.

Picking up her hand, he drew her over by the tree. "You should wear dresses more often."

"I should?" Her voice came out like a small croak.

He smiled. "I'll bet you've got your jeans on underneath."

"I do not!" she exclaimed indignantly.

He settled his hand on the small of her back, just below her waist, and squeezed gently. "You're right. I don't feel any jeans."

A tremor passed through her. He was standing so close that the heat of his body warmed her through the lace of her dress. "Shouldn't I get on the swing?" she asked, stumbling slightly over the words.

"Do you want to?"

"No, I—" She started to dip her head, but he caught her chin with the tip of his finger, making her look at him.

"Don't be afraid."

"I'm—I'm not afraid."

"Aren't you?"

"This wasn't my daydream," she said miserably. "It was the writers. They—"

"Who cares? It's a beautiful daydream. Why don't we enjoy it?"

She caught her breath at the husky intimacy in his voice, as if they were the only people left in the world. The sunlight filtering through the leaves of the tree threw lavender shadows across his features. They played hide-and-seek with his eyes and the corners of his mouth. She couldn't have torn her gaze away from him if she'd had to.

"How do we enjoy it?" she asked breathlessly.

"Why don't you touch my face, and then I'll touch yours."

Her hand trembled. It tingled at her side. She wanted to lift it, but she couldn't.

He gently clasped her wrist and drew it upward between their bodies until she touched him. As she brushed the side of his jaw, he released her, leaving her on her own.

With the tips of her fingers, she felt the slight hollow in his cheek, right beneath the ridge of bone. Her hand moved on to the corner of his jaw, his chin. She touched him as if she were blind, memorizing every dip and rise. Unable to stop herself, she slid her fingertips to his bottom lip and explored its contours.

He smiled beneath her touch and lifted his own hand to her mouth. Under the touch of his fingers, her mouth became beautiful. His eyes bathed her with admiration, and hard knots unraveled inside her until all of her became beautiful.

"I'm going to kiss you now," he whispered.

Her lips parted, and her heart raced. His breath fell softly on her skin as his head dipped. He drew her against his body so tenderly she might have melted there from the warmth of the sunlight. She anticipated his lips for a fraction of a second before they brushed against her own. And then her senses sang as he kissed her.

Castles and flowers and milk-white steeds danced through

her mind. His mouth was gentle, his lips chastely closed. A spell of wonder and innocence enveloped her. The kiss was pure, unsullied by awkwardness or lust, a kiss to awaken a sleeping princess, a kiss that had been formed from the gilded web of daydreams.

When their lips finally parted, he continued to smile down at her. "Do you have any idea how beautiful you look?"

Mutely, she shook her head, her customary glibness deserting her. He drew her away from the trunk of the tree into a patch of sunlight and kissed her again. Then he reached up, pulled a leaf from the tree, and tickled her nose with it.

She giggled.

"I'll bet you don't weigh anything." Without giving her a chance to reply, he picked her up in his arms and swung her in a slow, looping circle. The skirt of her dress tangled in his fingers and the sleeves of his shirt billowed. Thousands of tiny bubbles rose inside her. She tossed back her head, and her laughter seemed to mingle with the breeze and the sunlight that lit sparks in his dark hair.

"Are you dizzy yet?" he asked, laughing back at her.

"No . . . Yes . . ."

He set her on her feet, keeping his arm behind her waist so she didn't fall. And then he twirled her again, dancing her in and out of the shadows. She felt light and graceful and achingly alive, an enchanted princess in a fairy-tale forest. Pulling her into his arms, he kissed her again.

She sighed when he eventually drew away. The music swirled around them, bathing them in its magic. He cupped her cheek as if he couldn't get enough of her. He turned her again and again. Her lips tingled, and the blood sang in her veins. Finally she thought she understood what it was to be a woman.

They stopped moving. He held her still in front of him and looked beyond her. "Do you have what you need?"

His voice jolted her. It sounded different, harder.

"Cut and print!" Jack exclaimed. "Fantastic! Great work,

both of you. I may need a couple more close-ups, but let me check the tape first."

Eric stepped away from her. She felt a chill as he transformed himself before her eyes. All the warmth disappeared. He looked edgy, restless, and hostile.

His name seemed to stick in her throat. "Eric?"

"Yeah?" The day wasn't warm, but beads of sweat had broken out on his forehead. He walked behind the cameras toward one of the director's chairs and snatched up the cigarettes he had left there.

She followed him, unable to hold herself back. "I—It—uh—it went pretty well, didn't it?"

"Yeah, I guess." He lit a cigarette and took a deep, uneven drag. "I hope we don't have to do a piece of shit like that again. From now on do us all a favor and keep your adolescent sexual fantasies to yourself."

Her daydream shattered. He had been acting. None of it was real. Not his kisses, his whispers, his gentle, loving touch. With a soft exclamation of pain, she turned into an ugly duckling again. Picking up her skirts, she raced for the solitude of her trailer.

Dash stood less than twenty feet away observing it all. He had seen how skillfully Dillon had maneuvered her so the cameras could photograph them from different angles, and he couldn't remember the last time he'd felt such an urge to hurt someone. He told himself it wasn't any of his business. Hell, he'd done worse to women in his life. But Honey wasn't a woman yet, and as Dillon bent over to retrieve his script, Dash found himself walking up to him.

"You're a genuine sonovabitch, aren't you, pretty boy?"

Eric's eyes narrowed. "I was doing my job."

"Is that so? And what job is that?"

"I'm an actor."

Dash opened and closed his fist at his side. "A bastard is more like it."

Eric's eyes narrowed and he tossed his cigarette to the ground. "Go ahead, old man. Take a swing." He braced himself, the muscles beneath his shirt tightening.

Dash wasn't intimidated. Dillon had Hollywood muscles, built on high-priced gym equipment instead of hard work and barroom brawls. They were cosmetic muscles, no more real than the kisses he had given Honey.

And then Dash saw the sweat glistening on Eric's forehead. He had seen men sweat from fear before, and they always looked wild in the eyes. Dillon just looked desperate.

He knew then that Eric wanted him to hit him, and as abruptly as it had seized him, he lost his desire to draw blood. For a moment he did nothing, and then he pushed his hat back on his head and gave Dillon a long, steady gaze.

"I guess I'll pass for now. I don't want a young stud like you humiliating me in front of everybody."

"No!" A vein began to throb in Eric's temple. "No! You can't do that. You—"

"So long, pretty boy."

"Don't—"

The plea stuck in Eric's throat as he watched Dash walk away. He fumbled for another cigarette, lit it, and drew the poisoned smoked into his lungs. Coogan didn't even respect him enough to fight him. At that moment he admitted to himself what he had refused to acknowledge before. How much he admired Dash Coogan—not as an actor, but as a man. Now that it was too late, he knew that he wanted Coogan's respect, just as he'd always wanted respect from his father. Dash was a real man, not a pretend one.

The smoke was choking him. He had to get out of here. Someplace where he could breathe. An image of needy, light blue eyes swam before him. He stalked from the set, pushing his way through the equipment and the crew, trying to escape those eyes. But they stayed with him. She was so desperate for love that she didn't have any sense of self-preservation. She hadn't even put up a fight, just let him throw her right over the edge of the cliff.

His lungs burned. Stupid. She was so goddamn stupid. She didn't understand the first rule of fairy tales. She didn't understand that little girls weren't ever supposed to fall in love with the evil prince.

Air Time

1983

12

Liz Castleberry's Fourth of July beach party was in full swing when Honey arrived. She wedged the silver Mercedes Benz 380 SL she had purchased after the show's third season onto the side of the road between a Jag and an Alfa Romeo. As she stepped down onto the sandy soil, she heard the bang of a firecracker exploding from the beach on the other side of the house. This was the first of Liz's party invitations Honey had accepted, and then only because it was informal and because Dash was going to be here.

Slinging the faded denim slouch bag that contained her bathing suit over her shoulder, she locked the car. Three years ago last month she had arrived in Los Angeles, but she felt decades older than that sixteen-year-old girl. Thinking back, she decided the horrible day toward the end of the second season when Eric Dillon had humiliated her in that phony fantasy love scene was what had finally forced her to grow up. At least the experience had put an end to the childish crush she'd had on him. No one, not even Dash, knew how much the memory of that day still made her cringe.

As she approached the beach house, she found herself wondering what the new season held in store for her. They would begin shooting at the end of the month for the show's fourth year, and the producers were finally going to permit Janie to turn fifteen. It was about time, since she would be twenty in December.

After the painful adjustments of the first two seasons, last season had been relatively uneventful. She had gotten along well with the crew, stayed away from Eric, and deepened her friendship with Liz Castleberry. But her relationship with Dash had been the most important change in her life.

She spent a lot of her spare time on the set with him, as well as nearly every Saturday at the ranch, doing chores and helping out with the horses. Not only did she love being with him, but the work gave her a convenient excuse to get away from the new house in Pasadena that Chantal had nagged her into buying because she insisted it would help Gordon get back to his painting. It hadn't helped, a fact that didn't surprise Honey at all. She liked the house much better than that awful place in Topanga Canyon, but it certainly didn't feel like home. For one thing, Buck Ochs was still in residence, and for another, her relationship with Sophie hadn't improved at all.

Shaking off depressing thoughts of her family, she approached the front entrance of Liz's beach house. The house was deeper than it was wide, with salt-weathered gray siding and salmon shutters. A small garden lay off to one side, along a low stone retaining wall that marked the boundary of the neighboring house, where Guy Isabella's daughter Lilly lived. The walk was tiled in a fish-scale pattern and edged with clusters of crimson and white impatiens.

As she approached the front door, she hesitated. After three years in L.A., she still hadn't been to that many parties. She wasn't comfortable at social functions because she was always afraid she'd use the wrong fork and because everyone seemed so sophisticated. Besides, Ross's lie about how old she was had taken hold, and the few times she had tried to convince people of her real age, they hadn't believed her.

She rang the bell, and a sunburned middle-aged man in bathing trunks let her in. The hairy patch on his chest looked like a map of Indiana.

He threw up his hands. "Honey! Hi, I'm Crandall. I love, love, love your show. It's absolutely the only thing I watch on television. You should have won last year."

"Thanks." She wished people would stop bringing up her Emmy nomination. She hadn't won—a fact her agent attributed to her continuing refusal to take any of the other acting parts that were offered her. Eric had won two years in a row. The movies he had filmed during the last few hiatuses were turning him into a major box-office star, and it was no secret that he was going to break his contract so he could make movies full time.

"Lizzie's out on the deck," Crandall said, leading her through a white-tiled entryway decorated with misty impressionistic paintings.

The living room was filled with people in various forms of casual wear, from bathing suits to slacks, everything stylish and expensive compared to her khaki shorts and Nike T-shirt. Liz had been nagging her to dress better, but Honey didn't have the talent for it. She moved past overstuffed sofas and chairs upholstered in baby blue and pale salmon toward a wall of windows that provided a panoramic view of the sea. The room smelled of barbecue, suntan lotion, and Chloè.

Liz came through a set of French doors that opened onto the deck and made her way toward Honey. Puckering her lips, she blew a kiss into the air somewhere near her costar's ear.

"You actually showed up. Happy Fourth of July, darling. Dash told me he'd ordered you to appear, but I didn't believe you'd really do it."

"Is he here yet?" Honey gazed hopefully through the sophisticated crowd, only a few members of which she recognized, but she didn't spot him.

"I imagine he'll be along." Liz stared at Honey's hair. "I can't believe that it's actually starting to curl. Evelyn told me you've been letting her work with it. You're beginning to look like a woman instead of a grade-school bully."

Honey had too much pride to let Liz see how much she liked her new hair. On the final day of shooting last March, Liz had ordered Evelyn to soften the blunt edges and feather back the bangs. At first, since the hair was so short, Honey hadn't seen much of an improvement, but as it had grown these past four months and Evelyn had continued to touch it up, it now curled softly around her face and brushed the slopes of her jaw.

"But you still look so young," Liz complained. "And you dress like an absolute infant. Look at those shorts. They're too big, and the color is putrid. You don't have any style at all."

Honey had grown used to Liz's blunt judgments, and she was merely annoyed instead of angry. "Why don't you give up, Liz? You'll never make me into a fashion plate. I don't have the talent for it."

"Well, I do, and I can't imagine why you won't let me take you shopping."

"I'm not interested in clothes."

"You should be." Before Honey could protest, Liz was whipping her through the crowd and up a narrow circular staircase into a pink and rose bedroom that reminded Honey of an expensive flower garden. Chintz draperies were tied back from the windows with tasseled cords, and sea-green carpeting covered the floor. One corner held a watered-silk chaise, another an ornate armoire made of bleached oak. A misty pastel fabric that looked as if it had been painted by Cézanne draped the double bed. Honey spotted a pair of masculine cuff links on the table next to it, but as much as she would have enjoyed hearing the details of Liz's love life, she had always restrained herself from asking.

Liz opened one of the louvered closet doors and began to dig around inside. "You'd have more confidence in yourself if you dressed your age."

"I have lots of confidence. I'm the most independent person I know. I take care of my family, and I—"

"Confidence in yourself as a woman, darling. It's the most amazing coincidence—" She pulled out a navy sack with crimson lettering. "I bought this for myself last week in a little boutique just off Rodeo, but when I got home, I realized I'd picked up the wrong size. I'll bet this would fit you perfectly."

"I brought a suit with me," Honey said stubbornly.

"And I can just imagine what it looks like."

Honey's hand clamped over the top of the slouch bag that

contained the old red tank suit the maid at the Beverly Hills Hotel had bought for her the week she'd arrived in L.A.

Liz shoved the sack at her and fluttered her hand toward the bathroom. "Try it on. You can always take it off if you don't like it."

Honey hesitated and then decided if she tried on the suit she could at least postpone going back downstairs for awhile. Maybe by then Dash would have arrived and she wouldn't have to face so many strangers by herself.

The bathroom looked like a tropical grotto complete with lush flowering plants, a sunken pink marble tub, and gold faucets shaped like dolphins. She peeked into the sack. Tucked inside the folds of tissue paper lay a skimpy bikini in a soft peach-and-white Hawaiian print along with a short wrap skirt in the same fabric. She pulled out the separate pieces. They were certainly prettier than her red tank suit, but she didn't like the idea of letting Liz manipulate her. She began to stuff the suit back into the sack, but hesitated. What was the harm in trying it on? Slipping out of her clothes, she donned the separate parts of the bikini and turned to assess herself in the beveled mirror that lined the wall behind the tub.

She hated to admit it, but Liz was right. The suit fit her perfectly. The under-wire top made the most of her small breasts by pushing them together just enough to give her a hint of cleavage. The bottom covered up everything important and was cut high enough on the sides to make her legs look longer. Still, she wasn't used to having so much of herself exposed. She opened the short, sarong-style skirt, looking for the clasp. When she found it, she wrapped it around her waist and fastened it on the left side. It fell low on her hips, just revealing her navel.

With the curling halo of her hair, her enhanced bust line, and her navel peeking out over the top of the skirt, even she had to admit she looked a little bit sexy.

"Knock, knock. I hope you're decent." The door swung open, and before Honey could respond, Liz had entered and clipped a pair of gold hoops to her earlobes. "You really need to get your ears pierced."

Honey touched the swaying hoops. "I can't go swimming with these on."

"Why on earth would you want to swim? I haven't been in the ocean in years. At least you're wearing a decent shade of lipstick, but I think a dab of mascara would be lovely."

Liz pushed her down onto a stool, whisked some pale peach blusher over her cheeks, and then dabbed at her lashes with light-brown mascara.

"There. Now you look your age. Whatever you do, don't go near the water."

Honey stared at the gold hoops shimmering through the honey-colored tendrils at her ears and studied the soft, flattering makeup. Even her mouth was sexy. She looked like herself, and yet not like herself. Older, more mature. Much prettier. Her reflection was disconcerting. She liked the way she looked, and yet the young woman in the mirror wasn't altogether a person she could respect. She was a bit too soft, too feminine, not nearly tough enough to fight life's battles.

Liz must have sensed her indecision because she spoke quietly. "It's time to grow up, Honey. You're nineteen years old. You need to come out of your cocoon and start discovering who you are."

Awareness hit her, and Honey jumped up from the stool. "You set me up, didn't you? You didn't buy that bathing suit for yourself. You bought it for me." She snatched up the tube of light-brown mascara. "And why would someone with lashes as dark as yours happen to have this lying around?"

Liz didn't even look guilty. "I've been bored lately, and I must admit the challenge of transforming you into a reasonable facsimile of a young woman has its appeal. Of course Ross is going to have a coronary when he sees you, but that's his problem. All this secrecy about your age is ridiculous."

Honey shook her head. "You're a complete fraud."

"Whatever do you mean?"

"That bitch-goddess act you put on."

"It's not an act. I'm ruthless and unscrupulous. Ask anyone."

Honey smiled. "Dash tells everybody you're a pussycat."

"Oh, he does, does he?" Liz laughed, but then gradually her amusement faded. "You've seen a lot of Dash this past year, haven't you?"

"I like the ranch. I go out there on weekends. We ride and talk, and I help out in the stable. That housekeeper of his doesn't know how to fix the kind of food he likes. Sometimes I cook for him."

"Honey, Dash is— He can be hard on people who care about him. I don't think he means to, but he can't seem to help it. Don't make up too many fatherly fantasies about him. He only lets people so close before he pushes them away."

"I know. I think it's because of his childhood."

"His childhood?"

"He spent a lot of time in foster homes. As soon as he got attached to somebody, they'd make him move someplace else. After a while, I guess he decided it was better not to get close to anybody."

Liz stared at her in astonishment. "He told you all that?"

"Not exactly. You know how he is. But he's said a few things here and there, and I've sort of drawn my own conclusions. When you're an orphan yourself, it's not too hard to recognize the symptoms in somebody else. Dash and I have handled our situations differently, though. He doesn't attach himself to anybody, and I attach myself to just about everybody."

She looked down at her hands, embarrassed to have said so much. "My mouth is getting away from me again. It's like a disease."

Liz studied her for a moment before linking her hand through Honey's arm. "We'd better get back to the party. I have the most wonderful young man I want you to meet. He's the son of an old friend—cute, smart, and only a little bit arrogant. The best part—he's not in the business."

"Oh, I don't think—"

"Don't be a baby. It's time to test your wings. Not to mention the effect of that sexy outfit."

Ignoring Honey's reluctance, Liz led her downstairs. Honey was disappointed to see that Dash hadn't yet arrived. Lately, he'd been getting a little too bossy with her, and she couldn't wait to see how he reacted to her appearance. It was about time she showed him that she wasn't a child anymore.

Liz began introducing her to the other guests, and people greeted her with varying degrees of surprise.

"You look a lot younger on television, Honey."

"I hardly recognized you."

"How old are you, anyway?"

Ross appeared next to her just as this blunt inquiry was being made and quickly whisked her away. He had gained a few pounds over the summer and his stomach, visible beneath an open terry-cloth wrap, was sunburned.

"What do you think you're doing?" he growled, his eyes skimming from her hair to her flat, bare midriff. "You shouldn't be in public looking like that."

Liz hadn't left Honey's side. "Leave her alone, Ross. And stop being such a worrywart. There's nothing in the world —not even her real age—that would make audiences stop loving her. Besides, she's here to have fun."

They greeted several more people, and then Liz steered her out onto the deck and toward a young man standing alone by one of the umbrella tables. He had light-brown hair cut short, square, blunt features, and an athlete's trim build. Sunglasses dangled from a short cord around his neck, and a gold watch glimmered at his wrist. Despite the rumpled and faded purple polo shirt that accompanied his swim trunks, the easy assurance of his stance made Honey suspect he came from money. As Liz led her relentlessly forward, she felt herself begin to panic. She didn't know anything about men like this.

"No, Liz. I—"

"Darling, I want you to meet Scott Carlton. Scott, would you make certain Honey gets something to eat and drink?"

"My pleasure."

Honey gazed up into a pair of warm brown eyes that were regarding her with obvious admiration. Some of her tension eased.

"What are you drinking?" he asked, as Liz left them alone.

She started to request an Orange Crush, but stopped herself just in time. "Whatever you're having. I'm not particular."

"Coors it is." He went over to an ice chest and pulled out a can of beer. Returning to her side, he popped the top and handed it over to her. She took a nervous sip.

"I must be the only person in America who hasn't watched your show. I've been taking classes in the evenings for my M.B.A. I've seen photos of you, of course, in magazines." His eyes dropped momentarily to the little swell of cleavage rising from the cups of her bikini and he smiled. "You look lots different in person."

"The camera puts on weight," she said inanely. Where was Dash? Why hadn't he shown up? She hoped he wouldn't bring a date. Watching him with other women bothered her.

"Not something you need to worry about. So how long have you been in L.A.?"

She told him. He asked her a few questions about her work, and then began to tell her about his job with a well-known market research firm. She realized to her amazement that he was trying to impress her. Imagine somebody like him trying to impress somebody like her. Gradually she became aware of the fact that several of the young men were giving her sidelong glances, and her self-confidence took a baby step forward.

"If you don't mind a personal question, how old are you, Honey?"

She resisted the urge to look over her shoulder and see if Ross was nearby. "Nineteen. Twenty in December."

"Really. I'm surprised. You look older. Even though you're small, there's something about your eyes. A maturity."

She decided that she definitely liked Scott Carlton.

He was joking with her about one of his coworkers when Dash came out on the deck and her heart gave a crazy jolt. All the men around him faded like old photographs. He was taller than most of them, but it was more than his physical stature that made the others seem diminished. He was a legend, while they were merely mortals.

A young woman approached him, and Honey realized it was Lilly Isabella, Liz's next-door neighbor. She had met her once last fall when she had visited Liz. Lilly was tall and beautiful, with full breasts and slim hips. Her silver-blond hair swept back from her face like liquid silk, displaying a finely chiseled classical profile.

The sight of Lilly sapped some of Honey's confidence. She was so sexy and sophisticated, obviously born to money and privilege. She wore a light blue raw-silk top tucked into a pair of darker blue slacks that set off her long legs. A silver slave bracelet encircled her upper arm and a matching belt cinched her waist. As Dash smiled at her, jealousy nipped at Honey. He never looked like that when he talked to her.

"Do you know Lilly?" Scott asked, following the direction of her eyes.

"Not really. We've met, but that's all. Why? Do you know her?"

"We dated for a while. But Lilly's complicated. It's hard for an ordinary guy to compete with her father. Besides, she doesn't stay with any guy for long if he's not an actor."

Honey waited, but he didn't elaborate. She watched as Dash tilted his head attentively, treating Lilly as a mature, desirable woman, even though she wasn't all that much older than Honey. Her resentment grew, and she decided it was time she showed him that Lilly Isabella wasn't the only desirable woman around. She gazed up at Scott through her lashes. "If Lilly walked away from someone as attractive as you, then she's definitely not as smart as she looks."

He grinned. "You want to go down to the beach?"

She glanced toward Dash and saw that he still hadn't noticed her. "I'd love to."

They had to pass Dash and Lilly to reach the steps. As she and Scott drew close, Dash spotted her for the first time. To Honey's delight, Scott slipped his arm around her waist. A flicker of surprised crossed Dash's features, but she couldn't tell whether it was from the change in her appearance or Scott's familiarity.

"Hi, Dash." She greeted him as if she had just noticed him, then introduced Scott and spoke to Lilly.

"Honey! I didn't recognize you. You look terrific." Lilly gave her a friendly smile and exchanged a few pleasantries with Scott.

Dash's eyes surveyed Honey's bare midriff, then locked on to her breasts. He was obviously displeased, and his scowl deepened as he spotted the beer can she still held in her hand. "Since when did you start drinking?"

"Since absolutely forever," she replied in her best Liz Castleberry imitation.

"Honey and I were just going for a walk on the beach," Scott said, taking her elbow. "We'll talk to you later."

She fancied she could feel Dash's eyes boring into her back as she walked away. The idea pleased her, and she added a defiant swing to her hips.

Eric regretted accepting the invitation to Liz's party before he'd stubbed out his first cigarette. He had been filming a movie since hiatus had begun, and this was his first day off in weeks. He should have spent it in bed. Rubbing the stubble on his jaw, he looked for a corner where he could hide out undisturbed. He'd have a drink and then slip away.

As he walked across the deck, a young woman in a red sundress shot him an admiring glance. He wondered why. He was unshaved and disreputable looking, in keeping with his role as a renegade cop on the run from the kingpin of a drug ring. The movie role was a far cry from Blake Chadwick, and exactly what Eric needed to flush the saccharin of *The Dash Coogan Show* from his veins.

Even though he had two years left on his contract, he'd decided he had to get out now. He didn't care how much it cost or what his lawyers had to do. From now on he was concentrating on his film career and putting television behind him.

He spotted Coogan on the other side of the deck and turned his back to look out at the ocean. He avoided his costar as much as possible, maybe because he had the uneasy sense that Dash saw right through him. Being with

Dash Coogan always made him feel inferior, the same way he used to feel with his own father. Eric didn't like to think about how much he wanted Dash's respect. Every time Dash called him "pretty boy," Eric felt sick.

Sunlight sparkled the tips of the waves and he thought about going for a swim, but it was too much trouble. A couple stood talking on the beach in front of him. He dismissed the man but his eyes lingered for a moment over the woman. Squinting against the glare from the sand, he saw that she was tiny but well proportioned, with small round breasts and good legs. From a distance, she looked a bit too fragile to appeal to him, but she was still tempting. Maybe he'd take a closer look when she came up on the deck. He didn't bother to consider what he would do if she weren't interested in him. That never happened.

The man reached out and touched her arm. She tossed her curls and her earrings sparked in the sun. Turning her head, she laughed.

With a shock he realized it was Honey. What had happened to the tomboy with the cropped hair and perpetual scowl? Occasionally last season, she had shown up in lipstick and a skirt. But she hadn't looked like this.

She stretched out her arm and made a sweeping gesture toward the water. The wind whipped her skirt, revealing the V of her thighs. His gaze settled there, and then he was disgusted with himself because his instinctive response seemed vaguely incestuous. No matter how much she might have changed, Honey still reminded him of Jase.

"Haven't I seen your face on a post-office wall somewhere?"

A woman's voice, rich and musical, came from behind him. He turned toward her and forgot all about Honey.

"An innocent man wrongly accused," he said.

She took a sip of wine from her glass and regarded him with a pair of widely spaced light gray eyes. A long lock of silvery hair blew across her face. She hooked it with her little finger and pushed it away.

The corners of her mouth twitched. "Why don't I believe that?"

"It's the truth. I swear."

"I can't imagine anyone describing you as innocent."

He feigned hurt. "I'm a choirboy. Really."

She laughed.

He held out his hand. "Eric Dillon."

She gave it a lazy glance. "I know."

And then she walked away.

He stared after her, intrigued as much by her aplomb as by her beauty. She walked over to a group of men and was quickly surrounded. He heard her musical laughter. The crowd parted and he saw one of the men offering her a shrimp speared on a toothpick. She took it from him, brushed it over her lips before she tasted it, then nibbled it slowly, as if she were savoring each bite.

Liz Castleberry came up behind him. "I wondered how long it would take you and Lilly to find each other."

"Is that her name?"

Liz nodded. "She's Guy Isabella's daughter."

"That turkey?" Eric gave a snort of disgust. Guy Isabella was a movie star, not an actor.

"Don't let Lilly hear you say that. She thinks he's perfect. Not even the fact that he's a lush tarnishes the halo she's put on him."

But Eric wasn't interested in Lilly Isabella's father. As he watched her with the men, he lit a cigarette. She definitely intrigued him. Maybe it was because she didn't look like the type of woman who could be easily hurt.

Not even by him.

"I don't believe you." Honey laughed. "Nobody could break his arm three times in one summer."

"I did."

As dusk fell, Scott showed no signs of losing interest in her, and her self-confidence had grown by leaps and bounds. Now she found herself extending her leg ever so slightly through the slit in her skirt and hanging onto Scott's words as if each one were shaped from precious metal. Once she'd gotten the hang of it, flirting hadn't proved to be difficult at all. In a queer way it made her feel strong, although it was a different kind of strength from what she experienced when she cussed at somebody. Flirting gave her another sort of power, one she didn't fully understand but that she was definitely enjoying. She hoped Dash was watching.

"I can't imagine someone as athletic as you ever being awkward." Her voice held just the right degree of admiration.

"You should have seen me when I was fourteen."

He pitched his beer can over her shoulder toward the trash container that sat in the sand behind her. It bounced off the rim. This was their second trip to the beach. After their earlier walk, they had eaten and chatted with some of the other guests. She had spotted Eric, looking gorgeous and unsavory with a week's worth of stubble on his chin, but her old fascination with him had been murdered that day under the oak tree.

Dash, however, was definitely distracting her. Every time she looked at him he had a woman hanging on his arm. In retaliation, she concentrated on Scott. Lovely Scott, who licked her with his eyes and treated her as if she were every inch a mature, desirable woman.

"I'll bet you were cute when you were fourteen," she said as they waded at the edge of the water.

"Not half as cute as you are right now."

Incredibly, she felt her mouth forming a coquettish pout. "You make me sound like a puppy dog."

"Believe me, you don't look anything like a puppy dog."

She had only a few seconds to enjoy his compliment before he slipped his arms around her body and drew her against him. Her bare midriff brushed against the soft knit fabric of his shirt. He lifted his hand and cupped the back of her neck. Then he lowered his head and kissed her.

His kiss wasn't anything like those lying kisses Eric had once given her. This one was real. He opened his mouth to encompass hers. A wave swirled around her calves, unbalancing her enough so that she leaned into him. He held her more tightly, and warmth spread through her body.

"God, you're really something," he whispered against her open lips. "I want to make love to you."

"You do?" She suppressed the urge to look toward the deck and see if Dash was watching.

"Can't you feel how hard I am?"

He pressed his hips against her stomach. A delicious heat spread through her, along with a new sense of power. She had done that to him.

One of his hands slipped down from the small of her back to cup her bottom. He gave it a gentle squeeze. "You're terrific. Has anybody ever told you that?"

"Everybody." She gazed up at him. "Has anybody ever told you that you're a wonderful kisser?"

"You're not so bad yourself."

She smiled and he kissed her again. This time his lips parted and he slipped his tongue into her mouth. She received the intimacy with curiosity and decided kissing was definitely something she wanted to learn more about. An image of who she wanted her teacher to be flashed through her mind so quickly that she couldn't grab hold of it.

She pushed against his hips to make certain she hadn't lost her effect on him and discovered that she hadn't. His hand slid between their bodies and closed around her breast. She tensed, not wanting so much intimacy so quickly. He slipped his thumb inside the bikini bra and found her nipple. She began to pull away.

"Just what in the goddamn hell do you think you're doing?"

She sucked in her breath at the sound of the gruff, familiar voice coming from behind her.

Scott released her slowly, removing his hand from her breast and frowning at the interloper over the top of her head. "Do you have a problem?"

Turning slowly, she confronted a furious Dash Coogan, his face as dark as a thundercloud, invisible six-shooters riding on his hips. He was paying no attention to Scott, but was glaring at her instead, and he looked as if he were ready to take on all of Dodge City.

"You're drunk," he accused.

Lifting her chin, she returned his stare glare for glare. "I've had two beers. Not that it's any of your business."

"What's this all about, Mr. Coogan?"

Scott's respectful form of address seemed to make Dash even angrier, and the corner of his mouth curled unpleasantly. "I'll tell you what it's about, sonny. You're getting a little too free with your hands."

Scott looked puzzled. "I'm sorry, but I don't see what this has to do with you. She's a consenting adult."

"Not even close." Lifting his arm, he jabbed his hand toward the house. "You get your butt back there right this minute, little girl. That is if you're sober enough to walk that far."

She drew herself up to her full height. "Go to hell."

"What did you say to me?"

"You heard me. I'm not a *little girl,* and I have no intention of letting you order me around. Scott and I are leaving right now for his apartment."

He took a step closer, his eyes narrowing to slits. "I wouldn't bet on it."

She had to tilt her head all the way back so she could stare him down. A dangerous excitement had taken hold of her, a need to dance on the edge of a perilous cliff. "We're going to his apartment, and I'm going to spend the night there."

"Is that so?"

Scott was growing increasingly uncomfortable. "Honey, I don't know what kind of relationship you have with Mr. Coogan, but—"

"We don't have any relationship at all," she said, daring Dash to contradict her.

His voice was low and flat as he addressed Scott. "She's just a kid, and I'm not going to have you taking advantage of that. The party's over for tonight."

"Mr. Coogan—"

Ignoring him, Dash grasped Honey's arm and began steering her across the sand toward the house, just as if she were a disobedient five-year-old.

"Don't you do this to me," she hissed between her teeth. "I'm not a child, and you're ruining everything."

"That's exactly what I had in mind."

"You have no right to interfere."

"You don't even know that boy."

"I know that he's a great kisser." She tossed her head, deliberately making her curls fly. "And I imagine he'll be an even better lover. He'll probably be the best lover I ever had."

He didn't slacken his pace. Her shorter legs were having a difficult time keeping up with his longer ones, and she stumbled slightly in the sand. His grip tightened on her arm. "That wouldn't be too hard, would it?"

"You don't think I've had lovers before? That just goes to show what you know. I've had three lovers just this summer. No, four. I forgot about Lance."

Instead of taking her back up on the deck, he drew her around the side of the house. "Oh, I know you've had lovers. All the men on the crew talk about how easy you are."

She came to a dead stop. "They do not! I never did anything with a single person on the crew."

He pulled her forward. "That's not what I hear."

"You heard wrong."

"They told me you'll undress for anything in pants."

She was outraged. "I will not! I never undressed for a man in my life. I—" She clamped her mouth shut, realizing too late that he'd trapped her.

He shot her a triumphant look. "You're damned right, you haven't. And we're going to keep it that way for a while."

They had reached his car, a four-year-old Cadillac Eldorado. He opened the door and pushed her inside. "Just in case you're lying to me about how many beers you've had, I'm driving you home."

"I'm not lying. And you're not my father, so stop acting like one."

"I'm the closest thing you've got to a father." He slammed the door.

As he stalked around the front of the car, she remembered a time in her life not all that long ago when she would have given anything to hear him speak those words. But something inside her had changed. She didn't know when it had happened or why. She only knew that she didn't want him to act like a father any longer.

When he got behind the wheel, she confronted him, turning her head so swiftly that one of the gold hoops swung forward and bounced against her cheek. "You can't lock me up, Dash. I'm not a kid anymore. I like Scott, and I've decided to go to bed with him. If not tonight, then another night."

He pulled out onto the road, tires spinning in the gravel. He didn't speak until they had passed the guardhouse at the entrance of the private compound and were out on the highway. As the headlights of a passing car cast slanted shadows over his face, he said softly, "Don't give it away cheap, Honey. Make it mean something."

"Like *your* affairs?"

He snapped his head back to the road. She waited. When he didn't say anything in his own defense, her anger grew. "You make me sick. You'll go to bed with any woman who throws herself at you, but you still have the nerve to give me lectures on morality."

He hit the button on the radio, blasting George Jones through the car and drowning out any further conversation.

13

A light flicked on inside the house. Eric had been dozing, but his head snapped up. Music and muted conversation still drifted over from Liz's party next door. He glanced down at the illuminated dial on his watch and saw that it was nearly two o'clock. He had to be on the set in five hours. He should be home in bed instead of skulking in the shadows of Lilly Isabella's deck, waiting for her to return from the party.

Another light went on. Unzipping the dark green windbreaker he had slipped into earlier, he wandered over to the sliding doors that led from the deck into the house and lit a cigarette. There were no curtains on the windows, and he could see the room inside. It held low contemporary furniture in neutral tones that served as a background for the wall of enlarged color photographs that dominated the room. Some of them were portraits of Guy Isabella in various roles he'd played, others artistically posed male nudes. He rapped on the glass.

She appeared almost immediately. Her upper arm held a faint red mark from the silver slave bracelet she had just removed, and her feet were bare. When she saw who was standing on her deck, she gave him a mischievous grin and shook her head. He grabbed the back of one of the tubular deck chairs, turned it so it was facing the doors, and sank down into it.

She slid the door open and regarded him steadily for several seconds. "What do you want?"

"Bad question, sweetheart."

"You're a real tough guy, aren't you?"

"Not me. I'm gentle as a lamb."

"I'll bet. Listen, I'm tired and you're trouble. That's a bad combination, so why don't we just call it a night?"

He stood and flicked his cigarette over the rail into the sand. "Sounds like a good idea." Stepping past her, he entered the house.

She splayed one hand on the hip of her dark blue slacks. He saw that her fingernails were unpainted and bitten nearly to the quick. The flaw intrigued him.

"That's funny. I can't remember inviting you in."

He gestured toward several of the nude male photographs. "Friends of yours?"

"The Hall of Fame of my old lovers."

"I'll bet."

"You don't believe me?"

"Let's just say that most of them look like they'd be more comfortable in a steam bath than in bed with a woman."

She sank down on the couch and stretched like a cat who had gone too long without stroking. "Funniest thing. That's what I've heard about you."

"Is that so?"

"You know how rumors fly about good-looking actors. You're all supposed to be gay."

He laughed, then took his time enjoying the generous lines of her body.

She had enough self-confidence to be amused instead of insulted by his perusal. "Is this where I'm supposed to surrender to your mesmerizing sexuality and take off my clothes?"

"I don't know if I'm ready to give up the pleasures of those steam baths."

She laughed, a rich, throaty sound. "Why do I have the feeling my guardian angel was looking the other way when I let you in the door?" She stood and yawned, this time lifting her silken blond hair from her neck. "You want a nightcap before you leave?"

He shook his head. "I have an early call."

"I'll tell you what, Mr. Dillon. If you want to stop by some time next week, I might be persuaded to open a bottle of Château Latour and play my Charlie Parker tapes for you."

He had no intention of making it that easy for her. "Sorry, I'm going on location."

"Oh?"

Flipping up the collar on his windbreaker, he walked over to the patio doors. "Maybe I'll call you when I get back."

Her head shot up. "And maybe I won't be available."

"I guess I'll have to take my chances." He let himself out, then grinned and lit a cigarette.

Dash was in the paddock inspecting the fetlock of one of the three Arabians he was now boarding along with four other horses when Honey arrived at the ranch. She got out of her car and walked toward him, her full prairie skirt whipping around her legs, the eyelet trim at the hem playing peek-a-boo with the hot afternoon breeze.

She wore the skirt with a white knit tank top, powder-blue sandals, and tiny gold balls in her just-pierced earlobes. In the week and a half that had passed since the party, Liz had taken her on two shopping trips, and she now had a new wardrobe of flouncy little dresses, slacks and tops that had cost a fortune, designer jeans, silk T-shirts, belts and bangles and shoes in every style and color. These past few nights she had found herself standing in her closet simply staring at the beautiful fabrics. It was as if she had spent years suffering from a particularly acute form of malnutrition, only to be confronted by a banquet table laden with food that was irresistible. No matter how much she looked, she couldn't get her fill.

Some of the clothes even seemed to be taking on a life of their own. A few hours ago she had fingered a shimmery little ice-blue evening gown, an updated version of a flapper's dress, and had fought a nearly irresistible urge to put it on, even though she was planning to drive out to see Dash. The gown was hardly designed for a casual afternoon visit to a dusty ranch, but she'd barely been able to resist. *Slip me on,* the shimmery blue gown seemed to say. *If he sees you wearing me, he won't be able to resist you.*

Her hand felt clumsy as she lifted it to wave at him. "Hi!"

He nodded but didn't stop what he was doing. She gripped the top rail of the fence and watched. The sun felt good on her back and arms, but it didn't ease her tension. They hadn't spoken since the night of the party.

He finally finished inspecting the horse and walked over to her, all sweaty and smelling of the stable. He took in her feminine attire but didn't comment on the absence of her customary baggy jeans and faded T-shirt. One part of her wished that she had worn the blue evening gown after all.

"Nice of you to tell me you were stopping by," he said sarcastically.

"I called, but nobody answered." She slipped her foot off the bottom rail. "Why don't I go inside and make you some lemonade? You look hot."

"Don't bother. I don't have time to be sociable today."

She gazed at him steadily. "You're really mad at me, aren't you? You've given me the deep freeze ever since Liz's party."

"Is there any particular reason why I shouldn't?"

"Dash, I'm not Janie. There wasn't any reason for you to turn into Father Avenger."

She had uttered the statement mildly, but his temper immediately flared. "I turned into your friend is what I did. You were smearing yourself all over that boy like a bitch in heat. It was one of the most disgusting things I ever saw in my life. And I don't even know why I bothered to stop you. I'll bet he was on the phone to you that same night, and you were in bed with him by morning."

"It was a little later than that."

He cursed softly, and an emotion that almost seemed like pain furrowed his forehead. "Well, you got what you wanted, didn't you? I just hope you're ready to live with yourself knowing you gave it away so cheap."

"That's not what I meant. I meant that he didn't call me that night. He called me the next day. But I haven't gone out with him."

"Now why is that? I'm surprised that somebody so anxious to explore life's mysteries didn't just get right down to it."

"Please. Don't be so mad." She tried to curb her tongue, but a devil inside prodded her on. "I wanted to talk to you about it first."

He snatched off his hat and slapped it against the side of his jeans, sending up a puff of dust. "No. Uh-uh. I'm not going to turn into your damn sex therapist."

As if she had moved outside her body and was standing on the side observing, she heard herself say, "Liz told me I should go to bed with him."

His eyes narrowed and he slammed his hat back on his head. "Oh, she did, did she? Now why am I not surprised? The way I remember it, she was pretty free with her favors, too."

"What a rotten thing to say. As if you weren't?"

"That doesn't have the slightest thing to do with it."

"You make me sick." Turning on her heel, she stomped away.

He grabbed her arm before she'd taken two steps. "Don't you walk away from me when I'm talking to you."

"Mount Rushmore finally wants to talk," she scoffed. "Well, forgive me very much, but I'm no longer in the mood to listen."

The stable hand was watching them curiously, so Dash pulled her toward the house. The moment they were out of sight of the paddock, he lit into her.

"I never thought I'd see the day when you'd misplace your integrity, but that's just what you're about to do. You seem to be losing all sight of who you are. There's right and there's wrong, and you're not the kind of person who should be jumping into bed with somebody you don't love."

He spoke so fiercely that some of her anger faded. No one except Dash Coogan had ever given a damn about what she did. As she saw the lines concern had drawn in his face, her temper dwindled into a warm, cozy flame. Without thinking about what she was doing, she lifted her hand and flattened her palm against his shirt where she could feel his heart thudding beneath the damp cotton.

"I'm sorry, Dash."

He jerked away from her. "You should be. Start thinking before you jump into things. Think about the consequences."

The way he recoiled from her touch made her angry all over again. "I'm going to the doctor for birth control pills," she shot back at him.

"You're what? You're doing what?" Before she could respond, he launched into a tirade about young people and sexual promiscuity and was so obviously outraged that she almost wished she hadn't baited him. Even so, she couldn't stop herself from prodding him further.

"I'm ready to have sex, Dash. And I'm not going to be casual about protecting myself."

"You're not ready, dammit!"

"How do you know? I think about it all the time. I'm—edgy."

"Edgy isn't the same thing as being in love, and that's the question you have to ask yourself. Are you in love?"

She gazed into those hazel eyes that had seen it all and the word *yes* sprang to her lips, only to be bitten back before it could escape. The truth she had been trying so hard to shut out of her conscious mind refused to be contained any longer. At some point along the way, without knowing exactly when it had happened, her child's love for Dash Coogan had changed into a woman's love. The knowledge was new and old, wonderful and terrible. She couldn't meet his eyes so she gazed at the brim of his Stetson, just above his ear.

"I'm not in love with Scott," she said carefully, her voice sounding thin to her own ears.

"Then that should settle the issue."

"Were you in love with Lisa when you slept with her? Do you love those women who leave makeup smears in your bathroom sink?"

"That's different."

Heartsick, she turned away from him. "I'm going home."

"Honey, it really *is* different."

She looked back at him, but this time he was the one who wouldn't meet her eyes. He cleared his throat. "I'm sort of worn out when it comes to women. But it's not the same with you. You're young. Everything's new for you."

Her response was flat. "I haven't been young since I was six years old and I lost the only person who ever loved me."

"You're not going to find love in some stranger's bed."

"Since I haven't been able to find it anyplace else, I guess I might as well give it a try." She shoved her hand in her pocket and pulled out her car keys, angry with herself for sounding so self-pitying.

"Honey—"

"Forget it." She began walking to her car.

"If you'd still like to make some lemonade, I wouldn't object."

She looked down at the keys in her palm and wanted to cry. "I'd better go. I've got some things to do."

It was the first time since they'd known each other that

she was the one to walk away. As she looked back up, she saw that she had surprised him.

"You bought some new clothes."

"Liz and I have gone shopping a couple of times. She's making me over."

For some reason this seemed to reignite his anger, and his hazel eyes grew as hard as flints. "There wasn't anything wrong with the way you were."

"It was time, that's all."

As she climbed behind the wheel of the car, he held on to the top of the door so she couldn't close it. "You want to drive over to Barstow with me on Friday? A friend of mine wants to show me some quarter horses he's raising."

"Liz and I are going to the Golden Door for a week."

He looked at her blankly.

"It's a spa."

A muscle ticked in his jaw, and he released his hold on the door. "Well, now. I sure wouldn't want you to miss an intellectual experience like that."

She started the car. Her tires spit gravel as she sped down the drive.

He stood in front of the house and watched until the rooster tail of dust grew too small to see. A spa. What in the goddamn hell had gotten into Liz, taking Honey to someplace like that? She was just a kid. Smaller than a peanut. Not even as old as his daughter.

And the thought of her in bed with some good-looking young stud fill him with rage.

He turned his back to the road and stalked toward the stable. He told himself it was natural to feel protective toward her. For the past three years, he had been the closest thing she'd had to a father, and he didn't want to see her get hurt.

That was the reason he was upset. He cared about her. She was tough and fragile and funny. She had a conscience as big as all outdoors, and she was the most generous person he knew. Look at the way she treated that band of parasites she called a family. She was smart, too. Damn, she was smart. Good-hearted and optimistic, always certain there were at least three pots of gold at the end of every rainbow. But her optimistic nature made her vulnerable. He hadn't forgotten the crush she'd had on that bastard Eric Dillon, which was exactly why he didn't want to see her jumping into bed with the first young stud who caught her eye.

Now if the boy were somebody decent, someone who really cared about her and wasn't just looking to put a celebrity notch on his bedpost, he'd feel different. If she fell in love with somebody decent who would be good to her and not hurt her, he'd—

Smash the sonovabitch's face in.

The craving for a drink hit him hard. He pulled off his hat and wiped the sweat from his forehead with his shirtsleeve. He had just turned forty-three. He had three ex-wives and two kids. Already in his lifetime he'd lost more money than most people ever dreamed of making. Life had thrown him a second chance when he'd stopped drinking, but when it came to women there was an empty place inside him that had been formed when he was a child being moved from one family to another. He couldn't love the same way other men loved. Women wanted intimacy and fidelity from a man, qualities he had proven time and again that he couldn't give.

Disgusted, he slammed his hat back on. She was just like a pesky little termite, gnawing her way bit by bit through his different layers. But he couldn't deny that she made him feel young again. She made him believe that life still held possibilities. And he wanted her. Damn did he want her. But he'd put a bullet right through his brain before he'd let himself hurt that little girl.

"Lilly, sweetheart."

Eric watched Guy Isabella weaving through a rain forest of long silver streamers trailing from the huge crimson and black helium balloons that bobbed at the vaulted ceiling of his Bel Air home. Impeccably dressed in formal wear, he smiled at Lilly and then looked at Eric with distaste. Obviously, Eric's tuxedo didn't make up for his stubbly jaw.

Everything about Lilly seemed to glow at the sight of her

father. She hugged him and kissed his cheek. "Hi, Daddy. Happy birthday."

"Thank you, angel." Although he was speaking to his daughter, his attention was still on Eric.

"Daddy, this is Eric Dillon. Eric, my father."

"Sir." Eric carefully concealed his contempt as he shook Isabella's hand. Blond and boyishly handsome, both Guy Isabella and Ryan O'Neal had spent most of the seventies competing for many of the same roles. But O'Neal was a better actor, and from what Eric had heard, Guy had hated his guts ever since *Love Story*.

Guy Isabella represented everything Eric detested about motion picture actors. He was a pretty face, nothing more. He was also said to have a problem with alcohol, although that might not be anything more than rumor since Eric had also heard that he was a health nut. His worst sin in Eric's eyes was professional laziness. Apparently Isabella didn't think it was important to work at his craft, and now that he was pushing fifty and no longer capable of playing male ingenues, the parts were getting more difficult to come by.

"I saw that spy movie you made," Isabella said to him. "It was a little too gritty for my taste, but you did some fairly good work. I understand you're filming something new now."

Isabella's condescension set his teeth on edge. What right did an aging male bimbo have to pass judgment on his performance? Still, for Lilly's sake, he tempered his reply. "We finish shooting next week. It's gritty, too."

"Too bad."

Eric turned away to study the house. It was built in the style of a Mediterranean villa, but with a heavy Moorish influence that indicated it had been constructed in the twenties. The interior was dark and opulent. He could imagine one of the old silent-screen vamps being at home with the narrow stained-glass windows, arched doorways, and wrought-iron grillwork. The living room had priceless Persian rugs on the floor, custom-made chairs with leopard-skin upholstery, and an antique samovar over the fireplace. A perfect place for a man with a Valentino complex.

Isabella was still regarding Eric's unshaven jaw with disapproval. His cologne smelled heavily of musk, which mingled with the aroma of the whiskey in the heavy crystal tumbler he was carrying.

"I'll tell you what I like, Dillon. Your TV show. My people are trying to put together something like that for me, but you've got to have a special kid."

"Honey's hard to duplicate."

"Damn cute. She gets you right here, you know what I mean. Right in the heart."

"I know what you mean."

Isabella finally turned his attention to Lilly, who was dressed in pale raspberry silk and asymmetrical silver jewelry. "So how's your mother, kitten?"

Lilly filled him in on the latest news from Montevideo, where her stepfather was ambassador, while Eric surveyed the gathering. It was an old Hollywood crowd made up of megastars from the fifties and sixties, former studio heads, agents. Everyone eminently respectable. He wouldn't have been caught dead here if it weren't for Lilly.

Tonight marked their third date, and he hadn't even kissed her. Not because he didn't desire her or because he was bored with her, but because he liked being with her so much. It was a new experience for him to be both physically and mentally attracted to a woman.

He and Lilly had so many things in common. Both of them had been raised in affluence. She knew art and literature, and she understood his passion for acting. She was an irresistible combination of beauty and brains, aloofness and sensuality. Even more important, she had an air of worldliness that allowed him to relax when he was with her instead of worrying that somehow he would hurt her.

"Isn't he wonderful?" she said as her father left to greet a guest.

"He's something, all right."

"Most divorced men would have passed their daughters off onto their ex-wives, but my mother was never very maternal and he was the one who raised me. It's the funniest thing, but in a way you remind me of him."

Eric reached for his cigarettes without comment. Lilly's relationship with her father was her one drawback, but he had to admire her filial loyalty.

"Of course, you're dark and he's blond," she went on. "But both of you belong in the Greek god category." She lifted a champagne glass from the tray of a passing waiter and gave him a mischievous smile. "Don't let this go to that swelled head of yours, but each of you has a certain—I don't know—an aura or something." She dipped the tip of her index finger into her champagne glass and then brought it to her lips, where she sucked it. "Oh, sorry, you can't smoke in here."

He gazed around with irritation and saw that no one else was smoking. He remembered that Isabella was supposed to be a health nut. "Let's go outside then. I need a cigarette."

She began leading him along the limestone paved foyer to the back of the house. "You smoke too much."

"I'm quitting as soon as this movie's over."

"And the check's in the mail." She lifted one of her expressive eyebrows at him. He smiled. She never let him get away with bullshit, another thing he liked about being with her.

He gazed up at the coffered ceiling. "How long has your father lived here?"

"He bought the house right after he and my mother were married. Louis B. Mayer used to own it, or King Vidor. Neither of them remembers which one."

"Sort of a weird place to grow up."

"I guess."

She led him into the kitchen where she nodded absentmindedly at the help before she took him out through a service door. The grounds, lush with mature vegetation, sloped sharply in the back. Water splashed gently in a hexagonal-shaped fountain covered in blue-and-yellow-patterned tiles. He caught the scent of eucalyptus, roses, and chlorine.

"I want to show you something." Lilly was whispering, even though the grounds were deserted. He lit his cigarette. She danced ahead of him down along a curved path that ran roughly parallel to the house, her silver-blond hair flying, her skirt swirling around her long legs. He grew aroused just watching her. She was beautiful, but not fragile. And definitely not an innocent.

Recessed lights hidden in the landscaping softly illuminated the leafy branches of the magnolia and olive trees they passed. As the slope grew steeper and the red-tiled roof of the house slipped out of sight, she turned back and took his arm. They rounded a curve and another house came into view—a tiny replica of Snow White's cottage.

He laughed softly. "I don't believe it. Was this yours?"

"The perfect playhouse for a Hollywood kid. Dad had it built for me when he and Mother got divorced. I guess it was my consolation prize."

The story-book cottage was half-timbered and made of stucco with rustic patches of brick showing through. A small chimney rose from one end of a mock thatched roof. The front held a set of diamond-paned windows framed by wooden shutters.

"The window box used to be filled with geraniums," she said, letting go of his arm and walking up to the cottage. "Daddy and I planted them together every year." She pushed the latch on the wooden double door, and the hinges creaked as it opened. "Most of the original furnishings are gone now, and the place is mainly used for pool storage. You'll have to duck."

Eric took one last drag on his cigarette before he tossed it away. Bending, he entered the cottage. The ceiling was just above his head even though he wasn't standing completely upright.

"Give me your matches."

He passed them over and heard her moving about. A few seconds ticked by and then the interior was filled with flickering amber light as she lit a pair of candles on the mantelpiece of a miniature stone fireplace.

He shook his head in wonder as he looked around. "I don't believe this place."

"Isn't it wonderful?"

The ceiling of the playhouse cottage was beamed and

sloping, high enough for him to stand upright at the center but falling off at the sides. A muted but still colorful mural of elves, fairies, and forest creatures frolicked across the walls. The muralist had painted rustic cracks along with several patches of bricks, as if the plaster had broken away in places. Even the cans of pool chemicals and the neatly stacked pile of lounge cushions didn't spoil the cottage's enchantment.

"It's a little musty, but Dad keeps the place maintained. He knows I'd kill him if he let anything happen to it."

He couldn't tear his eyes away from her. In her pale raspberry gown with her silver-blond hair and exquisite features, she looked as enchanted as the figures in the mural.

She moved a cushion from the top of the stack to the floor. Sinking down on it, she leaned back against the others. "You're too big for the place. The boys I used to bring here were a lot smaller."

He lowered himself onto the cushion next to her, propping up one knee and loosening his tie. "Were there lots of them?"

"Only two. One lived in the next house, and he was boring. All he wanted to do was move the chairs around and make forts."

There was a husky, seductive quality in her voice that intrigued him. He turned her hand over in the lap of her gown and traced a circle in her palm with his fingernail. "And the other?"

"Uhm. That would have been Paulo." She leaned her head back against the cushions, her eyes drifting shut. "His father was our gardener."

"I see."

"He came here whenever he could." She drew her hand to the bodice of her gown and laid the tips of her fingers across her full breast.

His mouth went dry, and he knew he could no longer hold out against her. "What did the two of you do?"

"Use your imagination."

"I think"—he toyed with her fingers—"that you were naughty."

"We played"—she caught her breath as he stroked the center of her palm— "pretend games."

Leaning forward, he brushed his lips over the corner of her mouth. "What kind of games?"

The small, pointed tip of her tongue flicked out to lick the place he had kissed. "Uhmm . . . The usual ones children play."

"Such as?" He slid his finger over her wrist and along her inner arm.

"I was afraid of getting a shot. Paulo told me he could fix me up so I wouldn't have to go to the doctor."

"I like the kid's style."

"I knew what he was doing, of course, but I pretended I didn't." Her breath caught as his hand slipped down along her leg and crept under the hem of her dress. "It was all pretty comic."

"But exciting, too."

"Definitely exciting."

He rubbed her leg through her shimmery stocking, gradually moving higher until his thumb rested in the small cave at the back of her knee. "I like to play games, too."

"Yes, I know."

He stroked her lower thigh and then tensed with excitement as her stockings came to an end and he touched bare skin. He should have known that she wouldn't wear anything as ordinary as panty hose.

"And do you still hate going to the doctor?" he asked.

"It's not my favorite thing." At the slight pressure he was exerting, she eased her legs apart. The insides of her thighs were firm and warm where he stroked them.

"But what if you're sick?"

"I—I'm hardly ever sick."

She gasped as his thumb brushed her through her panties.

"I don't know about that," he said. "You feel warm."

"Do I?" she asked breathlessly.

"You might have a fever. I'd better check." He slipped his finger inside the leg opening. She made a small, moaning sound.

"Just as I thought."

"What?"

"You're hot."

"Yes." She squirmed beneath his intimate touch.

In the candlelight her lips were parted and her face flushed. His own excitement burned more fiercely as he saw how the sweet perversion of this fantasy had aroused her. Women had never been anything more than medicine to him, an over-the-counter drug to be taken at night in hopes that he'd feel better in the morning. He had never cared about his partner's satisfaction, only his own, but now he wanted to watch Lilly shatter beneath his touch, and he knew his own satisfaction wouldn't be complete without hers.

"I'm afraid I'll have to take these off." He met no resistance as he slipped the panties down over her hips. When they were off, he reached up and touched her breast through her dress. She moaned, and her forehead puckered in a frown, as if she were upset about something, but she pushed her breast against his hand, so he didn't stop.

"Your heart rate is fast," he said.

She didn't reply.

He found the zipper at the back of her dress. Sliding it down, he lowered the bodice and then removed her bra.

She lay, half sitting, half reclining in front of him, naked except for her shimmering stockings and the pale raspberry gown bunched at her waist, knees raised, legs open, wanton. He touched her breast and then gently squeezed on her nipple. She made an animal sound deep in her throat, almost a sound of distress, while at the same time she arched against his more intimate caress below, inviting him to touch more deeply.

The mixture of conflicting emotions she was exhibiting bothered him but at the same time aroused him so fiercely he could hardly hold himself back. Her moans grew guttural in her throat, and tears began to leak from beneath her eyelids.

Alarmed, he drew back, only to have her sink her fingers into the muscles of his forearms and pull him closer. He continued his caresses, sweat dampening his shirt. As his body demanded its own release, he held back to watch the disturbing fusion of emotions that played across her face: pleasure and pain, feverish arousal and a disturbing anguish. Her passion dewed his hand, and his breathing echoed harshly in the enchanted interior of the cottage as she splintered beneath his touch.

He moaned and held her through the aftershocks. "Lilly, what's wrong?" He'd never seen a woman react with so much distress to lovemaking. When she didn't answer, he crooned softly to her. "It's all right. Everything's all right."

And then he decided he had imagined her distress because her quick hands began working at the zipper on his trousers. When she had freed him, she grasped the loose ends of his bow tie in her fists and drew his mouth to hers, giving him her tongue. She stroked him until he lost all reason.

He fumbled in the pocket of his trousers for the foil packet he never went anywhere without and drew it to his teeth to rip it open with a shaking hand. She brushed it away. "No. I want to feel you."

Shifting her weight, she lowered herself upon him.

He was too far gone to heed the alarms that clanged in his brain, and only after he had spilled himself inside her did he feel a chill of foreboding. He had been attracted to her because she seemed so strong, but now he wasn't sure.

She began nibbling his ear and then she insisted on running back to the house to steal some food from the kitchen for them. Before long they were laughing together over lobster and petits fours, and his forebodings had evaporated.

The next day they went to a Wynton Marsalis concert together, and after that he continued to see her several times a week. Her beauty fascinated him, and they never ran out of conversation. They argued about art, shared a mutual passion for jazz, and could talk for hours about the theater. It was only when they climbed into bed that something was very wrong. Even as Lilly demanded that he bring her to orgasm, she almost seemed to hate him for doing it. He knew it was his fault. He was a bad lover. He had used women for so long that he had no idea how to be unselfish.

He redoubled his efforts to make certain that she was satisfied, giving her back rubs, kissing every part of her, caressing her until she begged him for release, but her distress continued unabated. He wanted to talk to her about the problem, but he didn't know how, and he realized that he could converse with Lilly on any topic except those intimate ones that mattered. As summer slipped into fall and nothing improved, he knew he had to put an end to it.

While he was making up his mind how to do it, she appeared unexpectedly at his house one night in early October just after he'd gotten back from the studio. He poured two glasses of wine and held one of them out to her. She took a sip. Once again he noticed her fingernails, bitten nearly to the quick.

"Eric, I'm pregnant."

He stared at her as a cold sense of dread crept through him. "Is this a joke?"

"I wish it were," she said bitterly.

He remembered that first night in the playhouse two months earlier when he hadn't used anything, and his gut tightened. Fool. What a goddamned fool.

She stared into the depths of her wineglass. "I've— Tomorrow I have an appointment for an abortion."

As quickly as her words sank in, rage exploded inside him. "No!"

"Eric—"

"No, goddamnit!" The stem of his wineglass cracked in his hand.

She gazed at him miserably, her light gray eyes swimming with tears. "There isn't any other way. I don't want a baby."

"Well, you have one!" He pitched the glass into the corner where it shattered, splattering its contents everywhere. *"We* have one, and there won't be any abortion."

"But—"

He could see that he was scaring her, and he tried to calm his breathing. Setting aside her glass, he grasped her hands. "We'll get married, Lilly. It happens all the time."

"I—I care about you, Eric, but I don't think I'd be a very good wife."

He attempted a shaky laugh. "That's another thing we have in common, then. I don't think I'll be a very good husband, either."

She smiled tremulously. He drew her into his arms and squeezed his eyes shut while he began to make promises to her, promises of roses and sunshine, daffodils and moonbeams, everything he could think of. He didn't mean any of it, but that made no difference. She had to marry him, because no matter what, he wouldn't be responsible for the death of another innocent.

14

INTERIOR. RANCH HOUSE LIVING ROOM—DAY.

Dash and Eleanor stand in the middle of the floor, their expressions combative.

> ELEANOR
> I have no respect for you. You know that, don't you?

> DASH
> I believe I've heard you mention it before.

> ELEANOR
> I admire men of education and refinement. True gentlemen.

> DASH
> Don't forget the necktie part.

> ELEANOR
> What are you talking about?

> DASH
> The last time we had this conversation, you said

you couldn't respect a man who wasn't wearing a suit and tie at the exact moment he died.

ELEANOR

I most certainly did not say that. I simply pointed out that I could never respect a man who doesn't even own a necktie, much less wear one.

DASH

I do so own one.

ELEANOR

It has a hula girl painted on it.

DASH

Only when you look at it straight on. From the side, it's more of a flamingo.

ELEANOR

I rest my case.

DASH

So what you're saying is that we've got a doomed relationship, is that it?

ELEANOR

Absolutely.

DASH

No hope.

ELEANOR

Not a bit.

DASH

Because we're too different.

ELEANOR

Polar opposites.

DASH
(taking a step closer)
So how's come I'm getting ready to kiss you?

ELEANOR

Because you're a crude, unprincipled cowboy.

DASH

Is that so? Then how's come you're going to kiss
me right back.

ELEANOR

Because—Because I'm crazy about you.

They move into each other's arms and exchange a long,
satisfying kiss. The door bangs open and Janie rushes in.

JANIE

I knew it! You're doing it again. Stop it! Stop that!

DASH

(still holding Eleanor in his arms)
I thought you were off polishing your fingernails
for that Bobby character.

JANIE

His name is Robert and you should be ashamed
of yourselves.

DASH

I don't see why.

JANIE

She's just using you. Ever since Blake went off to
join the air force, she's been hanging onto you
like a burr. She's afraid of getting old and
ending up alone. She's afraid—

DASH

(moving away from Eleanor to confront Janie)
That's enough, Jane Marie.

JANIE

The minute your back is turned, she laughs at
you. I've heard her, Pop. She makes fun of you
on the telephone to all her New York City
friends.

                                ELEANOR
                               (together)
Janie, that's not true.

                                 DASH
                               (together)
You go back to the house.

Janie regards them mutinously and then runs from the
house.
Dash and Eleanor stare at the door.

                                ELEANOR
                               (quietly)
And there goes the biggest reason of all why
this relationship doesn't stand a chance.

When the scene ended, Honey walked behind the cameras
to retrieve her script, tugging at the rubber band that held
back her ponytail and rubbing her scalp with her fingers. She
had refused to let them cut her hair, and the producers had
finally agreed to let Janie wear a ponytail, but they made
Evelyn scrape her hair back so tightly that Honey sometimes
got a headache. Even so, it was worth it. In the five months
that had passed since Liz's beach party, her hair had grown
long enough that it brushed the tops of her shoulders.

As she fluffed it with her fingertips, she watched Liz and
Dash, who were still on the set talking quietly with each
other. Jealousy gnawed at her. They were the same age, and
they had once been lovers. What if the two people to whom
she was the closest were slipping back into their old relationship?

One of the assistants broke up their tête-à-tête by telling
Dash he had a phone call. Liz walked over to her, and
Honey noticed that her lipstick was smeared slightly at one
corner. She looked away.

"Have you seen that boutique catalogue I put in your
dressing room this morning?" Liz asked as she picked up a
bottle of mineral water. "They have the most marvelous
belts."

Liz was the best female friend she had, and Honey determinedly repressed her jealousy. "I wish you'd stop tempting me. You're turning me into a shopoholic."

"Nonsense. You're just making up for lost time." Liz took a drink, holding the neck of the bottle so gracefully she might have been sipping from Baccarat.

"Clothes are starting to be an obsession," Honey sighed. "For months I've been reading every fashion magazine I can get my hands on. Last night I fell asleep dreaming about that new coral silk I bought." She grinned ruefully. "I read *Ms.* magazine, and I know that femininity is a trap, but I can't seem to help myself."

"You're just trying to find some balance."

"Balance! This is the most unbalanced thing I've ever done. For the first time in my life, I can't respect myself."

"Honey, regardless of the body parts you were born with, you grew up more as a boy than a girl. Now you're simply trying to discover yourself as a woman. Sooner or later you'll be able to bring all the different parts of yourself together. You're just not ready yet. And until you are . . ." She lifted the mineral water bottle in a toast. "Shop till you drop." With a grin, she set off for her dressing room.

Honey picked up her script and stuffed it in a tote bag silk-screened with splashy red poppies. She knew her obsession with her physical appearance was because of Dash, but her attempts to make him look at her as a woman were failing dismally. If anything, he had become more paternal, huffing and puffing and frowning at everything she did. No matter how hard she tried, she couldn't seem to please him. And playing Janie Jones five days a week didn't help. The role that had once fit so comfortably had begun to chafe.

She turned to leave the soundstage just as a pair of fingers jabbed her ribs from behind. "Damn it, Todd!"

"Hey, gorgeous. You want to run some lines with me?"

Honey glared at Todd Myers, the sixteen-year-old actor who was playing Janie's new boyfriend, Robert. He had been chosen for his well-scrubbed, all-American looks— brown eyes and hair, round cheeks, small build so he didn't overpower her. Beneath all that apple pie, however, he was an egotistical brat. Still, in light of her own past behavior problems, she hadn't quite had the heart to rip into him.

"I wasn't planning on eating lunch today. I've got a psych paper due, and I'm going to my dressing room to finish it."

"I don't see why anybody who's making as much money as you should be wasting your time with college."

"Just a correspondence course. I've been taking them on and off ever since I finished high school. I like to learn things. It wouldn't hurt you to spend a little more time with the books."

"You sound like my old lady," he said with disgust.

"You should listen to her."

"Yeah, sure." He stuck out his arms and wiggled his hips. "So, are you ready for our big love scene this afternoon?"

"It's not a love scene. It's just a kiss. And I swear to God, Todd, if you try to French me again—" She let her threat hang in the air.

"I won't French you if you promise to go out with me this weekend. One of my friends is having a Christmas party. There'll be plenty of grass and maybe even some coke. Have you ever had a coco-puff? You take a cigarette and sprinkle it with—"

"I don't do drugs, and I'm not going out with you."

"You're still stuck on that asshole Eric Dillon, aren't you? I heard all about the way you used to hang around him. I'll bet you cry yourself to sleep every night now that he's married and he knocked up his old lady."

She gave him a silky smile. "Has anybody ever told you that you're a wonderful argument for mercy killing?"

His face grew sulky. "You should be nice to me, Honey. Otherwise I might be tempted to tell everybody the birthday you're going to celebrate tomorrow is your eighteenth instead of your seventeenth like everybody thinks."

"It's my twentieth, Todd."

"Yeah, right," he scoffed.

She gave up. Ross's lie had become so commonly accepted that few people believed the truth, not even when she flashed her driver's license. For the past six months, her face had been plastered on the covers of half the teen magazines in the country celebrating the fact that Janie had turned fifteen. The event was receiving nearly as much press as Michael Jackson's new *Thriller* album.

Leaving Todd behind, she headed back to her dressing room to work on her psych paper. Two of the women writers broke up a whispered conversation as she came into view and then gave her mischievous grins. At one time she would have suspected that they were plotting against her, but now she knew it was more likely that they were part of the birthday surprise the cast and crew were planning for her. She chatted with them for a few minutes, and as she left, she remembered those early days when the writers had seemed like gods to her. That had ended when she and Dash had become friends.

Unlike her family, the cast and crew wouldn't forget her birthday. Last year they had surprised her with a leather-bound set of all the scripts of *The Dash Coogan Show*. She had been deeply touched, but she couldn't help wishing her family would remember the occasion just once. Even if they only gave her a card, she would appreciate the gesture.

Dash came stalking around the corner and she saw that he looked upset.

"What's wrong?"

"Wanda just called me. She always manages to get me going."

She had imagined that when people got divorced they would get out of each other's lives, but Dash always seemed to be having conversations with his first ex-wife. Of course, they had children together, and she supposed that made a difference, but since their son was twenty-four and their daughter twenty-two, she couldn't imagine what they had left to talk about. In general, she tried not to think about his kids, especially since both of them were older than she was.

"Didn't you tell me that Wanda had remarried?"

"A long time ago. A man named Edward Ridgeway. Not Ed, mind you. Edward."

"Why does she bother you so much?"

"Revenge, I guess. She still doesn't feel like she's settled old scores. She called to tell me that Josh is getting married the day after Christmas."

"That's only three weeks away."

"Nice of her to let me know my son's getting married, isn't it? Now I have to go to Tulsa for the wedding." He looked grim.

"You don't want him to get married?"

"He's twenty-four. I guess that's up to him, and anything that'll cut him loose from Wanda's apron strings is probably a good thing. I just hate the idea of letting her lead me around by the nose for two days. She was a sweet little thing when I married her, but over the years she's turned into a barracuda. Not that I should blame her. All that tomcattin' of mine hurt her pretty bad."

He began to walk away, and then slowly turned back. She could see that he had something on his mind, and she regarded him quizzically. He shoved his hand in his pocket.

"Honey, you wouldn't want to— Never mind. Bad idea."

"What?"

"Nothing, I was just—" He shifted his weight. "I was thinking about asking if you wanted to go to Tulsa with me for the wedding. Sort of act like a buffer. But I don't expect you'd want to leave your family so close to Christmas."

She thought of Chantal, who was growing plump and lazy on junk food and game shows right along with her idiotic stepfather, Buck. And of Gordon, who still hadn't picked up a paintbrush. She thought of Sophie, who spent more time in bed than out of it and refused to follow any of the doctor's orders. The idea of getting away from all that and being with Dash would be the best Christmas present she could have.

"I'd love to go with you, Dash. It'd do me good to get away for a while."

That evening she pulled down the sloping drive into the garage of their house in Pasadena. It was dark as she let herself in through the mudroom off the garage. She flicked the light switch, but the bulb seemed to be burned out, and she fumbled with the door leading into the kitchen. When she opened it, she was startled to see the glow of candlelight.

"Happy birthday!"

"Happy birthday, Honey!"

Flabbergasted, she saw all of her family standing in a half circle around the kitchen table. Sophie had dragged herself out of bed, Buck had thrown a sports shirt on over his undershirt, Chantal had poured the extra twenty pounds she'd gained into a pair of crimson slacks, and, reflected in the lenses of Gordon's new wire-rimmed spectacles, were the flames of twenty pastel candles sitting on top of a birthday cake.

They hadn't forgotten. They had finally remembered her birthday. Tears stung her eyes and she felt years of stored resentment melting inside her.

"Oh, my . . . It's—" Her words grew choked. "It's beautiful."

All of them laughed and even Sophie smiled, because the cake wasn't beautiful at all. Three layers tall, it was lopsided and unevenly coated with the ugliest shade of blue frosting Honey had ever seen. But the fact that they had done this for her, baked the cake themselves, made it the most precious gift she had ever received.

"I can't—I can't believe you did this." She struggled not to cry.

"Well, of course we did it," Chantal said. "It's your birthday, isn't it?"

They were off by one day, but that was meaningless. She was filled with love, joy, and an aching sense of gratitude.

Gordon gestured toward the cake. "I baked it, Honey. Me, myself, and I."

"I helped," Chantal threw in.

"We all helped," Buck said, scratching his belly like a beardless Santa Claus. "Except for Sophie."

"I picked out the icing color," Sophie said, looking hurt.

Their faces glimmered before her, soft, beautiful, and beloved in the golden light of the flickering candles. She forgave them all their foibles and knew that she was right to have stuck by them. They were her family. She was part of them and they were part of her, and every one of them was precious.

Gordon grinned like a schoolboy with a secret. Sophie's fat cheeks dented in a distracted smile, and Chantal's blue eyes glowed in the candlelight. Embarrassed by the depth of her emotions, Honey dabbed self-consciously at her cheeks.

"All of you— I—" She tried to tell them what was in her heart, but the feelings ran too strong and her throat constricted.

"Come on, Honey. Cut the cake!"

"Cut it, Honey. We're all hungry."

"It sure is going to taste good."

She laughed as Buck thrust a large knife into her hand and pushed her toward the cake. "Blow out the candles."

"Happy birthday to you, happy birthday to you . . ."

She blew out the candles, laughing through her tears. Once again, she tried to find the words that would express what this meant to her.

"I'm so happy . . . I—"

"Cut straight down through the middle," Gordon said, directing her hand. "I don't want you to ruin my artwork."

A tear dripped off her chin as she pointed the knife into the center. "This is wonderful. I'm so—"

The cake exploded.

Screams of laughter erupted as chunks of chocolate flew everywhere. Cake shot up into Honey's face, clots of blue icing stuck to her skin and clung to her clothes. Bits and pieces splattered against the wall and dropped to the floor.

They had all drawn back from the table in a single, unified motion just as she had cut into the center, and they were untouched. Only she had been hit.

Buck clutched his stomach. Their laughter grew louder. Even Sophie had joined in.

"Did you see her face?"

"We fooled you," Chantal cried. "It was all Gordon's idea. Gordon, you're so smart!"

"I told you it would work!" Gordon hooted. "I told you! Look at her hair!"

Chantal clapped her hands as she described her husband's cleverness. "Gordon cut a hole in the middle of the cake, and then he stuffed it with this big balloon blown up real full of air. We broke three of them trying to get it just right. Then we iced the whole thing so you couldn't tell, and when your knife poked through the balloon—"

Honey's chest heaved and she stumbled backward, staring at them. They were gathered around the ruined feast like a pack of jackals who had gorged on a banquet of malice. Their spitefulness choked her. She would leave them, pack her suitcase and never see them again.

"Uh-oh, she's mad," Gordon taunted. "She's going to be a bad sport, just like always."

"You're not going to be a bad sport, are you, Honey?" Chantal stuck out her lip. "We've had so much fun. You're not going to spoil it."

"Darn," Buck said. "We should of knowed."

"No," she said, her voice a tight, painful whisper. "I'm not going to be a bad sport. It—it was a great joke. Really. I'd—I'd better get cleaned up."

Turning her back on them, she fled through the hallway into the back wing of the house, clots of cake and icing dropping off her pretty silk blouse and linen slacks. The pain inside her made it hard to breath. She was going to move away. She would leave them and never come back. She would—

A choking sound slipped from her. And then what? Who would take their places? Not Dash. She had been building dream castles where he was concerned. He could have any woman he wanted, so why would he take her? This family was all she had.

The clattering began in her brain. The lonely clickety-clickety clattering of a ghost roller-coaster car creaking up a wooden incline. She squeezed her eyes shut trying to block out a painful, persistent voice that told her all of her success, all of her money, all the pretty clothes in the world wouldn't disguise the fundamental unlovableness that lived at her core.

Black Thunder's coaster car creaked up the lift hill. But no matter how hard she tried to imagine it, she couldn't make it shoot over the top.

15

Honey and Dash flew into Tulsa the day after Christmas for his son's wedding. They barely spoke to each other on the flight, and she suspected he regretted inviting her. She should have told him she couldn't come, but she had followed him just as she always did, ready to receive whatever crumbs of affection he tossed in her direction.

As she got off the plane, she told herself that anything was better than spending the rest of the holiday with her family. Even the birthday party the cast and crew had given her three weeks ago hadn't dulled the memory of what had happened. Since then, she had spent most of her time at home sequestered in her bedroom.

The Tulsa airport was crowded with holiday travelers. Inevitably, many of them recognized Dash, who was unmistakable with his tall stature, his Stetson, and an aged shearling jacket. She walked anonymously at his side. With her eyes shielded by large sunglasses and hair tumbling in sexy disarray, no one in the crowd recognized her as the tomboy Janie Jones.

She had chosen her clothes defiantly, not only because they were so unlike Janie's outfits but because she knew how much he would dislike them. A soft, golden-brown oversized sweater slipped off one shoulder. She wore it with a pair of slim-cut black leather pants, a belt of gold links, matching gold hoop earrings, and little black flats with a bronze diamond appliquéd over the vamp. A fur jacket was draped over her arm, completing an ensemble that looked both sexy and expensive.

Dash, predictably, had frowned when he met her at LAX. "I don't see why you had to wear something like that. Those pants are too damn tight."

"Sorry, Daddy," she had mocked him.

"I'm not your father!"

"Then stop acting like one."

He had given her an angry glare and looked away.

Now the holiday travelers gathered around him. "We love your show, Mr. Coogan."

"Could I have your autograph for my daughter? She wants to be an actress someday. Of course she's only eight, but—"

"We sure like that Janie. Is she a dickens in real life, too?"

Dash glanced over his shoulder at Honey, who had moved off to the side and was attracting her own share of attention from several of the men, although not because of her celebrity. "She's a dickens, all right."

Later, as they got into the rental car, he began to scold her again. "I don't know why you couldn't have worn something respectable. Everybody was looking at you like you were—I don't know."

"Like I was your Playmate of the Month?"

He threw the Lincoln into gear and refused to respond.

The wedding was scheduled for seven that evening. They checked in at the same hotel where the reception was being held. Honey discovered that Dash had booked them separate rooms on different floors, as if closer accommodations would contaminate him. After getting rid of their luggage, they headed for Wanda Ridgeway's house.

Thoroughbred Acres was one of Tulsa's newer upscale housing developments. As they drove through the entrance pillars, Honey noticed that all the streets were named after famous racehorses. The Ridgeway house, a large colonial, sat on Seattle Slew Way. Although it was only noon, the Christmas lights surrounding the porch were lit, and milk cans decorated with sprigs of greenery sat in a cluster beside the front door. As Honey followed Dash up the walk, she recalled what she knew about him and his first wife.

He and Wanda had met when the rodeo Dash was riding in had come to the small Oklahoma town where she lived. By the time he had left, she was pregnant, a fact he didn't find out about until three months later when she tracked him down in Tulsa. He was nineteen, she eighteen.

According to Dash, Wanda was the sort of woman who wanted to stay in one place all her life and organize charitable fund-raisers. From the beginning she had hated his nomadic life-style, and the marriage was over even before their second child was born. She had never forgiven Dash, not for his wandering eye or for throwing her life off track.

Her enmity was carefully concealed, however, as she admitted Dash and Honey into the two-story foyer and greeted her ex-husband with a hug. "Randy, darlin', I'm so glad to see you."

She was plump and pretty, a bit overdressed in ruffled silk. Her hair was arranged in the sprayed blond helmet so comfortable on the heads of well-to-do women in the Southwest, and her fingers flashed with diamonds. The Ridgeway Christmas tree stood directly behind her, decorated entirely with wooden hearts, burlap bows, and miniature flour sacks.

"Josh said you wouldn't show up, and you know how Meredith is with all that prayin', but I told him his daddy wouldn't miss his wedding, not for anything. And his bride, Cynthia, is just the sweetest thing. Josh! Meredith! Your daddy's here. Yoo-hoo! Oh, damn, Meredith's still at her Bible study and Josh had to make a last-minute trip to the travel agent."

She turned to Honey. "Now who's this? You didn't get married again, did you?"

But unlike the fans at the airport, Wanda had the eyes of a hawk, and even before Honey had slipped off her sunglasses, she recognized her ex-husband's traveling companion. Her lips thinned ever so slightly. "Well, if it isn't your sweet little costar. What a surprise. And aren't you the dearest little thang. Edward, you'll never guess who's here? Ed-*ward!*"

A middle-aged man with thinning hair, gentle eyes, and a slight paunch appeared in the foyer from the back of the house. "Well, hello there, Dash. I had the fan on in the bathroom and didn't hear you come in."

"Edward, look who Randy brought with him. Little Honey Jane Moon, one of your favorite TV people next to J.

R. Ewing and *Three's Company*. Isn't she just cute as a baby's *be*-hind?"

"Hello, Miss Moon, and welcome. Well, now, this is an honor. Yes it is. My, you sure do look grown-up in real life." His glance was admiring but not lecherous, and Honey decided she liked Edward, despite the fact that his red bow tie was embedded with blinking green lights.

After their coats and Dash's Stetson had been disposed of in a closet lined with peg hooks and organizer shelves, Wanda led them into a cavernous family room complete with every variety of painted wooden goose, straw wreath, and wicker basket. The room smelled of clove-scented potpourri bubbling away in ceramic pots printed with fat red hearts.

Wanda pointed toward a bar at one end decorated with pewter tankards and golf prints. "Get Randy a drink, Edward. And there's some soda pop in the refrig for Honey."

"If you don't mind, I'd rather have wine," Honey said, deciding she'd better assert herself before Wanda bulldozed her six feet under.

Dash frowned at her. "A Seven-Up'd be fine for me." He sank down onto a couch strewn with ruffled red-checked gingham pillows. Honey took the seat next to him and contemplated the character of a woman who would offer liquor to a recovered alcoholic.

The telephone rang. Wanda bustled off to answer it, and Edward was making enough noise with an ice-cube tray for Honey to whisper to Dash without being overheard.

"I don't know how you ever had the nerve to say that I talk more than any of your ex-wives. Wanda could set a land-speed record."

For the first time that day, he smiled at her. "Wanda settles down after a while. You never do."

Wanda had barely returned to the room before a young woman appeared in the doorway. She was thin and, at first glance, rather plain, with auburn hair and a wan complexion. Closer inspection, however, revealed fine, regular features that would have been attractive if they had been enhanced with a few basic cosmetics. When she saw Dash sitting on the couch, her pale lips drew up in a smile and she became almost pretty.

"Daddy?"

Dash had jumped up the moment he saw her, and he met her in the center of the room, where she disappeared into his arms like a rabbit diving into a hole. "Hi, there, pumpkin. How's my girl?"

As Honey watched them together, the ache of familiar pain spread through her. Despite separations and divorces, these people were still a family, and they had bonds that nothing could ever break.

"Praise the Lord," she said softly. "I knew He would bring you here today."

"A seven-forty-seven brought me here, Merry."

"No, Daddy. Our Lord did." An expression of intense certainty settled over her, and Honey watched curiously to see how Dash would respond.

He chose to retreat. "Meredith, I want you to meet somebody special. This is Honey Jane Moon, my costar on the show."

Meredith turned. As she spotted Honey, she looked as if her father had just kicked in her rabbit's hutch. Her pale lips narrowed until they almost disappeared, and her gray eyes grew opaque with hostility. Honey felt fried, as if Meredith had hit her with a lethal dose of electrical current.

"Miss Moon. The Lord be with you."

"Thank you," Honey replied. "You, too."

Wanda tossed down a Jack Daniels in one gulp. "No more Jesus stuff, Meredith. You could take the fun out of an orgy."

"Mother!"

Dash chuckled. Wanda looked over at him and smiled. For a few seconds the hostilities fell away and Honey had a brief glimpse of what it must have been like for them when they were young.

She was glad to see the moment fade as Wanda began outlining the afternoon's schedule. Relatives would be arriving any minute, she told them. The caterers had set up a buffet table in the dining room and she hoped no one was allergic to shellfish. Everybody needed to be at the church by six-thirty sharp. The dinner-reception at the hotel was dressy and she hoped dear little Honey had brought something special to wear.

Dear little Honey excused herself to use the powder room. A conch shell full of pastel soap conch shells sat on the basin along with another bubbling container of potpourri. The room smelled like pumpkin pie served with lilacs. When she emerged, Wanda had gone to the dining room to badger the caterer and the groom had returned.

Although Meredith Coogan bore little resemblance to her father, her twenty-four-year old brother Josh looked like a blurred and softened version of Dash, one in which all of the older man's angular lines and hard planes had been tamed and weakened. Josh acknowledged the introduction to Honey and was making a polite inquiry about their trip when Wanda returned to the room and interrupted.

"Did Josh tell you about his new job with Fagan Can?"

"No, I don't believe he did," Dash replied.

"He's going to be a supervisor in their accounting department. Tell your father all about it, Josh. Tell him what an important man you're going to be."

"I don't think I'll be all that important, sir. But it's steady work and Fagan is a well-established firm."

Wanda gestured toward him with a glass of bourbon. "Tell your father what a nice office they're giving you."

"It's very nice, sir."

"On the *corner* of the third floor," Wanda reported.

"The corner?" Dash tried to look suitably impressed. "Well, now."

"Two windows." She held up her fingers in case Dash couldn't count.

"Two. Isn't that something."

The doorbell rang, and Wanda once again excused herself. Dash and Josh regarded each other uncomfortably, each at a loss for anything more to say.

Honey stepped in to ease the tension. "Too bad you didn't have Josh working for you in your wild days, Dash. Maybe he would have kept the scum suckers away."

Dash smiled.

Josh looked puzzled. "Scum suckers?"

"She's referring to my well-known problems with the IRS," Dash offered.

Josh's forehead crumpled in an earnest furrow. "You shouldn't joke about the IRS, sir. Not with everything you've been through. Tax problems aren't a laughing matter."

Dash glanced longingly toward the bar.

Wanda and Edward's relatives began to arrive until the house was filled with a dozen more people. Honey's head had started to ache, and she tried to find sanctuary next to a silk ficus tree potted in a milk bucket. A brief lull fell over the room only to be broken by Meredith's small, sincere voice.

"I'm holding a prayer meeting in the living room at six o'clock. I'd like everyone to attend."

Wanda threw up her hands. "Don't be ridiculous, Meredith. I have a million things to do, and I certainly can't waste time praying."

One of the aunts giggled nervously. "I'm sorry, Meredith, but it's going to take me forever to do my hair."

Others chipped in with their excuses, obviously having already experienced one of Meredith's prayer sessions.

Dash took a few steps toward the door. "Honey and I have to go to the hotel to change, so it'll be easier if we just meet you all at the church."

Meredith looked crestfallen, and perhaps because Honey had been feeling so miserable herself, she experienced a moment's sympathy.

"The hotel's not that far away, Dash. We can stop here first."

Dash gave her his steeliest glare.

Meredith gazed at Honey, resentment oozing from every pore. "That's a wonderful idea," she said stiffly.

Dash, however, didn't think it was a wonderful idea at all, and as they drove to the hotel he told Honey he had no intention of going to Meredith's prayer meeting. "I love my daughter, but she's crazy when it comes to religion."

"Then I'll go by myself," she retorted stubbornly.

"Don't say I didn't warn you."

Honey dressed for the wedding in the gown that she had once considered wearing to the ranch, a delicately beaded silvery-blue sheath the exact color of her eyes. She fluffed her hair and clipped crystal clusters to her ears, but even though the mirror told her that she looked almost beautiful, she wasn't reassured. When Dash saw her, he would find something to criticize. The neck would be too low, the skirt too tight, her jewelry too flashy.

Dash had made arrangements to hitch a ride to the church with one of Josh's ushers, so she returned to the house by herself, hoping she wouldn't regret the impulse that had led her to accept Meredith's invitation. Meredith's face fell when she realized that Honey had come alone.

"Sorry," Honey said. "I guess your father isn't much for prayer meetings."

Honey could almost see Meredith's internal struggle as she tried to reconcile her obvious dislike of Honey with her need to evangelize. She wasn't too surprised when evangelism won.

Meredith led her into a living room that looked as it had just come out of plastic wrappers and gestured toward the velour sofa. As they took seats at opposite ends, Honey experienced an almost irresistible urge to delve into her handbag for lipstick and mascara. Meredith's lack of cosmetics combined with her dowdy polyester print dress made her much homelier than she needed to be. Honey began to understand what Liz Castleberry had gone through with her.

Meredith spoke stiffly. "Are you saved, Miss Moon?"

Honey had always rather enjoyed theological discussions and she gave the question serious consideration. "That's not an easy question to answer. And please call me Honey."

"Have you given yourself to the Lord?"

She remembered that long-ago spring when she had prayed to Walt Disney. "I suppose it depends. I consider myself a spiritual person, Meredith, but my theology isn't all that orthodox. I guess I'm a searcher."

"Doubts come from the devil," Meredith said harshly. "If you live in faith, there's no need to question."

"I have to question. It's my nature."

"Then you'll go to hell."

"I don't want to offend you, Meredith, but I don't think anyone has the right to pass judgment on somebody else's salvation."

But Meredith refused to back down, and Honey gave up all hope of a stimulating discussion. For the next half hour, Meredith quoted scripture and prayed over her. Honey's headache returned, but after a while, everything about Meredith softened. She prayed fervently, her face infused with joy, a young woman blissed out on Jesus.

"Smile, Randy. Everybody's watching us, dammit."

"They want to see if I'm gonna body-slam you to the dance floor."

The cloying scent of Wanda's hair spray was making Dash's stomach go crazy. He sidestepped to avoid another couple and told himself he didn't need a drink.

Wanda winced. "You stepped on my goddamn foot. Watch yourself, will you? God, you're a terrible dancer."

"You're the one who wanted to put on a show. You had to let all your friends see how well you've managed your ex-husband. Got him dancing with you, eating right out of your hand like a tame little puppy dog."

The stiff social smile never left her face. "I hate it when you're like this. At your own son's wedding. You are so mean, Randy Coogan. You've always been a mean, cold-hearted, lying, cheating bastard."

"You're never going to let it go, are you? We've been divorced for nearly twenty years, but you still want my last drop of blood."

"That's the only thing besides tits all your ex-wives have in common."

Honey swept past with Josh's best man, and the wedding photographer snapped her picture. Dash figured it would show up in one of the tabloids sooner or later. Several times during the fall photographers had caught her when she looked a lot older than seventeen. Instead of questioning her age, they ran the photos with captions like "Child star growing up too fast" or "Honey Jane Moon out past her bedtime."

Dash's jaw tightened. For somebody who didn't know how to dance, Honey had been doing a good job of it for almost four hours. And that wasn't all she was doing. More than a few times, he'd seen her reaching for a champagne glass.

All evening there had been something wild about her that he didn't like—the way she tossed her head, the throaty laughter that seemed to be coming from a woman instead of a kid. He tried to tell himself that he was just imagining the way all the men were looking at her. After all, she wasn't the most beautiful woman there, not even in that sparkly blue dress that fit too damn tight over her butt. She was cute, no doubt about it, but she was too little and baby-faced to be beautiful. He liked women who looked like women. Hell, there were lots of women who were prettier than Honey.

Still, he couldn't deny that there was something about her that might attract a certain type of man. The type who might like baby-faced little girls more than twenty years too young for them.

A voice that hadn't bothered him since the night of Liz's party when he'd caught Honey kissing that boy began to whisper to him. *A drink will make you forget about her. You don't need her when you can have me.* It was the siren's voice, the deceiving voice all drunks carry around inside them. *I can make you feel better. I can take away the pain.*

Wanda's words jabbed at him like her mascara-spiked eyelashes. "I don't know how you could bring her here and humiliate your own flesh and blood. Everybody's acting like Honey's your real daughter. Poor Meredith's been on the verge of tears all night."

Wanda called out a cheery greeting to one of the guests and then lowered her voice to a vindictive hiss. "I suppose I should be grateful that the people here don't know you as well as I do. I can see what's going on in your mind, and it makes me sick. How can you look at yourself in the mirror? She's younger than your own daughter."

He caught the enticing scent of the bourbon she had been drinking cutting through her hair spray, and his mouth went dry. "There's nothing going on in my mind—not like you mean—so just you get your own mind out of the gutter."

Her hand clamped his, trying to hurt. "Don't bullshit me, Randy. You might be able to fool everybody else here, but you can't fool me. I've seen the way you look at her when you think nobody's watching. And I'll tell you this, mister. It curdles my stomach. They're all cooing about how cute she is and how sweet it is that you act like father and daughter in real life. But that's not the way it is between you two at all."

"Now that's where you're wrong," he sneered. "It's just like that between us. Exactly. I've practically been raising that girl."

"Bullshit," she hissed through her frozen smile. "You make my skin crawl."

He'd had all he could take. He spotted Edward approaching with the bride in his arms and stepped in front of them. "The night's almost over, Edward, and I haven't had a chance to dance with my new daughter-in-law."

Wanda glared at him, but there were too many people around for her to dig in. The women changed places. Josh's new wife, Cynthia, was a pretty, vivacious blonde with blue eyes and big teeth. As he drew her close, he caught the scent of a new brand of hair spray.

"Did Josh tell you about his job, Father Coogan?" she asked as they took their first steps.

He winced at her form of address. "Why, yes. He did mention it." The netting on her headpiece poked dangerously near his eye, and he drew back his head. He felt as if he had been at the mercy of women with sharp points and razor edges all night. Honey whipped by in a soft cloud of champagne bubbles, laughing and dancing for all she was worth.

Forget about her, the siren whispered. *Let me soothe you. I'm smooth and soft, and I go down easy.*

". . . Fagan Can is an important company, but you know

Josh. Sometimes he needs a little push, so I told him when he was interviewing, I said, 'Now, Josh, you go in there and you look those men right in the eye and let them know you mean business.'" She winked. "The company's giving him a corner office."

"So I understand."

"An office with"—she lowered her voice to a stage whisper—*"two* windows."

The dance was endless. She chattered on about corner offices, china patterns, and tennis lessons. The ballad finally drew to a close, and she bustled off to claim her new husband. Josh sprang to her side, gazing at her earnestly to make certain he hadn't committed some unknown offense.

Congratulations, son, Dash thought sadly. *You managed to marry your mother, after all.*

He had to have a drink.

One of Cynthia's bridesmaids passed by and he grabbed her. She giggled at the honor of dancing with the legendary Dash Coogan, but he barely noticed because the siren's voice had grown more insistent, and he could feel all his years of sobriety slipping away.

Come to me, lover. I'm all the woman you need. I'll purr and I'll coo and I'll make you forget about Honey.

Honey swept by and shot him a hostile glare. Raucous, drunken laughter swirled around him, and the clatter of ice cubes was amplified in his head until it formed a crazed percussion to the music.

He hated to dance, but he moved from one bridesmaid to the next, afraid that if he stopped, the siren would claim him. The evening groaned on, and the bride and groom left. Before long, the guests began to depart. The seductive smell of liquor filled his lungs—wine, scotch, and whiskey over-powering the scents of food and flowers.

Just have one, the siren whispered. *One won't hurt.*

As the band finished its final set, the voice of the siren had grown so loud he wanted to clamp his hands over his ears. If he left the dance floor, he knew he would be lost.

"We haven't had a chance to talk, Daddy. Let's go talk."

He jumped as Meredith appeared from nowhere. His tongue felt cumbersome, and he was afraid she would notice he was sweating.

"We—we haven't danced, Merry. The evening's almost over and I haven't danced with my best girl."

She looked at him strangely. "The band's packing up. Besides, I told you earlier, Daddy. I don't believe in dancing."

"I forgot."

He had no choice but to follow her to one of the empty tables near the dance floor. Abandoned wineglasses and tumblers with amber residues floating in their bottoms sat on the linen tablecloths. They multiplied in front of his eyes until there seemed to be a battalion of them spread before him, like enemy soldiers on the march.

She pulled her skirt down over her knees as she took the seat next to him. "Stay at the house tonight, Daddy. You can have my room. Please. I hardly ever get to see you."

His fingertips brushed against a glass with an inch of precious watered-down liquor in the bottom. "I—I don't think that's a good idea. Your mama and I don't do too well when we're cooped up together."

"I'll keep her away from you. I promise."

"Not this time."

Pick me up, lover. Just one little sip and you'll forget all about her.

Her voice hardened. "It's Honey, isn't it? You've got plenty of time to spend with her, but not with me. You think she's perfect—a chip right off the old block. She talks like you. She even drinks like you. It's too bad she's not your daughter instead of me."

The glass burned his fingers. "Don't be childish. This doesn't have anything to do with Honey."

"Then spend some time with me tomorrow morning."

The world was reduced to the shimmering liquid in the glass before him and the agonizing need that pounded in his skull. "I'd love to spend time with you, Merry. I just don't want to do it praying."

Her voice broke. "You have to accept the Lord, Daddy, if you're going to have life eternal. I pray for you all the time. I tremble for you, Daddy. I don't want you to end up in hell."

"Hell's relative," he said harshly.

Gotcha!

His fingers clamped around the glass. It fit into his palm like a million old memories. Sweat broke out on his forehead as the siren gobbled him up. He couldn't stop himself, and he raised his head, ready to lift the tumbler to his lips, but before it got there, he spotted Honey on the other side of the nearly deserted room.

She was standing by the windows with a young stud smeared all over her like baby oil. His beautiful little Honey with the sassy mouth and big heart wasn't doing one thing to get away from him, just smearing herself closer and rubbing against him.

Meredith began to pray.

He shot up from the chair, knocking over the glass.

"Daddy!"

He barely heard her as he stalked across the room. The walls spun around him. His shirt clung to his chest beneath his jacket.

Come back! the siren wailed. *Don't go to her! I'm the one who'll never leave you! Only me!*

When he reached Honey's side, he didn't ask permission or beg anyone's pardon. With one hard yank, he pulled her away from the slimy bastard who was trying to dry-hump her right there in front of everybody and hauled her toward the door.

She made a small gasp, but he didn't give a shit if he hurt her. He didn't give a shit about anything except getting Honey away and putting an end to the jealousy that was eating him up.

"Dash, what's—"

"Shut up. You're acting like a goddamn whore."

She looked stunned, and then her eyes narrowed. "You bastard."

He wanted to whip the back of his hand right across her snotty little mouth. The silver chain on her evening purse had slipped from her shoulder and the purse bumped against the side of his leg, but he ignored it. Wanda was trying to get his attention, and several of the departing guests spoke to him. He stalked past them without replying.

He got her out into the hallway and around the corner, then dragged her down a carpeted ramp while the delicate beading on her little slip of a dress rustled in protest. Just as they reached a back set of elevators, he saw that she held an open bottle of champagne in one hand, and the siren gave a throaty, triumphant laugh.

Gotcha again!

His heart slammed against his ribs as he thrust her into the elevators. The doors slid shut; he stabbed the button.

And then he closed his hand into a fist.

16

Honey stared at Dash.

The elevator soared upward, and she clutched the bottle to her chest. She'd had too much to drink, but she wasn't so drunk that she didn't realize Dash had turned dangerous. His face was pale and stony, his bearing rigid. And the hand he held at his side was clenched tight.

"I should never have brought you here." He spit out the words, each one poisoned.

The alcohol in her blood made her reckless. "Obviously not, since you've ignored me all night."

The doors opened. She fled past him out into the hallway, the champagne bottle dangling from her fingertips, but she didn't move quickly enough to get away from him.

He reached out and snatched the purse from her shoulder. "You're drunk."

She wasn't drunk, but she wasn't entirely sober, either. "What do you care?"

His green eyes were hard chips. "I care, all right." They reached her suite, and he dug into her evening bag for the key. Unlocking the door with one hand, he shoved her inside with the other.

"Get out of here," she cried.

The door closed behind him. "Give me that bottle. I don't want you drinking."

She had forgotten about the champagne she had snatched from the table. She didn't want any more to drink, but now that he was demanding she hand over the bottle, she decided she wouldn't give it up. Why should she? He hadn't said a word when Wanda had separated them at the wedding or later when she'd seated them at different tables for the reception. He'd danced with everybody but her. She was hurt and angry, and she had just enough alcohol in her veins to challenge him.

"Why should I do what you tell me?"

"Because you'll be sorry if you don't."

He took a step toward her, and she immediately backed away, retreating across the living room until she bumped into a door frame. She sidestepped and moved backward into the bedroom.

"Give me the bottle." He came through the doorway after her, his face bleak and scary.

She realized that he was finally giving her his complete attention. Her pulse began a crazy thumping as she decided that his anger was better than his indifference.

Clutching the bottle to her breasts, she kicked off her shoes and confronted him. "You've ordered me around for the last time, Dash Coogan. You can go to hell."

"Hand it over, Honey."

Her calves bumped against the bed. She clambered up on it, knowing that she was playing a dangerous game but unable to stop herself. "Take it away from me."

Without warning, he lurched forward and snatched the bottle from her.

She had been so absorbed in her own misery that she'd forgotten about his alcoholism. Now as she stared at the open bottle in his hands, she froze.

Seconds ticked by, and then an expression of disgust crossed his face. In two steps he reached the bottom of the bed and flung the bottle into the trash can that sat nearby with such force that the container fell to its side. A small amount of champagne frothed onto the carpet.

He turned back to her as she stood in the center of the mattress. His features were harsh, impossible to read. She began to walk awkwardly away from him until she reached the headboard. She leaned against the wall for balance, a position that thrust her breasts slightly forward.

He went very still. She watched as his eyes slid down over her. Seconds slipped by, one giving way to another. The rush of blood in her ears grew louder. Following his gaze, she saw that her dress had ridden far up on her thighs. A dangerous excitement, stronger than fear, took hold of her. Placing the palms of her hands flat on the wall behind her, she angled her hips forward more sharply so that her dress rode higher.

"Stop it," he said hoarsely.

The wildness that had been skimming around her all evening took possession. She parted her thighs. "What's the matter, cowboy?" she said huskily. "Can't you take a little heat?"

"You don't have any idea what you're doing."

"Poor Daddy," she said, her voice soft and mocking.

"Don't call me that," he said harshly.

She pushed her spine away from the wall and began walking down the length of the bed toward him, her stockinged feet sinking into the mattress. The champagne fired her, giving her courage and daring and igniting a primitive instinct. She began a mocking croon to him, taunting him with a relationship that didn't exist, prodding him so that he would be forced to acknowledge that he was hiding behind a lie.

"Oh, Daddy mine. Sweet Daddy . . ."

"I'm not your daddy!" he burst out.

"Are you sure?"

"Don't—"

"Are you sure you're not my daddy?"

"I won't—"

"Be sure, Dash. Please."

He stood frozen before her, his head below hers for once. Her body moved in awkward rhythm to the unsteady surface beneath her feet. He didn't move as she leaned forward to wrap her arms around his neck.

"I'm sure," she said.

When he didn't reply, she took his mouth, kissing him hungrily, using her tongue and her teeth to have all of him. She drew his lips between hers, invading him as if she were the woman of experience and he the novice.

He was like ice and steel. Frozen. Unyielding.

She didn't stop. If they had just this one moment of truth between them, she would wring it dry and make it last forever. The only barriers that separated them were the ones he had erected in his mind. She stroked deep into his mouth.

A groan erupted from the back of his throat and his hand tangled in her hair. He drew her down until she fell against him and he was taking all her weight. His mouth opened, and he overpowered her.

His kiss was rough and deep, full of dark need. She wanted to drown in it. She wanted all of her body to fit through his mouth so she could hide herself away inside him. At the same time she wanted to grow in size and strength until she could overpower him and force him to love her as she loved him.

And then she felt him shudder. With an awful hiss, he drew his head back. "What do you think you're doing?"

She collapsed to her knees on the bed. Reaching out, she wrapped her arms around his hips and crushed her cheek against the strong, flat muscles of his abdomen. "Exactly what I want to do."

He grabbed her shoulders, pushing her away. "That's enough! You've gone far enough, little girl."

She leaned back on her heels. Speaking softly, she said, "I'm not a little girl."

"You're twenty years old," he said harshly. "You're a kid."

"Liar," she whispered.

His eyes grew dark with pain, but she had no pity. This was her night. Probably the only night she would have. Without questioning what she was about to do, she slipped her hands to the back of her neck and reached beneath her hair for the tiny hook and eye at the top of her gown. When it was free, she tugged on the zipper. It made a small hiss in the quiet of the room, and the dress fell from her shoulders.

She dropped her feet over the side of the bed and stood. The dress slipped off her hips to the floor, leaving her in a lacy bra, shimmery silver stockings, and ice-blue tap pants.

His voice was hoarse. "You're drunk. You don't even know what you're asking for."

"Yes, I do."

"You're hot, and you want a man. It doesn't make any difference which one."

"That's not true. Kiss me again."

"No more kisses, Jane Marie."

"You're pathetic," she retorted, refusing to let him hide behind a make-believe relationship.

"I'm not—"

She caught his strong wrist and drew his hand to her breast, pressing it over the fullness. "Can you feel my heart pound, Dash?" She rubbed the palm back and forth so that her nipple hardened beneath the silky fabric. "Can you feel it?"

"Honey . . ."

She clasped his large hand beneath both of her smaller ones and slid it down between her breasts, over her ribs. "Can you feel me?"

"Don't . . ."

She paused for only a moment before she slipped it over the silky fabric of the tap pants and then between her legs.

"Christ." He touched her, closed around her, then pulled back as if she had burned him.

"We're going to stop this right now, you hear me?" he roared. "You're drunk, and you're acting like a whore, and that's the end of it."

"You're scared, aren't you?" She lowered her eyes to the

221

front of his trousers. "I can see how much you want me, but you're too afraid to admit it."

"That's smut talking. You don't have the slightest idea what you're saying any more than you have any idea what sex is all about. I'm a hundred years older than you. You're just a kid."

"You're forty-three. That's hardly ancient. And you didn't kiss me like I was a kid."

"Not one more word. I mean it, Honey."

But she was in too much pain to stop. Setting her jaw, she attacked him.

"You're such a coward."

"That's enough."

"You don't have the guts to admit the way you feel about me."

"Stop it!"

"If I were a coward like you, I couldn't look at myself in the mirror."

"I said to stop!"

"I'd kill myself. I really would. I'd take a knife and stick it—"

"I'm warning you for the last time!"

"Coward!"

He grabbed her arm, nearly hauling her off her feet as he drew her up against him. His face twisted, and as his mouth drew near hers, he hissed, "Is this what you want?"

The kiss was hard and consuming, and she should have been frightened, but the fire inside her burned too hot.

Her responsiveness fanned his anger instead of cooling it. Drawing back from her, he stripped off his jacket. "All right. I'm done playing games with you. If that's what you want, I'm going to give it to you."

He whipped off his tie and tugged at the front of his shirt, sending the onyx studs flying. He was breathing heavily, and there was an air of desperation about him. "Don't you think for one minute that you can come crying to me afterward."

She watched as he stripped off his cummerbund and shirt. "I won't cry."

"That's only because you don't know a damn thing about

what's going to happen to you." He pitched a shoe across the room. "You don't know anything, do you?"

"Not—not from practical experience."

He yanked off his other shoe, throwing it against the bed stand with a curse. "Practical experience is the only thing that counts. And don't think I'm going to make it easy on you. That's not the way I do it. You wanted yourself a lover, little girl. Now you got yourself one big time."

All her muscles went weak, and her wildness was replaced by fear. But even fear couldn't make her flee the room, because she needed his love too badly.

"Dash?"

"What do you want?"

"Do you—Should I take off the rest of my clothes now?"

His hands froze on the waistband of his trousers. He sank down into the chair behind him. For a moment he did nothing. She held her breath, praying that the man she loved would reappear instead of this dangerous stranger who was trying so hard to frighten her and succeeding all too well. But as his mouth thinned, she knew he wasn't going to relent.

"Now that's a real good idea." He stretched out his legs and crossed them at the ankles as he inspected her. "You just take everything off nice and slow while I watch."

"Why are you making this so terrible?"

"What did you expect, little girl? Did you think it was going to be poetry and kisses? If you wanted that, you should have picked yourself a schoolboy. Somebody as new to the game as you are. Somebody with nice manners who'd take time with you and wouldn't hurt you like I'm going to."

"You won't hurt me."

"Now that's where you're wrong. I'm gonna hurt you, all right. Look at how much bigger I am. Get that underwear off. Or are you ready to admit you've made a mistake?"

She wanted to run from him, but she couldn't. No one had ever found her worthy of love, and if this was the only kind he could give her, then she would take what he had to offer. Her hands trembled as she reached behind her to the clasp of her bra.

He shot up from the chair, his face contorted with fury. "This is your last chance. Once that bra comes off, I'm gonna be all over you."

She opened the clasp awkwardly and let the straps slip from her shoulders.

A muscle near his cheekbone ticked. "When that bra comes off, it'll be too late. I mean it. You're gonna wish you'd never been born." The lacy garment dropped to the floor. "When that bra comes off, you're gonna wish—"

"Dash?" Her voice trembled, barely a whisper. "You're really scaring me. Could you—Could you just hold me for a minute first?"

All his bluster disappeared. His shoulders dropped, and his mouth contorted with raw pain. Groaning, he reached out and wrapped her in his arms. Her breasts nestled into the warmth of his bare chest like small birds.

His voice blew across her ear, soft and sad. "I'm so afraid for you, Honey."

"Don't be afraid," she whispered. "I know you can't love me back."

"Sweetheart—"

"It's all right. I love you enough for both of us. I love you so much."

"You only think you do."

"I do," she said fiercely. "More than I've ever loved anyone in my life. You're the only person who's ever really cared about me. Don't be mad at me."

"Sweetheart, I'm not mad at you. Don't you understand? I'm mad at myself."

"Why?"

"Because I'm no good for you."

"That's not true."

He sighed, a ragged sound. "You deserve so much better. I won't mean to hurt you, but before we're done, I'll break your heart."

"I don't care. Please, Dash. Please love me, just for tonight."

He stroked her hair for a very long time. Then his hands slid down over her bare back to her hips. "All right, sweetheart. I'll love you. God forgive me, but I can't help myself."

He kissed her forehead and cheeks. He stroked her until his own breathing grew labored, then laid claim to her mouth. His kiss was demanding, and she lost herself in its wonderful strength. The power of his arousal pressed against her belly as his hands moved up along her sides. Dropping his head, he kissed her young breasts and suckled on them until she was weak with need.

"I never knew," she gasped.

"I'll show you, sweetheart," he replied.

Laying her on the bed, he drew off her panties and stockings. For a moment she was afraid she would do something wrong, and she tensed.

"You're so beautiful."

Relaxing, she let him separate her legs and stroke the soft, firm skin of her inner thighs. Before long, she felt herself surrendering, every part of her trusting him. When he parted her, she yielded up to him. She didn't fight his fingers as they made the passage easier. She welcomed him with hot, racing joy when he was naked and lying between her open thighs.

"Easy now, sweetheart," he said, his voice a rasp as he continued to stroke her. "Don't tense up on me."

She didn't. She let her arms fall wide and open on the bed, all of her open and trusting. He knew where to touch, where to stroke. He'd been making love to women for longer than she'd been alive, and he understood the mysteries of her body better than she did.

When he took slow possession, she received him with wonder and passion, barely feeling the pain because he had prepared her so well. He fondled her and caressed her, displaying infinite patience even though his own body was slick with sweat. Again and again he took her up to the peak, but he wouldn't let her fly.

She began to plead with him in short gasping breaths. "Please. I need . . ."

"Quiet now."

"But I have to . . ."

"No more. Hush."

He kissed her and stroked her and drew back his head to watch her as she begged for release.

"I'm going to . . . die."

"I know, sweetheart. I know."

His eyes filled with smoky tenderness, and she began to cry.

He smiled and let her soar.

17

Honey lay in his arms afterward, her head on his shoulder. He toyed idly with her hair, wrapping silky curls around his big brown fingers while she discovered the textures of his chest and explored old scars that she had seen but never touched.

He was quiet.

She wasn't.

"I never thought it would be so wonderful, Dash. It didn't hurt at all, and I wanted it to last forever. I was worried— You know, you read about it in books, and that sort of gives you high expectations. But then you've got to ask yourself, is that the way it really is?" She touched a scar near his nipple. "Where did this one come from?"

"I don't know. Montana, maybe. I worked on a ranch up there."

"Uhmm. I can't imagine anything more wonderful than sex. I was afraid that I'd be—You know, since I haven't had any practice, I thought I might be sort of a dud." She lifted her head, her forehead wrinkling. "I wasn't a dud, was I?"

He kissed the tip of her nose. "You weren't a dud."

Reassured, she lay back down and resumed her stroking. "But I still don't know a lot, and really, I don't see why we can't do it again. I'm not sore. Really, I'm not. And I want to make sure I satisfy you—I know that's important. And I haven't done any—you know—oral sex or anything."

"Jesus, Honey."

She propped herself up on her elbow to look at him. "Well, I haven't."

A faint, ruddy glow stained his cheekbones. "For pete's sake, where do you get your ideas?"

"I may not have had a lot of experience, but I'm a big reader."

"Well, that explains it."

"And another thing . . ."

He groaned.

"Everything happened so fast. Well, not fast. Really slow, which was wonderful. But I got a little crazy. Which wasn't my fault because everything you were doing to me was making me crazy. Not crazy, exactly, but—"

"Honey?"

"Uh-huh?"

"Do you think you could sort of wander toward the point you're trying to make before both of us die of old age?"

She toyed with the edge of the sheet where it lay over his waist. "My point—" She hesitated. "It's a little embarrassing."

"It's hard to imagine there's anything much left that *could* embarrass you."

She gave him a glare that was supposed to be withering, but she was so happy that it fell short of the mark. "What I'm trying to say is that—In the heat of passion, so to speak, I didn't get a chance to . . . I didn't actually . . . " She stroked the edge of the sheet. "The point is . . . " She took a deep breath. "I want to look."

His head shot up. "You what?"

Now she was the one with the ruddy cheekbones. "I want to . . . *look* at you."

"Sort of like a science experiment?"

"Do you mind?"

He chuckled and then dropped his head back to the pillow. "No, sweetheart, I don't mind. Look away."

She drew back the sheet, and within a very short time

Dash seemed to set aside all his reservations because they were making love again.

He was in the shower when room service banged on the door the next morning. He had ordered coffee and she had ordered waffles, sausage, toast, juice, and blueberry cheesecake. She wanted to eat everything, taste everything, do everything. She smiled and hugged herself. She was all woman. One hundred and two pounds of female dynamite. The meanest and toughest hombres in the West hadn't been able to whip Dash Coogan, but she had brought the king of the cowboys right to his knees.

Sashaying through the living room, all sexy and full of herself, she secured the belt of the robe she had thrown on after she had come out of the shower and opened the door. "Bring it right—"

Wanda Ridgeway pushed past her and stormed inside. "He's here, isn't he? He wasn't in his room. I know he's here."

"Mother, please." Meredith reluctantly followed.

Dash and Wanda had been divorced for years, but Honey was immediately guilt-stricken. "Who—who are you talking about?"

The sound of the shower could be heard clearly from the direction of the bedroom, and Wanda gave her the sort of look that grown women give children who are caught in a lie.

"Mother thinks my father is here," Meredith said stiffly.

"Dash?" Honey widened her eyes just as Janie did when she was trying to wiggle out of a tight spot. "You think Dash is here?" She gave a phony laugh and widened her eyes even more. "Why, that's ridiculous." Another phony laugh. "Why would Dash be using my shower?"

"Then who is it?" Wanda asked.

"A man—I—I met a man at the wedding. . . ."

Reddening, Meredith turned toward her mother. "I told you he wasn't here. You always think the worst of him. I told you—"

"She's lying, Meredith. Your whole life you've blamed me for the divorce. Despite all your hellfire talk, you still think your father walks on water. You think that he's all lit up with a great big halo just like Jesus. Well, your father couldn't walk on water if it was made out of concrete. His zipper broke up our marriage; not me."

The shower stopped.

Honey darted a nervous glance toward the doorway. "I don't mean to be rude, but if there's nothing else. . . ."

"Hey, Honey. Come in here and dry my back."

Meredith sucked in her breath at the sound of her father's voice. Wanda lifted her head in triumph.

"His shower was broken," Honey stammered. "I was with another man, but he left. And then Dash called and said his shower was broken, and he asked if he could use mine."

Dash came through the door, drying his hair with one towel, another wrapped around his hips. "Honey—"

He broke off.

Wanda crossed her arms over her chest, her expression smug. Meredith gave a hiss of outrage.

Dash went still for only a moment before he resumed drying his hair. "What are the two of you doing up so early?"

"How could you?" Meredith gasped.

"It's not what you think, Meredith." Honey rushed to his side. "Dash, I was just telling Wanda and Meredith about how the shower in your room wasn't working. And you called to ask if you could use mine. And since my— uh— companion for the night had left, I said that would be fine, and—"

Dash looked at her as if she'd lost her mind. "What the hell are you talking about?"

"Your broken shower?" Honey inquired weakly.

He slipped his towel down around his shoulders, grasping the ends with his hands as he turned to Meredith. "There wasn't any broken shower, Merry. Honey and I spent the night together, and since we're both consenting adults, it's nobody's business but ours."

Wanda's eyes glittered with malicious satisfaction. "Your daughter finally gets to see for herself exactly what kind of man her father is."

Meredith's lips trembled and then contracted bitterly. "I'm going to pray for you, Daddy. I'm going to spend the rest of this day on my knees praying for your everlasting soul."

Dash whipped the towel from his neck. "Don't goddamn bother! I don't need anybody praying for me."

"Yes, you do. You need all the prayers you can get." Meredith glared at Honey. "And you! You're an affront to every woman who values the sanctity of her own body. You tempted him just like the whores of Babylon."

Meredith had hit too close to the truth, and Honey winced. Dash, however, took a step forward.

"You stop right there," he said, his voice low with warning. "Don't you say another word."

"That's what she is. She—"

"Enough!" Dash roared. Before Honey knew what was happening, he had drawn her to his side. She went weak from the rush of feelings that his protectiveness evoked within her.

"If you want to stay part of my life, Meredith, you're going to have to accept Honey, because she's going to be part of it, too."

Honey's head lifted to look at him.

"I'll never accept her," Meredith said bitterly.

"Maybe you'd better think about what you're saying before you go slamming too many doors."

"I don't have to think about it," she replied. "If I accepted this sordid relationship, it would become my sin, too."

"You're going to have to work that out for yourself," he said.

Wanda stepped forward. "Go hold the elevator for us, Meredith. I'll be along in a second."

Meredith obviously had more on her mind that she wanted to say, but she didn't have the nerve to defy her mother. Refusing to look at her father, she darted Honey a hate-filled glance and did as she was told.

"You had to bring her here, didn't you?" Dash said after Meredith had left.

Wanda stiffened. "You haven't had to live with her.

You've been the good guy who breezes into town every few years with an armload of presents. I've been the nasty bitch who sent her daddy away. She's twenty-one years old, and I'm sick of living with her blame."

His mouth drew tight. "Just get out."

"I'm on my way." She slipped her purse strap higher on her shoulder, and then some of her malice seemed to fade. She looked from Dash to Honey and back to Dash. She shook her head.

"You're getting ready to screw everything up again, aren't you, Randy?"

"I don't know what you're talking about."

"Every time you start to get your feet back on solid ground, you do something to spoil it. As long as I've known you, that's been your way. Just when things are getting good for you, you always manage to ruin it."

"You're crazy."

"Don't do it, Randy," she said quietly. "This time, don't do it."

Silence fell between them. His face was rigid, hers pensive. She gave his arm an awkward pat and left them alone.

Honey's eyes raced from the closed door to Dash. "What did she mean? What was she talking about?"

"Never mind."

"Dash?"

He sighed and gazed out the window. "She knows I'm going to marry you, I guess."

Honey swallowed hard. "Marry me?"

"Go on and get dressed," he said harshly. "We've got a plane to catch."

He wouldn't talk about his startling announcement during the flight, or even after they reached Los Angeles. Finally, she gave up trying. On the freeway from the airport, he swore at other drivers and cut them off. But even his bad temper couldn't dampen the choir of angels singing inside her.

He had said he was going to marry her. Her world had split open like an egg, revealing a jeweled center.

He swore darkly and cut between two vans. She realized they were heading toward Pasadena instead of to the ranch, and her stomach began to cramp. He was taking her home. What if he hadn't meant what he'd said at all? What if they weren't getting married, and he was trying to find a way to tell her he'd changed his mind?

"I'll bet you didn't pack a single pair of jeans in that suitcase."

He sounded so accusing that she grew defensive. "We were going to a wedding."

"You always have a smart comeback, don't you?"

She opened her mouth to respond, but before she could speak, he went on. "Now here's the way we're going to do this. I figure the best thing is to go down to Baja. We'll get married there and then camp for a few days. We've got another week before we have to be back on the set, and we might as well make the most of it."

The choir of angels burst into a chorus of alleluias. "You mean it?" she breathed softly. "We're really getting married?"

"What do you suggest as an alternative? Did you want to have an *affair?*" He spit out the word as if it were a particularly loathsome obscenity. "Did you want to *live together?*"

"Everybody else does it," she said tentatively, trying to understand his mood.

He looked completely disgusted with her. "Is that all the value you put on yourself? I'll tell you one thing, little girl. I've been low in my life, but I've never been so low that I didn't marry a woman I loved."

He loved her! The knowledge radiated inside her like a sunburst. She no longer cared about his bad mood or anything else. He had said that he loved her, and she was going to be his wife. She wanted to throw herself into his arms, but there was something so forbidding about him that she didn't quite have the nerve.

He didn't speak again until they arrived at her house. "I'll give you ten minutes to get rid of all those fancy clothes and pack some jeans and boots. We'll spend the night at the ranch and then set out first thing tomorrow morning. It'll get cold at night, so bring a set of long underwear. And you're going to need your birth certificate."

Birth certificate! They really were going to do it. Giving a little whoop of happiness, she reached across the car to hug him, then raced into the house to do as he had directed.

None of her family seemed to have noticed that she'd been gone. She packed quickly and told Chantal she wouldn't be home for a few days. Chantal wasn't curious enough to ask for an explanation, and Honey didn't give one. Part of her still couldn't believe that Dash Coogan was really going to marry her, and until it had happened, she didn't want to jinx herself by telling anybody.

He was drumming his fingers impatiently on the steering wheel when she returned to the car. "You didn't have to wait out here," she said as she climbed in. "You could have come inside."

"Not with that bunch of cannibals."

She decided there would be time enough to sort out his opinion of her family after they were married, but she couldn't as easily dismiss something he had said earlier. As the car shot onto the Ventura, a small chill clouded her happiness.

"Dash? What you said earlier about always marrying the women you loved. I don't want to be loved the same way you loved your other wives. I want—I want it to be forever."

He glared at the freeway in front of him. "That just goes to show what you know."

18

They were married the next afternoon in Mexicali, just across the border. The ceremony took place in some sort of government office—Honey wasn't certain what kind since she couldn't read the Spanish signs and Dash still wasn't being communicative. Both of them were wearing jeans. She held a bouquet of flowers he had bought from a street vendor outside, and her ring was a plain gold band from a nearby jewelry shop.

The walls were thin and a radio blared Spanish rock songs from the next office. The official who married them had a gold tooth and smelled like cloves. As the ceremony ended, Dash grabbed the copy of their marriage certificate and dragged her outside, all without kissing her.

The warm afternoon air was fetid from the stench of the irrigation canals and fertilizer spray, but she breathed it in joyously. She was Mrs. Dash Coogan. Honey Jane Moon Coogan. She was finally part of someone else.

He pulled her toward his jeep, which was parked at the curb and filled with their camping gear. She knew from past discussions that the vehicle had been specially modified to handle the rough terrain of the wilderness camping he enjoyed. As he drove into one of the government-owned Pentex gas stations to fill the thirty-gallon tank, she remembered all the times he'd set out on one of these camping trips without her and how she had dreamed of going along. Now she was doing it in a way she had never imagined.

They headed west from Mexicali on Highway 2. Heat waves rose off the pavement, and litter blew across the highway. Abandoned tire treads lay at the side of the road like dead alligators, and tired old billboards scarred the bleak landscape. A truck filled with field workers blasted by, its horn squalling. Honey stuck her hand out the open window and waved at them gaily.

"Do you want to get your arm ripped off?" Dash snarled. "Just keep those hands inside."

Having the marriage ceremony behind them obviously hadn't improved his mood. She told herself that sooner or later he would let her know what was eating at him, but until then she was going to hold her tongue.

She had visited Tijuana several times with Gordon and Chantal, but this part of Baja was new to her. The land was parched and forbidding, a gnarled finger poking into the sea. Several miles west of Mexicali, the highway crossed the top of Laguna Salada, a wide, dry lake bed that extended as far as she could see. Its surface was marked with tire tracks from jeeps and ATVs.

As she stared at the dry moonscape of the lake bed, her eyes began to feel heavy. They had arrived at the ranch just after dark and eaten a silent meal. Afterward, he had brusquely directed her to one of the guest rooms, where she had tossed all night, unable to sleep because she was afraid he would change his mind by morning. She glanced down at the gold circlet on her finger and tried to absorb the fact that they were truly married.

Her shoulder banged against his as he abandoned the highway and began heading across the dry lake bed. "We're camping for the night in one of the palm canyons," he said brusquely. "It's not too accessible, so the developers haven't gotten hold of it yet."

"Not too accessible" proved to be an understatement. The gears of the jeep ground painfully when the small vehicle finally cleared the lake bed and assaulted the steep, rocky slopes that rose off its western edge. For an hour they followed a road that was little more than a rutted track, jolting and jarring her until she felt bruised. Finally, it passed through a narrow cleft in the rocks into a tiny palm-shaded canyon.

Granite walls, wild and rugged, rose high on the sides. She saw the twisted silvery limbs of elephant trees interspersed with palm and tamarisk. As Dash stopped the jeep, Honey heard the sound of running water. He climbed out and disappeared into the trees. She got out herself, stretched her limbs, and looked around for the source of the sound. Behind her, a small waterfall tumbled in a lacy silver mist from the harsh cliff face.

Dash came out of the trees, zipping his pants as he walked. Honey quickly looked away, both embarrassed and fascinated by this intimacy that was exactly the sort of thing she had always imagined a man would do in front of his wife.

He nodded toward the waterfall as he began unloading the jeep. "These canyons are one of the few places with fresh water in all of Baja. There's even a hot springs. Most of the peninsula is dry as dust, and water's a lot more precious than gold. Grab those tent poles."

She did as he told her, but as she was pulling the poles from the back, she caught the end of the longest one on the jeep's frame and they all clattered to the ground.

"Damn it, Honey, watch what you're doing."

"Sorry."

"I don't want to have to spend this entire trip cleaning up your messes."

She bent down to retrieve the poles.

"And do you mind telling me why you're wearing those sandals? I distinctly remember telling you to bring boots."

"I did," she said. "They're with my clothes."

"What good are they going to do with your clothes if we're in the middle of the desert and you run into a rattler?"

"We're not in the middle of the desert," she pointed out as she rose to her feet with the tent poles clutched in her arms.

"You've been spoiling for a fight ever since yesterday, haven't you?"

She stared at him, unable to believe his gall. He was the one who'd been acting as if he'd sat on a porcupine.

He poked the front brim of his Stetson back with his thumb, his expression belligerent. "We might as well set down a few rules right now. That is if you're not too busy dropping things to listen."

"I've never been camping before," she said stiffly. "I don't know anything about it."

"I'm not talking about camping. I'm talking about the two of us." He advanced on her until only a few feet separated them. "First off. I'm the boss. I'm set in my ways and I don't have any intention of changing a single one of them. You're going to have to do a lot more accommodating than me, and I don't want to hear any bitching about it. Understood?"

He didn't wait for her response, which was a good thing.

"I don't concern myself with housework. Expressions like 'splitting the work load' aren't even part of my vocabulary. I don't run a washing machine; I don't worry about whether there's coffee in the cupboard. We hire somebody to do that or you take care of it. Either way." His eyes narrowed. "And that parasite family of yours. If you want to keep supporting them that's your business, but I'm not giving them a penny, and they're not coming within ten miles of the ranch. Is that understood?"

He sounded as if he were giving her terms for parole.

"And another thing." His scowl grew blacker. "Those birth control pills I saw in your case. From now on they're one of your basic food groups, little girl. I already ruined one set of children, and I don't have any intention of ruining another."

"Dash?"

"What?"

She set the tent poles on the ground, then looked up at him, trying to keep her gaze steady. "I've been doing my best not to lose my temper with you, but you've pushed me right to the edge. You know that, don't you?"

"I've barely got started."

"Now that's where you're wrong. You're all done."

His jaw jutted forward. "Is that so?"

"It's so. I never used to be much of a crybaby, Dash Coogan, but since I fell in love with you, I've done more than my share. And I'm warning you right now that you're upsetting me, which means I'll probably start crying pretty soon. I'm not proud of it—as a matter of fact, I'm ashamed—but that won't change the outcome. So if you don't want to spend the rest of this sorry excuse for a honeymoon with a crying wife, I suggest you start acting like the gentleman I know you can be."

His head dipped. He kicked at the ground with the toe of his boot. When he spoke, his voice was soft, a bit hoarse. "Honey, I've never been faithful to a woman in my life."

A spike of pain drove right through her.

He gazed at her, his eyes unhappy. "When I think about my track record and all these years we've got stretching between us, not to mention the fact that we're going to put an end to two careers, I can't believe I'm doing this. It doesn't matter so much about me, but I can't stand the idea of hurting you. I know I must be crazy, Honey, but I don't seem to be able to help myself when it comes to you."

All of her resentment faded, and she was filled with tenderness. "I think I'm a little crazy, too. I love you so much I can hardly stand it."

He pulled her against his chest. "I know you do. And I love you even more. That's why there's no excuse for what I've done."

"Please, Dash, don't talk like that."

He stroked her hair. "You got under my skin when I wasn't even looking, just like a chigger. Everything would have been all right if you hadn't grown up on me, but all of a sudden you weren't a kid anymore, and no matter how hard I tried, I couldn't make you turn back into one."

For a long time the only sound was the rush of the waterfall behind them.

By the time they had set up camp, the sky had clouded over and a chilly drizzle had plunged the temperature down into the forties. Honey was cold, wet, and happier than she could ever remember.

"Do you mind getting the last of the food?" He zipped the front of the small tent he had set up.

She reached inside the jeep, but before she could pull out the large food tin he had sprung to her side and taken it from her.

"It's not heavy," she protested. "I can do that."

"I expect you can." Leaning down, he brushed his lips over hers.

She smiled to herself as she remembered all the chest-pounding he'd been doing. Dash Coogan had more bluster than any man she'd ever known.

An icy gust of wind blew through the camp site, rattling the wet palm fronds, and she shivered. "I thought this was supposed to be a tropical climate."

"You cold?"

She nodded.

"That's good."

She looked at him quizzically.

"The weather can change fast around here, especially in the winter." He sounded pleased. "This is about the only time of year you need a tent. Normally, I'd have just brought a sun fly to give us shade, keep out the bugs, and let the breeze through. Grab some dry clothes for both of us and that long underwear of yours while I put this away."

She did as he asked, but as she began to head toward the tent to change, he stepped in front of her. "Not that way." Taking her hand, he wrapped a poncho around their dry clothing and began to lead her into the palms.

The temperature was dropping by the minute, and her teeth had started to rattle. "I'm afraid I'm too cold for a hike, Dash."

"Come on now. You're tougher than that. A little nip in the air never hurt anybody."

"It's a lot more than a nip. I can see my breath."

He grinned. "Is it my imagination or are you starting to whine?"

She thought of the tent and those fluffy down sleeping bags where they could be curled up right now and where she could be getting more lessons in lovemaking. "It's definitely not your imagination."

"I can see I'm going to have to get you toughened up."

He led her through a breach in the trees and she caught her breath. Before them in a nest of ferns and mossy rocks lay a small pool with steam curling from its surface into the chilly air.

"I told you there was a hot springs here," he said. "Now what do you say the two of us strip off these clothes and get down to some serious hanky-panky?"

She was already unbuttoning her blouse, but her fingers were clumsy with the cold and he finished undressing first. When he was naked, he helped her peel the wet denim from her legs and then drew her into the pool until he was standing waist deep, but only her breasts and shoulders were exposed. The water felt hot and wonderful against her cold skin. Above the surface her breasts were covered with gooseflesh, her nipples puckered into hard little pebbles. He dipped his head and caught one in the warmth of his mouth. She arched her neck at the gentle suction. His mouth moved to the other nipple.

After a while he released her and began sluicing warm water over her chilled shoulders, not letting her dip beneath the surface, but warming her with the water and the palms of his big brown hands.

She began to stroke his hips and the fronts of his thighs beneath the water. Her nipples softened and spread like summer buds beneath his warm fingers. Her hands grew more adventuresome. She stroked him until he groaned.

They were near the center of the pond now, and the water had grown deeper until the tops of her shoulders were covered. "Wrap your legs around my waist," he said huskily.

She licked at the beads of moisture that had formed on his cheekbones and did as he asked.

He played with her beneath the water, his fingers on a rampage, making her gasp as they explored every part of her.

"Dash . . ." She tightened her strong young thighs around him.

He groaned out her name and drove home.

They stayed in the palm canyon for two days, and during that time Dash seemed to grow younger before her eyes. The harsh lines at the corners of his mouth faded and the bleakness in his green eyes disappeared. They laughed and wrestled and made love until sometimes she wondered which of them was the twenty-year-old. She cooked bacon and eggs on the Coleman stove, and had tears in her eyes the morning of the third day when they left their canyon behind. Dash wanted her to see everything, and since the weather had once again grown hot, they were to spend the next few nights camping along the Gulf of California, or the Sea of Cortés, as it was also called.

"That was the best time I ever had in my life," she sighed when they were back on the highway heading south.

"We'll come here again." His voice grew surprisingly

grim. "I imagine we'll have time for a lot of camping in the future."

"What's wrong with that? You love to camp."

"I like to camp when I'm on vacation. Not because both of us are going to be unemployed."

She set her jaw. "I don't want to talk about it."

"Honey—"

"I mean it, Dash. Not now."

He let her have her way and began identifying some of the vegetation and pointing out the volcanic rock formations. As they drove farther south with the hot breeze blowing through the open windows of the jeep, she saw abandoned automobile bodies everywhere, and she began to feel uneasy. There was something almost apocalyptic about the landscape: bleak, parched vistas scabbed with rusted automobile hulks lying on their backs like dead beetles, skeletal vegetation sucked dry of moisture, crumbling roads spotted with animal carcasses. Even the most dangerous switchbacks had no guardrails, just clusters of memorial crosses marking the spot where loved ones had been lost.

An irrational fear came over her, not for herself but for Dash. "Let me drive," she said abruptly.

He looked over at her quizzically. She knew he was a good driver, but she wanted to be behind the wheel. Only if she were in control of every motion of the automobile, every nuance of the road, could she protect him from harm.

"There's a beach-shack restaurant not far from here where we can eat lunch," he said. "The food's real good. You can take over from there."

She forced herself to draw a series of deep breaths and, gradually, she began to relax.

"Shack" was a generous description for the restaurant. It was made of adobe that had once been painted a bilious shade of green, and the mismatched tables were set outside on a crumbling patio overlooking the sea. The patio was shaded by a dilapidated roof covered with flapping tar paper and supported by splintered wooden posts.

"I know the IRS still takes most of your paycheck, Dash, but I thought you could afford better than this."

"You just wait," he said with a grin as he led her to a wooden table with a square of well-scrubbed linoleum nailed over the top.

"Señor Coogan!"

"Hola! Cómo estás, Emilio?"

Dash rose as an elderly man came toward them. They exchanged greetings in rapid-fire Spanish and then Dash introduced her, but since she didn't speak the language, she wasn't certain exactly how he identified her. Eventually Emilio bustled off through a banging screen door into the kitchen.

"I hope you're hungry." Dash took off his hat and set it on an empty chair.

For the next half hour, they feasted on one of the best meals Honey had ever eaten: quesadillas made of tender flour tortillas with goat cheese bubbling from the sides, succulent lime-seasoned chunks of abalone, avocados stuffed with plump shrimp that hinted of saltwater and cilantro. Occasionally one of them would spear an especially tender morsel and feed it to the other. Sometimes they kissed between bites. Honey felt as if she'd known how to be a lover all her life.

She was too full to eat more than a few bites of the fat fig tart that was their dessert. Dash had put down his fork, too, and was gazing out at the sea. She saw a ridge in his hair where he had taken off his hat, and she reached out to smooth it, barely able to believe that she now had the right to do this sort of thing.

He caught her hand and drew it to his lips. When he let her go, his expression was solemn. "As soon as we get back—"

She tugged her hand away. "I don't want to talk about it."

"We have to talk. This is serious, Honey. The first thing I want you to do is see a good lawyer."

"A lawyer? Are you trying to divorce me already?"

He didn't smile. "This isn't about divorce. Every penny of your money has to be locked up tight so the IRS can't take it away from you because of me. I won't have you paying for my financial mistakes. It was stupid of me not to have thought of it right away so we could have taken care of it before we ran off to get married. I don't know—I'm not good about money."

She saw how distressed he was, and she smiled at him. "I'll take care of it, okay? Don't worry."

Her reassurance seemed to satisfy him, and he leaned back in his chair. But now that he had raised the specter of their future, it hung between them. She knew she had to stop being such a coward and face the topic she wanted to avoid. She toyed with the label on the bottle of mineral water she had been drinking.

"Maybe it'll be all right, Dash. Nobody has to know. We can keep our marriage a secret."

"Not a chance. The tabloids have probably already found out. You think that guy who married us is going to keep his mouth shut?"

"He might."

"And what about the clerk who did the paperwork? Or the jeweler who sold us your wedding ring?"

She sank back in her chair. "So what do you think will happen?"

"Our P.R. people will fall all over each other trying to do damage control. It won't do a damned bit of good, but they'll go through the motions anyway so they look like they're earning their paychecks. The tabloids will have helicopters flying over the ranch trying to get photos of the two of us naked. Columnists will write about us in the newspapers. The comics are going to have a field day. We'll be fair game for every monologue on the Carson show. We won't be able to turn on the set without hearing some smartass take a poke at us."

"It won't be—"

"The production company and bullshit artists at the network will convince each other they can make script adjustments and revise the concept. But no matter what they try to do, audiences are going to puke, and *The Dash Coogan Show* will be history."

She was furious with him. "You're wrong! You're always looking at the bad side. That's one thing I can't stand about you. When the slightest little thing happens, you have to act like it's the end of the world. Audiences aren't stupid. They know the difference between real life and a television program. The network wouldn't drop the show for anything. They've made millions. It's one of the most successful shows in history. Everybody loves us."

"Who are you trying to convince? Me or yourself?"

His gentleness was her undoing. She looked out at the ocean where the waves were sparkling in the afternoon sun, and her shoulders sagged. "We haven't done anything wrong. We love each other. I'm not going to be able to stand it if people try to make something obscene out of the two of us. This is real life. Not a television show."

"But our audience doesn't know us, Honey; they only know the characters we play. And the idea of Janie Jones and her pop running off to get married is just about as repulsive as you can get."

"It's so unfair," she said softly. "We haven't done anything wrong."

His eyes were steady and searching. "Are you sorry?"

"Of course not. But you seem to be."

"I'm not sorry. Maybe I should be, but I'm not."

Their tension eased as each looked into the other's eyes and saw only love.

That afternoon they set up camp on a crescent-shaped white-sand beach tucked into a secluded cove. Dash showed her how to chip fist-sized oysters from the rocks with a hammer and chisel. They squeezed fresh lime juice over them and ate them raw.

It was too chilly for swimming, but Honey insisted on wading, and afterward Dash warmed her feet between his thighs. They made love to the sound of the surf.

The following night they took a room in a small hotel so they could bathe in warm water. After Honey discovered the pleasures of showering together, she went on tiptoe to whisper what she wanted to do to him.

"Are you sure?" he asked, his voice husky.

"Oh, yes. I'm sure, all right."

This time, she was the one who led him to the bed.

The next day they drove deep into the desert and pitched camp. She saw the contorted trunks of elephant trees and granite boulders sculpted by the wind into fearful shapes. Stretches of cardon cactus with vultures perched in their upthrust arms were etched in stark relief against the sky. That evening as they sat around the small fire Dash had made, she watched with apprehension while the sun faded.

"I don't know if I'm going to like this."

"You haven't seen the stars until you've seen them from the desert."

The sun dipped beneath the horizon and a great swarm of birds flew up. She caught her breath. "How beautiful. I've never seen so many birds."

He chuckled. "Those are bats, sweetheart."

She shuddered and he drew her down beside him on the sleeping bag he had unfolded. "Nature isn't prettied up here. That's why I like it. This is life stripped down to its bare bones. Don't ever be afraid of it."

Gradually, she relaxed as she lay on his shoulder and he covered her breast with his palm. The desert was alive with night sounds. Time slipped by as one star after another poked through the sky. Without any city lights to blur their brilliance, she felt as if she were seeing stars for the first time.

Slowly she came to understand what he meant. Everything was so elemental that the two of them seemed to have been peeled bare until nothing was left separating them. No subterfuge, no secrets.

"When we get back, Honey, it's not going to be easy. I just hope you're tough enough to take it."

She propped herself up on one elbow and gazed down at his familiar, beloved face. "Both of us know I'm tough enough," she said softly. "But are you?"

She could almost see him withdrawing from her, and the closeness between them dissolved.

"That's ridiculous." He angled up until he was sitting on the sleeping bag, his back toward her.

Perhaps it was the spell cast by the desert, but she felt as if a blindfold had been pulled away from her eyes. She could finally see him clearly—not just what he wanted her to see, but everything there was. The vision scared her, but his love had given her courage so she sat up and gently touched his back. "Dash, it's way past time for you to finish growing up."

His muscles stiffened beneath her hand. "What are you talking about?"

Now that she had begun this, she didn't want to finish it. What if she was wrong? Why did she think she knew things about him that the grown women he'd married didn't? And then she reminded herself that those grown women had all lost him.

Getting on her knees, she moved around so that she could see his face. "You have to accept the fact that this marriage is the end of the line for you. And you're not going to get out of it by conveniently tumbling into another woman's bed just so I'll divorce you."

His eyes narrowed, and he shot up from the sleeping bag. "You're not making one bit of sense."

"Bull. You've been using your zipper as an escape hatch since the first time you got married. Your other wives let you get away with it, but I won't." Her heart began to thud, but she'd gone too far to back down, and she rose to stand beside him. "I'm telling you right now that if I find you in bed with another woman, I might take a gun to you, I might take a gun to her, but I'm not divorcing you."

"That's the stupidest thing I ever heard you say! You're practically giving me permission to be unfaithful to you."

"I'm just telling you how it is."

"See, this is exactly what I was afraid of." His speech grew choppy, a clear sign that he was agitated. "You're too young. You don't know the first thing about being married. No woman with half a brain in her head tells her husband something like this."

"I just did." She bit down on her bottom lip to keep it from trembling. "I'm not divorcing you, Dash. No matter how many women you sleep with."

Even in the firelight she could see that his face had grown

ruddy with anger. "You're just plain stupid, you know that?"

Some of her fear began to slip away, and she gazed at him with wonder. "I'm really scaring you, aren't I?"

He scoffed at her. "I'm not scared. Hell, no. It's just hard to believe how stupid you are."

She pushed some more. "I can't do anything about the way you grew up. Those welfare people shifted you from one family to another, not me."

"That doesn't have anything to do with it."

"I'm not going to disappear on you like those families did. You can love me as much as you want, and nothing bad's going to happen. I'm your wife for the rest of your life, and no matter how hard you try, there isn't anything you can do to drive me away."

She could see him trying to find a way out. He even opened his mouth to retort, but then a great stillness came over him. Reaching out, she closed her hand over his.

The cactus creaked in the night wind. He spoke softly, still not looking at her. "You really mean it, don't you?"

"I really mean it."

He gazed at her, and even though he cleared his throat, his voice was husky with emotion. "You're the damnedest, most aggravating female I've ever met."

At first she thought it was a trick of the firelight, but then she knew it was no trick at all. Dash Coogan had tears in his eyes.

The
Drop
1989-1990

19

"Do you still feel bitter toward Dash and Honey?"

The *Beau Monde* reporter crossed her legs as she asked the question and regarded Eric through the red metal frames of her glasses. Laurel Kreuger reminded him of a Gap ad. She had a New York intellectual look—slim and attractive with short no-fuss hair and minimal makeup. Her clothes were casual and oversized: turtleneck, baggy khaki trousers, boots, a Soviet army watch.

A *Beau Monde* cover story was worth some inconvenience, but she had been interviewing Eric on and off for several days; it was Sunday, his only day off, and he was getting tired of it. Trying to channel his restlessness, he rose from one of the hotel penthouse's two facing couches and wandered over to the window, where he lit a cigarette and gazed down at Central Park. The trees were still bare of leaves, and their branches whipped in the March wind. He felt a momentary nostalgia for California, even though he'd only been away for a month.

He finally replied to her question. "Dash and Honey got married at the end of eighty-three, more than five years ago. I've been too busy since then to give it much thought. Besides, I was basically already off the show when it happened."

As he exhaled, the smoke spread skeletal fingers against the glass, blurring but not quite obscuring his reflection. His face seemed both sparer and harder than it had been during his years on the Coogan show, although it had lost none of its male beauty. If anything, the sullen, brooding quality he had exhibited in his twenties had, in his thirties, matured

Susan Elizabeth Phillips

into a dark sexuality that made the alienated antiheroes he frequently played on-screen so dangerously compelling.

The Manhattan Sunday traffic crept by far below as the reporter continued her probing. "Regardless of the fact that you were no longer a regular on the Coogan show, you were certainly outspoken at the time."

He drifted back over to the couch where he had been sitting facing her. "A lot of us were. If you'll remember, we had four seasons of that show in the can, and the producers were just getting ready to put it up for syndication. We were all expecting to make a lot of money on that deal. When news of Dash and Honey's marriage broke, it went right down the toilet. Ross Bachardy had to give the show away."

"That sounds bitter to me."

"Money's money." He sank back onto the striped cushions. "If I'd known what was going to happen with my career, I wouldn't have worried."

"Apparently being nominated for this year's Best Actor Oscar changes one's perspective."

"Not to mention one's bank account."

"So you decided to forgive the lovebirds their transgressions?"

"Something like that."

"Do you still talk to either one of them?"

"I was never close to either Dash or Honey. I speak to Liz Castleberry every few months."

"Coogan still shows up once in a while in commercials and doing guest shots, but Honey's pretty much a mystery lady," Laurel said. "Occasionally somebody will spot her on the Pepperdine campus taking a class, but other than that, she doesn't seem to leave their ranch very much."

"A major waste of talent. She never had any idea how good she was. Still, I'm not surprised she's made herself scarce. The press beat up on her pretty badly."

"She lied about her age for so long that no one believed her when she finally told the truth. The fact that people thought she was seventeen instead of twenty when she and Coogan ran off made it even worse."

He stabbed his cigarette into the ashtray next to him.

"Ross Bachardy was the one who concealed her age, not Honey."

"You sound like you're defending her."

"In some ways, she got a bum rap. In other ways, she and Dash screwed over a lot of people's futures."

"But not yours."

"Not mine."

She glanced at the notebook in her lap. "You've been getting some heady press lately. Gene Siskel said he expects you to be the premier actor of the nineties."

"I appreciate the vote of confidence, but predictions like that are a bit premature."

"You're only thirty-one years old. You've got a lot of time to prove the critics right."

"Or wrong."

"You don't believe that, do you?"

"No, I don't believe that."

"You certainly are self-confident. Is that why you decided to come to New York to do *Macbeth?*" She glanced down at her tape recorder to make certain the cassette wasn't running out.

He put his finger to his lips. "The Scottish play."

She regarded him quizzically.

"Actors consider it bad luck to refer to this play by its title. It's an old theatrical superstition."

Her mouth gave a wry twist. "Somehow I don't think you're the superstitious type."

"We have another two weeks before we finish our run, and I'm not taking any unnecessary chances, especially in a production this risky."

"I'll say it's risky. Casting you and Nadia Evans, two of the screen's reigning sex symbols, as Lord and Lady Macbeth was hardly conventional. The critics walked into the theater with their fangs bared. Both of you could have fallen on your faces."

"But we didn't."

"It's the sexiest production of *Mac*—er the Scottish play I've ever seen."

"Sexy's easy. It's all that blood and guts stuff that's hard."

She laughed, and a current of sexual chemistry sparked between them. It wasn't the first time it had happened, but once again he dismissed the idea of taking her to bed. It was more than the AIDS crisis that had made him selective about his bed partners. His first year with Lilly, when he had tried so hard to establish real sexual intimacy with her, had stripped him of his ability to enjoy sex for its own sake. He no longer went to bed with women he didn't like, and he definitely didn't go to bed with members of the press.

"You don't give a lot away, do you, Eric?"

He reached for his cigarettes, stalling for time. "What do you mean?"

"I've been interviewing you for several days, and I still don't have the foggiest notion what makes you tick. You're probably the most closed person I've ever met. And I don't just mean the way you dodge personal questions about your divorce or your past. You don't ever let anything slip, do you?"

"If I could be any tree in the world, I'd be an oak."

She laughed. "I must admit you've surprised me. Tell me why—"

But before she could begin another line of questioning, the door of the penthouse burst open and Rachel Dillon charged in. Her dark, tangled hair flew back from a small, delicate face whose soft features were marred only by a smear of chocolate near her mouth and a round Band-Aid plunked at the center of her forehead. Along with purple jeans and pink high-top sneakers, she wore a Roger Rabbit sweatshirt accessorized with a cast-off rhinestone necklace that had belonged to her mother. She was six weeks shy of her fifth birthday.

"Daddy!" She squealed with delight as if she hadn't seen him in weeks when, in fact, they had only been separated for a few hours. Throwing out her arms and nearly sending a vase of silk flowers toppling in the process, she raced toward him.

"Daddy, guess what we saw?"

She didn't notice the copy of the Sunday *Times* that lay on the floor directly in her path. Rachel never noticed any obstacles between herself and what she wanted.

"What did you see?" With a well-practiced motion, he swept her up just as she slid on the papers, catching her before she could bang her head on the nearby coffee table. She threw her arms around his neck, not out of gratitude for being rescued from potential disaster but because she always gave him crushing bear hugs after even the shortest separations.

"You guess, Daddy."

He drew her wiggling, energy-charged form into his lap and breathed in her particular strawberry scent of little-girl's hair faintly overlaid with sweat, since Rachel never walked when she could run. A panda-shaped barrette dangled from the very end of a dark brown lock. While he gave her question serious consideration, he slipped it off and set it on the end table. Rachel's barrettes were everywhere. He'd even pulled one out of his pocket in the middle of a press conference thinking it was his cigarette lighter.

"You saw a giraffe or Madonna."

She giggled. "No, silly. Daddy, we saw a man do peepee on the sidewalk."

"And that's what we love about the Big Apple," he replied dryly.

Rachel nodded her head vigorously. "Daddy, he did. Right on the sidewalk."

"Your lucky day." He gently touched the Band-Aid on her forehead. "How's your owie?"

But Rachel refused to be distracted. "Daddy, even Becca the goody-goody looked."

"Did she now." Eric's eyes grew soft, and he gazed across the room toward Rachel's twin sister Rebecca, who had just come through the door and was holding hands with Carmen, the girls' nanny. She gave him her sweet smile. He winked at her over the top of her sister's head in the secret signal they had developed. *Rachel got here first as usual, but she'll soon be bored, and then you and I can settle in for a nice long cuddle.*

"Daddy, did Mommy call on the telephone?" Rachel bumped his chin with the top of her head as she spun around. "Daddy, she said she'd call me today."

"Tonight, honey. You know she always calls at bedtime on Fridays."

Growing bored right on schedule, Rachel bounced off his lap and raced over to her nanny to grab her hand away from Becca. "Come on, Carmen. You said we could do finger paints." Before she left for the bedroom, she turned back to her sister. "Becca, don't be mushing with Daddy all day, you pokey. After me and Carmen finish, I'm gonna show you how to tie your shoe." Her face grew stern. "And this time you better do it right."

Eric resisted the urge to leap in and protect his fragile, damaged daughter from her domineering sister. Rachel was impatient with Becca's slowness, but she was also big-hearted and fiercely protective of her. Although he had discussed her sister's Down syndrome with her as soon as she was old enough to understand, she refused to accept Becca's slowness and was merciless in her insistence that she keep up. Maybe in part because of her unrelenting demands, Becca was progressing more rapidly than the doctors had expected.

Eric knew that, despite public perception, children born with Down syndrome were not all the same. They ranged from being mildly to moderately retarded, with a wide variation in mental and physical abilities. The extra forty-seventh chromosome that caused Rebecca's Down syndrome had left her mildly retarded, but there was no reason to believe she couldn't live a full and useful life.

As Rachel disappeared, Becca came toward him, her thumb in her mouth. The girls were fraternal twins instead of identical ones, but despite Becca's slightly slanted eyelids and the gently depressed bridge of her nose, they still bore a strong resemblance to each other and to him. Smoothly extracting her thumb, he gathered her into his arms and kissed her forehead. "Hi, sweetheart. How's Daddy's girl?"

"Becca is boo-tee-full."

He smiled and hugged her. "You certainly are."

"Daddy boo-tee-full, too." Becca's speech was slower than Rachel's, full of word omissions and sound substitutions. Although it was difficult for strangers to understand her, Eric had no trouble.

"Thanks, champ."

As she settled back against his chest, a deep sensation of peace came over him, just as it always did when he held her. Although he could never have explained it to anyone, he felt as if Becca were the universe's special gift to him, the only absolutely perfect thing in his life. He had always feared himself around the defenseless, but protecting this fragile child had begun to remove that haunting burden. In a way that he didn't entirely understand, the gift of Rebecca had let him atone for what he had done to Jason.

He had gotten so wrapped up in his daughters that he had nearly forgotten Laurel Kreuger, who was avidly taking in this scene of domesticity. Although he had never made any attempt to hide Becca's condition, he hated exposing his children to the press, and he absolutely forbade having them photographed. Even though it wasn't Laurel's fault the children had come back early from their outing, he resented this intrusion into his privacy.

"That's it for today, Laurel," he said abruptly. "I have some business to attend to this afternoon."

"We were scheduled for another half hour," Laurel protested.

"I didn't know that the girls would be back so soon."

"Do you always drop everything for them?" Her question held the faintly judgmental undertone of someone who has never been a parent.

"Always. Nothing in my life—not *Beau Monde,* not even my career, is as important as my daughters." It was the most revealing statement he had made to her since their interviews began, but he could see that she didn't believe him. Despite the fact that she had been dismissed, she made no move to gather up her tape recorder or notebook.

"You and your ex-wife have joint custody, don't you? I'm surprised you didn't leave the girls with her for the past few months instead of uprooting them by bringing them all the way across the country."

"Are you?"

She waited for him to explain, but he remained silent. He had no intention of letting her know that Lilly was incapable of dealing with the girls for very long. In theory, the girls were supposed to divide their time equally between their parents, but in practice they were with him ninety per cent of the time.

Lilly loved both her daughters, but for some reason that he couldn't fathom, she blamed herself for Becca's condition and her guilt made her ineffectual at meeting her daughter's special needs. In some ways the situation was even worse with Rachel. For all Lilly's intelligence, she seemed to lack the resources to deal with her strong-willed daughter, and Rachel rode roughshod over her.

Laurel continued to watch him cuddle Becca. "You're going to spoil your reputation as the last of the tough guys. Although that might not be a bad idea. Some critics call it your fatal flaw. They say that no matter what role you play, you always seem alienated."

"That's crap."

"Not according to a recent critical analysis of your work." She flipped over some pages in her notebook. "I quote, 'Eric Dillon's solitary performances mark him as one of society's loners. He is an actor who lives on the edge: sexually dangerous, permanently alienated, a voluntary discard. We feel his pain, but only as much as he allows. He gives us a twisted sort of brilliance, hard and difficult to crack. Ultimately, Dillon is gorgeous, hostile, and ruined.'"

He shot up from the couch, his daughter caught firmly in his arms. "I said that's enough for today."

Becca looked up at him, her eyes widening with alarm. He forced his muscles to relax and rubbed her arm. Then he glared at the reporter.

Apparently Laurel decided she'd pushed him far enough because she immediately gathered up her things and stuffed them into her tote bag. When she was on her way to the door, however, she hesitated.

"I have a job to do, Eric. Maybe after all this is over, we could—You know. Have a drink or something."

"Or something," he said coldly.

After Laurel had left, he soothed Becca, then sent her off to play with her sister while he made some phone calls. When he was done, he went into the spacious room the girls shared and nodded at Carmen so she could slip away to take a much-needed break. Crossing to the end of the room, he observed Becca sitting at the low table patiently finger-painting red circles on white butcher paper.

Transporting the girls across the country for three months hadn't been easy. The hotel room was set up with their play equipment, along with multicolored plastic milk crates filled with toys and books. He'd arranged for a special school and a speech therapist for Rebecca and put Rachel into a private nursery school. Still, he believed the advantages of keeping the girls with him outweighed the disadvantages of uprooting them.

Rachel, growing bored with finger-painting, began to practice her cartwheels. There was too much furniture in the room for gymnastics, and he waited for the inevitable, which wasn't long in coming. As she threw herself over, she caught her heel on the corner of one of the milk crates and gave a howl of outrage.

He squatted down. "Here, let me rub it."

She glared at him, transferring the sole responsibility for her gymnastic failure onto him.

"Daddy, you ruined it! I was doing it right till you came in! It's all your fault."

He lifted one eyebrow, letting her know that he had her number.

She was one of the few people in the world who didn't have any qualms about facing him down and she returned him raised eyebrow for raised eyebrow. "Cartwheels are stupid."

"Uh-huh," he replied noncommittally. "Doing them in here isn't too smart, either."

He straightened and walked over to stand behind Becca, brushing his hand along the side of her neck. "Good work, champ. Give it to me when it's dry, and I'll hang it in my dressing room at the theater." He turned back to Rachel. "Let me see your painting."

She regarded him sullenly. "It's stupid. I ripped it up."

"I think somebody needs a nap."

"Daddy, I'm not cranky. You always say I need a nap when you think I'm being cranky."

"My mistake."

"Daddy, only babies take naps."

"And you certainly aren't a baby."

Becca piped up from the table. "Me want to show Patches Becca's painting, Daddy. Me want to show Patches."

Rachel's crankiness instantly vanished. She jumped up and raced over to grab Eric's leg. "Yeah, Daddy! Let Patches play with us. Please."

Both girls regarded him with eyes so full of entreaty that he laughed. "Couple of con artists. All right. But Patches can't stay too long. He told me he has to perform some major carnage this afternoon. Not only that, he has a meeting with his agent."

Rachel giggled and ran for her bureau, where she quickly pulled open a drawer and extracted a pair of her navy blue tights. She raced back to him, the tights extended, and then rushed for the Band-Aid box.

"Not a Band-Aid again," he protested as he sat down in one of the small chairs, wrapped the navy tights around his head, and then knotted the legs to the side in the manner of a pirate's scarf. "You're going to end up with a father who's lost half of his right eyebrow. Let's just pretend."

"Daddy, you got to do the Band-Aid," Rachel insisted, just as she always did when he protested. "You can't be Patches without a patch, can he, Becca?"

"Becca want to see Patches."

He grumbled as he peeled the wrapper from the adhesive strip and secured it at a diagonal across his right eye, from the inside corner of his eyebrow to the outer edge of his cheekbone. Becca's thumb crept toward her mouth. Rachel leaned forward in anticipation. They watched in silent fascination, waiting for that magical transformation when their daddy changed into Patches the Pirate. He took his time. No matter how humble his audience, that special moment of transformation was sacred to him, the time when the boundary between illusion and reality grew indistinct.

He breathed once. Twice.

Rachel squealed with delight as he squinted his eye beneath the Band-Aid, crooked one edge of his mouth, and completed the transfiguration.

"Well, now, and what do we 'ave 'ere? Two bloodthirsty wenches, if me eyes ain't deceivin' me." He gave them his fiercest glower, and was rewarded with piercing squeals. Rachel began to run away from him, as she always did. He jumped up from the small chair and quickly scooped her off her feet.

"Not so fast, me pretty. I've been lookin' for some 'earty mates to carry off on me pirate ship." His eyes traveled from Rachel, squealing with delight and squirming beneath his arm, to Becca, watching gleefully from her seat at the table. He shook his head. "Nah. On second thought, I'll be throwin' you back. The two of you look puny." He set Rachel down and, arms akimbo, regarded her ferociously.

Rachel immediately grew indignant. "We're not puny, Patches. Feel this." She raised her arm and made a muscle. "Becca, show Patches your muscle."

Becca did as she was told. Eric dutifully leaned down and examined both sets of thin little arms. As always, the fragile delicacy of their bones struck fear into his heart, but he hid it and whistled with admiration. "Stronger than you look, the both of you. Still . . ." He fixed Becca with a dark scowl. "Are you good with a rapier, lass?"

"He means a sword," Rachel whispered loudly to her sister.

Becca nodded. "Vewwy, vewwy good."

"Patches, me too," Rachel squealed, "I'm great with a

rapier." She launched them into the part of the game she liked the best. "And I can cut off a bad guy's head in a single swoop."

"Can you now?"

"I can even open his stomach and let his blood and guts and brains spill out without blinkin' me eye."

Eric was noted for his faultless concentration, but he nearly lost it as Rachel tried, for the first time, to copy his accent. He had invented the rules of this particular game, however, and he checked any display of amusement. Instead, he regarded them doubtfully.

"I don't know. Raidin' and plunderin' is serious work. I need somebody with a strong 'eart fightin' at me side. The truth of it is . . ." He sank down into the chair next to Becca and whispered conspiratorially. "I'm not too fond of the sight of blood."

Becca reached out and patted his shoulder. "Poor Patches."

Impish lights sparked Rachel's eyes. "Patches, what kind of pirate can't stand blood?"

"Lots of 'em. It's a 'azard of the occupation."

"Patches, me and Becca love blood, don't we, Becca? If you let us come with you, we'll protect you."

"Me protect Patches," Becca offered, winding her arms around his neck.

He shook his head doubtfully. "Mighty dangerous, it is. We'll be raidin' ships full of lions with jaws powerful enough to eat up little girls." They listened wide-eyed as he described the perils of their raid. He'd learned from experience that they were especially taken with cargoes of exotic animals, but any reference to either robbers or big dogs frightened them.

Eventually Rachel spoke the words she said each time. "Patches, can my mommy come with us?"

He paused for only a moment. "Is she strong?"

"Oh, yes. Very strong."

"She's not afraid of blood, is she?"

Rachel shook her head. "She loves blood."

"Then we'll take her right along with us."

The girls giggled their pleasure and his heart swelled. In fantasy at least, he could give them the mother who was so frequently absent from their daily lives and so very ineffectual when she was present.

Then Patches the Pirate settled down to spin magic yarns of sea voyages, tales complete with valiant little girls sailing the seven seas and vanquishing all their enemies. They were tales of bravery and determination, tales where little girls were expected to stand their ground right along with the men and fight to the end.

Spellbound, the children clung to every word. As they listened, they heard only the rich bounty of their father's imagination. They were too young to understand that they were watching the man who was perhaps the best actor of his generation play the only role of his career in which he was alienated from absolutely no one.

20

"Did Daddy win?" Rachel raced into the living room, her red nightgown flying behind her, bare feet slapping the black and white marble floor.

Lilly reluctantly drew her attention from the television entombed in a pebbled gray cabinet. She had just finished redecorating the Coldwater Canyon home she and Eric had once shared. The doorways were now framed by Ionic columns topped with broken pediments, and the neo-Roman furniture was upholstered in white canvas. The light gray walls served as a background for first-century marble sculptures, French torchère lamps, and a wall-sized surrealistic canvas of a supersonic jet flying through the center of an enormous red apple. At first she had adored the new decor, but now she had begun to think so much neo-classicism was too cold.

"Don't run, Rachel," she admonished her daughter. "Why aren't you asleep? It's after nine. I hope you didn't wake Becca."

"I want to see if Daddy winned his Oscar. And I'm scared of a thunderstorm."

Lilly looked through the windows and noticed the trees were whipping in the wind. Southern California was having a terrible drought, and she suspected this storm would pass over without a drop falling as the others had, but she knew she would have trouble convincing her strong-willed daughter of that. "It's not going to rain, Rachel. It's just some wind."

Rachel gave her the mutinous look that seemed to be permanently stamped on her face. "I don' like thunderstorms."

In the background the Academy Award broadcast faded into a commercial. "There's not going to be a thunderstorm."

"Yes there is."

"No, there isn't. We're having a drought, for God's sake."

"Yes there is."

"Dammit, Rachel, that's enough!"

Rachel glared at her and stomped her foot. "I hate you!"

Lilly squeezed her eyes shut and wished Rachel would disappear. She couldn't handle her as Eric did. Yesterday when she'd picked the girls up at their father's, Rachel had started to go outside in her socks. When Eric had ordered her to put shoes on, she'd screamed that she hated him, but it hadn't seemed to bother him. He'd glared right back at her and said, "Tough luck, kiddo. You're still going to wear your shoes."

Lilly knew that she would have given in. It wasn't that she didn't love her daughter. At night when Rachel was asleep, Lilly could stand forever by her bed and simply gaze at her. But during the daytime, she felt so incompetent. She was like her own mother, a woman who simply wasn't maternal. Her mother had left Lilly to be raised by her father, and Lilly was doing the same with her daughters. Sometimes it was better that way.

Even so, she found herself resenting Eric's relationship with the girls. She knew they loved him more than they loved her, but being a parent was easier for him. He never lost his temper with Rachel, and Becca's condition didn't terrify him the way it terrified her.

"Look, there's Daddy!" Rachel squealed, her quarrel with her mother temporarily forgotten. "And Nadia. She's real nice, Mommy. Not like when her and Daddy was in *Macbeth* and she screamed all the time. She gave me and Becca Gummi Bears."

The camera was panning the front rows of the star-studded audience that was packed into the auditorium of the Dorothy Chandler Pavilion. Eric's date for the Academy Awards was Nadia Evans, his *Macbeth* costar. Lilly was jealous, although she knew she had no right to be. Eric had been a faithful husband; it was her infidelities that had ended their marriage.

Even after Eric had discovered she was having an affair with Aaron Blake, one of Hollywood's more exciting young actors, he hadn't insisted on a divorce. But Lilly hated the frustrations of trying to be a wife and mother, she hated the relentless intimacy of the marriage bed, and she hadn't seen any point in postponing the inevitable. Eric had never loved her—she knew he wouldn't have married her if she hadn't been pregnant—but he had treated her well, and having been the child of a hostile divorce, she wanted to retain at least the semblance of an amicable relationship with him.

Lilly studied Nadia Evans as the camera lingered on her and tried to take some satisfaction from the fact that she was just as beautiful as the actress. She was even slimmer now than she had been before her pregnancy, and she loved the deeper hollows in her cheeks. Recently she had been wearing her silver-blond hair in a ballerina's knot low on her neck to further emphasize her facial bones.

The Best Actor nominees were read off, and Lilly's resentment settled in deeper. She was a child of Hollywood, and every part of her yearned to be at his side now, sharing this moment.

"Mommy, do you think Daddy will win?"

"We'll see."

Rachel, for once motionless, stood in the center of the black and white marble floor and gazed at the television.

"And the Oscar goes to . . ."

Lilly snatched the remote control and punched up the volume.

"Eric Dillon for *Small Cruelties!*"

Rachel giggled and clapped her hands. "Mommy, he winned! Daddy winned!"

Lilly sagged back into the couch. This was what she got for divorcing him. She should have been the one sitting with him when he won, not Nadia Evans. If only they were still married, this would have been her night of triumph, too.

But it was too late for regrets. She remembered his icy fury when he had discovered she was having an affair and wondered what he would have done if he had known that Aaron Blake wasn't the only lover she had taken while they were married. Her stomach coiled in self-disgust. Every time she took a lover, she thought he would be the one who could fill up the empty spaces in her life. But it never happened. The only man who had given her lasting happiness was her father.

Nadia kissed Eric. He got up from his seat and took a hop step down the aisle, stopping as people rose to thump him on the back. When he got to the stage and received the Oscar, he turned to the audience and grinned, holding the gold statue high over his head.

The audience finally quieted, and he began to speak. "This shouldn't mean so much, but it does . . ."

She couldn't watch any more, and she snatched the remote control and punched the power button.

"I want to see Daddy!" Rachel protested.

"You'll see him tomorrow. It's bedtime."

"But I want to watch. Why did you turn off the TV?"

"I've got a headache."

A clap of thunder boomed outside the window, bringing noise but no rain. Rachel's finger plopped into her mouth, a clear sign that she was upset.

"Tuck me in, Mommy."

As Lilly gazed down at Rachel, her heart filled with love for this child who so seldom asked for any affection from her. They walked down the hallway together, temporarily at peace. She paused for a moment outside the door of Becca's room and gazed inside at the still little bundle lying under the covers.

What if that damaged child were punishment for her own sins? She tried to redirect the agonizing path her thoughts always took when she looked at Becca and found herself wondering what her life would be like if she hadn't let Eric talk her out of the abortion. But as she turned away from the room, she knew that no matter how ineffectual and resentful these children made her feel, she didn't regret having given birth to them.

They passed the group of enlarged photographs she had taken before she'd married Eric and abandoned her cameras. She had always meant to do portraits of the girls, but somehow she'd never gotten around to it. They entered Rachel's bedroom, which was decorated in pink and lavender hearts, although the feminine ambience was spoiled somewhat by Rachel's Hulk Hogan posters.

Rachel climbed on the bed, her small round bottom sticking up in the air for a moment before she slipped beneath the covers. Lilly was arranging them over her when another clap of thunder rattled the windows.

"Mommy!"

"It's all right. It's just thunder."

"Mommy, would you sleep with me?"

"I'm not ready to go to bed yet."

Rachel looked mulish. "Daddy lets me sleep with him. Daddy sleeps with me and cuddles me all night long."

Lilly froze. A painful, high-pitched noise began to whine in her head, gradually growing more shrill. She could barely summon the breath to speak. "What—What did you say?"

"Daddy . . . He sleeps with me if I'm scared. Mommy, what's wrong?"

The noise in Lilly's head became a great whirlpool sucking her into its center. The whirlpool spun her faster, and the noise shrieked in her brain until she felt as if she were coming apart. She collapsed on the side of the bed and tried to keep from fainting.

Rachel's voice called to her from far away. "Mommy? Mommy?"

The room began to settle around her, and she tried to tell herself there was nothing in Rachel's innocently spoken words to have inspired such a deep, unreasonable fear, but she felt as if she had been threatened at the most fundamental level of her existence.

Her fingers clasped the edge of the cover as she slowly pushed out the words. "Does Daddy sleep with you very often?"

Another clap of thunder rattled the windows. Rachel gazed out with trepidation. "Mommy, I want you to sleep with me."

Lilly tried to keep her voice from trembling, but the coldness in her limbs made that impossible. "Tell me about Daddy."

Rachel's eyes didn't move from the window. "Thunder's scary. Daddy says I don't have to be scared. His hair tickles."

Lilly's heart began to race so fast that she could barely breathe. "What—what do you mean his hair tickles?"

"It tickles my nose, Mommy."

"The hair on his—on his head?"

"No, silly. His tummy." She pressed her hand to the center of her chest. "Here."

Lilly's knuckles had turned white from gripping the edge of the cover. "Doesn't Daddy—Well, of course he does." She tried to force a laugh through her stiff lips, but it emerged as a sob. "Of course Daddy has his—his pajamas on when you get in bed with him, doesn't he?"

Rachel once again looked toward the window. "I'm scared of boomers, Mommy."

"Listen to me, Rachel!" Her voice rose to a shriek. "Does Daddy wear his pajamas when you get in bed with him?"

Rachel's forehead puckered. "Daddy doesn't wear jammies, Mommy."

Oh, God. Dear God. She wanted to run from the room, run from the awful black whirlpool sucking her toward the unspeakable. Her teeth began to chatter. "Does Daddy—Has he ever . . . touched you, Rachel?"

Rachel's thumb crept into her mouth and she nodded.

Blood no longer flowed through her veins, but knife-sharp slivers of ice. She gripped her daughter's shoulders. "Where does he touch you?"

"Becca's asleep."

She wanted to disappear, to jump from her own skin and from the monstrous whirlpool that seemed about to carry her away, but she couldn't abandon her daughter. "Think very carefully, Rachel. Has Daddy ever touched you—" *No! Don't say it. You're not allowed to tell.* "Has Daddy—" Her voice broke on a sob.

Rachel's eyes were wide with alarm. "Mommy, what's wrong?"

The words spilled out in a rush. "Has he ever . . . touched you . . . between your . . . legs?"

Rachel nodded again and rolled over, facing the window. "Go away, Mommy."

Lilly began to sob. "Oh, baby." She pulled her small daughter into her arms, covers and all. "Oh, my sweet poor baby."

"Mommy, stop! You're scaring me!"

Lilly had to ask the final question, the unspeakable one. *Don't let it be true. Please don't let it be true.* She drew back enough to see her daughter's face, no longer rebellious but pale with apprehension. Lilly's tears dropped onto the satin binding of the cover.

"Did Daddy—Oh, Rachel, sweetheart. . . . Did Daddy ever show you—show you his penis?"

Wide-eyed and frightened, Rachel nodded. "Mommy, I'm scared."

"Of course you are. Oh, my poor, poor baby. I won't let him hurt you. I won't ever let him hurt you again."

Lilly rocked her and crooned, and as she clasped her daughter's small body to her breast, she made a vow to protect her. She might have failed Rachel in some ways, but she wouldn't fail her in this.

"Mommy, you're scaring me. Mommy, why are you calling me Lilly?"

"What, sweetheart?"

"You said Lilly. That's your name. That's not my name. You said 'poor Lilly.' "

"Oh, I don't think so."

"You did, Mommy. 'Poor Lilly.' "

"Go to sleep, sweetheart. Shh. . . . Mommy's here."

"I want my daddy."

"It's all right, sweetheart. I won't ever let him hurt you again."

Eric didn't return home until seven that morning. There had been interviews, photographers, three different parties ending with a buffet breakfast. Nadia had finally given out at four, but it was the biggest night of his life, and he hadn't been ready for it to end.

He stepped out of the limo onto the cobbled entryway that led to his house. His collar was open, his bow tie undone, and the jacket of his tuxedo was draped over his arm. In his hand the gold statue of Oscar glimmered in the early morning sun. He had the feeling that everything in his life had come together. He had his work and his daughters, and for the first time since he was fifteen, he didn't hate himself.

The limo pulled away, and he saw Lilly standing by her car waiting for him. His euphoria faded. Why couldn't she have let him have one day to enjoy his success? But as she came toward him, his annoyance was replaced with alarm. Lilly was always meticulous about her appearance, but her clothes were wrinkled and her hair had come undone from its careful ballerina's knot.

He hurried over to her, noticing that she had eaten off her lipstick and old mascara had smudged under her eyes. "What's wrong? Is something wrong with the girls?"

Her face tightened, looking pinched and ugly. "Something's wrong, all right, you perverted bastard."

"Lilly . . ."

As he reached out to take her arm, she jerked away, snarling at him like a cornered animal. "Don't touch me! Don't ever touch me!"

"Maybe you'd better come inside," he said, forcing his voice to sound calm.

Without giving her a chance to refuse, he went to the front door and unlocked it. She followed him into the house, moving through the foyer and off to the living room on the left. Her breathing was heavy and agitated.

The room was sparsely furnished, with white walls, pale wood, and some comfortable sofas upholstered in light, nubby fabric. He laid his coat and the Oscar on a chair that sat near a rough-hewn cupboard displaying baskets, Mexican tinware, and figures of saints. The early morning sun streamed through the windows, casting rectangles of light on the floor. He walked into one of them.

"Let's get this over with so I can go to bed. What is it this time? Do you need more money?"

She spun toward him, her face pale with distress, her lips quivering. Guilt replaced his annoyance, the guilt he always felt when he was with her because she wasn't a bad person, yet he hadn't been able to love her the way she needed.

He softened. "Lilly, what's wrong?"

Her voice broke. "Rachel told me. Last night."

"Told you what?" His forehead puckered in alarm. "Is something wrong with Rachel?"

"You should know that better than anyone. Did you do it to Becca, too?" Her eyes filled with tears. She sagged down onto the couch, her hands crumpling into fists in her lap. "My God, I can't bear to think that you might have touched Becca, too. How could you, Eric? How could you be so sick?"

Genuine fear had begun to grip him. "What's happened? Jesus, tell me!"

"Your dirty little secret is out," she said bitterly. "Rachel told me all about it. Did you threaten her, Eric? Did you threaten to do something terrible to her if she told?"

"Told what? For God's sake, what are you talking about?"

"What you've been doing to her. She told me—She told me that you've been sexually molesting her."

"What?"

"She told me everything."

A deathlike stillness came over him. His voice was a soft rasp. "You'd better explain what you're talking about. Start at the beginning. I want to hear everything."

Lilly's eyes narrowed with hatred. Her speech was rushed and shrill. "Last night I was tucking Rachel into bed. There was some thunder, and she asked me to get in bed with her. When I said no, she told me that you let her sleep with you."

"Sure I let her sleep with me when she's scared. What's wrong with that?"

"She said you don't wear pajamas."

"I never have. You know that. When the girls are around, I sleep in a pair of briefs."

"That's sick, Eric. Letting her in bed with you."

His alarm was changing into anger. "There's nothing sick about it. What the hell's wrong with you?"

"So much righteous indignation," she scoffed. "Well, don't bother, because she told me all of it, you bastard." Lilly's face twisted until it was ugly with hatred. "She said she's seen your cock."

"She probably has. Christ, Lilly. Sometimes they walk in on me when I'm getting dressed. I don't go out of my way to flaunt myself in front of them, but I've never made a big deal out of it."

"You bastard. You think you've got an answer for everything. Well, that's not all she said. She told me you touch her between her legs."

"You're a liar! She wouldn't say that. I've never touched her—" But he had. Of course he had. Carmen usually bathed the girls, but sometimes he did.

"Listen to me, Lilly. You're putting some kind of sick interpretation on something that's perfectly normal. I've bathed those girls on and off since they were babies. That's what Rachel was talking about. Ask her. No, we'll ask her together."

He moved toward her, ready to drag her back to her house and his daughters if necessary, but she jumped up from the couch and the fear on her face stopped him.

Her teeth were bared, her too-thin face fierce. "You're not going to get within a mile of her. I'm warning you right now, Eric. Stay away from those girls or I'll have you thrown in jail so fast your head will spin. I may not be much of a mother, but I'll do whatever I have to do to keep them safe. If I think you're posing the slightest threat to them, I'll go to the authorities. I will. I mean it. I'll keep quiet as long as you stay away, but the moment you come near those girls, you'll find this filthy perversion of yours smeared over every paper in the country."

She fled from the room.

"Lilly!" He started to go after her, but then he made himself stop. He had to pull himself together and think.

His cigarette pack was empty. Crushing it in his fist, he threw it across the room toward the fireplace. The conviction he had seen in Lilly's eyes chilled him. She truly believed what she was saying. But how could she believe he was capable of something so obscene when she knew how much he loved those girls? He began pacing the floor, trying to remember everything he had ever done with his daughters, but it was so impossible, so ridiculous.

Gradually, he grew calmer. He had to stop reacting emotionally and think logically. This was another one of Lilly's trips off the deep end, and he should be able to prove that without any difficulty. The whole thing was so patently absurd. Fathers all over the country bathed their children and took them into bed when they were frightened. His lawyer would straighten it out in no time.

"I've been taking a crash course in child sexual abuse since your phone call, Eric, and I'm afraid this may not be quite as easy as you think."

Mike Longacre leaned forward over his desk. He was in his late thirties, but thinning hair and a tendency toward pudginess made him look older. He had been Eric's lawyer through the divorce, and the men had developed a distant sort of friendship. They'd done some deep-sea fishing together, played racquetball, but they had little else in common.

Eric shot up from his chair and thrust one hand back through his hair. He hadn't had any sleep; he was running on cigarettes and adrenaline. "What do you mean it's not easy? The whole thing is incredible. I would no more harm my daughters than I'd cut off my arm. Lilly's paranoia is the danger to them, not me."

"Sexual abuse of children is a tricky area."

"Are you telling me you actually think Lilly can make this stick? I told you what she said. She obviously twisted some innocent remarks Rachel made. There's nothing more to it."

"I understand. I'm simply advising you that we have to tread carefully here. Sexual abuse of children is the one area of the law where the accused has no rights. You're guilty until proven innocent. Remember that a sickening number of these charges are true, and the court's primary concern is protecting the children. Countless fathers are molesting their daughters every day."

"But I'm not one of them! My God, my children don't need protection from me. Goddamnit, Mike, I want this thing stopped before it goes any farther."

The lawyer toyed with his gold pen. "Let me tell you a little about what can happen here. Everyone used to believe that children never lied about sexual abuse, but we've discovered that they can be coached. Let's say the mother has gotten a lousy divorce settlement. Her husband is driving a BMW and she can't pay her grocery bill. Maybe he wants to challenge the custody arrangement, or he isn't making his child support payments."

"None of this applies to Lilly. I've given her everything she's wanted."

Mike held up his hand. "For whatever reason, women frequently feel powerless in divorce cases. Maybe the kid says something that starts her thinking. She begins asking questions. 'Daddy touched you here, didn't he?' She pops a piece of candy in the kid's mouth, and when the kid says no, she hands out another piece of candy. 'Are you sure? Now think hard.' The kid is getting all this extra attention and begins to fabricate to keep Mom happy. There have even been cases where mothers have threatened to kill themselves if the children don't say what she tells them."

"Lilly wouldn't do that. She's not a monster. Jesus, she loves the girls."

There was a moment of silence in the office. "Then what's going on here, Eric?"

Eric swallowed hard and looked up at the ceiling. "I don't know. God help me, I don't know."

He turned back to the attorney, struck by a new thought. "Rachel's a hardheaded little girl. Even though she's just turned five, I don't know how much she could be influenced. We'll hire the best psychiatrists in the field. Let them talk to her."

"In theory, that's a good idea, but in practice it backfires all the time."

"I don't see how. Rachel's well adjusted. She's articulate. She's—"

"She's also a child. Listen to me, Eric. We're not dealing with an exact science. Most of the professionals who specialize in child abuse cases are well trained and competent, but it's still a relatively new discipline. Even the most capable make mistakes in judgment. There have been a lot of scary cases. For example, a little girl is given an anatomically correct male doll. She's never seen anything like this before, and she pulls on its penis. Bingo. The overzealous expert takes this as a sign of abuse. I'm not exaggerating. These things happen all the time, and there aren't any guarantees. I'm sorry. I'd like to be able to reassure you that a psychiatric exam of Rachel would exonerate you, but I simply can't. The truth is, you'll be playing Russian roulette if you press the issue."

Mike gave him a slow, steady gaze. "You also have to remember that Rebecca would be questioned. I imagine she could be influenced quite easily."

Eric squeezed his eyes shut, his flicker of hope dying. His sweet little Becca would do anything or say anything if she thought it would please.

Mike's chair squeaked as he shifted his weight. "Before you even think about challenging Lilly, you need to understand the consequences. Once she goes public with her accusations, everything happens quickly and none of it is good. The girls will be taken away from you while the investigation goes on."

"How can that happen? This is America. Don't I have any rights?"

"It's as I said. In child abuse cases you're guilty until proven innocent. The system has to work that way for protection, and the best you can hope for while the investigation goes on is supervised visitation. The investigations themselves are supposed to be kept confidential, but the girls' teachers will be questioned, friends and neighbors, all the hired help. Anyone with half a brain will be able to figure out what's going on, and since you're involved, I can guarantee it'll hit the papers long before the courts get hold of it. I don't think I need to elaborate on what being accused of child molestation will do to your career as a leading man. The public will put up with a lot, but—"

"I don't give a shit about my career!"

"You don't mean that." He held up his hand and went on. "The girls will be forced to undergo medical examinations. A series of them if this drags on."

Eric felt sick. How could he put his babies through something like that? How could he hurt them that way? They were innocents. When they were born, he had thought he had broken the cycle, but once again it had caught him up. Why did he always have to hurt the innocents?

"The examinations will prove they haven't been abused," he said.

"Maybe in an ideal world. The truth of the matter is that in the majority of cases, there isn't any physical evidence. Most sexual abuse involves fondling or oral copulation. An intact hymen is no proof that a child hasn't been molested."

Eric felt as if the walls of the office were closing in on him. He hadn't believed—He hadn't even let himself consider the possibility that he might lose his daughters. Any minute now he'd wake up, and this would only be a nightmare.

The lawyer shook his head. "The minute these charges become public, a man has a loaded gun pointed at his head. For someone who's a celebrity, it's even worse. On the positive side, I've seen some fathers go bankrupt defending themselves in these cases, and you don't have to worry about that."

Pain and frustration made Eric's voice sharp. "Is that the best you can do for hope? That I can afford to defend myself? What the fuck kind of comfort is that?"

Longacre stiffened. "It probably wasn't wise for you to have taken your daughters into bed in the first place."

Eric's rage exploded. He vaulted across the desk and grabbed the attorney by the collar of his shirt. "You son of a—"

"Eric!"

As he drew back his fist, the alarm in Longacre's eyes stopped him, and he forced himself to let go.

Mike gasped for breath. "You fool."

Eric was trembling as he pulled away. "I'm sorry. I—"

Unable to say more, he fled from the office and drove frantically to Lilly's house. He had to get to his children. But when he arrived at the house, everything was locked and the curtains were drawn.

He found the gardener working by the pool in the back. The man said Lilly had left the country. And she had taken the girls with her.

Three weeks later Eric flew to Paris, where his team of private investigators had located Lilly and the girls. As he stared blindly out the window of the taxi that was moving through the traffic on the quai de la Tournelle, he knew that the last weeks had been the longest in his life. He had smoked too much, drunk too much, and, in the wake of his Oscar triumph, been unable to concentrate on his work.

As the taxi crossed the pont de la Tournelle to the tiny Ile Saint-Louis that sat in the center of the Seine, the driver kept grinning at Eric in his rearview mirror. Eric had long ago accepted the fact that there were few places left in the world where his face wasn't recognized. He looked off to his left toward the neighboring Ile de la Cité's famous landmark, but Notre-Dame's slender spire and flying buttresses barely registered in his mind.

The Ile Saint-Louis sat between Paris's Right and Left banks where it formed the period to the Ile de la Cité's exclamation mark. The island was one of Paris's most exclusive and expensive neighborhoods and had housed a number of luminaries over the years, including Chagall and James Jones as well as current residents such as Baron Guy de Rothschild and Madame Georges Pompidou.

The taxi let Eric out in front of the address the investigators had given him, a seventeenth-century town house located on the fashionable quai d'Orléans. Across the Seine the Left Bank glimmered in the late morning light. As Eric paid the fare, he looked up toward the second floor windows and saw the draperies move. Lilly had been watching for him.

As desperately as he yearned to see his daughters, he knew the situation was too explosive for him to give in to the urge to arrive unexpectedly, and so he had called Lilly early that morning. At first she had refused to see him, but when she realized he was going to come whether she wanted him to or not, she had agreed to meet him at eleven when both girls would be gone.

The town house was built of limestone, and the intricately carved wooden front door was enameled a rich shade of blue. White shutters, their top halves open to reveal pots of trailing pink ivy geraniums, graced the long, narrow windows. He was about to lift the knocker when the door swung open and Lilly stepped out.

She looked tired and drawn, even thinner than he remembered, with faint purple smudges lodging in the hollows beneath her eyes. "I warned you to stay away," she said, hugging her arms beneath her silk blouse, although the morning was warm.

"We have to talk."

He saw a group of tourists coming toward them and turned his head away. The last thing he needed to do while he was trying to reclaim his life was sign autographs. He snatched a pair of sunglasses from the pocket of his white cotton dress shirt and shoved them on. "It's too public here. Can't we go inside?"

"I don't want you near their things."

The cruelty of her comment filled him with rage, and he wanted to strike her. Instead, he grasped her upper arm so hard that she winced and pulled her along the tree-lined quay toward a bench that faced the river.

The setting was idyllic. Tall poplars cast dappled shadows over the walk. A fisherman stood on the banks near a graceful iron light pole. A pair of lovers walked by, their bodies so intertwined it was difficult to tell where one began and the other ended.

She sat down on the iron bench and began clenching and unclenching her hands. He remained standing and stared blindly out toward the water. For the rest of his life, he would hate this beautiful city.

"I'm not giving in to your threats any longer, Lilly. I'm going public. I've decided to take my chances in court."

"You can't do that!" she cried.

"Just watch me."

He looked down at her. Her fingernails had been bitten so far down that the cuticles were bloody.

She gasped for breath as if she had been running. "The publicity will ruin your career."

"I don't care anymore!" he exclaimed. "My career doesn't mean anything without my children."

"What's the matter?" she sneered. "Can't you find anybody else who'll give you your sexual thrills?"

He grabbed her. She gasped, trying to pull away from him by cowering into the bench. His rage was a blinding white light, and he knew that if he didn't let her go, he would hurt her.

With a dark oath, he dropped her arm and whipped off his sunglasses. They snapped in his hands, and he hurled them into the Seine. "God damn you!"

"I won't let you near them!" she cried, jumping up from the bench. "I'll do whatever I have to. If you go to court or do anything to try to get them back, I'll send them underground."

He stared at her. "You'll do what?"

A pulse beat frantically in a thin blue vein near her temple. "There's an underground system that protects children when the law won't. It's illegal, but effective." Her gray eyes darkened with bitterness. "I knew you'd try to get to them, so I've learned a lot about it in the past few weeks. All I have to do is say the word, Eric, and the girls will disappear. Neither of us will have them then."

"You can't mean that. You wouldn't send them into hiding with strangers."

"The strangers won't molest them, and I'll do whatever I have to do to keep them safe." Her face sagged. He saw how tired she looked, but he felt no pity for her.

"Please," she whispered. "Don't make me send them away. They've already lost their father. Don't make them lose their mother, too."

Beneath her exhaustion he saw determination, and he knew with sickening certainty that she wasn't making an idle threat. Her conviction in his guilt was absolute.

The ball of pain spun inside him, growing larger with each revolution. "How can you believe I'd hurt my daughters?" he asked hoarsely. "What did I ever do to make you think I'm capable of something like this? Jesus, Lilly, you know how much I love them."

Tears rolled down her cheeks. "I don't know anything anymore except that I have to protect them. I'll do that, even if it means giving them up to strangers. No little girls should have to suffer what they've suffered."

She turned to leave.

He took a quick step after them, his voice raw with

desperation. "Just tell me how they're doing. Please, Lilly. At least do that for me."

She shook her head and walked away, leaving him more alone than he'd ever been in his life.

21

EXTERIOR.
PASTURE FENCE NEAR THE RANCH HOUSE—DAY

Dash and Janie are standing by the fence. Dash holds a crumpled letter in his fist.

JANIE
Did Blake write you? When's he coming home on leave?

DASH
This letter isn't from Blake. It's from your grandmother.

JANIE
(excited)
My grandmother? I didn't even know I had one of those!

DASH
Do you remember all the stuff I told you about your ma?

JANIE
(cheerfully)
I remember. You said she was the sweetest thing you'd ever met and you couldn't figure out how she gave birth to a spawn of Satan like myself.

281

DASH

She was sweet, Janie. But I also told you she was
an orphan, and that was a lie.

JANIE

A lie? Why'd you lie, Pop?

DASH

Your mama's parents kicked her out of the house
when she was only seventeen years old. They
were pretty strict people. She wasn't married.
And she was pregnant with you.

JANIE
(puzzled)
You mean you and Ma had to get married?

DASH

I married your ma because I wanted to. There
wasn't any *have* to about it.

He gazes down at the letter.

DASH

Apparently your grandfather died last year,
and your grandmother's getting old. She wants
to see you, so she hired some private detectives
to track us down. According to this letter, she'll
be here day after tomorrow.

JANIE

Wow! I can't believe this. Do you think she'll
have one of those buns on top of her head and
bake pies?

DASH

Janie, there's somethin' I got to tell you. Maybe I
should have told you a long time ago, but—I
don't know—I couldn't seem to bring myself to
do it. Now I guess I don't have any choice. Your
grandmother knows the truth, and if I don't tell
you, she will.

JANIE

You're starting to make me nervous, Pop.

DASH

I'm sorry, Janie. I don't know how else to say
this but straight out. Your Ma was already
pregnant with you when I met her for the first
time.

JANIE

But that doesn't make sense. How could—Are
you trying to tell me—Do you mean that you're
not really my father?

DASH

I'm afraid that's about the size of it.

"Stupid, stupid, stupid." Honey slammed the covers holding the final script of *The Dash Coogan Show.*

"I hope you're not talking about me." Dash came through
the door of the motor home where Honey was curled up on
the couch. He wore jeans and cowboy boots with a tweed
sports coat. A silver and turquoise thunderhead bolo glimmered at the collar of his denim shirt.

Although they'd been married for five years, her heart
gave the funny jump-skip that still happened when he came
up on her unexpectedly. She didn't think she'd ever get
enough of looking at that legendary face—those rough
hewn features so elemental that they seemed to have been
carved by the wind and then baked by the desert sun.

He pocketed the key he'd used to open the door, leaned
down, and kissed her. "I know I haven't taken all those
fancy college classes like somebody I could mention, but I
don't consider myself stupid."

She laughed and wrapped her arms around his neck to
pull him closer. "You're sly as a fox, you old cowboy."

He kissed her again, sliding his hands beneath the baggy
powder-blue knit sweater she was wearing with a short white
denim skirt. "I thought you were going to work on that
paper you got due."

"I am. I just—" She released him. "Yesterday I was straightening up that mess you call a den, and I found the scripts from our final season. I decided to bring the last one along to reread. See if the Fatal Episode was as bad as I remembered."

He took off his sports coat and tossed it over a chair. "You could have asked me. I'd have told you it was even worse than you remembered."

She rose from the couch and walked a few steps to the coffeepot she kept going whenever she went on location with Dash. They were in a rough East Los Angeles neighborhood where he was shooting a low-budget television movie about a Texas cop on assignment with the LAPD. She handed him a mug and then poured another for herself. Leaning back against the small counter, she crossed her ankles, which were encased in the powder-blue socks she was wearing with her white Keds. When she had gotten dressed that morning, Dash had told her she looked all of thirteen and he would appreciate it very much if she didn't get him arrested for something unsavory like statutory rape.

She took a sip of coffee. "I don't know why the writers thought that kind of stupid explanation about Dash not really being Janie's father would make audiences forget they were watching a married couple pretend to be father and daughter."

He sat down on the couch and leaned back. When he stretched out his legs, his cowboy boots reached halfway down the center of the motor home. "By the time the Fatal Episode aired, we didn't have any viewers left anyway, so I guess it didn't matter."

"It mattered to me. I hated the idea that they tried to save the show by deciding that Dash and Janie weren't really father and daughter. That was even stupider than Bobby's dream on *Dallas*."

"It was Pam's dream, not Bobby's. And nothing could be that stupid."

A police siren from the street outside penetrated the thin shell of the motor home. Dash scowled. "Damn. I don't know why I let you talk me into bringing you along today. This neighborhood's too dangerous."

Honey rolled her eyes. "Here we go again. Papa Dash being overprotective."

"Overprotective! Do you have any idea how many drug murders and gang shootings have happened around here just in the last few months? And this two-bit production company didn't hire any security people. They probably don't even have a city permit to film."

"Dash, I've kept the door locked, and I'm not going out. You know I have to write my English lit paper, and this is a perfect place to do it because there aren't any distractions. If I were home, I'd be out riding, or digging in the flower bed, or baking you a chocolate cake."

He sputtered some more, and she gave him a sympathetic smile. She tried not to tease him too much about his overprotectiveness because she understood that he couldn't help himself. No matter how certain he was of her love, he could never completely set aside the little boy buried inside him who was afraid the person he loved most was going to be snatched away.

"It's my fault," he grumbled. "I like having you around so much I lose my common sense. Rub my neck, will you? That fight scene yesterday got me all stiff."

He turned sideways, and she went over to the couch, where she knelt in back of him. She pushed her hair behind one ear. As she cocked her head, it tumbled forward on the opposite side and fell in a honey-colored waterfall over his shoulder. He leaned against her and she began massaging the muscles of his shoulders, closing her eyes for a moment to absorb the solid, familiar feel of him. Their marriage had brought her more happiness than she had ever believed possible, and even all the professional and financial difficulties that had followed had never made her regret what they had done.

"I'm too old for these cops and robbers pictures," he grumbled.

"You won't be fifty till summer. That's hardly ancient."

she'd used most of it to put a big dent in his IRS debt. He'd been furious when he'd found out, but she didn't regret a single penny. The debt was finally paid off, and they had begun to set aside money for the future.

A worse problem was the beating his professional career had taken as a result of their marriage. It saddened her to see him forced to accept roles in second-rate television movies such as the one he was shooting now. He shrugged off her concern by saying he'd never been much of an actor anyway, and any work was good work.

Maybe he wasn't a versatile actor, but to her mind, he was something even better. He was a legend, the last of the solitary individualists who wore a white hat and stood for decency. No matter how much they had needed the money, she wouldn't let him accept any parts that tarnished that image.

As her nose brushed against his shirt collar, she knew that the biggest conflict between them—the one that never went away—was Dash's refusal to let her have a child. The issue lurked like an unwelcome visitor in all the invisible corners of their existence together. She yearned for his baby, dreamed of bassinets and snap-legged sleepers and a sweet little down-covered head. But he said he was too old for a baby and that he'd already proven he didn't know how to be a father.

She no longer believed his excuses. She knew he was afraid something would happen to her in childbirth, and he needed her too much to take the risk. What she didn't know was how she could fight a fear that was rooted in love.

He poked his finger through one of her curls. "I almost forgot to tell you. Apparently there was a news report about Eric Dillon on television a couple of hours ago."

"That arrogant little bastard."

"Dillon's at least six feet tall. I don't know why you call him little."

"Six feet is still four inches shorter than you. That makes him little in my book."

"That's a pretty narrow definition of short, especially

coming from somebody who can't even reach the top shelf of her kitchen cupboards."

"I notice that you're not debating the fact that I called him a bastard. Since he won his Oscar last month, he's probably even more insufferable than I remember."

"He wasn't that bad, Honey. You shouldn't blame him for the fact that you fell in love with him and he had to spend all his spare time hiding out from you."

"I did not fall in love with him, Dash Coogan. I just had a crush. You were the one I fell in love with."

He grinned. "I've been thinking. How do you feel about going up to Alaska this summer and doing some backpacking along the Chilkoot Trail?"

"That's a wonderful idea. I've always wanted to go to Alaska."

"We don't have to. I may not be a multimillionaire, but I can afford something better for you than a tent. If you want to go to Paris or something—"

"I do. But not with you. I can just hear you complaining about the traffic and the fact that everybody's speaking French. Maybe the next time Liz goes to Europe, I'll go with her."

"That sounds like a good idea."

They smiled at each other, both of them knowing she wouldn't go anywhere without him. She'd lived through an entire childhood without anyone to love her, and now that she had Dash, she didn't want to be with anyone else. She was dependent on him in a way that she had never permitted herself to be dependent on anyone, even when she was a child. He was both her greatest strength and her greatest weakness.

She shifted her weight to avoid the corner of his belt buckle where it was digging into her waist and remembered that she had interrupted him. "So what did you hear about Eric?"

"Oh, yeah. Apparently he tried to straighten out a curve on Mulholland last night. He was driving drunk, the stupid son of a bitch."

"I hope he's all right."

"I guess it was pretty serious. Some broken bones; I don't know what all. Luckily, no one else was involved."

"It's hard to feel a lot of sympathy for him, isn't it? He just won an Oscar. He's rich and successful, at the top of his career. And he's got two little girls. How could he be so self-indulgent?"

"Remember that he grew up with lots of money. I doubt he ever had to work too hard for anything. People like that don't have a lot of depth to them."

"It's funny, though, how somebody who's so obviously shallow can turn in the performances he does. Sometimes when I watch one of his films, he makes me shiver."

"That doesn't have anything to do with his performance. It's your leftover sexual attraction to him."

She laughed and threw herself against him, toppling him back against the couch so that he bumped his head on the wall.

"Damn little hellcat," he murmured against her mouth.

She pulled his shirttail from his jeans. "How much time do we have before you need to be back on the set?"

"Not much."

"Doesn't matter." The snap on his jeans gave way beneath her fingers. "You've been so quick on the trigger lately that I'm sure we can manage."

He reached back to close the open set of blinds on the motor home window. "Are you casting aspersions on my staying power?"

"I absolutely am."

His hands slid beneath her sweater and unfastened her bra. He brushed his thumbs over her nipples. "If you wouldn't wiggle around so much and make all those moaning sounds in my ear, I might last longer."

"I do not moan. I——" She moaned. "Oh, that's not fair. You know I'm sensitive there."

"And about a hundred other places."

Within minutes, he had located half a dozen of them.

Their lovemaking was filled with laughter and passion. As

sometimes happened when they were finished and Honey lay against his chest, she could feel tears welling in her eyes. *Thank you for giving him to me, God. Thank you so much.*

Dash locked the door of the motor home behind him when he left. She opened the blinds so she could watch him walk away with that rolling, bowlegged gait she loved. Her very own cowboy husband. If she could only convince him to let her have a baby, she'd never ask for anything else again.

The view from the window was grim and depressing. The production vehicles and motor homes were grouped together in what had once been the parking lot for the abandoned light-bulb factory across the street, where the crew was gathered to film today's scenes. The factory's brick walls held spray-painted obscenities and gang messages. As always happened on location, a small crowd had formed to watch the actors: kids truant from school, people who had wandered out from the local shops, an assortment of vagrants. A street vendor was even selling ice cream bars.

Still, she didn't let the festive atmosphere delude her. For once, Dash was right to be cautious; this was a dangerous neighborhood. When they'd gotten out of their car that morning, she'd seen a broken hypodermic needle lying in a weedy hole in the asphalt.

She turned away from the window and walked over to the table where she was working on the paper for her lit class. She regarded the notes she had made without enthusiasm. She was twenty-five years old, too old to be going to school. Maybe that was why she was having so much difficulty getting started on this paper. Since she had no specific career goal in mind, she took classes more to fill time than for any other reason. All she wanted from life was to be Dash Coogan's wife, the mother of his child, and to play Janie Jones for the rest of her life. But if she told Dash school had begun to seem pointless, she knew exactly what he would say.

"Damn right it is. Give that underworked agent of yours a

phone call and get your cute little butt back to work in front of the cameras where you belong."

Dash persisted in believing that she was a great actress despite the fact that she'd only played one part. She wished he were right and her talent was genuine instead of a gimmick. Not even to him would she confess how much she missed acting.

Occasionally when he was away from the ranch, she read scenes from plays aloud: everything from Shakespeare to Neil Simon and Beth Henley. But it was always a disaster. She sounded phony and stilted, like an actor in a junior high play, and any fantasies she had about going back in front of the cameras quickly dissolved. In the past five years she'd lived through a humiliating amount of abuse from the press and the public. The only thing they hadn't been able to take away from her were her performances as Janie Jones, and she wouldn't let anything tarnish that.

She settled at the table to work, but she couldn't seem to concentrate. Instead, she found herself thinking about her last phone conversation with Chantal. As usual, Chantal had wanted money, this time so she and Gordon could take a cruise.

"You know I can't afford that," Honey had said. "I don't have a source of income now, and I've been telling you for the past year that I can't keep up the payments on your house much longer. Instead of cruises, you need to start thinking about finding some place less expensive to live."

"Don't start nagging me, Honey," Chantal had replied. "I can't take any more pressure now. Me and Gordon have both been under a lot of stress these last six months, ever since those doctors told me about my fallopian tubes and all. It's hard facing the fact that I can't ever have a baby."

Chantal had said the one thing guaranteed to win Honey's sympathy, and she had immediately softened. "Chantal, I'm sorry about that. You know I am. Maybe I should send you to another doctor. Maybe—"

"No more doctors." Chantal had said. "They've all told me the same thing, and I can't stand any more of those examinations. Besides, Honey, if you can find the money to pay all those doctor bills, I don't see why you can't come up with enough for a cruise."

Last night when Honey had mentioned the conversation to Dash as the two of them were getting ready for bed, he'd started badgering her again.

"Chantal's just using you. To tell the truth, I think she's more relieved than sorry that she can't get pregnant. She's too lazy to have a baby. Don't you realize that by making Gordon and Chantal so dependent on you, you've robbed them of the chance to become productive people? I know you always think you know what's best for everybody else in the world, but that's not necessarily true."

She'd slapped down her hairbrush and glared at him. "You don't understand, Dash. It's not in Chantal's nature to be productive."

"It's in anybody's nature if they're hungry enough. And what about Gordon? He's got two arms and two legs. He's perfectly capable of carrying his own weight."

"But you don't understand how it was when I first came to L.A. Gordon threatened to take Chantal away from me. She was all I had, and I couldn't let that happen."

"He was manipulating you, is what he was doing."

"That may be, but I can hardly turn my back on Chantal now that Sophie's gone. It's been three years since Sophie died, and she still hasn't gotten over it."

"If you ask me, you've mourned your Aunt Sophie a lot longer than Chantal ever did."

"That's a dirt-rotten thing to say."

He'd begun noisily brushing his teeth, effectively shutting off further conversation. She'd stomped into the bathroom and closed the door, not wanting to admit even to herself that he was at least partially right. Sophie's death seemed to have hit her harder than Chantal. But it had been so unnecessary, so lacking in dignity. Her aunt had choked on the wing bone in some store-bought fried chicken Gordon had heated up in the microwave.

At least Buck Ochs was gone. Sophie hadn't even been cold in her grave before he'd brought home a hooker. To

Gordon's credit, he'd thrown Buck out, and the last Honey had heard, Sophie's former husband had gone to work in a park near Fresno.

She pushed away thoughts of her family and forced herself to get to work on her paper. Two hours later, with her notes organized and the first few pages written, she rose to pour herself a fresh mug of coffee. As she glanced through the back window, she saw Dash walking across the narrow, dirty street toward the motor home.

Once again, her heart gave that silly hop-skip. She looked at her watch and saw that it was nearly four o'clock. Maybe he was done for the day and they could go home early. With a smile, she set down her coffee, unlocked the door, and stepped outside.

The late afternoon was hot and humid, more like July in South Carolina than May in southern California. The vans and trucks surrounding her were jammed so close together that the air couldn't circulate, and everything smelled of gasoline and exhaust fumes. As Dash crossed from the street into the parking lot, she waved at him.

He lifted his arm to wave back, but halfway up, his hand stalled. He was close enough that she could see him frown. Just then, she heard the muffled sound of a woman's cry. She turned sharply.

Off to her right, two of the larger motor homes were parked parallel to each other, forming a narrow, dark tunnel less than five feet across. She saw a flash of movement toward the rear of the vehicles and took a quick step forward.

A thin, swarthy-faced man wearing a ripped red T-shirt and shiny black pants was dragging a young Hispanic woman into the confined space. Horrified, Honey watched as the man rammed the woman against the side of the larger vehicle and made a grab for the purse she held clamped in her arms. The woman screamed, hunching her shoulders to protect the purse at the same time she struggled to free herself from him.

The woman and her assailant were less than thirty feet away, and, instinctively, Honey began to rush forward, but before she could go far, she heard the thud of running feet behind her. Dash shot past, giving her a hard shove in the center of her back that sent her sprawling.

She gasped as her bare knees scraped on the asphalt and the heels of her hands slid over the rough surface. The pain was sharp, but not as sharp as the sense of dread that swept through her. She jerked her head back up.

From the ground she could see it all. She could see the pattern of bright yellow flowers on the skirt of the woman's dress, hear her cries for help as she foolishly clung to her purse.

Dash stood not far from the point where Honey lay, his back to her, legs braced. Her heart pounding, she opened her mouth to yell at him to be careful, not to play the hero, not to—

"Let her go!" Dash called out.

Time hung suspended, so that the most insignificant details would be forever etched in her mind with grotesque clarity. The veins of cracked asphalt that led to her husband's boots, the raveling hanging from the hem of his jeans. She felt the hot sun beating down on her back, smelled the asphalt, saw the long shadow cast by his tall frame. Dominating it all was the wild, drug-crazed expression in the eyes of the woman's assailant as he stood at the end of that dark tunnel formed by the production vehicles and spun to face Dash.

In one grotesque motion, the man snatched a snub-nosed pistol from the waistband of his shiny black pants and raised it. A horrible scream spilled from her throat as she watched the wild-eyed addict fire two shots.

Dash twisted and crumpled to the ground in a slow, awkward movement. A cloying gray fog enveloped her, making everything seem unreal. In the narrow tunnel the woman fell, too, a bright yellow blur, as the addict shoved her down and ran away, the purse lying forgotten at her side.

Dash's arm lay over the cracked pavement. Honey saw his bare wrist, the broad back of his hand. Sobbing like a wounded animal, she began to crawl toward him on her hands and her bloody, scraped knees. Through the gray fog, she told herself that everything would be all right. Just seconds ago she had waved at him. None of this was real because nothing this ghastly could happen without warning. Not so quickly, not without an omen.

She was barely aware of the shouts of the crew members as they came running from the other side of the street. She saw only her husband's fingers clawing at the asphalt.

She struggled to her knees beside him, her body shaking with wrenching sobs. "Dash!"

"Honey . . . I'm . . ."

Gripping his arms, she turned him so that his head and one shoulder were resting in her lap. A big stain was spreading over his chest like a sunburst. She remembered that he'd had a wound like this in one of his films, but she couldn't think which one it was.

She cupped his cheeks and whispered on a sob, "You can get up now. Please, Dash . . . Please, get up . . ."

His eyelids flickered, and his mouth began to work. "Honey . . ." He whispered her name on a horrible wheeze.

"Don't talk. Please, God, don't talk . . ."

His eyes locked with hers. They were full of love and bleak with pain. "I knew . . . I'd . . . break . . . your . . . heart," he gasped.

And then his outspread hand went limp.

Inhuman, wrenching sounds slipped from her throat. The asphalt was so black, his blood so red. His eyes stared up at her, open but unseeing.

One of the crew members touched her, but she shook him off.

She cradled her husband's head in her lap, stroked his cheek while she rocked and whispered to him. "You're going . . . to be fine. You're all right . . . My darling . . . My own . . . cowboy."

His warm blood seeped through her skirt, making her thighs sticky. She continued to rock him. "I love you, my darling. I'll . . . love you . . . forever." Her teeth were chattering and her body convulsing with shivers. "Nothing bad can happen. Not a thing. You're the hero. The hero never . . ."

She pressed kisses to his forehead, the ends of her hair dipping in his blood, tasting the blood in her mouth, muttering that he wouldn't die. She would die instead of him. She would take his place. God would understand. The writers would fix everything. She stroked his hair. Kissed his lips.

"Honey." One of the men touched her.

She lifted her head and her face contorted with fury. "Go away! Everybody go away! He's all right."

The man shook his head, his cheeks wet with tears. "Honey, I'm afraid Dash is dead."

She pulled her husband's beloved head closer against her breasts and rested her cheek against his hair. She spoke fiercely in a flood of words. "You're wrong. Don't you understand? The hero can't die! He can't, you stupid God! You can't break the rules. Don't you know? The hero never dies!"

It took three medics to pull her away from Dash Coogan's lifeless body.

22

The room was stifling, but she lay on the bed wrapped in Dash's old sheepskin coat. Beneath it her nylons stuck to her legs and the black dress she had worn to the funeral was soaked with perspiration. She kept her face buried in the collar of the coat. It held his scent.

Sweaty tendrils of hair clung to the back of her neck, but she didn't notice. Liz had come and gone, bringing a plate of food that Honey couldn't eat and trying to talk her into staying at the beach house for a few weeks so she wouldn't be alone. But Honey wanted to be alone so she could find Dash.

She curled tighter into the coat, her eyes pressed closed. *Talk to me, Dash. Let me feel you. Please, please let me feel you so I know you're not gone.* She tried to make her mind go blank so Dash could reach her, but a terror so black she wanted to scream swept through her. Her mouth opened against the soft collar.

She wasn't aware that someone had come into the bedroom until she felt the mattress sag next to her. She wanted to strike out at all of them and make them leave her alone. They had no right to intrude on her privacy like this.

"Honey?" Meredith spoke her name and then began to cry. "I—I want to ask you to forgive me. I've been hateful and jealous and vindictive. I knew it was wrong, but I couldn't stop myself. All I—All I ever wanted was for Daddy to love me, but he loved you instead."

Honey didn't want Meredith's confidences, and she had no comfort to give. She pushed herself up on the bed and sat on the edge with her back to Meredith. She clutched the lapels of Dash's sheepskin jacket around her. "He loved you, too." She spoke woodenly, knowing she had to say the words. "You were his daughter, and he never forgot that."

"I—I was so hateful to you. So jealous."

"It doesn't matter. Nothing matters."

"I know Daddy is at peace and we should be giving praise instead of grieving, but I can't help it."

Honey said nothing. What did Meredith know of a love so strong that it was as fundamental as oxygen? All of Meredith's emotions were directed safely toward heaven. Honey willed herself to disappear inside Dash's jacket until Meredith left.

"Could you—Could you forgive me, Honey?"

"Yes," Honey replied automatically. "I forgive you."

The door opened and she heard Wanda's voice. "Meredith, your brother's leaving. You need to come and say good-bye."

The mattress moved as Meredith rose. "Good-bye, Honey. I'm—I'm sorry."

"Good-bye, Meredith."

The door shut. Honey rose from the side of the bed, but as she turned toward the window, she saw that she still wasn't alone. Wanda stood watching her. Her eyes were red with weeping, her sprayed blond bubble flattened on one side. At the funeral she had carried on as if she were the widow instead of Honey.

She dabbed at her eyes and sniffed. "Meredith's been jealous of you from the first time she saw you and Randy on TV. He wasn't much of a father to her—I guess you know about that—and watching the two of you being so close was like an open wound to her."

"It doesn't matter now."

Wanda's perfume bore the heavy scent of carnations. Or maybe it wasn't her perfume. Maybe Honey was smelling the overpowering scent of all the funeral floral arrangements.

"Is there anything I can do for you?" Wanda asked.

"Make everybody go away," Honey replied dully. "That's all I want."

Wanda nodded and moved to the door where she blew her nose, then spoke briskly. "I wish you well, Honey. I admit I didn't think Randy should have married you. But all of his ex-wives were at that funeral today, and the three of us together never gave him as much happiness as you did in a single day."

Dimly, Honey realized that it had taken a generosity of spirit for Wanda to make that statement, but she only wanted to be rid of her so she could lie down on the bed again and close her eyes and try to reach Dash. She had to find him. If she couldn't find him, she would die herself.

Wanda left, and within an hour, the rest of the guests were gone, too. As night fell, Honey walked aimlessly through the house in her stockinged feet. His coat hung so long on her that when she slipped her hands into the pockets, her fingers couldn't touch bottom. Eventually, she curled up in the big green leather chair where he used to sit watching television.

The man who had murdered Dash was an addict out on parole. He'd been killed in a gun battle with the police several hours after Dash had died. Everybody seemed to think she should feel better because Dash's murderer was dead, but revenge meant nothing to her. It couldn't bring Dash back.

She must have dozed because when she awakened it was past two in the morning. She went into the kitchen and began aimlessly opening cupboard doors. His favorite coffee mug sat on the shelf; an open pack of his spearmint LifeSavers lay by the sugar bowl waiting for him. She walked into their bathroom and saw his toothbrush in a blue china holder on the counter. She rubbed her thumb over the bone-dry bristles and then slipped it into her pocket. On her way out of the bedroom, she extracted a pair of his socks from the laundry hamper and put them in the other pocket.

There was no moon overhead when she went outside, only the faint glow from the light bulb above the door of the stables. As she crossed the yard toward the paddock, the stones tore holes in the feet of her nylons, but she paid no attention. She made her way to the fence where they had stood together so many times.

She waited and waited.

Finally, her legs gave out and she sank down into the dirt. She pulled his toothbrush from one pocket and his socks from the other. They formed a warm damp ball in her hand. Tears wet her cheeks as the silence suffocated her.

She slipped his toothbrush into her mouth and sucked on it.

As the weeks passed she grew thin and frail. Occasionally she remembered to eat, more frequently she didn't. She slept at odd times and in short snatches, sometimes in his chair, sometimes in their bed with an article of his clothing pressed to her cheek. She felt as if she had been tipped over and emptied of every emotion except despair.

The newspapers had relentlessly chronicled Dash's death, and helicopters hired by the paparazzi buzzed the ranch for a photograph of the grieving widow, so she spent most of her time inside the house. Ironically, Dash's death had given their marriage a posthumous respectability, and instead of being the butt of everyone's jokes Dash was a martyred hero, while her name was spoken with respect.

Newspaper articles described her as brave and courageous. Arthur Lockwood drove to the ranch to tell her he was being plagued with requests to interview her and that several important producers wanted to cast her in their next pictures. She stared at him blankly, unable to understand.

Liz began tormenting her with healthy casseroles, vitamins, and unwanted advice. Chantal and Gordon appeared to plea for money. Her hair began to fall out, but she barely noticed.

One afternoon early in August, three months after Dash's death, she was maneuvering the narrow canyon road coming back from a visit with Dash's attorney when she realized how easy it would be to take one of the bends too wide. With a quick press on the accelerator, she could fly through the guardrail and crash into the canyon. The car would roll, then become a blazing fireball incinerating all her pain.

Her hands trembled as they clutched the steering wheel. The burden of pain had grown too crushing, and she simply couldn't bear it any longer. No one would care very much if she died. Liz would be upset, but she had a full, busy life and she would soon forget. Chantal would cry at her funeral, but Chantal's tears were cheap; she wouldn't cry much harder than she did when one of her soap opera characters died. When people didn't have a real family, they could pretty much die unmourned.

Family.

It was all she had ever wanted. A person who would love her without condition. A person she could love back with all her heart.

A sob racked her body. She missed him so much. He had been her lover, her father, her child, the center of everything good in her life. She missed his touch and scent. She missed the way he swore, the sound of his footsteps crossing the floor, the scrape of his whiskers against her cheek. She missed the way he turned the newspaper inside out so that she could never find the front page, the sounds of Sooners games blaring from the television. She missed his daily rituals of shaving and showering, the abandoned towels and underwear that never quite hit the hamper. She missed all the flotsam and jetsam that had been part of Dash Coogan.

Through the blur of tears, she watched as the needle on

the speedometer edged upward. The tires squealed as she careened around a curve. A push on the accelerator, a twist of her hands, and all the pain would be gone.

Unbidden, the memory of a young girl with chewed hair and worn-down flip-flops came back to her from another lifetime. As the speedometer inched higher, she wondered what had happened to that fierce little sixteen-year-old who had believed anything was possible. Where was the child who had taken off across America in a battered pickup truck with only guts to keep her going? She could no longer remember what that kind of courage felt like. She could no longer remember the child she had been.

Find her, a voice inside her head whispered. *Find that little girl.*

Gradually, her foot eased on the accelerator, not from any renewed desire to live, but simply because she was too tired to maintain the pressure.

Find her, the voice repeated.

Why not? she thought dully. The only thing she had better to do was die.

Ten days later the humid South Carolina heat consumed her as she stepped out of her air-conditioned Blazer onto the crumbling asphalt parking lot of the Silver Lake Amusement Park. Knee-high weeds grew through the gaping holes in the pavement and rust-streaked concrete obelisks showed where light posts had once been mounted. Her legs were rubbery. She had been on the road for several days, stopping at odd times to check into a motel and sleep for a few hours before she drove on. Now she was exhausted to the very marrow of her bones.

She squinted dispiritedly into the blazing sun and gazed at the boarded-up park entrance. She had owned the park for years, but she had never done anything with it. At first she simply hadn't had enough time to manage both her career and the park. After she'd married Dash, she'd had time, but not the money.

The roof on the ticket booth had collapsed and the flamingo-pink paint on the six stucco gate pillars was peeled and dirty. Over the entrance the letters on the sign that dangled crookedly were barely visible.

S lver Lak Amusem   Par
Home of th Legendar Bl ck Thu der
Roll r Coast
Thrillz 'n' Ch llz fo th Entir Fam ly

She lifted her head and took in the view she had crossed a continent to see—the ruins of Black Thunder. Above the decay of the park, the mighty wooden hills still soared into the scorched Carolina sky. Neither time nor abandonment had been able to destroy it. It was indomitable, the greatest wooden roller coaster in the South, and nothing could spoil its majesty—not the dilapidated buildings, the sagging signs, the tangled undergrowth. It hadn't been operable for eleven years, but it still waited patiently.

She lowered her eyes to escape the flood of painful emotion. In the old days she would have been able to see the top half of the Ferris wheel and the curving arms of the Octopus rising above the ticket booth, but the rides were gone and the parched sky held only a fireball sun and Black Thunder.

The humidity enshrouded her, thick and suffocating, making her perspire through the waistband of her khaki shorts. The sun beat down on her thin shoulders and bare legs as she began walking along the perimeter of the fence, but the pines and undergrowth prevented anything more than an occasional glimpse inside the park. Eventually she came to the old delivery entrance. It was fastened with a length of chain and a rusted padlock, both without purpose since the fence nearby had been slit long ago. The park must have been a popular place for scavengers when it still held the possibility of salvage. Now, even the vandals seemed to have abandoned it.

The chain-link prongs scratched her legs as she climbed over the fence. She made her way through the scrub and then slipped between two disintegrating wooden buildings that had once held heavy equipment. She walked on, passing beneath Black Thunder's colonnade of weathered southern-pine support columns but unwilling to look upward into the massive curving track for fear of the damage she would see. She moved out into the center of the park.

A chill gripped her as she saw the disintegration. The Dodgem Hall had collapsed and, farther on, the picnic pavilion was overgrown with scrub. Broken sidewalks led nowhere; circles of barren earth marked the spots where the Scrambler and Tilt-a-Whirl had once stood. Through the trees she could glimpse the murky surface of Silver Lake, but the *Bobby Lee* had long ago sunk to the bottom.

Dirt sifted through the open weave of her sandals as she made her way to the abandoned midway. Her footsteps padded the ground in the silence. A pile of rotted timbers lay in the weeds, and a tattered blue plastic pennant, dull with dirt, was snared on a nail head. The hanky-panks were gone, the scent of popcorn and candy apples replaced by the smell of decay.

She was the only person left on earth.

As she stood in the park's vacant heart, she finally lifted her eyes back to the sky so she could take in the entire skeleton of Black Thunder as it encompassed her abandoned universe. Her eyes stung as she followed the invincible lines of the mythic coaster: the great lift hill followed by the plunge toward the earth at an angle sharp enough to penetrate the very bowels of hell, all three hills with their glorious, thrice-delivered promises of death and resurrection, the heart-stopping spiral down to the water and the smooth, fast delivery into the station. Somewhere on that wild, racing ride she had once been able to touch eternity.

Or had she? She began to tremble. Was the certainty that she had been able to find her mother when she had ridden that coaster nothing more than the fancy of a child? Had the coaster really delivered her into the presence of God? She knew that her belief in God had been born on that coaster as surely as that same belief had been washed away by Dash Coogan's blood.

As she stared at the great ribs of Black Thunder etched against the parched sky, she cursed and begged God, both at the same time. *I want him back! You can't have him. He's mine, not yours! Give him back to me. Give him back!*

The ferocious sun burned through her hair into her scalp. She started to sob and sank to her knees, not to pray but to curse. *You fucker. You awful fucker.*

But even as she squeezed her eyes shut the silhouette of Black Thunder's three mighty hills stayed etched on her lids. The horrible obscenities continued to spill from her until they gradually assumed the cadence of ritual.

Exhausted, a stillness came over her. She opened her eyes and lifted them to the mountaintops as those in despair had done for centuries. Hope. Black Thunder had always given it to her. And as she stared at those three wooden peaks, she was filled with the absolute certainty that the coaster could transport her to some eternal place where she could find her husband, a place that existed beyond the temporal, a place where love could live forever.

But Black Thunder had no more life left in it than Dash Coogan's body, and it was incapable of transporting her anywhere. The massive skeleton stood crippled and impotent against the August sky, no longer bearing promises of hope and resurrection, no longer promising anything except dry rot and decay.

She stumbled back to her car, the weight of her weariness overwhelming. If only she could make Black Thunder run again. If only . . .

Climbing inside the suffocating interior of the car, she leaned back against the seat and fell into an exhausted sleep.

23

Sheri Poltrain had been working behind the register at the Gas 'n' Carry in Cumberland County, North Carolina, for three years. She'd been robbed twice and threatened with bodily harm half a dozen times. Now as the stranger approached the register of the convenience store, she tensed. She was better acquainted with trouble than most women, and she knew when it was walking toward her.

He looked like a biker, except the wrists and hands exposed beneath the sleeves of his unzipped brown leather jacket were clean and free of tattoos. And he didn't have a beer gut. Not even close. Through the open front of his jacket, she saw a belly as flat as the stretch of rainy county highway that ran past the gas pumps outside. He was at least six feet tall, with good shoulders, a muscular chest, and faded jeans that clung to one of those narrow, tight butts men never had the good sense to appreciate. No. There was definitely nothing wrong with his body. In fact, it was pretty incredible. What was wrong with him was his face.

He was just about the meanest-looking son of a bitch she'd ever seen. Not ugly mean. Just cruel mean. Like he might put out cigarettes on sensitive parts of a woman's body without ever changing his expression.

His hair, damp with the chilly late November drizzle that fell outside, was dark brown, almost black, and it hung nearly to his shoulders. It was clean but shaggy. He had a strong, perfectly shaped nose and the kinds of bones she'd once heard somebody describe as chiseled. But great bones couldn't make up for those thin lips and that hard mouth that didn't seem to have learned how to smile. And great bones couldn't make up for the coldest, single blue eye she had ever seen in her life.

She told herself not to stare at the black patch that covered his other eye, but it was hard to ignore. With that black patch and emotionless expression, he looked like some kind of modern-day pirate. Not the blow-dryer kind on the cover of one of the romance novels that sat on the rack next to her register, but the nasty kind who might pull a Saturday night special out of his back pocket and empty it into her belly.

She looked uneasily down at the digital display on her register that told her how much gas he had pumped into the mud-splattered gray GMC van that sat outside. "That'll be twenty-two even." She wasn't the type to let any man see that she was afraid, but this one gave her the heebie-jeebies, and her voice wasn't as firm as usual.

"Also a bottle of aspirin," he said.

Her eyes flickered with surprise at his faintly accented speech. He wasn't an American, but a foreigner. He sounded like he was from the Middle East or somewhere. The notion sprang into her mind that he might be some kind of Arab terrorist, but she didn't know if Arab terrorists could have blue eyes.

She removed an aspirin bottle from the cardboard display behind her and slid it across the counter. There was something dead in that single visible eye, an absence of any sort of life force that gave her the creeps, but when he withdrew nothing more threatening than a wallet from his back pocket, her curiosity poked through one small corner of her fear.

"You stayin' around here?"

The look he gave her was so threatening she quickly returned her attention to the register. He laid thirty dollars on the counter, picked up the aspirin bottle, and walked out of the store.

"You forgot your change," she called after him.

He didn't bother to look back.

Eric removed the seal from the aspirin bottle. As he rounded the back of the van, he pulled off the lid and took out the cotton wad. It was a chilly, drizzly Saturday afternoon in late November, and the dampness was bothering the leg he had injured in his auto accident. When he was behind the wheel, he swallowed three pills with the cold coffee dregs in his Styrofoam cup.

After his car had crashed through the guardrail last May, he'd spent a month in the hospital and another two months in physical therapy as an outpatient. Then in September, he'd started work on a new film. They'd considered delaying shooting because of his injuries, but he'd made good progress, and they had eventually decided to work around them instead, giving him a stunt double for a number of scenes he would normally have done himself.

The picture had been finished ten days ago. Afterward, he was scheduled to fly to New York to discuss a play, but at the last minute he'd decided to drive instead, hoping the solitude would help him pull himself together. After a few days, the solitude had become more important than his destination, and the closest he'd gotten to Manhattan was the Jersey Turnpike.

He was heading south on the back roads, traveling in a GMC van because it was less conspicuous than his Jag. At first he'd had vague ideas of visiting his father and step-mother on Hilton Head, where they'd retired a few years ago. But it hadn't taken him long to figure out that they were the last people he wanted to see, even though they'd been urging him to visit for years, ever since he'd grown famous. Still, he had six more weeks to kill before he had to start work on another film, and he had to do something to fill the time, so he kept on driving.

As he pulled away from the pumps, he caught sight of the female attendant watching him through the plate-glass window. She hadn't recognized him. No one had recognized him since he'd left L.A. He doubted that even his friends would have known him unless they looked closely. The phony accent he'd used in his last film, along with the longer hair he'd grown, had successfully concealed his identity for three thousand miles. Even more important than anonymity, the disguise afforded him at least temporary escape from being himself.

He turned out onto the wet county road and automatically patted his jacket pocket for his cigarettes only to remember he no longer smoked. They wouldn't let him smoke in the hospital, and by the time he was dismissed, he'd fallen out of the habit. He'd fallen out of the habit of enjoying all of life's sensory pleasures. Food no longer held any appeal, and neither did liquor or sex. He could no longer even remember why they had once been so important. Ever since he'd lost his children he felt as if he belonged more to the world of the dead than the living.

In the seven months since Lilly had taken the girls, he'd learned more than most lawyers knew about the sexual abuse of children. While he had lain in his hospital bed, he'd read stories of fathers violating tiny babies in unspeakable ways, of perverted, twisted men who preyed upon one daughter after another, betraying the most sacred trust that could exist between two human beings.

But he wasn't one of those monsters. He was also no longer the naive hothead who had stormed Mike Longacre's office demanding that his attorney put an end to Lilly's false accusations. Now he knew that the law was also full of injustice.

No matter what personal sacrifices he had to make, he wouldn't let his children end up in the underground, where they would be deprived not only of their father but of their mother as well. So he stayed away from them, relying on the international fleet of detectives he had hired to keep them under watch. With an increasing sense of dull resignation, he followed Lilly's wanderings with the girls, first to Paris and then to Italy. They'd spent August in Vienna, September in London. Now they were in Switzerland.

Everyplace she went, she engaged new governesses, new tutors, new specialists, all of whose bills he paid. From the interviews the detectives held with those she had hired, he knew that Becca was regressing and that Rachel had become increasing difficult to control. Lilly herself was the only stability the girls had, and forcing them into the underground would end even that.

Even so, he ached for his daughters so badly that he was sometimes tempted. Over the past seven months his pain had gone beyond the torture of a raw, gaping wound into something more primal, a desolate emptiness of the soul that was worse than any physical anguish because it was a living death. For a while he had been able to direct his despair into the role he was playing, but when the filming was done, he had lost his place to hide.

He had also gradually lost the ability to see any of the world's beauty, and now he only registered its horror. He could no longer read newspapers or watch television because he couldn't endure another account of a newborn baby abandoned in a trash can, umbilical cord still attached to its small, blue body. He couldn't read about another severed head found in a cardboard carton, or a young woman gang raped. Murders, mutilations, evil. He had lost his ability to separate his own pain from the suffering of others. All the world's pain belonged to him now, one atrocity after another, until his shoulders were bowed with the weight and he knew he would break if he didn't find a way to protect himself.

And so he was running, hiding away inside the skin of someone he'd invented, a persona so menacing that ordinary people drew away from him. He played jazz tapes instead of listening to the radio, slept in his van rather than a motel room with its beckoning television, avoided big towns and newspaper stands. He sheltered himself in the only way he knew how because he had grown so fragile he was afraid he would shatter.

A tractor-trailer rig kicked water at his van as he turned from the county access road out onto a state highway. The wipers made several half-moon passes over the windshield before he could see. Through the blur he spotted a blue road sign imprinted with the white H that indicated a nearby hospital. It was what he'd been looking for, the fragile thread that allowed him both to protect himself and try to save his soul at the same time.

He followed the blue and white hospital signs through a two-stoplight town until he came to a small, unassuming brick structure. He parked in the farthest corner of the lot away from the hospital building and climbed into the back of the van. The seats had been removed so there was an area big enough to stretch out his bedroll, which was now neatly folded away next to an expensive leather suitcase that held his clothes. He pushed it aside and drew forward a cheap vinyl suitcase.

For several moments he did nothing. And then, with something that might have been either a curse or a prayer, he opened the lid.

"'Ow does a bloke get some service around 'ere?"

Nurse Grayson's head shot up from the chart she had

been studying. She was generally unshockable, but her mouth dropped open at the improbable figure who stood on the other side of the nurse's station desk, grinning devilishly at her.

He wore a frizzy red wig topped with a black pirate's scarf knotted at the side. A purple satin shirt was tucked into voluminous black trousers that were spangled with saucer-sized red and purple polka dots. A single exaggerated eyebrow arched into the clown white that covered his face. He had a bright red mouth, another dot of red on the end of his nose, and a purple patch shaped like a star covering his left eye.

Nurse Grayson quickly recovered. "Who are you?"

He gave her a naughty grin that made her forget she was fifty-five years old and long past the age where she could be taken in by a charming scoundrel.

He sketched an overly dramatic bow before her, tapping his forehead, chest, and waist. "Patches the Pirate is me name, me pretty, and a more pitiful excuse for a sea dog, you'll never set eyes on."

Despite herself, his mischievous manner drew her in. "Now why is that?"

"Can't stand the sight of blood." He gave a comical shudder. "Miserable stuff. Don't know 'ow you tolerate it."

She giggled, and then belatedly remembered her professional responsibilities. Casually lifting her hand to tidy any errant salt-and-pepper curls that might have escaped her cap, she inquired, "Can I help you with something?"

"It's the other way around, now isn't it? I'm 'ere to entertain the kiddies. The bloke from the Rotary Club told me to show up at three. Did I get the time wrong again?" His look was devilish and unrepentant. "In addition to bein' afraid of blood, I'm also unreliable."

The single eye not covered by the patch was the brightest turquoise she had ever seen—as crystal clear as a candy mint. "No one told me that the Rotary had arranged for a clown to visit the children."

"Didn't they now? And I 'ave to be in Fayetteville by six

to entertain at the Altar Guild bazaar. It's lucky for me that you've got an understanding 'eart, in addition to a beautiful face. Otherwise, I wouldn't be able to earn the fifty bucks the Rotary's payin' me."

He was full of the devil, but so charming she couldn't resist. Besides, the rain had kept visitors down this afternoon, and the children could use a little entertainment. "I suppose there's no harm."

"Not a bit."

She came out from behind the desk and began to lead him down the hall. "As you can see, we're a small hospital. We only have twelve beds in Pediatrics. Nine of them are filled."

"Anyone I should know about?" the clown asked softly, all traces of mischievousness fading.

If she'd had any doubts about letting him onto the floor without official authorization, they vanished instantly. "A six-year-old named Paul. He's in one-oh-seven." She pointed toward the end of the hall. "He's had a rough time with pneumonia, and his mother's been too busy with her boyfriend to visit very often."

The clown nodded and made his way to the room she had pointed out. Moments later, Nurse Grayson heard the cheerful gravel of his voice.

"Ahoy, there, mate! Me name's Patches the Pirate, and I'm the mangiest dog that ever sailed the seven seas. . . ."

Nurse Grayson smiled as she made her way back to the nurses' station and congratulated herself on her good judgment. There were times in life when it paid to bend the rules.

Eric spent that night parked off the side of a dirt road in a small clearing just over the South Carolina border. When he emerged from the van the next morning, still dressed in his jeans and T-shirt from the day before, his mouth felt like dull metal from bad food and too many nightmares.

He'd bought the clown costume a week ago in a shop near Philadelphia, and since then he'd stopped at a small-town hospital nearly every day. Occasionally he called ahead, posing as a civic leader. Most of the time, however, he just followed the blue and white signs as he'd done yesterday and talked his way in.

Now he couldn't shake off the suffering of the little boy at the hospital yesterday. The child was thin and frail, and his lips bore a faint bluish rim. But it was the boy's pathetic delight at receiving Eric's undivided attention that had been wrenching. Eric had stayed with him for the rest of the afternoon and then gone back that evening and done magic tricks until the child had fallen asleep. But instead of feeling good about what he'd done, he could only think about all the children he hadn't been able to comfort, all the pain he couldn't stop.

The chilly dampness seeped through his T-shirt. As he worked the kinks out of his muscles, he gazed up into the gunmetal-gray sky. So much for sunny South Carolina. Maybe he should get back on I-95 and head directly for Florida. For a while now, he'd had vague ideas of hanging around the clowns at Ringling Brothers winter quarters in Venice for a few weeks. Maybe he'd get a chance to perform for well children, for a change, instead of sick ones. The idea of being with children who weren't suffering tantalized him.

He climbed back into the van. He hadn't showered in two days, and he needed to check into a motel so he could clean up. In the past he'd always been impeccable about personal cleanliness, but since he'd lost his children he'd grown lax. But then he'd grown lax about a lot of things, like eating and sleeping.

Half an hour later, he felt a tug on the steering wheel and knew he had a flat. He pulled over to the shoulder of the two lane highway, climbed out of the van, and went around to the back to get the jack. It had started to drizzle again, and at first he didn't see the splintered wooden sign that leaned in the palmettos at the side of the road. But the bad tire was mud slicked, and when he pulled it off, it got away from him and rolled into the ditch.

He spotted the sign as he bent over to reclaim the tire. The letters were faded, but he could still make them out:

SILVER LAKE AMUSEMENT PARK
Home of the Legendary Black Thunder
Roller Coaster
Thrillz 'n' Chillz for the Entire Family
Twenty Miles Straight Ahead,
Left 3 Miles on Rt. 62

Silver Lake Amusement Park. He felt the tug of familiarity, but he couldn't remember why. It wasn't until he secured the last lug nut on the spare that he recalled the name. Wasn't that the place Honey had talked so much about? He remembered the way she had entertained the crew with stories about growing up in an amusement park in South Carolina. She had spoken of a boat that had sunk to the bottom of the lake and a roller coaster that was supposed to be famous. He was almost certain it had been the Silver Lake Amusement Park.

He secured the hubcap with the heels of his hands and then looked thoughtfully back at the sign. His jeans were wet and muddy, his hair dripping down the back of his neck. He needed a shower, clean clothes, and a hot meal. But so did the majority of the world's population, and as he stood where he was, he wondered if the park was still in existence. The condition of the sign made it doubtful. On the other hand, anything was possible.

Maybe the Silver Lake Amusement Park was still open. And maybe they needed a clown.

24

"Honey, it's raining!" Chantal shouted. "You stop working right now."

From Honey's perch high atop Black Thunder's lift hill, she looked down at the miniature figure of her cousin gazing up at her from beneath the small red dot of an umbrella

"I'll be down in a few minutes," she shouted back. "Where's Gordon? I told him to come right back."

"He's not feelin' good," Chantal yelled. "He's taking a little rest."

"I don't care if he's dying. You tell him to get back up here."

"It's the Lord's day! You shouldn't be workin' on the Lord's day."

"Since when did either of you ever care about the Lord's day? Neither of you likes to work on any day."

Chantal walked away in a huff, but Honey didn't care. Gordon and Chantal's free ride was over. She drove another nail into the catwalk she was building at the top of the lift hill. She hated rain and she hated Sundays because the restoration work on the coaster ground to a halt. If she had her way, the construction crew would be on the job seven days a week. They weren't union members, so they could work longer hours.

Ignoring the rain, she continued to nail together pieces of the catwalk. It frustrated her that she wasn't strong enough to do the harder jobs, such as repairing the track. The crew, under the supervision of the roller-coaster restoration expert she had hired to oversee the job, had spent the first two months removing the old track and repairing the frame wherever it was damaged. Luckily, much of it was still sound. The concrete footings had been installed in the sixties, so they didn't have to be replaced. All of them had been worried about cracks in the ledgers, the giant boards the track rested on, but there hadn't been as many as they'd feared.

Still, rebuilding the entire track was a massive and expensive project, and Honey was rapidly running out of money. She had no idea how she would finish financing the new lift chain and engine that still had to be installed, not to mention the electrical system, as well as air-compressor brakes to replace the old hand-operated ones.

The rain was falling more steadily and her footing had

grown precarious. Reluctantly, she lowered herself over the side and began the long climb down the frame that they were using like a ladder until the catwalk was complete. Her body no longer screamed in protest as she made the arduous descent. She was thin, hard-muscled, and weary from two months of backbreaking work, seven days a week, as many as fourteen hours a day. Her hands bore a ridge of calluses across the palms as well as a network of small wounds and scars from mishaps with the tools she had gradually learned to use with some degree of competence.

When she reached the ground, she pulled off her yellow hard hat. Instead of heading to her makeshift home, she walked through the dripping trees toward the other end of the park. Any fleeting thoughts she'd had about living in Sophie's trailer had vanished upon her first inspection. The roof had collapsed, the robin's-egg-blue shell had caved in on one side, and vagrants had long ago stripped it of everything useful. After having the wreckage removed, she'd installed a small silver trailer on the same site.

Now, however, her destination wasn't her own temporary home but the Bullpen, the ramshackle building that had once housed the unmarried men who worked in the park. Currently Gordon and Chantal lived there. She was glad the Bullpen sat at the opposite end of the park from her trailer. It was bad enough being around people all day. At night, she needed to be alone. Only when she was alone could she feel the possibility of some connection with Dash. Not that she really thought it would happen. Not until she could ride Black Thunder.

She'd snared her hair in a rubber band at the back of her neck, but wet strands stuck to her cheeks and her sweatshirt was soaked through to her skin. If Liz could see her now, she'd be wringing her hands. But Liz and California were part of another universe.

"Who is it?" Chantal said in response to Honey's knock. Honey set her teeth in frustration and jerked open the door. "Who do you think it is? We're the only people here."

Chantal jumped up nervously from an old orange Naugahyde couch where she'd been reading a magazine and sprang to attention like an employee whose boss had caught her loafing. The interior of the Bullpen was made up of four rooms: a crude living area that Gordon and Chantal had furnished with odds and ends bought from Good Will; the sleeping area that used to hold wooden bunk beds but now contained an old iron-framed double bed; a kitchen; and a bathroom. Although the interior of the house was shabby, Chantal was keeping it neater than she'd kept any of their houses.

"Where's Gordon? You told me he was sick."

Chantal tried to slide the magazine under an ugly brown velour pillow. "He is. But he still went out back to change the oil on the truck."

"I'll bet he didn't go out until after you told him I was looking for him."

Chantal quickly changed the subject. "You want some soup? I made some nice soup a little while ago."

Honey threw off her wet sweatshirt and followed Chantal into the kitchen. Old metal cupboards covered with bile-green paint lined two of the walls, one of which held the park's only working telephone. The gold Formica counter-tops were dull and stained with use, and the linoleum floor had cracked like drought-stricken earth.

Because Honey and Gordon were working on the coaster all the time, Chantal was the only one free to take care of their meals, and she had learned that if she didn't cook, none of them ate. Surprisingly, the work seemed to have been good for Chantal. She'd lost a lot of the weight she had gained over the years and had begun to look like a more mature version of the eighteen-year-old who had won the Miss Paxawatchie County beauty contest.

"Opening a can and heating up the contents doesn't constitute *making* soup," Honey snapped as she took a seat at one end of an old picnic table they had moved inside. She knew she should encourage her cousin instead of criticizing her, but she told herself she simply didn't care about Chantal's feelings anymore.

Chantal's mouth tightened with resentment. "I'm not as good a cook as you, Honey. I'm still learning."

"You're twenty-eight years old. You should have learned a long time ago instead of spending the past nine years heating up frozen dinners in the microwave."

Chantal reached into the cupboard for a bowl, then took it over to the old gas stove and began filling it with chicken noodle soup. "I'm doing my best. It hurts my feelings when you're so critical."

"That's too bad. If you don't like the way I'm running things around here, you can leave any time." She hated her surliness and bad temper, but she couldn't seem to stop. It was like those early days on the Coogan show when any sign of weakness would have broken her.

Chantal's hand tightened around the ladle. "Me and Gordon don't have any place to go."

Honey set her mouth in an unforgiving line. "Then I guess you're stuck with me."

Chantal regarded her sadly, her voice quiet. "You've changed, Honey. You've gotten so hard. Sometimes I barely recognize you."

Honey took a spoonful of soup, refusing to let Chantal see that her words hurt. She knew that she was hostile. The men on the crew never joked around with her like they joked with each other, but she told herself she wasn't trying to win any popularity contest. All she cared about was finishing Black Thunder so that she could ride it again and maybe find her husband.

"You used to be so sweet." Chantal stood by the sink with her arms hanging at her side, her face full of regret. "And then after Dash died, I think something twisted inside you."

"I just decided to stop letting you and Gordon freeload off me, that's all."

Chantal bit down on her bottom lip. "You sold our house right out from under us, Honey. We loved that house."

"I needed the money. And I sold the ranch, too, so it wasn't like I was singling you out for persecution." Selling the ranch was the most difficult decision she'd ever had to make, but she'd ended up liquidating almost everything to finance the restoration of the coaster. All she had left was her car, some clothes, and this park. Even so, she still didn't have enough money, and she would be lucky to make it to January before what she had left ran out.

She refused to think about it. She wouldn't let anything sway her from the determination that had been born in her the day she had returned to the park and had seen Black Thunder again. Sometimes she thought her decision to rebuild the coaster was all that was keeping her alive, and she couldn't let sentiment weaken her.

"This whole thing's crazy," Chantal cried. "Sooner or later, you're going to run out of money. And then what'll you have? A half-finished roller coaster that no one will be able to ride sitting in the middle of a place where nobody ever comes."

"I'm going to find a way to raise more money. There are some historical groups interested in restoring wooden coasters." Honey avoided meeting Chantal's eyes. None of those groups had the resources to come up with the large amount of money she needed, but she wasn't going to admit as much to Chantal. Her cousin already thought she was crazy. And maybe she was.

"Just suppose a miracle happens and you finish Black Thunder," Chantal said. "What good will it do you? Nobody's going to come to ride it because there isn't a park here anymore." Her eyes grew dark with urgency. "Let's go back to California. All you'd have to do is pick up the phone and somebody'd hire you to be in a TV show. You could make lots of money."

Honey wanted to put her hands over her ears. Chantal was right, but she couldn't do it. As soon as audiences saw her trying to play a part other than Janie Jones, they'd realize what a fraud she had been as an actress. The record of those performances was the only thing that she had left in which she could take pride, the only thing she couldn't sacrifice.

"This is crazy, Honey!" Chantal exclaimed. "You're throwing away everything. Are you trying to put all three of us in a grave right along with Dash Coogan?"

Honey slammed down her spoon, splashing soup everywhere, and jumped up from the table. "Don't you talk about him! I don't even want to hear you mention his name. I don't care about houses or California or anybody coming to the park. I don't care about you and Gordon. I'm restoring this coaster for *me* and not for anybody else."

The back door had opened, but she didn't notice until Gordon spoke. "You shouldn't yell at Chantal like that," he said quietly.

She spun around, her teeth barred. "I'll yell at her any way I want. You're both worthless. The two most worthless people I've ever met in my life."

Gordon studied a point just above her right eyebrow. "I've been working right by your side, Honey, ever since we came out here. Ten, twelve hours a day. Just like you."

It was the truth. Today's absence was rare. Gordon worked with her on Sundays and in the evenings after the men had left. She had been surprised to see that hard work even seemed to agree with him. Now as she noticed how pale he was, she realized he had probably been telling the truth when he had said he wasn't feeling well, but she didn't have any sympathy left to waste on anyone, not even herself.

"The two of you had better not push me. I'm in charge, and you need to decide right now how it's going to be." Her mouth twisted bitterly. "The old days are gone when you could get anything out of me you wanted just by threatening to leave. I don't care anymore if you go. If you don't think you can live with my decisions, then pack your bags and be out of here by tomorrow."

Brushing past him, she stalked out the back door and down the crumbling concrete steps. Why did she let them stay? They cared about her money, but not about her. And she didn't care about them anymore. She didn't care about anyone.

A chilly, wet blast of wind hit her, and she remembered that she'd left her sweatshirt behind. Off to her left she could see Silver Lake, its rain-cratered surface slate gray and fetid under the December sky. A vulture swooped over the ruins of the Dodgem Hall. The land of the dead. The park was a perfect place for her.

She slowed her steps as she entered the trees and the

emptiness enveloped her. Wet brown needles stuck to her work boots and the bottoms of her jeans. She wished she could rebuild the coaster by herself so she could get rid of everyone else. Maybe in the solitude Dash would talk to her. She sagged against the scaly bark of a longleaf pine, her breath forming a frosty cloud in the air, grief and loneliness overwhelming her. *Why didn't you take me with you? Why did you die without me?*

Only gradually did she grow aware of the fact that a man was standing in the far end of the clearing near her trailer. Chantal had said it wasn't safe for her to live so far away from them, but she had paid no attention. Now the hair at the back of her neck prickled.

He lifted his head and spotted her. There was something ominous about the still way he held himself. She'd encountered several vagrants since she'd returned to the park, but they'd run away when they saw her. This man didn't look as if he intended to run anywhere.

Until that moment she hadn't thought she cared enough about her personal safety to experience fear again, but even from sixty feet away, she could feel the man's menace. He was much larger than she, broad-shouldered and strong, with long, wild hair and a frightening black eye patch. Rain glistened on his leather jacket, and his jeans were muddy and soiled.

When he didn't come any nearer, she experienced a flicker of hope that he would turn away. But he began to move toward her instead, taking slow, threatening steps.

"You're trespassing." She barked out the words, hoping to intimidate him in the same way she'd intimidated so many others.

He said nothing as he came closer, then stopped in the shadows less than twelve feet away.

"What do you want?" she demanded.

"I'm not certain." His words were colored by a faint foreign accent she couldn't quite identify.

An icy finger of dread trickled down her spine. She was alarmingly aware of the emptiness of the clearing, the fact that even if she screamed, Gordon and Chantal wouldn't hear her.

"This is private property."

"I am not hurting anything." There was no intonation to his speech, just that soft, alien accent.

"You go on and get out of here," she ordered. "Don't make me call my watchman."

She wondered if he suspected there wasn't a watchman, because her empty threat didn't intimidate him.

"Why would you do that?" he asked.

She wanted to run, but she knew he would overtake her long before she could reach Chantal's trailer. As he stood staring at her, she had the frightening sense that he was trying to make up his mind about something. Her own brain quickly supplied a possibility. He was trying to decide whether he should kill her or just rape her. For a moment something about him seemed familiar. She thought of all those true-crime television shows Gordon and Chantal watched and wondered if she could have seen him on one of them. What if he was a fugitive?

"You don't know me, do you?" he finally said.

"Should I?" Her nerves were stretched so tautly she wanted to scream. One wrong word and he would be on her. She stood frozen until he took another step forward.

She instinctively moved back, holding out her arm as if that frail barrier could keep him away. "Don't come any closer!"

"Honey, it's me. Eric."

Only gradually did his words penetrate her fear, but even then it took a few moments before she realized who it was.

"I didn't mean to scare you," he said, in a flat, dead voice that no longer held any trace of accent.

"Eric?"

It had been years since she had seen him in person, and the many newspaper and magazine photographs of him bore no resemblance to this menacing-looking one-eyed stranger. Where was the sulky young heartthrob she had known so long ago?

"What are you doing here?" Her voice was harsh. He had no right to frighten her like that. And he had no right to intrude on her privacy. She didn't care if he was Mr. Big Shot in Hollywood. She was long past the point when she was impressed by movie stars.

"I noticed a sign about twenty miles from here and remembered how you used to talk about this place. I was just curious."

She took in the eye patch and his unkempt appearance. His clothes were muddy and wrinkled, his hands dirty, his jaw dark with stubble. It was no wonder she hadn't recognized him. She remembered his automobile accident, but she no longer felt pity for people who were lucky enough to emerge from accidents with their lives intact.

She didn't like the fact that she had to tilt her head to look him in the eye. "Why didn't you tell me who you were right away?"

He shrugged, his face blank of any expression. "Habit."

Uneasiness crept through her. He stood silently, making no attempt to explain either his presence in the park or his menacing appearance. He simply returned her gaze with one clear blue, unflinching eye. And the longer he looked at her, the more she had the disturbing sense that she was staring into a mirror image of her own face. Not that she saw a physical resemblance there. It was something more fundamental. She saw a bleakness of the soul she knew all too well.

"You're hiding out, aren't you?" she said. "The long hair. The phony accent. The eye patch." She shivered against the cold.

"The eye patch is for real. They wrote it into the script for my last film. As for the rest, I wasn't trying to scare you. The accent's automatic. I use it to keep the fans away. I don't even think about it anymore."

But he seemed to be trapped in something more fundamental than a ruse to avoid being recognized by his fans. As a runaway herself, it wasn't difficult to recognize another, although what he had to run from she couldn't imagine.

He stared off into the distance. "No neighbors. No satellite dish. You're lucky to have this place."

He hunched his shoulders against the damp wind, still not bothering to look at her. "I'm sorry about Dash. He never liked me much, but I genuinely admired him."

His condolences sounded begrudging, and she bristled. "Not as an actor, I bet."

"No. Not as an actor. He was more a personality than anything else."

"He always said he played Dash Coogan better than anybody." She clamped her teeth together so they wouldn't chatter. She didn't show her weaknesses to anybody.

"He was his own man. Not many people can say that." Turning his head, he looked past her toward the sliver of lake visible through the trees.

She remembered a newspaper photograph she'd seen of him the day before the Academy Awards: mousse-slicked hair, RayBan sunglasses, unstructured Armani suit. The photograph hadn't shown his feet, but they had probably been sockless and stuffed into a pair of Gucci loafers. It struck her that he was a man of a thousand faces, and his vagabond's guise was merely one of them.

"You've got a lot of space here," he said.

"And not very many people," she replied. "Which is the way I want to keep it."

He didn't take the hint. Instead, he glanced toward the trailer. "You wouldn't happen to have a shower rigged up in there with some hot water?"

"I'm afraid I'm not in the mood for company."

"Neither am I. I'll be back as soon as I get some clean clothes from my van."

By the time she opened her mouth to tell him to go to hell, he had disappeared into the trees. She stalked into the trailer and momentarily considered locking the door. But an enormous weariness had settled over her, and she realized she simply didn't care. Let him take his shower. Then he would go away and she could be alone again.

She was shivering, and she wasn't about to wait around in wet clothes while Mr. Movie Star used up all her hot water. Let him take the leftovers. As she peeled out of her work clothes and stepped into the shower, she wondered what had happened to him. Other than his divorce and the automobile accident he had obviously survived, she had never heard of a single traumatic event in his life. He was one of God's chosen, given fame and fortune as if he'd been sprinkled with fairy dust at birth. What right did he have to act as if he were living out a Greek tragedy?

After she had dried off, she slipped into a pair of worn gray sweats she kept on the back of the door, then left the bathroom for the tiny, utilitarian bedroom that occupied the back. She didn't bother to look toward the trailer's living area to see if he had returned, but a few moments later she heard the bathroom door click shut and then the sound of the shower running.

When she had finished combing the snags out of her wet hair, she went to the small kitchen that ran along one side of the living area. She thought about making a pot of coffee, but she didn't want Eric to stay that long, so she filled the sink with water and began washing the dirty cups and glasses that had accumulated over the last few days.

When he emerged from the bathroom, he was wearing clean jeans and a flannel shirt. His long hair was slicked back from his face, and he had shaved. She hadn't intended to ask any questions that would prolong his visit, but once again the eye patch caught her attention.

"Is your eye injury permanent or temporary?"

"Permanent. At least until I have surgery. Even then, who knows? It's not a sight for weak stomachs."

This time a stirring of pity disturbed the shell she had erected around herself. The loss of an eye would be difficult for anyone, but it must be especially devastating for an actor who was being deprived of one of the most fundamental tools of his trade.

"I'm sorry," she said. The apology sounded resentful, and she thought how much she disliked this tough, hard person she had become.

He shrugged. "Shit happens."

Doesn't it just, she thought. So that was the reason he was running away. He had injured his eye in an accident, and he couldn't face up to it.

He wandered across the short-pile gray carpet to the back window and gazed through it. She began retrieving cups from the soapy dishwater.

"You don't have any TV here. That's good."

"Most of the time I don't even see a newspaper."

He nodded brusquely. And then, "What are you doing here?"

She'd been waiting for the question. Everyone was full of questions. The townspeople, the workmen, Liz. Everybody wanted to know why she had left L.A., and why she was spending a fortune trying to rebuild a roller coaster that sat in the middle of a dead amusement park. Since she could hardly tell people she was rebuilding it so she could find her husband, she generally explained that the country's great wooden coasters were endangered historical landmarks, and she was trying to save this one. But she didn't owe Eric any explanations, and so she said brusquely, "I needed to get out of L.A., so I'm restoring Black Thunder. The roller coaster."

She waited for him to prod her with more questions, but instead he turned to face her. "Look, it's obvious that you don't want company, but I'd like to hang around for a couple of days. I'll stay out of your way."

"You're right. I don't want company."

"That's fine. Neither do I. That's why this is a good place for me."

She pulled a mug out of the water and rinsed it. "There's nowhere for you to stay."

"I've been sleeping in my van."

She grabbed a dish towel and dried her hands. "I don't think so."

"Afraid?"

"Of you? Hardly."

"Rebuilding that coaster must be a lot of work. Maybe you could use another set of hands."

She gave a short laugh. "Construction work isn't for movie stars. It plays hell with those hundred-dollar manicures."

He didn't rise to her taunt; he barely seemed to have heard her. "Just do me a favor. Don't tell anybody who I am."

"I didn't say you could stay."

"You won't even know I'm here. And one more thing. Every couple of days I'll be taking some time off. Since I won't be on the payroll, it shouldn't be a problem."

"Need to get your hair done?"

"Something like that."

She didn't want him around, but she could use another set of hands—especially since she didn't have to pay him wages.

"Fine," she snapped, "but if you get on my nerves, you have to go."

"I won't be around long enough to get on your nerves."

"You're already just about there, so don't push it."

He shoved one hand in the back pocket of his jeans and studied her openly, taking in her damp hair, the worn gray sweats, her feet stuck in a pair of Dash's old wool socks. The only jewelry she wore was her wedding band, but in the past few months tools had deeply notched the gold in several places. She couldn't remember the last time she'd used makeup. Her twenty-sixth birthday wasn't for another few weeks, but her face was lined and tired, her eyes haunted. She knew from her infrequent glances in the mirror that nothing of the girl she had been remained.

He stared at her without apology and she began to experience a strange sense of commonality. For some reason that she didn't understand, nothing mattered to him. She could tell him everything or withhold it all. He was encapsulated in his indifference, and no matter what she revealed, he wouldn't offer either sympathy or condemnation. He simply didn't care.

The irony wasn't lost on her. For years she had regarded Eric Dillon with antipathy. Now, he was the first person she'd met since Dash's death whose presence she could tolerate.

The next morning Chantal came running to her as soon as she met Eric to launch a vehement protest against Honey hiring such a dangerous-looking stranger.

"That Dev is going to murder us in our beds, Honey! Just look at him."

Honey glanced over at Eric, who was stacking a pile of two-by-sixes in the frosty morning air. Dev? So that was the name he was using. Short for devil?

He was wearing a hard hat like everyone else, but he had snagged his hair into a ponytail that formed a blunt comma at the back of his neck. His flannel shirt was open at the throat, and she could see a T-shirt beneath. He had on a pair of scuffed work boots and jeans with a hole at the knee. His current outfit seemed just as much a part of him as the Armani suits. The curious thought flashed through her mind that everything he wore was costume instead of clothing.

"He's all right, Chantal. Don't worry about it. He used to be a priest."

"He did?"

"That's what he said." Honey swallowed the last of her coffee and tossed aside her paper cup. She smiled cynically as she mounted the frame and began to climb the lift hill. The idea of Eric Dillon as a priest was the first thing that had struck her funny in a long time.

When she arrived at the top, she attached her safety line and gazed back down to the ground. Eric was reaching up to fasten a two-by-six to the rope that hauled up the lumber. Ponytails weren't normally a hairstyle she liked on men, but with his thin nose, sharp-bladed cheekbones, and dramatic eye patch, he definitely pulled it off. She could just imagine what Dash would have said about it, and she smiled to herself as she created a little dialogue between them, something she liked to do to give herself a sort of bittersweet comfort.

"Now why would anybody who calls himself a man want to wear something like that?" he would say.

She'd look dreamy-eyed in a way that would be guaranteed to aggravate him. "Because it's incredibly attractive."

"Makes him look like a pansy."

"You're wrong, cowboy. He looks all man to me."

"Well, then, if you think he's so damn good-looking, why

don't you use him to satisfy that itch that's starting to wake you up at nights."

She nearly hit her thumb with her hammer, something she hadn't done in a month. Where had that thought come from? There wasn't any itch. None at all.

She took a vicious swing, but her imagination refused to be stifled, and she could hear Dash say, *"I don't see what's so wrong with having an itch. It's long past time. I didn't raise you to be a nun, little girl."*

"Stop talking to me like a father, dammit!"

"Part of me is your father, Honey. You know that."

She began frantically running numbers from her dwindling bank account in her head to block out any more imaginary conversations.

25

True to his word, Eric stayed out of her way, and she had little conversation with him after that first day. His van was parked between two of the old storage buildings not far from the delivery entrance. In the evening, while she was eating dinner with Chantal and Gordon, he used her shower.

From the beginning he managed to blend in with the workmen, and what he lacked in skill he made up for in muscle and tenacity. After two weeks she had to remind herself that he truly was Eric Dillon and not the man he had created; a long-haired, one-eyed foreigner who had introduced himself to everyone as Dev.

Several times each week he disappeared for part of the afternoon. Despite herself, she began to wonder where he went for those four- or five-hour stretches. The third time he disappeared it finally occurred to her that he must have a woman somewhere. A man like Eric Dillon was hardly going to give up sex just because he'd lost an eye.

She slammed her hammer down on a nail she was driving into the catwalk. Lately, when she should have been thinking about coming up with the money she needed to finish the coaster, she had been thinking about sex, and last night she'd had another disturbing dream, one in which a faceless man approached her, obviously with the intention of making love. She wanted that part of her buried with Dash, but her body seemed to have other ideas.

She shoved the hammer back into her tool belt, determined not to think about it. Even thinking about sex was a betrayal of what she and Dash had meant to each other.

That evening during dinner, Chantal and Gordon were abnormally quiet. Chantal picked at the too-salty tuna casserole she had prepared, then finally pushed it away and went to the refrigerator for a Pyrex casserole full of red Jello.

Gordon cleared his throat. "Honey, I've got something to tell you."

Chantal fumbled the casserole as she set it on the table. "No, Gordon. Don't say anything. Please . . ."

"I'm just about broke, so if you're after money, forget it." Honey pushed aside the soggy potato-chip crust with the vague hope of finding a small chunk of tuna.

Gordon banged down his fork. "It's not money, dammit! I'm going away. Tomorrow. They're hiring construction workers up near Winston-Salem, and I'm going to get a job."

"Sure you are," Honey scoffed.

"I mean it. I'm not going to work for you anymore. I'm tired of taking your money."

"Why do I find that hard to believe?" She shoved back her plate and said sarcastically, "What about your great career as an artist? I thought you weren't ever going to compromise yourself."

"I guess I've been doing that since you picked me up on that Oklahoma highway," he said quietly.

Honey felt the first prickle of uneasiness as she realized that he was serious. "What brought about this sudden change of heart?"

"These past few months have reminded me that I like hard work."

Chantal was staring down at the table. She sniffed. Gordon regarded her miserably. "Chantal doesn't want to go. She—uh—she may not be coming with me."

"I haven't made up my mind yet."

"He's bluffing," Honey said sharply. "He won't leave you behind."

Gordon gazed at Chantal, and his eyes were tender. "I'm not bluffing, Chantal. Tomorrow morning I'm driving out of this place with or without you. You have to make up your mind whether you're going to stand by me or not."

Chantal started to cry.

Gordon rose from the table and turned his back on them. His shoulders heaved, and Honey realized he was near tears, too. She hid her own growing panic beneath anger.

"Why are the two of you doing this? Just go! Both of you." She sprang to her feet and spun on her cousin. "I can't support you any longer. I've been trying to find a way to tell you, and it looks like this is it. I want you out of here tomorrow morning."

Chantal jumped up from her chair and confronted her husband. "See what I mean, Gordon? How can I leave her like this? What's going to happen to her?"

Honey stared at her. "Me? You're worried about leaving me? Well, don't be. I'm tough. I've always been tough."

"You need me." Chantal sniffed. "For the first time in as long as I can remember, you need me. And I don't have any idea how to help you."

"Help me? That's a laugh. You can't even help yourself. You're pitiful, Chantal Delaweese. If you wanted to help me, why didn't you take some of the responsibility off my shoulders when I was busting my rear on the Coogan show? Why didn't you do something to help out then instead of lying around on the couch all day? If you wanted to help me, why didn't you act like you cared about somebody other than Gordon? If you wanted to help me, why didn't you bake me a birthday cake that didn't *blow up?*"

To Honey's dismay, her eyes stung with tears. There was a long silence broken only by the harsh sound of her breathing as she struggled for control.

Finally, Chantal spoke. "I didn't do any of that because I sort of hated you then, Honey. All of us did."

"How could you hate me?" Honey cried. "I gave you everything you wanted!"

"Remember when you made me enter the Miss Paxawatchie County contest because you were trying so hard to keep us off welfare? Well, it's like me and Gordon have been on welfare all these years. Not because we needed help like somebody with lots of kids and no way to feed them. But because it was easier to take a free handout than work. We lost our dignity, Honey, and that's why we hated you."

"It wasn't my fault!"

"No. It was ours. But you made it so easy."

Gordon turned back to Chantal, his expression miserable. "I need you, too, Chantal. You're my wife. I love you."

"Oh, Gordon." Chantal's lips trembled. "I love you, too. But you can take care of yourself. Right now, I don't think Honey can."

Honey's throat closed tight with a nearly uncontrollable rush of emotion. She fought against it, struggling to keep her dignity. "That's the stupidest thing I ever heard you say, Chantal Booker Delaweese. A woman belongs with her husband, and I don't want to hear another word about you staying here with me. As a matter of fact, I'll be glad to have you gone."

"Honey . . ."

"Not one more word," she said fiercely. "I'm saying my good-byes right now, and both of you had better be out of here first thing tomorrow." She grabbed her cousin and drew her into her arms for a crushing hug.

"Oh, Honey . . ."

She pulled away and extended her hand toward Gordon. "Good luck, Gordon."

"Thanks, Honey." He took her hand, and then he hugged her, too. "You take care, you hear?"

"Sure." Moving away, she headed toward the back door, where she forced a smile that made her jaw muscles ache, then rushed outside.

She ran across the park. Her hair came free and flew about her head, lashing her cheeks. Her feet thudded on the hard ground. As the trailer came into sight, she gasped for air, but she didn't stop running.

She stumbled on the step and caught herself just before she fell. When she got inside, she pushed the door shut and leaned back against it, using her body to stave off the monsters. Her chest heaved, and she tried to calm herself, but she had passed the point of reason, and her fear consumed her.

For months she had been telling herself she wanted to be left alone, but now that it had happened, she felt as if she had been cast loose in space, aimlessly whirling, disconnected from all human life. She was no longer part of anyone. She had no family left. She lived alone in the land of the dead, only her obsession with Black Thunder keeping her alive. But Black Thunder had no plasma, no skin, no heartbeat.

Gradually, she became aware of the noise of water running. At first she couldn't think what it was, and then she realized that Eric was using her shower. Normally he was gone by the time she returned from her dinner, but she had come back earlier than usual.

She pressed her hands to her temples. She didn't want to be alone. She couldn't be alone. *I can't bear it anymore, Dash. I'm so afraid. I'm afraid of living. And I'm afraid to die.*

Her teeth began to chatter. She stepped away from the door, holding onto the counter for support. The fear was sucking at her bones, gobbling up little bits of her. She had to make it go away. She needed a connection with someone. Anyone.

Numbly, she turned toward the short, narrow hallway and stumbled the few short yards that took her to the bathroom door. She told herself not to think. Just to keep herself alive.

Forgive me. Oh, please, forgive me.

The knob turned in her hand.

Steam enveloped her as she entered. She pressed the door shut behind her and stood against it, struggling to breathe.

He had his face turned to the nozzle, his back toward her. His body was too large for the rectangular shower stall, and when he moved, his shoulders bumped into the sheets of cheap plastic that formed the walls, making them rattle. She could discern the outline of his back and buttocks through the steam-clouded walls, but none of the details. His body could have belonged to any man.

Squeezing her eyes shut, she kicked off her shoes. Then she crossed her arms over her chest and peeled both her sweatshirt and T-shirt over her head. Her bra was lacy and delicate, pale shells of mint green, the remaining token of femininity she hadn't been willing to abandon to the world of hard hats, work boots, and Skil saws. With a dull sense of inevitability, she unsnapped her jeans and pulled them slowly down over her legs, revealing the fragile pair of panties that matched her bra.

Her legs had begun to shake and she steadied herself with a hand on the rim of the sink. If she didn't find a human connection, she would break apart. A connection with anyone.

Her reflection floated before her in the steam-fogged mirror above the sink. She could make out tangled hair, the indistinct outlines of her features.

The water stopped running. She whirled around. Eric turned in the shower stall and went absolutely still as he saw her standing there.

She said nothing. The steamy plastic panels continued to blur the distinguishing lines of his features in a way that comforted her. He could be any man, one of the faceless men in her dreams, an anonymous man whose only purpose was to take away her fear of being alone and unloved.

Slowly he turned his back to her, and the shower door made a hollow *ping* as he opened it. Reaching through with one dripping arm, he retrieved his towel from the wire hook outside. His eye patch dangled from a black cord beneath. Still standing in the shower, he passed the towel through his wet hair, pushing it away from his face, then reached for the black patch and secured it over his head to spare her the sight of his mutilated eye.

"Right now I feel like it is. Maybe trying to keep up with the sexual excesses of my twenty-five-year-old child bride has something to do with it."

She buried her lips in the side of his neck while her hands trailed down along the front of his shirt to the waistband of his jeans. "Want to knock off a quickie?"

"Didn't we do that early this morning?"

"Anything that happens before six o'clock counts for the day before."

"Now why's that?"

"It's all a matter of relativity. I learned about it in that philosophy class I took last year." She slipped her fingertips inside his waistband. "It's far too complex for me to explain to an ignorant cowpoke, so I'm afraid you'll have to take my word for it."

"Is that so?" He leaned forward so abruptly that she upended over his shoulder.

"Hey!"

He caught her in his lap before she could sprawl to the floor. "It seems to me somebody's getting a little too smarty-pants to fit into her britches."

She squirmed into a more comfortable position in his arms and gazed up into that wonderful face. "Are you ever sorry you married me?"

He cupped her breast and gently kneaded it. "About a hundred times a day." And then the teasing light faded from his green eyes and he drew her against him with a muffled groan. "My sweet little girl. Sometimes I think my life didn't start until the day I married you."

She lay contented against him. Maybe their marriage was even more precious to her because it wasn't perfect. They'd had so many problems right from the beginning: their guilt over the demise of the TV series, the humiliation they had suffered from the press, the fact that his daughter hated her guts.

Most of their problems hadn't gone away. They'd only recently emerged from their financial troubles. Instead of sheltering the money she'd brought into their marriage,

Her heart thudded relentlessly in her chest. The steam was beginning to make her skin glisten. Naked except for the fragile pieces of mint-green lace, she waited for him to emerge.

He stepped through the shower door, watching her as he rubbed the towel in slow circles over the dark, matted hair on his chest. The bathroom was small, and he was so close she could have touched him. But she wasn't ready to touch, and her gaze dropped to his sex. It lay heavy against his thigh, the heat distending him. This was what she wanted from him. Only this. The connection.

She kept her eyes averted from his face so that she would know him only as a body. His torso was perfectly sculpted, the musculature deliberately defined. She saw an angry red scar near his knee and looked away, not because she was repulsed, but because the scar personalized him.

He passed the towel over his buttocks and thighs. She could feel her hair curling in the steam, forming baby corkscrews around her face. Beads of moisture had gathered between her breasts. They dampened her thumb as she unfastened the front clasp on her bra and let the pale green lace drop away like fragile teacups.

She sensed his eyes upon her breasts, but she would not look at his face. Instead, she studied the indentation at the base of his throat where a trickle of water had collected. His arm moved toward her, the tendons strong and clearly defined. She caught her breath as he passed his hand over her breast.

The dark tan of his arm looked foreign and forbidden against the paleness of her skin. He flattened his palm against her rib cage, slid it down over her stomach and inside the waistband of her panties. Tendrils of fire licked at her nerve endings. Her body felt hot and swollen. He slipped down her panties.

As soon as she stepped out of them, she knew she had to touch him. Leaning forward, she dipped her mouth to the moisture that had cupped at the base of his throat. Her nostrils quivered as she caught the clean scent of his skin.

She pressed her nose to his chest, a nipple, turned her head toward his underarm, softly breathing him in.

Ribbons of her pale hair streamed over his damp chest, adorning his darker skin with gentle ornamentation. He flattened his hands over her back. She trembled at the sensation of once again being enclosed in a man's arms. He slid his hands down along her back to her buttocks, cupping them to draw her against him. She felt him hard and moist against her belly.

She waited for him to speak, to ask all the "why's" and "what's" that would send her flying away from him. But instead of speaking, his head dipped to the curve of her neck. She caught the backs of his thighs and squeezed them. Then she arched her neck and offered him her breasts.

He lowered his lips to her collarbone before claiming the swell of flesh below. Her skin was alive to sensation: the dampness of their flesh, the pleasuring pain of his whiskers, the soft whip of his wet, dark hair. And then she felt the demands of his mouth as he encompassed her nipple and drew it deeply inside. His eye patch brushed over her skin.

He reached between her legs from behind and opened her. She moaned and encircled his calf with her leg, trying to climb his body so that she could take him in. But he held her off, stroking her and touching her in ways that made her gasp with need.

Only once did she turn cold. When he put her away from him and reached for his pile of clothing on the floor.

Keeping her eyes averted from his face, she watched his hands, too befuddled by the urgency of her need to understand why he should be taking a wallet from his jeans. What he wanted there. And then as he slid out the small foil packet she understood and hated the necessity because faceless men should have no need for small foil packets. Faceless men should have bodies that blindly served, without the power to reproduce, without the dangers of disease.

She turned her back while he readied himself.

And then his hands came around her to toy again with her breasts until she sobbed. He turned her. She propped her arms over his shoulders as he lifted her, wrapped her legs around her waist. He pressed her to the thin bathroom wall so that her spine was flat against it.

"Are you ready?" he whispered, his voice smoky.

She nodded her head against his cheek and pressed her eyes shut as he pushed himself inside her.

Her hair tumbled down over his back, and her thighs clasped him with their work-strengthened muscles. She clung to him, whispering *yes* and *yes*. Her body was so starved, so desperate.

Gently, he used her.

Tears seeped from her eyes and trickled along his damp spine. He held her in his strong arms, stroked her so deeply, caressed her so tenderly. She cried out with her climax, and then gripped his shoulders tighter while he drove to find his own release. She stoically bore his weight as he leaned shuddering against her.

Gradually he withdrew and lowered her to the floor. His breathing was harsh and uneven. She saw his arm move and knew he was about to draw her close. Quickly, she backed away, not looking at him, not letting him touch her. Within seconds, she had left him alone while she closed herself in the small bedroom across the hallway.

Much later, when she emerged, he had disappeared. She could find no sign that he had even been there except for the droplets of water still clinging to the walls of the shower. She dried them off before she stepped inside herself.

He couldn't take any more hurt!

Eric's knuckles were white as he gripped the van's steering wheel. Why had he let another wounded person into his life? He had been trying to get away from suffering, not plunge in deeper. He wanted to drive away, but he had not even been able to put the key in the ignition.

Her face was imprinted on the windshield in front of him: those luminous, haunted eyes, that full mouth trembling with need. God, he'd been dreaming about that mouth from the moment he had seen her again. It was soft and sensual, and it drew him as if it had magic powers. But he hadn't even kissed her, and he doubted she would have let him if he'd tried.

Instead of finding sanctuary in this dead amusement park, he had plunged himself deeper into hell. Why was he so drawn to her? She was cold and tough, with a grim, single-minded determination that was at odds with her small stature. Even the men on the construction crew shied away from her. They had been stung too often by her razor-sharp tongue. She was the same little monster she'd been that second season of the Coogan show, a hundred years ago.

Over the trees he could see the top of the lift hill. He didn't understand what there was about the coaster that obsessed her, but he had begun to hate those moments when he looked up from the ground und saw her small body entwined with the frame of the great wooden beast until she and the coaster almost seemed to be one. Her obsession frightened him.

Who was she? Not the needy, love-struck girl who had once reminded him of his little brother. Not the tough, sharp-tongued boss lady in the yellow hard hat, either. Sometimes when he looked at her, he thought he saw another woman standing slightly apart from her —a saucy, laughing woman with a loving heart and wide-open arms. He told himself the image was an illusion, a mental hologram he had created out of his own despair, but then he wondered if he might not be seeing the woman she had been when she was married to Dash Coogan.

Tonight, her beauty had clawed at his guts. The strength, the tragedy, the awful vulnerability. But they had come together like animals instead of human beings. Even when their bodies were locked together, they had given nothing of themselves to each other, so that in the end he could use her as she was using him, impersonally, as a safe receptacle.

But it hadn't worked that way. The thing that terrified him—the thing that made sweat break out on his body and his stomach clench—was the way she had made him feel.

For the space of time while he had held that fragile female body—a body that demanded nothing more from him than sexual release—he had felt all the fiercely protective layers he'd erected around himself slip away, leaving him ready to go to the ends of the earth to console her.

As he sat staring blindly through the window of the van, he knew that he should leave just as surely as he knew he was going to stay. But he would never let himself be so vulnerable to her again because he had no place left inside him to hold anyone else's pain. They said he was the best actor of his generation, and he was going to use his talent. From this moment on, he would wrap himself so tightly inside his identities that she would never again be able to touch him.

The next day Honey drove herself relentlessly, trying to shut out the events of the night, but as she inspected a section of track with the project foreman, the images washed over her. How could she have done it? How could she have betrayed her marriage vows like that? Self-hatred gnawed away at her, a bleak antipathy toward the person she had become.

For the rest of the day she threw herself into her work with a ferocity that, by evening, left her drained and weak. As she dropped to the ground and unfastened her tool belt, she heard someone approaching her from behind. Even before she turned, she could feel who it was and she tensed.

Eric regarded her with a face empty of any expression. Instead of feeling relieved that he wasn't forcing her to acknowledge what had happened, she felt chilled. If it weren't for the small aches in her body, she would think that she had imagined the whole thing.

"I understand that your cousin and her husband have left," he said in his carefully accented English. "Would you mind if I move my belongings into the Bullpen? It's more comfortable than my van."

She had tried to forget about the empty Bullpen. All day she had looked down at the vacated building expecting to see Gordon's truck parked there, but he and Chantal were gone.

"Suit yourself," she said stiffly.

He nodded and walked away.

When she returned to her trailer, she heated a can of beef stew for her own dinner and tried to block out her loneliness by running numbers on her calculator. The figures hadn't changed. She could meet her payroll through the first week of January, and then she would have to shut down.

Grabbing a soft blue cable-knit cardigan, she let herself outside. The night was clear, the sky dotted with silver stars. She hoped Chantal and Gordon were all right. It would be Christmas in less than two weeks. Last Christmas, she and Dash had camped in the desert and he'd given her handmade gold earrings shaped like crescent moons. She'd put them away in her jewelry box after he died because she couldn't bear looking at them.

She picked her way along the overgrown path that led to the lake and stood on the bank to gaze out over the water. The government had finally forced the Purlex Paint Company to stop its pollution, but it would be several years before the lake began to come to life again. Now, however, the darkness concealed its polluted condition, and moonlight formed silver streamers on its still surface.

She turned her back on the lake and let her eyes rise above the trees to the hills of Black Thunder, dimly visible in the moonlight. Everybody thought she was crazy to be rebuilding the coaster. How could she explain this unrelenting drive to find some sign that Dash was not lost to her? In saner moments she told herself that Black Thunder was only an amusement-park ride and that it held no mystical powers. But her rational mind was silenced by the driving urgency that insisted she could only restore her soul by taking a ride through her nightmares on Black Thunder.

Her shoulders sagged. Maybe everybody was right. Maybe she was crazy. She could feel her eyes fill and the wooden hills wavered before her. *You damned old cowboy. You broke my heart, just like you said you would.*

A movement in the pines distracted her. Alarmed, she saw the dark figure of a man standing there. He stepped out of the shadows, and she realized that it was Eric. She felt a jolt of panic at the idea of being alone with him.

As had become her practice when she wanted to hide her fear, she grew angry. "I don't like being spied on. You just wore out your welcome."

His single blue eye regarded her dispassionately as he came toward her. "Why would I be spying on you? Actually, I was here first."

"It's my lake," she retorted, dismayed at her own childishness.

"And you're welcome to it. From what I can see, nobody else would want it."

Even though they were alone, she realized that he was speaking to her with the faint tinges of a Middle Eastern accent. She also realized that if she continued to snap at him, he might think last night had some real meaning to her. She took a shaky breath and attempted to regain her dignity.

"The lake's starting to come back," she said. "A paint company used it as a dumping ground for years."

"This place is too isolated for you to be living alone. I found a vagrant hanging around the Bullpen this evening. Now that your relatives are gone, maybe you should consider renting a room in town instead of staying out here by yourself."

He didn't realize that he was more dangerous to her than any vagrant, and her slim hold on composure snapped. "I don't remember asking for your opinion."

The face that was so expressive on the screen slammed shut like a screen door with a too-tight spring. "You're correct. It's not my business."

Despite the accent he had thrown up like a barrier, memories of the night before rushed over her and she struggled against her panic in the only way she knew. "You hide behind that accent, don't you?" she said contemptuously. "And you're hiding more than your famous face. Well, you may forget who you are, but I don't, and I'm sick of you acting like some kind of nut case."

His jaw tightened. "The accent's automatic, and I'm

hardly the nut case." She sucked in her breath, waiting for him to confront her with having come to him. But instead, he said, "I'm not the one who's building a roller coaster in the middle of nowhere. I'm not the one running around like some pint-sized version of Captain Ahab obsessed with her own goddamned Moby Dick."

"Better than Moby Dickless!" She wasn't obsessed. *She wasn't!* This was simply something she had to do so she could live again.

"What does that mean?" His accent was gone, his face shadowed.

She went on the attack, trying to sink her teeth into the softest part of his flesh, trying to make the kill first. "What kind of coward are you, running away just because you lost your stupid eye? *At least you're alive, you bastard!"*

"You little shit. You don't know what it looks like under here." He jabbed his fingers in the direction of the black patch. "There isn't an eye there. Just a mass of ugly red scar tissue."

"So what? You've got a spare."

For a moment he didn't say anything. Her stomach felt sick at what she was doing, but she didn't know how to take back the words.

His lips curled in mockery, and he spoke softly. "I always wondered what happened to Janie Jones, and now I know. Life threw her one too many hard knocks and now she's right back where she started— a bossy little bitch hiding behind a big mouth."

"That's not true!"

"Jesus. It's too bad Dash isn't still alive. I'd lay money he'd throw you over his knee and beat some sense into you just like he did when you were a kid."

"Don't you talk about him," she said fiercely. "Don't you even speak his name." Tears were glistening in her eyes, but he appeared unmoved.

"What in the hell are you doing here, Honey? Why is rebuilding that coaster so important to you?"

"It just is, that's all."

"Tell me, damnit!"

"You wouldn't understand."

"You'd be surprised at how much I can understand."

"I have to do it." She looked down at the hands she was twisting in front of her and her anger faded. "When I was a child that coaster meant a lot to me."

"So did my Swiss army knife, but I wouldn't give up everything to get it back."

"It's not like that! It's about—it's about *hope.*" She winced, appalled by what she had revealed.

"You can't make Dash come back," he said cruelly.

"I knew you wouldn't understand!" she exclaimed. "And when I need lectures from you, I'll let you know! You're running away just as much as I am and for a lot less reason. I read the papers. I know you have children. Two little girls, right? What kind of father are you to disappear on them like this?"

He gave her a look so taut with restrained rage that she wished she'd kept her mouth shut.

"Don't make judgments about things you don't know anything about." Without another word, he stalked away from her.

For the next few days Eric only spoke to her when the men were around, and he always used the voice of Dev, the construction worker. The voice began to haunt her dreams and make her body ache with sensations she didn't want to acknowledge. She kept reminding herself that Eric was a gifted and disciplined actor with complete control over any character he created, but the menacing-looking construction worker was assuming an identity separate from Eric in her mind. She did everything she could to stay away from him, but in the end her escalating money problems made that impossible.

On a Tuesday afternoon, four days after their confrontation by the lake, she made up her mind to approach him. She waited until the men stopped for lunch. Eric had been loading old sections of track into the back of a flatbed, and he pulled off his gloves as she came near.

She held out a brown paper bag. "I noticed you haven't been eating lunch, so I fixed this for you."

He hesitated for a moment, then took it from her. He was clearly wary, and it occurred to her that he had been avoiding her as much as she was avoiding him.

"I only brought along one thermos, though, so we'll have to share." She began to walk, hoping he'd follow. After a few seconds, she heard his footsteps.

She moved away from the men to the spot where the carousel had once stood. Not far away an old sycamore had fallen in a storm. She sat down on it, put the thermos on the ground, and opened her lunch sack. A moment later he straddled the trunk and pulled out the peanut butter sandwich she'd made that morning. She noticed that he bunched the plastic wrap around the bottom part to protect it from his grimy hands, and she remembered that he had grown up in a wealthy family where clean hands would have been required at the dinner table.

"I cut it into triangles instead of rectangles," she said. "It's the closest I come to gourmet cooking these days."

The corner of his mouth ticked in something that might have been his version of a smile. She felt a sharp pang as she remembered how much she and Dash used to laugh.

He gestured toward the barren circle of earth in front of them. "One of the rides must have been here."

"The carousel." The first time she had seen Eric, his eyes had reminded her of the bright blue saddles on the horses. She opened her own lunch bag, trying to overcome her uneasiness as she pulled out her sandwich. She knew this was a bad idea, but she hadn't been able to come up with a better one.

Slipping a corner of the peanut butter sandwich in her mouth, she chewed it without tasting, swallowed, then set it in her lap. "I have something I want to talk to you about."

He waited.

"I'm going to have to call off the restoration work if I can't come up with some cash in the next few weeks."

"I'm not surprised. It's an expensive project."

"The truth of the matter is, I'm broke. What I wanted to

ask you—" The chunk of sandwich seemed to be stuck in her throat. She swallowed again. "I was thinking that you . . . That is, I was hoping you might—"

"You're not going to hit me for a loan, are you?"

Her carefully planned speech vanished from her mind. "What's so horrible about that? You must have a few million stashed away, and I only need around two hundred thousand."

"That's all? Why don't I just whip out my checkbook right now?"

"I'll pay you back."

"Sure you will. That coaster's going to be earning you a fortune. What do you figure? Maybe five bucks a week?"

"I'm not planning on paying you back from the coaster. I know it won't make a profit. But as soon as I finish Black Thunder and it's running again, I'm—" She stumbled on her words. This was going to be even harder than she had thought. As she spoke, she knew she was giving up the only thing she had left that was of any value to her. "I'm calling my agent this evening. I'm going back to work."

"I don't believe you."

She felt sick. "I have to. If acting is the only way I can get Black Thunder running, then I'll do it."

"Something good might come out of this after all."

"What do you mean?"

"You should never have stopped performing, Honey. You didn't even give yourself a chance to find out what you could do."

"I can do Janie Jones," she said fiercely. "That's it. I'm a personality, just like Dash. I'm not an actress."

"How do you know that?"

"I just do. I used to listen to all that talk of yours about internal technique, affective memory, the Bucharest school. I don't know anything about those things."

"That's just vocabulary. It doesn't have anything to do with talent."

"I'm not going to debate this with you, Eric. All I'm saying is that I can pay you back. I'll have my agent put together some ironclad contracts—film roles, TV movies, commercials—anything that pays. By the time people figure out I'm not Meryl Streep and the job offers stop, you'll have your money back with interest."

He stared at her. "You'd sell your talent that cheap?"

"It's not exactly talent I'm selling, is it? Notoriety might be a better word."

His lips thinned. "Why don't you just pick up the phone and call one of the big men's magazines? They'd give you a fortune for a nude layout. Think about it. You'd have the money you need to finish rebuilding your roller coaster, and guys all over America could jerk off to naked pictures of Janie Jones."

He had made a direct hit, but she wasn't going to let him see it. "How much do you think they'd give me?"

He balled the paper sack and, with an exclamation of disgust, threw it on the ground.

"I'm kidding," she said tightly. "You were getting so sanctimonious."

"I wonder. If nude photos were the only way you could get the money, would you do it?"

"I guess I'd have to think about it."

"I'll bet you would." He shook his head in wonder. "Damn it, I think you'd actually do it."

"So what? My body doesn't mean anything to me anymore."

A subtle tension came over him, and she suspected he was remembering the way she had offered herself to him. She seized the chance to tell him indirectly that their lovemaking had no significance to her.

"My body isn't important, Eric. It doesn't mean anything! Now that Dash is dead, I just don't care anymore."

"I sure as hell think he'd care."

She looked away.

"He would, wouldn't he?"

"Yes. Yes, I guess he would." She drew a shaky breath. "But he's dead, Eric, and I have to rebuild this coaster."

"Why? Why is it so important to you?"

"It's—" She remembered the night by the lake. "I tried to tell you before, and you wouldn't understand. It's just something I have to do, that's all." A long silence fell as she attempted to get herself back under control.

He studied the scuffed toe of his work boot. "Exactly how much do you need?"

She told him.

He gazed out toward the clearing that had once marked the site of Kiddieland. "All right, Honey. I'll make a deal with you. I'll loan you your money, but on one condition."

"What's that?"

He turned to her, his single blue eye regarding her so intently she felt burned. "You'll have to sign yourself over to me."

"What are you talking about?"

"I mean that I'll own your talent, Honey. Every bit of it until the loan's paid off."

"What?"

"I choose your projects. Not you and not your agent. Only me. I decide what you can and can't do."

"That's ridiculous."

"Take it or leave it."

"Why should I? You'd never hand your career over to someone else."

"Not in a million years."

"But you expect me to."

"I don't expect anything. You're the one who wants the money, not me."

"What you're talking about is slavery. You could put me in hemorrhoid commercials or make me do auto shows at a hundred dollars a pop."

"Theoretically."

"I don't have any reason to trust you. I don't even like you."

"No, I don't expect you do."

He said the words so matter-of-factly that she was ashamed. Obviously, he didn't expect anything more from her.

Snatching up her uneaten lunch, she rose from the log and gave him a hostile glare. "All right. You've got a deal. But you'd better not cross me, or you'll regret it."

He watched her as she stalked away. *Big talker,* he thought to himself. She was still swinging those fists just as she had when she was a kid. Still daring the world to cross her. And had it ever.

He couldn't tolerate watching her shadowbox with ghosts much longer. And the worst ghost of all was that damned roller coaster. She had said the coaster was about hope, but he had the uneasy sense that she somehow thought Black Thunder could bring her husband back. He stood and picked up the remnants of his lunch. He couldn't imagine what it would be like to be loved as Honey loved Dash.

Even though he didn't have to be back in L.A. for two weeks his mind screamed at him to leave now. Take himself as far from the grieving Widow Coogan as he could get. That's what he should do. But instead of disengaging himself from her, he had just become even more entangled, and when he asked himself why, he could only come up with one answer.

In some strange way, he felt as if he had just taken a giant step toward finally earning Dash Coogan's respect.

26

Not a single red bow or a sprig of holly decorated the interior of her trailer on Christmas morning. Honey had planned to endure the holiday rather than celebrate it, but when she got out of bed, she couldn't make herself climb into her work clothes for another day of solitary labor.

As she stared at herself in the bathroom mirror, some small shred of vanity poked at her. Dash used to tell her how pretty she was, but the small face that looked back at her was gaunt and haunted, a street urchin grown old too quickly. She turned away in disgust, but instead of walking out of the bathroom, she found herself kneeling down to search the tiny storage space below the sink for the hot rollers she had stuck there when she had moved in, along with her makeup.

An hour later, dressed in a silky turtleneck and pleated trousers of antique rose wool, she finished brushing out her hair. It fell in loose waves to her shoulders and shone like warm honey from the conditioner she had used. Makeup camouflaged the circles under her eyes while mascara thickened her lashes and emphasized her light blue irises. She dusted her cheekbones with blush, slicked on a soft pink lipstick, and fastened the gold crescent moons Dash had given her into her lobes. Her eyes began to sting as she watched one of the moons tangle with a tendril of hair, and she quickly turned away from her reflection in the mirror.

When she reached the trailer's living area, she poured herself a cup of coffee and went to the table next to the couch for the brown envelope she had put there several days earlier. It had a message scrawled across the front in Chantal's childish handwriting. "Do Not Open Until December 25. This Means You!" She tore apart the envelope flap and pulled out a lumpy package wrapped in white tissue paper with a note affixed to the top.

Dear Honey,

Hope you have a Merry Xmas. Me and Gordon like Winston-Salem. We found a place to stay in a real nice trailer park. Gordon likes his job. He said to tell you he's got a present for you, but you won't get it for a while. I made a friend. Her name is Gloria and she taught me how to croshay.

I'm still thinking you should go back to L.A. I don't think Dash would like what your doing to yourself. I miss you. I hope you like your present.

Love,
Chantal (and Gordon)

P.S. Don't worry. If you go back to L.A., me and Gordon won't come with you.

Honey blinked her eyes and unwrapped the tissue paper. With a shaky smile she drew out the first real present she had received from Chantal since they were children, a hand-crocheted cover for a roll of toilet paper. It was made of neon-blue yarn and ornamented with misshapen yellow loops to represent flowers. She carried it to the bathroom, where she stuffed it with a spare roll and set it in a place of honor on the back of her toilet.

That done, she tried to think of something else to occupy her time. Impulsively, she snatched up a gray wool jacket, grabbed her purse, and headed for her Blazer. She would turn the radio up and take a long drive.

Only Christmas carols were playing on the local stations, so she snapped the radio off before she reached the town limits. The weather was in the high fifties and clear, and she had just decided to drive over to Myrtle Beach to watch the ocean when she spotted Eric's van stopped at a traffic light several blocks ahead of her. She remembered his mysterious disappearances and wondered if he were on his way to meet a woman. The idea made her feel sick.

She wasn't planning to follow him, but when he turned off Palmetto Street, she found herself turning, too. A number of holiday travelers were on the road, and she didn't have any trouble keeping several car lengths between them. To her surprise, he pulled into the parking lot of Paxawatchie County's major hospital.

She parked her car a few rows over from the van and waited. Several minutes ticked by. Her mind drifted to Dash, and because that was too painful, she thought about the work that lay ahead before Black Thunder could once again fly over the tracks.

She returned her attention to the van as the back doors swung open. And a clown stepped out.

He was dressed in a purple shirt tucked into baggy polka-dotted trousers, and his hair was covered by a frizzy red wig tied with a pirate's scarf. In one hand he held a bundle of multicolored helium balloons, in the other a plastic trash bag that looked as if it might be stuffed with presents. Just as she decided she had followed the wrong van, the clown tilted his head and she caught a glimpse of a purple star-shaped eye patch. For a moment she felt disoriented.

Eric Dillon had still another face.

Who was he? How many identities did he have? First Dev. Now this. She wanted to drive away, but she couldn't. Without stopping to think about what she was doing, she followed him inside.

He had disappeared by the time she got to the lobby, but it wasn't difficult to find his trail. An elderly woman sat in a wheelchair holding a red balloon. A child with an arm cast held a green one. Further on, she came upon a patient lying on a gurney with an orange balloon floating overhead. But the trail ran out in a back hallway.

She tried to talk herself into leaving, but instead she approached a nurses' station. "Excuse me. Did you happen to see a clown go by earlier?" The question sounded ridiculous.

The young nurse behind the desk had a sprig of artificial holly stuck in her plastic name tag. "You mean Patches?"

Honey nodded uncertainly. This must not be Eric's first visit to the hospital. Was this where he came when he disappeared?

"He's probably doing a show for the kids today. Hold on." She picked up her phone, asked a few questions of the person on the other end, then hung up. "Pediatrics on three. They're starting now."

Honey thanked her and headed for the elevators. As soon as she stepped out onto the third floor, she heard squeals of laughter. She followed the sounds to a lounge at the end of the corridor and stopped. It took all of her courage to look inside.

A dozen very young children, probably between four and eight years old, were gathered in the cheerfully decorated room. Some wore hospital gowns, others robes. They were black, Asian and white. Several sat in wheelchairs and a few were hooked up to IVs.

Beneath his curly red wig, Eric's face was disguised in clown white. He had one large eyebrow drawn on his forehead, a scarlet mouth, a red circle at the end of his nose, and the purple star-shaped eye patch. He was concentrating on the children and didn't see her. Fascinated, she watched.

"You are not Santa Claus!" one of the children called out, a small boy in a blue robe.

"Now that's where yer wrong," Eric retorted belligerently. "I got a beard, don't I?" He stroked his smoothly shaven chin.

The children greeted this observation with vigorous shakes of their head and shouts of denial.

He patted his flat waist. "And I got a big fat stomach?"

"No, you don't!"

"And I got a red Santy Claus suit." He plucked at his purple shirt.

"No!"

A long pause fell. Eric looked bewildered. His face puckered as if he were about to cry, and the children laughed harder.

"Then who am I?" he wailed.

"You're Patches!" several of them squealed. "Patches the Pirate!"

His face cracked open in a smile. "That I am!" He pulled at the waistband of his baggy red and purple polka-dot trousers and half a dozen small balloons floated up and out. Then he broke into "Popeye the Sailor Man," substituting the name Patches and performing something close to an Irish jig.

Honey watched in bewilderment. How could a person who was driven by so many private devils set them aside to perform like this? His accent was a comic mixture of Cockney, Long John Silver, and Popeye's nemesis Bluto. The children were clapping with delight, completely caught up in the enchanted spell he was so effortlessly weaving about them.

As he wound up for his finish, he pulled three rubber balls

from his pants pocket and began juggling them. He was a clumsy juggler, but he was so enthusiastic that the children loved it. And then he saw her.

She froze.

One of the balls slipped from his grasp and bounced across the lounge. Several seconds ticked by as he stared at her, and then he immediately returned his attention to the children.

"I missed it on purpose," he growled, planting his hands on his hips, glaring at them, daring them to contradict him.

"You did not!" a few of them countered. "You dropped it!"

"You all think yer so smart," he glowered. "I'll 'ave you know I was trained in the arts of juggling by Corny the Magnificent 'imself!"

"Who's that?" one of the children asked.

"You never 'eard of Corny the Magnificent?"

They shook their heads.

"Well, then. . . ." He began spinning a magical yarn of jugglers and dragons and a beautiful princess with a wicked spell cast upon her that had made her forget her name and left her cursed to wander the globe trying to find her home. With facial expression and gesture, he created imaginary pictures so vivid they could have been real.

She had seen what she'd come for, but she couldn't make herself leave. Strands of the snare he had woven about the children entrapped her, and as she listened, it became impossible to remember who existed behind that clown's face. Eric Dillon was dark and damned; this pirate clown exuded a joyous, enchanting charm.

Patches shook his head dolefully. "So beautiful the princess is, and so sad. 'Ow would you like it if you couldn't remember yer name or where you lived?"

"I know my name," one of the bolder little boys called out. "Jeremy Frederick Cooper the third. And I live in Lamar."

Other children called out their names, and Patches congratulated them on their excellent memories. Then his shoulders hunched forward and he looked doleful. "Poor princess. If only we could 'elp her." He snapped his fingers. "I got me an idea. Maybe all together we can break that wicked spell."

There was a chorus of agreement from the children, and one little girl wearing eyeglasses with clear plastic frames lifted her hand.

"Patches? How can we help the princess if she's not here?"

"Did I say she wasn't 'ere?" Patches looked befuddled. "Naw, I didn't say that, mate. She's 'ere, all right."

The children began to look around, and Honey felt the first twinge of alarm.

"'Course she's not wearin' 'er princess clothes," Patches said.

Her palms began to sweat. Surely he wouldn't . . .

"On accounta the fact that she doesn't remember who she is. But she's beautiful just like a princess should be, so it's not 'ard to pick 'er out, now is it?"

A dozen sets of eyes landed on her. She felt as if she had been pinned to the wall like a dead butterfly. She spun toward the door.

"She's leaving!" one of the children called out.

Before she could clear the doorway, a rope dropped over her head and tightened around her waist, pinioning her arms to her side. Stunned, she stared down.

She'd been lassoed.

The children shrieked with laughter while she stared at the lariat, unable to believe what she was seeing. He began to reel her in. The children cheered. She stumbled backward, embarrassment making her even more awkward. How could he do this to her? He knew that she wasn't ready for anything like this. Her body bumped against his.

"She's shy around strangers," Patches said, beginning to untangle her from his lariat. As soon as he freed her, he threw his arm around her shoulder, ostensibly to give her a hug but, in reality, to pin her to his side. "Don't worry, Princess. None of these blokes'll 'urt you."

She looked out at the children and then back at him, her expression beseeching.

"Poor princess. Looks like she's lost 'er voice, too." He actually seemed to be teasing her. She wanted to push herself away in outrage, but she couldn't do it with the children watching.

"Where's your crown?" one skeptical little boy with an IV in his arm asked.

She waited for Eric to respond, but he kept silent.

The seconds ticked by.

He looked down at the fingernails on his free hand, then began an elaborate show of inspecting and buffing them while he waited for her to speak.

"Tell us, Princess," the little girl with the eyeglasses said softly.

"I—uh—I don't remember," she finally managed.

"See wot I told you?" Patches snapped one suspender with the hand he'd been buffing. "Memory like a piece a Swiss cheese. Full of 'oles." He sounded smug, and it irritated her.

"Did you leave it under your bed?" the little girl asked. "I left my Lite Brite under my bed."

"Uh—no, I don't think so."

"In the closet?" another child offered.

She shook her head, conscious of the clown's arm clamped around her shoulders.

"In the bathroom?" said a little boy with a lisp.

She realized they weren't going to let up on her, and she blurted out, "I—uh—I think I left it at the Dairy Queen." Now where had that ridiculous notion come from?

Patches's arm dropped from her shoulders, but instead of helping her out, he sounded distinctly skeptical. "You left yer princess crown at the Dairy Queen?"

He clearly wasn't going to make this easy. "It—It was giving me a headache," she said. And then, a bit more firmly as her sense of pride poked through, "Crowns do that."

"I wouldn't know. I only wear me pirate's scarf." She waited for him to give her a way out, but instead he said, "I 'eard a rumor about princesses and wicked spells."

"You did?"

"It came to me on good authority."

"Is that so?" She had begun to relax a little.

"I 'eard that a wicked spell on a princess can be broken if the princess in question . . ." He winked at the children. ". . . kisses a 'andsome man."

The boys groaned and the girls giggled.

"Kisses a handsome man?"

"Works every time." He began to preen for the children, tidying his wig and smoothing his painted eyebrow with his little finger. The children, anticipating what was coming, laughed harder.

His mischief was contagious, and she concealed a smile. "Is that so?"

"Bein' a charitable person and all . . ." He dusted the seat of his pants. ". . . I've decided to offer meself fer the job."

With comic lechery, he leaned toward her, his mouth outrageously puckered.

She almost laughed. Instead, she studied his pursed lips for several beats. Then she looked at the children and rolled her eyes. They giggled, and the sound filled her with a glow of pleasure.

She turned back to the clown. "A kiss?" She said the word as if he'd suggested cod liver oil.

Patches nodded. And with his mouth still puckered said, "A big smacker, Princess. Right 'ere." He pointed toward his painted lips.

"From a handsome man?" she inquired.

Still puckered, he flexed his muscles and preened.

She looked back at the children, and they laughed harder. "A kiss from a handsome man, huh? Well, all right, then."

Stepping past him, she approached a little boy with chocolate-brown skin and a leg cast. Bending down, she offered him her cheek. He blushed, but dutifully planted a quick kiss there. The children hooted at his embarrassment.

She straightened. Patches's painted smile had stretched like elastic over his face. And then the noise died down as all of them waited to see if the kiss would work.

She went very still in the time-honored manner of a princess shaking off a wicked spell. Gradually, she widened her eyes until they were huge with wonder.

"I remember! I'm from . . ." *Where?* Her muse deserted her. "I'm from Paxawatchie County, South Carolina!" she exclaimed.

"That's right here, Princess," a child with a lisp said.

"Is it? Do you mean I'm home?"

The children nodded.

"Do you 'member your name?" one of them asked.

"Why, I do. My name is—Popcorn." It was the first word that came into her head, inspired, no doubt, by the smell drifting into the lounge from the small kitchenette next door.

"That's a dumb name," one of the older boys observed.

She stood her ground. "Princess Popcorn Amaryllis Brown from Paxawatchie County, South Carolina."

The clown's blue eye twinkled in the white face paint. "Well now, Princess Popcorn. Since you've remembered yer name, maybe you'd 'elp me give out some Christmas presents 'ere."

And so she helped him distribute the presents he had brought, which turned out to be expensive hand-held video games. The young patients were delighted, and as she laughed with them, she felt lighthearted for the first time in months.

Finally the nurses appeared to lead the children back to their beds. Patches promised to stop by their rooms to see each one of them before he left.

When they were alone in the lounge, he turned away from her to pack up his tricks. While he gathered up his lasso and stowed it in the bag he had brought, she waited for him to speak, but he said nothing. She bent down to pick up one of the balls he had dropped. When he turned back toward her, she held it out.

"How long have you been doing this?" she asked quietly.

She had expected him to sidestep her question, but, instead, he looked thoughtful. As soon as he began to speak, she realized why.

"Well, now, Princess. Corky musta taught me to juggle not long after we sunk the *Jolly Roger.*"

Not only had he deliberately misinterpreted her question, but he had retained his identity as Patches. She shouldn't have been surprised. When Eric was in character, he stayed that way. She didn't stop to examine her sense of relief. She only knew that she felt safe talking with this pirate clown, and she didn't feel at all safe with Eric Dillon.

"You said his name was Corny," she corrected.

"There were two of 'em. Twins."

She smiled. "All right, Patches. Have it your way."

He had packed up his props and now he turned toward the door. "I'm gonna visit some of the older kids now, Princess. You want to come with me?"

She hesitated, and then she nodded.

And so Patches the Pirate and Princess Popcorn Amaryllis Brown spent Christmas afternoon visiting the children on the third floor of the Puxawatchie County Hospital, dispensing comfort, magic tricks, and video games. Patches told all the older boys that she was his girlfriend, and Princess Popcorn Amaryllis said that she most certainly was not. She said that princesses didn't have boyfriends; they had suitors instead. And that none of those suitors were clowns.

Patches said the only suit he owned was the one he was wearing, but he'd buy a new one if she'd give him a kiss. And so it went.

That afternoon, she heard something she had not heard in months. She heard the sound of her own laughter. There was something magical about him, a gentleness that drew in the children and made them feel free to clamber on his lap, to tug at his legs, a mischievous charm that let her set aside her grief if only for a few hours and wish that she could crawl into his lap, too. The thought brought her no pangs of guilt, no sense of disloyalty to Dash's memory. After all, there was nothing at all wrong with wanting to embrace a clown.

It was nearly dark when they left the hospital. Even then, he did not set aside the character of Patches. As they walked across the parking lot, he continued to flirt outrageously with her. And then he said, "Visit the kiddies with me later this week, Princess. We can try out this trick with daggers I been thinkin' about."

"Would it happen to involve using me as a target?"

"'Ow'd you know?"

"Intuition."

"It's perfectly safe. I 'ardly ever miss anymore."

She burst into laughter. "No, thank you, you rascal."

But as they reached his van, her laughter faded. When he climbed inside, this pirate clown would disappear, and he would take the princess with him. She felt just like all the sick children who had called out to him not to go. She thought of her empty trailer and the harsh, grim-faced man who shared the park with her. The soft, wistful words slipped out before she could stop them.

"I wish I could take *you* home with me."

She heard the briefest hesitation before he set down his bag and said, "Sorry, Princess. I promised me mates I'd go on a raid with 'em."

She felt incredibly foolish. In an attempt to recover, she clucked her tongue. "Carousing on Christmas night, Patches? You don't have any shame. And I was going to fix a real dinner, for a change."

There was a short silence. For the first time that afternoon, the clown seemed to lose some of his cockiness. "Maybe I'll—I could send one of me mates over instead. To keep you company."

His reply was a dash of cold water. It also made her feel vulnerable. She looked quickly down at the toes of her shoes. "If his name is Eric, I don't want to see him."

"Don't blame you," he replied without a lost beat. "Bad piece a work, that one."

Silence fell between them. The parking lot was quiet and the night clear. As if compelled, she lifted her chin and gazed into the clown's white face. Her brain knew who resided behind the makeup, but it was Christmas, the night ahead was long, and her heart stepped across the boundary of logic.

"Tell me about him," she said softly.

He shoved his hands in his pockets and said dismissively, "'E's not a subject fit fer the tender ears of a princess."

"My ears aren't all that tender."

"Just watch out for 'im, that's all."

"Why's that?"

"Yer too pretty, doncha see? Threatens 'im if 'e thinks a woman might be as good-lookin' as 'e is. Vainest man I ever knew. Doesn't like anybody sharin' 'is mirror space. First thing you know, 'e'll be stealin' yer 'air rollers, and walkin' off with yer makeup mirror."

She smiled, suddenly glad that he wasn't being serious. But then his brow puckered beneath the red eyebrow, and she could feel him growing tense.

"The truth is, Princess . . ." He pulled a key from his pocket and fit it in the rear door lock. "I think yer need to stay as fur away from 'im as yer can. Seems like you've 'ad enough trouble in yer life—wot with that wicked curse and everything—without addin' to it. 'E's got a ice cube for a 'eart, that one."

She thought of the children clamoring for his attention, the hugs he had given, the comfort he had offered. Some ice cube.

"I used to think that was true," she said stiffly, "but I don't believe it anymore."

"Now don't you turn soft on me, Princess, or I'll 'ave to go against me better judgment and give you some advice."

"Go ahead."

He leaned against the back of the van and met her eyes unflinchingly. "All right. You were smart to take 'is money for one. The bloke's so rich 'e won't miss a penny. And you need to do wot 'e says about yer career. 'E won't steer you wrong there, and you can trust 'im." He pushed one hand into the pockets of his baggy trousers. "But that's all yer gonna get from 'im. 'E's not good with fragile people, Princess. 'E doesn't mean to 'urt 'em, but it always 'appens."

She was the one who looked away. "I shouldn't have— That night in the bathroom—I was tired, that's all."

"It wasn't a smart thing to do, Princess." His voice grew

husky. "Yer not the kind of woman can take somethin' like that lightly."

"Yes I am!" she exclaimed. "That's exactly how I took it. It didn't mean anything because I'm still in love with my husband. And he would have understood!"

"Would 'e?"

"Of course. He understood about sex. And that's all it was. Just sex. There was nothing wrong."

"That's good, Princess. Then you don't 'ave anything to regret."

It should have been true, but it wasn't, and she didn't understand why.

He gave her a gentle smile and climbed into the van. "So long, Princess."

"So long, Patches."

The engine started immediately, and he pulled out of the parking lot. She watched as the van turned the corner and disappeared. In the distance church bells softly chimed. Above her head the stars popped out one by one.

Grief settled over her in a great heavy cloud.

27

Eric appeared at the door of her trailer that night. He wore black jeans and a dark jacket over a charcoal-gray sweater. His long hair was windblown, his single eye just as mysterious and unrevealing as the black patch that covered its mate. A creature of the night.

He hadn't visited her trailer since he'd moved into the Bullpen, and the belligerent set to his mouth indicated that he wasn't going to ask her if he could enter. Instead, he stood outside glaring at her as if she were the interloper.

She was ready to make a nasty comment when she was

struck with the irrational sense that the pirate clown would be disappointed in her if she didn't offer hospitality to his friend. The idea was crazy, but as she stepped back from the door to let him in, she reminded herself that everything had been crazy that fall. She was living in a dead amusement park, building a roller coaster that led to nowhere, and the only person she had been happy with was a one-eyed pirate clown who wove magic spells around sick children.

"Come in," she said begrudgingly. "I was just getting ready to eat."

"I don't want anything." His tone was equally hostile, but he stepped inside.

"Eat anyway." She pulled a second plate from the cabinet and ladled out a chicken breast for him along with a generous serving of rice and one of the rolls she had defrosted from the freezer. She set a place for him opposite hers at the small table and sat down to eat.

Silence fell between them. The chicken tasted dry in her mouth, and she picked at her food. He ate mechanically, but rapidly enough that she knew he was hungry. She found herself searching for some microscopic dab of clown white that he had missed when he showered, or a tiny speck of rouge at his hairline, anything to link him with the gentle, playful clown, but she saw nothing except that hard mouth and those darkly forbidding features. His transformation was complete.

He pushed back his plate. "I've been in touch with your agent, and I've had some scripts sent to me. I'm going to make a decision about your first project soon." His voice was brusque and businesslike, without even the slightest trace of the clown's humor.

She gave up any further attempt at eating. "I'd like a little say in this."

"I'm sure you would, but that wasn't our agreement."

"You didn't waste any time."

"You owe me a lot of money. I want you to know up front that I'm not going to chose a comedy, and that the part won't bear any resemblance to Janie Jones."

She stood and snatched up her plate. "That's all I can do, and you know it."

"You did a pretty good job of playing a princess."

She walked over to the sink and wrenched on the faucet. She didn't want to talk to him about the princess or what had happened between them today. The afternoon had been too wonderful, and she couldn't bear to have it corrupted.

"It's the same thing," she said, hoping to put an end to the discussion.

"It's not even close." He brought his own plate over and set it in the sink.

She shoved it under the faucet. "Of course it is. Janie was me and so is the—princess."

"That's the mark of a good actor. Instead of trying to create a character from whole cloth, the best actors create characters from aspects of themselves. That's all you did with Janie, and it was the same thing today."

"You're wrong. Janie wasn't just part of me; Janie was me."

"If that were true, you'd never have married Dash."

She clenched her teeth, refusing to let him force her into an argument.

He walked across the trailer toward the table. "Think about all the battles you fought over the years with directors. I can remember dozens of times when you'd complain about a line of dialogue or a particular action by saying that Janie wouldn't do something like that."

"I hardly ever won those battles, either."

"Exactly my point. You were forced to say the line the way it was written. You did whatever the script required. And it wasn't you."

"You don't understand." She spun around to confront him. "I've tried. I've read aloud all sorts of different parts, and I'm terrible."

"That doesn't surprise me. You were probably *acting* instead of just *being*. Open up some of those plays again, but this time don't try so hard. Don't act. Just be." He sat down on the straight-back chair near the table and stretched out his legs, not quite looking at her. "I've just about decided on a television miniseries that you've been offered. It's set during World War Two."

"Unless I get to play a feisty woman from the South who was raised by a broken-down rodeo rider, I'm not interested."

"You'd be playing a North Dakota farm woman who becomes involved with one of the detainees at a Japanese internment camp that adjoins her property. The hero is a young Japanese-American doctor who's imprisoned there. The farm woman's husband is fighting in the South Pacific; her only child has a life-threatening disease. It's good melodrama."

She stared at him, aghast. "I can't do something like that! A farm woman from North Dakota. You have to be joking!"

"From what I've seen, you can do anything you set your mind to." He gazed toward the front window of the trailer, which was pointed in the direction of Black Thunder.

"You're going to be a real bastard about this, aren't you?"

"Haven't you figured it out yet? I'm a real bastard about everything."

"You weren't this afternoon." The words slipped out before she could stop them.

His face stiffened as if she had committed some breach of protocol, and when he spoke, his voice was full of cynicism. "You really fell for that clown routine, didn't you?"

Every part of her turned to ice. "I don't know what you mean."

"My favorite part was the way you stood out there in that hospital parking lot and pretended it was all real." He leaned back in the chair and scoffed at her. "God, Honey, you really made an ass of yourself."

Pain swelled inside her. He was taking something beautiful and making it ugly. "Don't do this, Eric."

But he was on the attack, and he didn't waver. This time he would make certain he drew first blood. "You're—what? Twenty-five, twenty-six years old. I'm an actor, sweetheart. One of the best. I get bored sometimes and practice on the little kids. But it's all bullshit, and I sure as hell didn't expect you to get sucked in."

Her head had begun to pound and she felt ill. How could someone so physically perfect be so very ugly? "You're lying. It wasn't like that at all."

"I've got news for you, sweetheart. There's no Santa Claus, no Easter Bunny, and there aren't any magical clowns." He banged the front legs of the chair to the floor and swooped in for the kill. "About the best you can hope for in life is a full belly and a good fuck."

She drew in her breath. His upper lip had curled in a sneer and he was looking her over from head to toe as if she were a whore he might buy for the night. All the screen's bad boys flashed before her eyes. Every one of them was sitting before her right now, sullen, insolent, cruel—arms crossed, legs stretched out to kingdom come.

All the screen's bad boys.

And at that moment she saw through the smoke screen he had thrown up with his actor's bag of tricks. He was playing another part. With perfect clarity, her vision penetrated the insolence to find the pain, and it so perfectly matched her own that all her anger dropped away.

"Somebody ought to wash your mouth out with soap," she said softly.

"I'm just getting started," he sneered.

Her voice was a whisper. "Let it go, Eric."

He saw the compassion in her face and shot up from the chair, a world of pain coloring his words as he shouted at her. "What do you want from me?"

Before she could respond, he grabbed her shoulder and turned her toward the back of the trailer where the bedroom lay. "Never mind. I already know." He gave her a nudge forward. "Let's go."

"Eric . . ." She understood right then exactly what he was trying to do. Turning back to him, she gazed up into a face that was contorted with cynicism, and she felt no anger at all because she understood it was an illusion.

He wanted her to tell him to go to hell, to kick him out of the trailer, out of her life, to call him every despicable name she could think of. He wanted her to control something he couldn't control himself—the mysterious force that was drawing them together. But the December night on the other side of the trailer's silver shell loomed huge and empty, and she could not send him out into it.

He cursed softly. "You're going to let me do it, aren't you? You'll let me take you in there and fuck you."

She squeezed her eyes shut to hold back the tears. "Shut up," she whispered. "Just, please . . . shut up."

The armor of his defenses crumbled. With a groan, he pulled her into his arms. "I'm sorry. God . . . I'm sorry."

She felt his lips in her hair, on her forehead. His sweater was soft under her palms, the muscles beneath it taut and hard. He caressed her through her clothing—breasts, belly, hips, claiming everything, his touch sending fire licking through her veins.

She grew drunk with his scent: the wool of his sweater, piney soap and clean skin, the citrus tang of the shampoo he had used in his hair. He tilted up her chin to kiss her. Her mind screamed an alarm. Kissing was taboo. Only that.

Ducking her head, she worked the snap on his jeans, and they were naked by the time they reached her bed. It was narrow, designed for one instead of two, but their bodies were so intertwined it didn't matter.

Their passion was a hot, slick monster. She gave him all her secret parts to do with as he wished and took the same from him in return. Primordial serpent, soft devouring beast. They used their hands and mouths; probing, demanding, starved with need.

She did not know the man she accepted between her thighs. He was not a movie star, not a construction worker or pirate clown. His language was rough, his face grim, but through it all, his hands were as giving and gentle as the tenderest of lovers.

In the brief seconds afterward when her body hadn't yet settled back to earth but while he still lay atop her, she stroked his cheekbones with the pads of her thumbs. Inadvertently, her thumb slipped beneath the black eye patch. Without conscious thought, she felt for the disfiguring ridge of scar tissue he kept hidden away.

And encountered only the thick fringe of his eyelashes.

She sucked in her breath. Her thumb brushed over the configurations of a normal eye.

There isn't an eye there, he had said, *just a mass of ugly scar tissue.*

He drew away from her. Sat up on the edge of the narrow bed. "I wish I still smoked," he murmured.

She pulled the sheet over her naked body and stared at the strong muscles of his back. "There's nothing wrong with your eye."

His head shot up, and then he gathered his clothes and went into the bathroom.

She tucked the sheet high under her arms, drew up her knees. She began to shiver as all her misery washed back over her.

He came out of the bathroom wearing his jeans and drawing the sweater over his head, his black eye patch anchored firmly in place. He stopped in the doorway, looming there in the shadows, mysterious and dangerous.

"Are you all right?" he asked.

Her teeth were chattering. "Why did you lie to me about your eye?"

"I didn't want anyone to recognize me."

"I already knew who you were." Her voice broke on a quiver. "Don't lie, Eric. Tell me why."

He braced his arm on the door frame, and his voice was so low she barely heard the words.

"I did it because I couldn't live in my own skin any longer."

Turning on his heel, he left her alone in the small silver trailer.

Eric pulled off the interstate at a rest area in northern Georgia, one of the state-operated facilities with toilets, water fountains, and vending machines. It was three in the morning, and he had been keeping awake on coffee and the sugar hit from a stale Reese's Cup he'd found in his glove compartment. He hadn't made up his mind whether he would ditch the van in Atlanta and fly back to L.A. or whether he would keep driving.

The rest stop was nearly empty on this Christmas night. Not empty enough, however, for him to abandon his eye patch. He slipped it back over his head, then got out of the van and walked past the glass case that held a map of the Georgia highway system. Inside the low brick building a poorly dressed teenage girl sat on one of the benches holding a sleeping baby. She looked hungry, exhausted, and desperate.

Pity stirred the numbness inside him. She was too young to be alone in the world. He dug into his pockets trying to see how much change he had left and hoping it was enough to leave her with some food, but at that moment she looked up at him, and fear joined the other tragedies in her eyes.

She clutched her baby more tightly to her chest and sank back into the bench as if the wood could protect her from his menace. He could hear the quickened sound of her breathing and was sickened by the fear he was causing her. Quickly, he turned away to the vending machines. She was little more than a baby herself, another one of the innocents. He wanted to buy her a house, send her to college, give her a teddy bear. He wanted to buy a future for her baby, warm clothes, turkey dinners, teachers who cared.

The injustices of the world again overwhelmed him, and his head bowed under the crushing burden. He had money and power, and he should be able to fix it all. But he couldn't. He couldn't even protect the people he loved the most.

He shot the vending machines full of change. Instead of houses and college educations, packets of junk food clanked out, potato chips and candy bars, cookies shaped like elves and cupcakes shot full of chemicals—the bounty of America. He gathered it up and snatched the remaining bills from his wallet without counting them. Then he placed it all in a mute offering on the empty bench across from where she sat and left her alone.

By the time he reached the van, he knew he had to turn back. He had tried to run from all the evils that he wasn't able to correct, but even at the Silver Lake Amusement Park he hadn't been able to find sanctuary. It was a kingdom of the dead, ruled by a princess who was dying from grief. And she was the one innocent left that he might be able to save.

In less than a week, he needed to be back in L.A., but before he left he had to try to help her. Except how could he do it? When he was with her, he only hurt her. He remembered the way she had been at the hospital with the children, full of laughter and love, free of ghosts. And the person who had brought her back to life was a pirate clown, a jokester with an endless capacity for giving and a fearlessness about offering himself.

He knew he couldn't help her, but maybe the clown could.

When Honey returned to her trailer after work on Wednesday, two days after Christmas, she found a dress box sitting inside the door. Taking it over to the table, she opened it. Inside lay a white tulle princess dress spangled with silver moons and stars the size of half dollars. She lifted it out and saw what was beneath. A rhinestone tiara and a pair of purple canvas basketball sneakers.

With it was a note that said simply, "Thursday, 2:00 P.M." Instead of a signature, at the bottom of the card was a drawing of a small, star-shaped eye patch.

She pulled it all to her chest: the dress, the purple sneakers, the tiara. Blinking hard, she bit down on her lip and tried to think only of the clown and not what had transpired between herself and Eric on Christmas night. He had showed up for work today, but the only time he had looked in her direction had been with Dev's cynical eye.

The following afternoon when she entered the hospital, she was both nervous and excited. She didn't know whether it was because she'd see the clown again, or simply because, wearing the white tulle princess gown, she no longer felt like herself. Still, she knew she had to be cautious. After Eric's taunting, there was no way she would again fall under the spell of the pirate clown. The kinship she had imagined with him didn't exist. This time she wouldn't forget who lay beneath the white face and silly wig.

When she reached Pediatrics, the nurse directed her to one of the rooms at the end of the corridor. There she found two empty beds. Their occupants were sitting on the clown's lap, and they were wide-eyed as they listened to him read *Where the Wild Things Are*.

He must have read the book many times because she noticed that he seldom looked down at the words. Instead, he maintained eye contact with his small audience as he alternated between playing the parts of Max and the fearsome Wild Things.

He turned the last page. ". . . and it was still 'ot."

The girls giggled.

"I was pretty scary when I read that story, wasn't I?" he boasted. "I scared all of you, didn't I?"

They nodded their heads so agreeably that he laughed.

She stepped hesitantly into the room. The girls had been so absorbed in the story that they hadn't noticed her until then. Their eyes widened and their mouths formed small round ovals at the sight of her costume.

The clown's eyes swept over her, and he made no effort to hide his appreciation of her appearance. "Well now, look who's 'ere. It's Princess Popcorn 'erself."

One of the children on his lap, an earnest brown-skinned moppet with a bandage covering the left side of her face, leaned toward him and whispered, "Is she really a princess?"

"I absolutely am," Princess Popcorn said, stepping forward.

They continued to regard her in wide-eyed amazement. "She's beautiful," the other offered.

Awe-struck, they took in the tiara that nestled atop her tumble of honey curls, the white tulle princess gown with its glimmering moons and stars, the purple canvas basketball sneakers. Their small mouths gaped. She was glad she'd taken extra care with her hair and makeup.

"I couldn't agree more," Patches said softly. "Definitely the most beautiful princess in America."

Just like that, she could feel herself slipping under his spell, but this time she fought against it by primly pursing her soft rose lips. "Pretty is as pretty does. What's inside a person is a lot more important than what's outside."

Patches rolled his single turquoise eye. "'Ew writes yer material, Princess? Mary Poppins?"

She threw him a haughty look.

"What's that under your eye?" one of the girls asked, sliding down off his lap.

She had momentarily forgotten about the small purple star she had drawn high on her left cheekbone. Avoiding the clown's gaze, she reached inside her tote bag for her sable makeup brush and a pot of orchid eye shadow.

"It's a star, just like Patches's. Would you like one, too?"

"Could we?" they inquired breathlessly.

"You certainly could."

The visit flew by. Patches told jokes and performed his magic tricks while she painted stars on the children's faces. Some of the children had been there on Christmas Day, but a number of them were new patients. While the boys were more interested in Patches's magic tricks, the girls stared at her as if she had just stepped out of the pages of their favorite fairy tale. She combed their hair, let them try on her tiara, and reminded herself to buy another pot of orchid eye shadow.

Patches, in the meantime, flirted with all the little girls, the nurses, and most of all with her. She couldn't resist him any more than the children could, and even though she had promised herself she wouldn't again fall under his spell, there was something so irresistible about him that she let all of her sensible resolutions dissolve.

When it was finally time to leave and they were riding the elevator downstairs, she warned herself to be wary. But he would disappear in a few more minutes, and what real harm was there in holding on to the illusion just a little longer?

"Next time you're not lassoing me," she said.

"You don't know 'ow to 'ave a good time, Princess."

"We'll do knives instead."

His face brightened as the doors slid open. "Really?"

"Yes. I'll throw."

He laughed. They walked through the lobby and out into the parking lot. The days were short and dusk had settled.

He led her toward her car, but when they got there he hesitated, as if he, too, weren't ready for them to part.

"Will you come back with me on New Year's Day?" he asked. "It'll be me last visit before I take off to sail the seven seas."

New Year's was just four days off. If only Eric would go away and leave Patches behind. "Sure." She pulled her keys from inside her tote, knowing she had to separate herself from him but not willing to climb into her car.

He took her keys. She looked up at him and saw that he seemed troubled.

"I've been thinking about that coaster of yers," he said. "I'm worried about you."

"Don't be."

He unlocked the door and handed over her keys. "It won't bring back yer 'usband, Princess."

She stiffened. The headlights of a car pulling out of the parking lot turned the moons and stars on her dress into shimmering sparks. Her brain warned her that if she tried to explain, he would mock her later, but her heart couldn't believe this pirate clown could ever harm her. And maybe he would understand what Eric couldn't.

"I have to." She bit her lip. "The world isn't much good without hope."

"What kind of 'ope are you talkin' about?"

"Hope that there's something eternal about us. That it wasn't just some random cosmic accident that put us here."

"If yer tryin' to find God on that coaster of yers, Princess, I think you'd better look somewhere else."

"You don't believe in God, do you?"

"I can't believe in somebody that lets so much evil 'appen in this world. Little children suffering, murder, starvation. Who could love a God who 'as the power to stop all that, but doesn't use it?"

"What if God doesn't have the power?"

"Then 'e's not God."

"I'm not sure about that. I can't love the kind of God you're talking about, either—a God who would decide it was time for my husband to die and then send a dope addict to murder him." She took a quick breath, swallowed. "But maybe God isn't as powerful as people think. Maybe I could love a God who didn't have any more control over the random forces of nature than we have. Not a Santa Claus God of reward and punishment . . ." Her voice became a whisper. ". . . but a God of love who suffers with us."

"I don't think a roller coaster can teach you that."

"It did once. When I was a child. I'd lost everything, and Black Thunder gave me back hope."

"I don't think it's 'ope you want. And I don't even think it's God. It's yer 'usband." He pulled her into his arms. "Dash isn't comin' back, Princess. And it would tear 'im apart to see you sufferin' like this. Why don't you let 'im go?"

She felt the gentle pressure of his jaw on the top of her head and the warmth of his arms seemed like the safest place she had been in longer than she could remember. But because this silly clown had begun to mean too much to a woman who was still grieving over her husband's death, she pulled away from him and spoke fiercely.

"I can't let him go! He's the only thing I've ever had that was all mine."

She threw herself inside her car, but not until she had cleared the parking lot did she look back in her rearview mirror. The clown had disappeared.

28

Honey stood in the fading afternoon light on the porch of the Bullpen and asked herself what she was doing there. It was New Year's Day, and she had spent her entire hospital visit avoiding the clown. She had even slipped out early so she wouldn't have any more private parking-lot conversations with him. Tomorrow he was leaving, and it would all be over.

As she turned the knob and walked inside, the tulle skirt of her princess gown rustled in the stillness. She knew she had to hurry. Although he had been occupied with the children when she had left, she didn't know how much longer he planned to stay, and she would be mortified if he caught her going through his things.

She bit her lip as she stepped inside the musty room, ashamed of herself and yet unable to leave. His identities swirled in her head, separating, melding, and separating again: the menacing Dev, the warm, loving clown, and Eric himself, a dark enigma. Surely there would be something in his belongings that would tell her who he was. She had to put an end to this sick fascination. Otherwise, she would be left with another ghost.

His windbreaker was thrown over the orange vinyl couch, and through the doorway she could see a pair of jeans tossed on top of the old iron-framed double bed. Eric's clothes. An old flannel work shirt that belonged to Dev hung over the back of a chair. As she looked at these bits and pieces of his identity, she felt a despondency that was different from the ever-present pain of Dash's death.

Once he left tomorrow, she probably wouldn't ever see him again, not even when she went back to L.A. Eric lived in the insulated world of the superstars, so their paths weren't likely to cross by accident, and the decisions he made about her career would be handled through her agent. She had only now to solve the mystery, and to convince her heart that Eric and the clown were really one.

She smelled the particular odor of greasepaint even before she walked into the bathroom. Like many actors, he stored his makeup in a fishing-tackle box, which lay open on the lid of the toilet. A tube of clown white and small round tins of red and black rested on the back of the sink, along with a dark pencil and several sable brushes. She slumped against the door frame and stared blindly at the makeup. It was true then.

She gave a small, shaky laugh at her own silliness. Of

course it was true. She knew they were the same person. Her mind did, anyway. But somehow her heart kept refusing to make the final connection. Again, she wished Eric would go and leave the clown behind. Everyone loved clowns. Caring about a clown wasn't a betrayal.

"Well, now, look who came callin'. Princess Popcorn 'erself."

She spun around.

He stood a few feet away, the painted smile on his face curling around a genuine one beneath. She began to stammer an explanation for her presence, but then realized he didn't seem to care. It was almost as if he had been expecting to find her waiting for him.

"Yer crown's crooked," he said with a grin.

"It's not a crown. It's a tiara." She was nervous, and when she reached up to take it off, her hair became tangled in the combs that secured it.

"'Old on there, Princess. Let me 'elp you."

He stepped forward and extracted the tiara from her hair. The touch of his hands was so gentle she had to fight against the soft sensations spreading through her. "You do that like you've had lots of practice."

"I'm good friends with a couple of little girls who've got long 'air, too."

His easy manner disappeared. He turned his back on her and walked out into the living area. She followed him.

"Tell me about them," she said.

He stood by the window with its shabby, water-spotted curtain and toyed with her tiara. His strong, thin fingers, tan from the sun, looked out of place against the delicate filigree of metal and rhinestones. They were indisputably Eric's hands—hands that knew her intimately—and she looked away from them.

"Their names are Rachel and Rebecca. Rachel's a lot like you, Princess. She's tough and stubborn, and she likes gettin' 'er own way. Becca is—Becca is sweet and soft. 'Er smile could stretch yer 'eart wide open."

He fell silent, but even from the other side of the room, she could feel the strength of his love for his daughters.

"How old are they?"

"They're five. Six in April."

"Are they ugly like you?"

He chuckled. "They're the prettiest little girls you ever saw. Rachel's 'air is dark like mine. Becca's is lighter. They're both tall for their age. Becca was born with Down syndrome, but that 'asn't stopped 'er one bit." He turned the tiara in his hands and ran his thumbnail over the small combs, making a soft, pinging sound. "Becca's got lots of determination—always 'ad, right from the beginning—and her sister Rachel makes 'er keep up." Again, his thumbnail scraped over the prongs. "At least she used to. . . ."

He gazed at her, cleared his throat. "They would 'ave loved you in that outfit, Princess. Both of 'em are suckers for royalty."

He looked as if he wished he hadn't said so much, but there was even more he hadn't told her. Why was he separated from these daughters he obviously loved so much?

He walked over to her and handed back the tiara. "I'm leavin' tomorrow, you know."

"Yes, I know."

"I'm gonna miss you. Princesses like you don't grow on trees, now do they?"

She prepared herself for the joke that would come, but the mouth beneath his clown's painted grin was unsmiling. "You don't know 'ow beautiful you are, do you, Princess? You don't know 'ow just lookin' at you makes me old 'eart thump."

She didn't want to hear this. Not from the clown. She was too vulnerable with him. But if not from the clown, then who? She tried to smile. "I'll bet you say that to all the princesses."

He reached out and touched her hair. "I never said it to a one. Only you."

A traitorous weakness spread through her. She looked up at him with pleading eyes. "Don't . . ."

"Yer the sweetest princess I ever met," he said huskily.

She no longer knew who she was talking to, and tiny wings of panic began to beat at her insides. "I have to go now."

She turned her back on him and walked to the door. But when she got there, she stopped. Keeping her eyes straight ahead so that she didn't have to look at him, she whispered, "I think you're wonderful."

She groped for the door knob. Twisted it in her hand.

"Honey!"

It was Eric's voice, not the clown's. She spun around.

"I'm tired," he said, "of being a prisoner."

And then, as if it were happening in slow motion, he pulled off his wig and eye patch with a single movement of his arm.

His silky hair looked as black as the midnight sky next to his stark white face. His turquoise eyes were full of agony. *Run away!* her mind screamed. But she stood paralyzed as he withdrew the oversized white handkerchief that protruded from his pocket and lifted it to his face.

"Eric, no . . ." She took an involuntary step forward.

The lip rouge smudged into the white, the large eyebrow blurred. Helplessly she watched as he removed the layers of makeup.

It was a little murder.

Her eyes began to sting but she blinked the tears away. Bit by bit, the clown disappeared. She told herself she wouldn't give in to grief. She was already mourning the passing of one good man, and she would not mourn another. But the tears continued to form.

He was the instrument of his own destruction. When he was done, he dropped the soiled handkerchief and met her gaze full on.

Residues of his clown's makeup still clung to his skin and eyelashes, but there was nothing comical about his appearance. The face that had been revealed was one she knew— strong, handsome, unbearably tragic. She understood that he had made himself vulnerable to her in a way he had never done with anyone else, and it filled her with fear.

"Why are you doing this?" she whispered.

"I wanted you to see me."

There was a naked, hungry expression in his eyes that she

had never witnessed before, and in that moment she knew he was going to tear her apart just as Dash had done. Even so, she couldn't turn away. All of her old assumptions about him no longer worked, and she realized she would never be free of him if she couldn't unlock his mysteries. "What are you running from?"

He gazed at her with haunted eyes. "From myself."

"I don't understand."

"I destroy people." He spoke so quietly she barely heard him. "People who don't deserve it. The innocents."

"I don't believe you. You're the gentlest man I've ever seen with children. It's as if you can read their minds when you talk to them."

"They need to be safe!" he exclaimed, the statement exploding into the quiet of the room.

"What do you mean?"

"Children are real and precious, and they need to be safe!" He began to pace, and she felt as if the room had grown too small to contain him. When he spoke, the words tumbled from his lips as if they had been dammed up for too long.

"I wish there was a place where I could keep them all safe from harm. Where there weren't any car accidents or diseases or anyone who could hurt them. A place where there were no sharp corners or even any Band-Aids, because no one would ever need them. I wish I could make a place where all the kids that nobody wanted would come to stay."

He stopped walking and gazed into space. "And I could spend my time in this clown's costume making them laugh. And the sun would shine, and the grass would be green." His voice faded to a whisper. "The only rain that fell would be gentle, with never any thunder. And my arms would be as wide as the world so that I could stretch them out and protect everything that was too small and too tender to protect itself."

Tears glistened in her eyes. "Eric . . ."

"And my daughters would be there. Right in the middle where nothing bad could ever get to them."

It was his children. He had stripped himself bare, and she understood that whatever haunted him, whatever was driving him to the edge, was connected with his children.

"Why aren't you with them?"

"Their mother won't let me see them."

"But how could she be so cruel?"

"Because she believes—" His mouth twisted. "She won't let me near them because she believes I molested them."

The word, coming from his lips, wouldn't register in her mind. "Molested them?"

He spoke through clenched teeth, every syllable tortured. "She believes that I sexually abused my daughters." His face was ageless and emptied of all hope.

Stunned, she watched as he twisted away from her and fled from the Bullpen. His feet pounded on the wooden steps, and then all was quiet.

She stared at the empty doorway. Seconds ticked by as she tried to take in what he had said. Her brain dredged up old newspaper stories about scoutmasters, teachers, priests— men who ostensibly loved children but were found to have been molesting them. But her heart dismissed the possibility that he could be one of these men. There were many things in life of which she was uncertain, but nothing on earth could ever convince her that Eric Dillon, in any of his guises, could willfully hurt a child.

She ran outside after him. It was dusk and the sky was streaked with garish ribbons of scarlet, lavender and gold. He had disappeared. She ran through the trees toward the lake, but both the eroding shoreline and the crumbling pier were vacant. For a moment she didn't know what to do, and then a stillness inside her told her where he must be.

As soon as she cleared the trees, she saw him climbing Black Thunder to the top of the lift hill. Despite his hostility toward the coaster, he had instinctively chosen the same destination that so relentlessly drew her. Human beings had always gone to the mountaintop whenever they needed to find the eternal.

His purple shirt and polka-dot trousers blended in with the blazing Technicolor sunset behind him as he made his purposeful climb to the top. She understood the necessity of his journey because she had made it so many times herself, but something inside her couldn't let him make it alone.

Drawing the billowy tulle of her skirt through her legs from the back, she tucked as much of the excess material into the gown's sash as she could manage and began her ascent. She had made the climb a hundred times before, but never with the encumbrance of five yards of white tulle, and she moved awkwardly. Halfway up she tripped. She caught herself just before she lost her footing and swore softly.

The sound was enough to draw Eric's attention and he called down to her in alarm. "What do you think you're doing? Get down. You're going to fall."

Ignoring him, she stuffed the gown back into her sash with one hand while she held on with the other.

He was over the rail in a second, on his way down the side of the frame to meet her. "Don't come any farther. You're going to trip."

"I've got the instincts of a cat," she said, as she resumed her climb.

"Honey!"

"Quit distracting me."

"Jesus . . ."

His shiny black pirate's boots and then the legs of his purple trousers came into view. "I'm under you," she warned. "Don't come any farther."

"Hold still. I'm going to move alongside you and help you back down."

"Forget it," she said breathlessly. "We're a lot nearer the top than the bottom, and I don't have the energy to climb back down right now."

He must have decided it was more dangerous to argue with her than to let her do as she wanted because he stayed at her side until they reached the top. Then he slid under the rail and, grasping her arms, drew her up beside him.

They collapsed next to each other, sitting on the track, their legs hanging through the spaces between the ties. "You're crazy," he said.

"I know." Her skirt billowed over both of them and down

through the open framework. Pieces of tulle snagged on rough surfaces in the wood, and the moons and stars in her lap caught fire from the sunset.

They were silhouetted against the color-streaked sky with the world in miniature below them—treetops like small green sponges, the lake a mirrored sliver, the tiny finger of a faraway church steeple. From their perch in the sky, they were forced to remember that another more dangerous world existed beyond the safe parameters of this dead amusement park.

She gazed down the legendary first drop. "Do you know what happens when you hit the bottom?"

"What?"

"You go back up again," she said softly. "Always back up. With a roller coaster, hell is only temporary." *Please, God, let it be true.*

"When you've been accused of molesting the two people you love the most, hell is a way of life," he said harshly. "Fathers do it all the time, you know. Inhuman, perverted bastards, desecrating the most sacred responsibility a man can have."

"But not you," she said. She spoke the words with certainty, not questioning.

"No, not me. I'd kill myself before I'd hurt my daughters. I don't mean that as a figure of speech, Honey. I mean it literally. I love them more than my own life."

"Why did their mother accuse you?"

"I don't know!" he exclaimed. "I don't know why. I only know that she believes it's true. She truly believes I've done these—these unspeakable things to them." He ran his fingers through his hair, his speech growing agitated. The words had been held back for too long, and now they came in torrents. As they sat in the fading light of a new year at the top of the lift hill, he told her of the death of his stepbrother Jason and how his guilt had haunted him for years. He spoke of his marriage to Lilly and the birth of his twin daughters, of the joy the girls had brought him and the horror of their mother's accusations.

As she listened to him, she didn't once doubt that he was telling the truth. She remembered the games he had played with her: the harsh words, the air of menace he could assume at will. All of it was illusion. Only the clown's gentleness had spoken the truth about who he was.

She heard what he wasn't saying, too, and glimpsed the awful sense of responsibility he seemed to bear for all of the evil in the world. Finally, she understood his curse. He thought he should fix everything.

She couldn't address that pain, but she could address the other. "You may be hurting your daughters even more by not fighting for them," she said gently. "Losing a parent when you're so young is a terrible thing. It changes you forever. My mother's death shaped everything I've ever done, even the way I fell in love. Because of her death, I've spent my whole life trying to make a family for myself. Dash had to be my father before he could be my husband. You don't want that for them, Eric. You don't want them to spend their adult lives looking for you in every man they meet."

His face was haunted, his despair so absolute that she yearned to give him physical comfort, but she was afraid to reach out to him. Afraid he would misunderstand. She had allowed him to make love to her, but now a simple touch on the knee was too intimate.

"I can't do anything," he said. "Lilly's going to put them into the underground if I make a move to get them back. Then they won't have anyone."

Honey felt sick. She couldn't imagine any woman being so vindictive. Why did Lilly hate Eric so much? For the first time, she truly grasped the complexity of his dilemma.

"I'm sorry," she said.

He stood up, rejecting her pity. "Let's climb back down. Stay with me."

The descent was easier than the ascent. Even so, Eric stayed beside her, his hand catching her arm whenever he thought she looked unsteady. By the time they reached the ground, the sunset had faded and it was nearly dark.

They stood quietly for a moment. His face was in deep shadow. Beneath all the masks he had thrown up, all his identities, she felt the goodness that ran like a core of gold straight through him. "I can't imagine what your daughters must be feeling to have lost you."

To her surprise he lifted his arm and buried his hand in her hair. At first he said nothing, simply wove a strand through his fingers. When he spoke, his voice was husky and vulnerable. "And what are you going to feel when you lose me?"

The flutters of panic returned. He mustn't touch her. Not like this. She wasn't his to touch. "I don't know what you mean."

"Yes, you do. Tomorrow when I leave. Will it make any difference to you?"

"Of course it'll make a difference." She pulled away from him and walked toward a pile of scrap lumber.

"One fewer pair of hands to work on your coaster?"

"That's not what I mean."

"Then what?"

"I'll—" She turned back to him. "Don't ask me questions like that."

"Come back with me, Honey," he said quietly. "Leave the coaster and come back to L.A. with me. Now. Not three months from now when it's done."

"I can't."

"Why not?"

"I have to finish building it."

All his softness disappeared, and his mouth set in a grim, harsh line. "How could I forget? You have to build your great monument to Dash Coogan. Why did I think I could compete with that?"

"It's not a monument! I'm trying to—"

"To find God? I think you've got God and Dash tangled up in your mind. It's Dash you want to find on that coaster."

"I love him!" she cried.

"He's dead and no roller coaster in the world has the power to bring him back."

"He's not dead to me! Not ever to me. I'll always love him."

The light was too dim to see clearly, and so she wasn't certain that she saw him wince. But the sorrow in his voice was unmistakable. "Your body wasn't as faithful as your heart, was it?"

"That was just sex!" she cried, as much to herself as to him. "Dash wouldn't have cared about that. He understood about sex."

His voice was low and flat. "What did he understand?"

"That sometimes it's—Sometimes it's meaningless."

"I see."

"We've both been lonely, and—Don't try to make me feel guilty. We didn't even kiss, Eric."

"No, we didn't, did we? You did other things with that beautiful mouth of yours, but you wouldn't kiss me."

He took a step toward her, and she knew he was about to change that. She told herself to move away, but her feet remained rooted to the ground. At that moment she would have given all she had for him to slip one of his masks back on—any of them. She finally realized how much his protective identities had also protected her. Stripped bare as he was now, no barriers separated them. Not skin or bone. She could feel the pain of his yearning as if it were coming from her own heart.

"Do you know that I've been dreaming about your mouth?" His eyes were dark, his voice husky.

"I'm cold," she said. "I'm going back to the trailer."

"How it would feel. What it would taste like." He cupped her arms in his palms. His breath was soft. She couldn't move as he lifted his hand and gently brushed his thumb over her lips.

They parted automatically. It had been so long since she had been kissed, and he was so very beautiful, right to the center of his soul. His thumb outlined her bottom lip, touched the bow at the top. He dipped his head, and his thick, dark lashes fanned his cheekbones.

She felt the warmth of his mouth draw nearer and was

pierced with a longing so fierce that she knew if she gave into it, she would have committed such an unforgivable act of betrayal that she could never again live with herself.

Just as his lips were about to settle over hers, she jerked away. "No! No, I won't do this! I won't betray my husband."

She had never seen anything as sad as the expression on his face. His eyes shimmered with pain that pierced her to the very core, and he seemed to collapse into himself.

"I'll bet you would have kissed the clown," he whispered.

She ran from him then, fleeing his presence and the sweet, sad seduction she had almost not been strong enough to resist.

Eric stood next to the coaster long after she had disappeared into the trees. His eyes were dry and scratchy. He told himself he had been living with pain for so long that a little more wouldn't make any difference, but logic couldn't ease the anguish. As the night wind whipped the trees, he found himself remembering the child she had been, the way she had followed him with those puppy-dog eyes, begging him to pay attention to her. Even then, something about her had drawn him in.

Now she was a woman, and he loved her. Despite her hostility and her rejection, he knew that she understood him in a way no one else ever had. Although she had never had a child herself, she understood the depth of his love for his children. And her fierce, disciplined drive to finish her coaster—no matter how much it might alarm him— mirrored his own obsession with his work. She even seemed to know why he had to live in other people's skins. Despite the differences in their backgrounds, despite the lies and deceptions, she felt like the other half of himself.

And she didn't want him. Instead she wanted a dead man.

A fresh attack of pain began to rush at him, howling and yipping, ready to sink its teeth in. Before that could happen, his mouth gave a savage twist, and he flung up his shield of cynicism.

He was the Prince of Studs. Women came after him, not the other way around. All he had to do was snap his fingers and they lined up for his pleasure. He could have them any way he wanted: blond, brunette, old, young, big tits, long legs, step right up and let the big star take his pick. The women of the world were his to command.

Upside down? *Certainly, sir.*

Two for one? *We aim to please.*

But this woman didn't understand the rules.

She didn't understand the most basic fucking rule of the universe! She didn't understand that big movie stars were *entitled to any woman they wanted!*

This woman didn't care that he might be the best god-damn actor of his generation. He could be a bricklayer for all the difference it would make to her. She didn't care that he was a millionaire twenty times over, or that she was the only person in the world he had ever spilled his guts to. And she didn't even read goddamn *People* magazine, so how could she know that he was Sexiest goddamn Man Alive?

Eric turned away and headed back to the Bullpen to pack his things. As he left Black Thunder behind, he knew that he had done a lot of stupid things in his life, but the stupidest thing he'd ever done was to fall in love with the grieving Widow Coogan.

Into the
Station

1990

29

"Daddy!" Lilly jumped up from her living room couch where she had been resting from her unpacking chores and raced across the black and white marble floor to her father.

"Hello, darling." In the seconds before Lilly was encompassed in Guy Isabella's arms, she noted with relief that he looked as handsome as ever. His thick, silvered-blond hair gleamed in the late January sunlight that streamed through the windows. A cantaloupe-colored sweater lay knotted over the shoulders of his Egyptian-cotton shirt. His pleated linen trousers were baggy and stylishly wrinkled. When he'd visited her in London four months earlier, she'd suspected he'd had a face-lift, but he was secretive about the exotic cosmetic treatments that kept him looking closer to forty than fifty-two, and she hadn't asked.

"I'm so glad to see you," she said. "You don't know how horrible everything's been." Drawing back, she gazed up at him. "You have an earring." She stared at the small gold hoop in his earlobe.

His eyes crinkled at the corners of his tightly stretched skin as he smiled. "You noticed. One of my lady friends talked me into it not long after our visit in London. What do you think?"

She hated it. There had been enough changes in her life recently, and she wanted her father to stay the same. Still, she wasn't going to ruin their reunion with criticism. "Quite dashing."

His tawny eyebrow arched as he regarded her critically, taking in the long red knit sweater that hung too loosely from her shoulders over a pair of silky black leggings. "You look terrible. Didn't you say you were going to spend New Year's in St. Moritz with André and Mimi? I thought you'd be rested."

"Hardly," Lilly replied bitterly. "The new nanny quit so I had to take the girls with me. Becca wasn't a problem. She doesn't talk very much anymore, but Rachel was uncontrollable. After the first day, André and Mimi were aching to ask me to leave, but they're much too polite, so Mimi contented herself with helpful comments about my shortcomings as a disciplinarian. Then Rachel deliberately knocked a glass of grape juice on Mimi's Daghestan rug, and Mimi reverted to her fishwife roots. It was dreadful. We left for Washington two days later."

"Did your visit with your mother go well?"

"What do you think? Rachel has always exhausted her, and Becca— You know mother. She's not good with any sort of imperfection."

"I can imagine." He began to look around him, rubbing his hands together. "Where are my granddaughters? I can't wait to see Rachel again. And Becca, too, of course. I'll bet they've grown like weeds."

"Like nasty little weeds," Lilly murmured under her breath. Guy looked at her quizzically. "I called a service to get a sitter for the afternoon. She's taken them out for pizza and then to the park. I told her to keep them there for a couple of hours, but I doubt that they'll last that long. Rachel will attack another child or Becca will wet her pants or there'll be some other disaster and they'll be back."

"You need to discipline Rachel, Lilly."

"Don't you lecture me, too." She turned away from him and walked toward the windows. "How am I supposed to discipline her? She's hostile and difficult, and if I try to punish her, she runs away. I lost her for three hours last fall. After we found her, she went into my closet with a pair of scissors and deliberately cut up my new evening gown."

"I was hoping things would get better."

"How can they get better? She hates me, Daddy." Lilly crossed her arms over her chest and, biting her bottom lip, murmured, "And sometimes I hate her."

"You don't mean that?"

"No, of course I don't," she said wearily. "Except sometimes I do mean it. She makes me feel like such a failure." She reached down for the cigarette pack she'd left on the table that sat between the windows.

"You're smoking!"

Her hands faltered as she opened the pack. She hadn't intended to smoke in front of her father. He might sometimes be a bit too liberal in his use of alcohol, but he was a fanatic when it came to tobacco. "You have no idea of the strain I've been under."

He eyed her with such disapproval that she set down the pack. He walked over to the couch and carefully tugged on his trouser legs as he took a seat. "I can't understand why you're putting such pressure on yourself. I know you love to travel, but you've had so many addresses in the past nine months even I can't keep up with you. You're obviously exhausted. But I won't lecture you anymore, darling. At least you've had enough sense to come home so I can look after you."

"I'm only here for a few days. Just long enough to clear up some business affairs, and then we're going back to Paris."

"That's ridiculous, Lilly. You can't keep on moving around like this. Why do you have to leave so soon?"

"Eric's in town."

"All the more reason to stay. The way you've let him abdicate responsibility for the girls baffles me. You know I never liked him, Lilly, but I still can't believe how he's turned his back on his daughters."

Lilly looked away so she didn't have to meet his eyes. She had never told him about Eric. She was too ashamed. "Fatherhood was just another acting role for him. Once he mastered the part, he got tired of it."

"It's still hard for me to understand. He seemed to care about the girls so much."

"He's an actor, Daddy."

"Even so—"

"I don't want to talk about it."

He stood and came over to her. "But Lilly, you can't keep

running. It's not good for the girls, and it's not good for you. You've always been high-strung, and it's obvious that raising Rachel and Rebecca by yourself is too much for you. You're as thin as a rail and you look exhausted. You need some pampering, darling." He gave her a smile that gently crinkled the creases at the corners of his eyes. "How about a few weeks at a spa? There's a new place near Mendocino that's wonderful. I'm going to send you there as soon as possible. It'll be my Christmas present."

"You've already given me a dozen presents."

"Nothing's too good for my baby." He drew her into his arms, and she pressed her cheek against his smoothly shaven jaw. As he held her there, she began to feel nauseated. She took a deep breath, waiting for the comfort his presence always gave her, but the musky smell of his cologne seemed to make her even queasier. Disturbed, she pulled away from him.

"Is something wrong?"

"Jet lag, I guess. I feel—It's all right. My stomach is just a little upset."

"That settles it. I'm taking the girls home with me tonight."

"No, really—"

"Not another word. Every time I offer to take them, you put me off. Do you realize that you've never once let me have my granddaughters? Not once since they were born. And I can't count the number of times in the past nine months that I've asked you to fly them to California to stay with me for a few weeks, but you always have excuses. No more, darling. You're under enormous strain, and if you don't get some rest soon, you'll be ill."

A headache had begun to throb at her temples. "They're too big a handful, Daddy."

"That's what you always say."

"Becca's been wetting the bed, and she's having so many problems with her speech that it's hard to understand her. Rachel gets more rebellious all the time; she won't do anything she's supposed to. I'd put her in a school somewhere, but I don't want Eric—" She broke off. "Anyway, you're not used to young children. They'd be too much for you."

"Not for a few nights. That won't be a problem at all. And don't forget that I raised you, Princess."

Lilly's stomach began to roll again, but before she could say anything, she heard the sound of the front door crashing open.

"I'm not one bit sorry!" Rachel shrieked in that loud, determined voice that made Lilly want to cover her ears. "It was my swing, and that boy tried to take it!"

Lilly pressed her thin fingers to her temples to try to keep her head from blowing apart. The argument between her daughter and the sitter who was supposed to have kept the girls occupied accelerated.

Rachel stormed into the living room, her dark hair flying wildly around her face. "You're a stupid baby sitter! And I'm not doing anything you say!"

The sitter appeared with Becca in tow. She was an elderly woman, and she looked frazzled and angry. "Your daughter deliberately attacked a little boy," she announced. "And when I reprimanded her, she cursed me."

Rachel's light blue eyes were hostile, her mouth set in a mulish line. "I only said the S word, and he took my swing."

Guy stepped forward. "Hey, sweetheart. How about a kiss for your grandfather?"

"Grandpa Guy!" Rachel's hostility evaporated as she raced toward him. He hoisted her into his arms. Her legs were long, and her sneakers banged against the knees of his linen trousers. Lilly felt something horrible uncoiling inside her chest at the sight of her daughter in her father's arms. She suspected it was jealousy and she was ashamed.

While her father talked to Rachel, she got rid of the sitter and pulled Becca out from behind one of the neo-Roman chairs where she had gone to hide. To her disgust, she saw that Becca's pink corduroy slacks were wet.

"Becca, you wet yourself again."

Becca sucked on her thumb and watched her sister and grandfather with dull, disinterested eyes.

"Daddy," Lilly said nervously. "Don't you want to say

hello to Becca?" Guy reluctantly set Rachel down and turned toward her.

"She's W-E-T," Lilly warned.

"Mommy just told Grandpa you wet your pants again," Rachel announced to her sister. "I told you not to be a baby anymore."

"Well, now, accidents happen, don't they, Rebecca?" Guy patted Becca on the head but didn't pick her up. Lilly's father was no more comfortable with Rebecca than her mother, Helen, but at least he was more discreet about it. He pulled some cinnamon candies from the pockets of his linen slacks and handed them to the girls, just as he had done with her when she was a little girl. The familiar sight of those candies made her feel queasy again. She wondered if she were coming down with the flu.

"Unwrap it like this, Becca." Rachel extended her own candy toward her sister and showed her how to pull on the ends.

"Here, let me help," Guy said.

"No, Grandpa. Becca has to do things for herself or she won't learn. That's what Daddy says. Everybody keeps doing things for her, and it's made her lazy." She splayed her small hand on her hip and glared at her sister. "Unwrap it yourself, Becca, or you can't have it."

Guy plucked the candy from Becca's fingers. "Now, Rachel, there's no need for that." He unwrapped the candy and gave it to Becca. "Here, sweetheart."

Rachel gazed at him with disgust. "Daddy says—"

"What your father says isn't important anymore," Lilly snapped. "He's not here, and I am."

Guy saw that Lilly was upset and he came over to comfort her. Becca began to cry. Red syrup from the candy leaked from the corner of her mouth. Rachel glared at her mother and then turned to her sister.

"Crying's for babies, Becca. Daddy'll stop being so busy soon and have time for us. He will! How many times do I have to tell you?"

"That son of a bitch," Guy muttered, his voice so low that

only Lilly could hear. "How could he do this to them? Still, I suppose it's all for the best. They're young enough now to adjust. If he had abandoned them when they were older, it would have been doubly traumatic."

Lilly couldn't imagine how anything could be more traumatic than what had already happened. She was ruining her own life trying to protect children who weren't the slightest bit grateful, but she couldn't weaken. Even if her daughters hated her for it, she would protect them from their father's perversion.

Guy had gone back over to the girls, and Rachel gave a squeal of delight at something he had said. "Really? Can me and Becca get pizza, too? And can I watch television before I go to bed?"

"Absolutely." Guy tousled her hair.

Lilly's heart slammed against her rib cage. "Daddy—"

"Not another word, Lilly." He regarded her sternly. "You need a rest, and the girls are going to stay with me for a few days so you get it."

"No, Daddy, I don't—"

"Help your sister change into some dry clothes, Rachel, and then we'll go."

Lilly tried to protest, but her father paid no attention. Her head was pounding, her stomach rolling. She hated the idea of her daughters going off with her father, and she hated herself even more for being so jealous. What kind of mother was she to resent a loving grandfather's relationship with his own grandchildren?

She forced herself to return several changes of their clothing to the suitcase she had just unpacked. The upheaval in her stomach grew worse. While her father was occupied with the girls, she slipped into her bathroom and vomited.

She felt better with her stomach empty, but her head was still pounding. She quickly swallowed three aspirin and went back into the bedroom.

The excitement of staying with her grandfather had overstimulated Rachel. She was running up and down the back hallway and screeching at the top of her lungs. Guy, however, seemed to have the magic touch with her and when he told her to settle down, she obeyed.

They were ready to leave when they discovered that Becca had disappeared. Rachel found her hiding in the back of Lilly's closet. Her pants were wet again, and Lilly had to change her.

"Don't forget, Mommy," Rachel said as she stood at the front door holding her grandfather's hand. "If Daddy calls while we're gone, tell him to come get us."

For nine long months, every time she left the house, Rachel had said the same thing. Lilly clenched her teeth, an action that intensified the throbbing in her head, but painful experience had taught her that Rachel would refuse to leave if her request was ignored. "I won't forget," she said stiffly.

"Kiss your mother good-bye, girls," Guy said.

Rachel obediently gave Lilly a loud smack. Becca was unresponsive.

Guy pecked Lilly's cheek. "Don't worry about a thing, darling. Call some friends and enjoy yourself for a few days. The girls and I will be fine."

Lilly felt as if someone had taken a hammer and chisel to her head. "I don't know. The girls are so . . ."

"Don't fret, darling. Come along, girls. How about a stop for ice cream on the way?"

Rachel gave an earsplitting shriek and tugged on her grandfather's hand. Becca followed obediently. Guy held the door of his Jaguar sedan open and they clambered inside. His hair glinted in the California sunshine, and his straight white teeth flashed as he smiled. He was so handsome. So horribly, obscenely handsome.

"Their seat belts!" Lilly called out. "Don't forget their . . ."

Guy had already fastened the belts, and he waved his hand to indicate that he had heard. Moments later, he was backing down the drive.

Lilly rushed forward. "Be good!" she called out. "Don't do what Grandpa tells you." She caught her breath. What was wrong with her? "I mean—"

She felt cold and feverish at the same time, and she stumbled slightly as she made her way back inside the house and to her bathroom. Even though it was still light outside, she swallowed two sleeping pills. Her father was right. She was falling apart, and she had to get some rest. She climbed into bed without removing her clothes.

Afternoon slipped into evening, and the nightmares engulfed her. In her dreams she was running. A faceless woman raced after her, hands with blood-red fingernails extended and splayed. One by one those long blood-red nails shot off the ends of her fingers, turned into daggers, and stabbed her in the back. Lilly turned to her father for help, only to realize that he held the biggest dagger of all and it was pointed at Rachel. The horror enveloped her. And then it wasn't her father coming after her, but Eric, and he wanted Rachel. Mustering all of her strength, she cried out.

The strangled sound of her own scream awakened her. The room was dark, and for a moment she didn't know where she was. She gripped the cover, afraid to sit up, afraid to move for fear some indefinable horror would claim her. Her hair was stuck to her cheeks like a web, and she could hear a horrible pounding in her ears.

Eric's face swam before her eyes, a vision of filth and decay all the more obscene because of his physical perfection. As she struggled to clear her mind from the aftereffects of the sleeping pills she had taken, she was flooded by a paralyzing realization that she had made a horrible mistake by not telling her father about Eric. What if Eric went to Guy's house and took Rachel? Her father didn't know about Eric's perversion. He wouldn't know that he shouldn't hand her over. What if Guy let Eric have her?

Through the fog of her sleeping pills and the lingering horror of her nightmare, she was gripped by the awful certainty that Eric had done just that. He had taken Rachel, and her daughter was in desperate trouble.

Her body was leaden, and the bile rose in her throat as she remembered that Becca was with her father, too. But then she knew that Eric would never molest Becca. Her condition would repulse him. Rachel was his target. The stronger daughter.

Whimpering, she climbed from the bed and groped for her shoes. Then she staggered from the room, still trying to escape from her narcotic-induced fog. Her purse lay on the glass-topped credenza in the hallway, and she dug through the rubble of crumpled tissues, animal crackers, and boarding passes until she found her car keys. Gripping them in her fist, she picked up her purse and stumbled through the kitchen on her way to the garage. She had to get to Eric before he could hurt Rachel.

A set of Danish cutlery mounted in a polished block of teak caught her eye. After only a moment's hesitation, she pulled a heavy knife from its slot and placed it in her purse. She squeezed her eyes shut, the lids trembling. She knew she wasn't a good mother. She was self-centered, impatient, and she never seemed to do the right thing. But she loved her daughter, and she would do whatever was necessary to protect her.

Eight miles away in the hills of Bel Air, Guy Isabella tucked the covers around his granddaughter's small body with one hand while he clasped a tumbler of whiskey with the other.

"Why can't I sleep with Becca, Grandpa Guy?" Rachel gazed apprehensively up at the room's high ceiling and then over at the tall windows with their diamond-shaped leaded-glass panes. Grandpa Guy had told her this used to be her mother's room, but Rachel didn't like it. It was dark and spooky.

"Rebecca has been asleep for almost an hour," her grandfather said. The ice cubes clinked in his glass. "I didn't want you to wake her."

"I'd be real quiet. I might get scared if I have to sleep by myself."

"Nonsense. You won't be scared." He ran the tips of his fingers over Rachel's lips. "Grandpa Guy will check on you before he comes to bed."

"I want to sleep with Becca."

"Don't be afraid, sweetheart. Grandpa Guy will be near."
Bending down, he pressed his lips lightly over Rachel's.

Eric rubbed his eyes and stared at the telephone next to
his bed as he unbuttoned his shirt. How many times in the
three weeks since he'd returned had he wanted to call
Honey? A hundred? A thousand? He told himself that it was
a good thing the park's only telephone was in the Bullpen
where she wouldn't hear it if he finally gave into temptation.
She had already let him know in every way possible that he
couldn't compete with a ghost, and he had no intention of
groveling.

It was nearly midnight, and he had been up since five, but
even though he was exhausted, he knew he wouldn't be able
to sleep for more than a few hours. His new role was both
physically and emotionally demanding, and he wasn't giving it his best, but he couldn't seem to manage all the peeling
away of layers that he had to go through to get to the heart of
a character. Maybe because he still hadn't managed to put
himself back together since the night he had peeled himself
away for Honey. How could he do his actor's job of entering
another person's soul when he felt so personally exposed? It
was as if he had left part of himself behind with her, and
until he was complete again, he would drift.

The idea made him angry. He had to scrub her memory
from his mind, erase the sound of her laughter as she had
played with the children at the hospital, drive out the images
of the two of them making love. Most of all, he had to forget
her soft, sweet compassion the night he had taken off his
clown's mask and laid himself bare to her.

The ringing of the doorbell interrupted his disturbing
thoughts. He frowned. His Nichols Canyon house was
tucked away on a nearly inaccessible road, hardly a convenient spot for drop-in company. He didn't bother to rebut-
ton his shirt as he made his way from his bedroom to the
front entry. When he reached the door, he peered through
the peephole and then quickly turned the knob.

"Lilly?"

Her teeth were chattering, and her skin looked pale and

pinched. She had cut her hair since he had seen her and it hung about her face in silvery-blond wisps that made her eyes look huge and haunted.

She stared at him as if she were looking at something profane. Her eyes took in his unbuttoned shirt and then dropped to the open snap on his jeans. Her mouth began to quiver. "Where is she?"

He shoved one hand wearily back through his hair. "What do you want, Lilly?"

"What have you done with her?"

She grabbed the door frame for support and he reached for her arm, beginning to grow alarmed. "What's wrong?"

She tried to pull away from him, but he drew her inside. He led her into the living room and pushed her down on the sofa. Her breathing was quick and shallow, and she was clutching her purse to her chest. He grabbed a bottle of brandy from the bar and splashed some into a glass.

"Drink this."

The rim of the glass clinked against her teeth. She swallowed and then coughed.

"Tell me what's happened?" he demanded. "Is something wrong with the girls?"

She passed a trembling hand over her mouth and rose unsteadily to her feet. Instinctively, he reached out to catch her, but she drew back. "Where is she?"

"Who?"

"Rachel! I know you have her."

His heart missed a beat. "I don't have her. For God's sake, what's going on?"

"I don't believe you. You took her from my father. Where have you put her? Where is she?"

"I didn't even know you were back in town. How could I have taken her? Are you telling me you don't know where she is?"

"Liar!" she shrieked. Bolting past him, she ran toward the back of the house.

He rushed after her and then watched as she threw open the door of the guest room. When she saw that it was empty, she moved onto the next room and the next until she reached his bedroom. His gut churned as he stopped inside the doorway. She stood in the center of the room clutching her purse to her chest, her eyes opalescent with terror.

"What have you done with Rachel?" she whispered hoarsely.

He forced himself to stay calm. She was barely holding onto the threads of reason, and if he said the wrong thing, he could push her over the edge. Sounding as composed as he could manage, he stepped cautiously into the room.

"When did you last see her?"

"Daddy took her for the night." Her speech was choppy, and she was twisting her purse strap around her fingers. "Becca, too. He took Becca, too. I knew I shouldn't let them go, but I was so tired."

"It's all right, Lilly," he said soothingly, moving a little closer. "You didn't do anything wrong."

"Yes, I did!" She began to whimper. "You don't understand. I never told him about you. He didn't know that you could hurt Rachel."

"I haven't hurt Rachel," he said quietly. "You can see she's not here. I love her. I'd never hurt her."

"Liar!" she shrieked. "Daddy loved me! He loved me, and he hurt me."

He could feel the hair begin to stand up on the back of his neck. "Lilly, what are you talking about?" He moved too quickly and she shrank back.

"Don't touch me!" Her eyes were wild, the pupils dilated. "You'll hurt me. You'll hurt me like you hurt Rachel."

He froze in his tracks.

She began to cry. "She doesn't like it when you hurt her . . . but she can't make you stop." Her voice grew higher in pitch, more childlike. "You tell her not to . . . make any noise . . . when you touch her. Don't make any noise, sweetheart. I won't hurt you. Just shut your eyes. But she can't . . . shut her eyes. And you . . . smell like whiskey."

"Lilly, I don't even drink whiskey."

"She doesn't like . . . that whiskey smell," Lilly sobbed.

"And she doesn't like it when—when you turn on the radio." She gulped for air. "And you say, 'Just shut your eyes and—and listen to the music, Lilly.'"

The horror of complete comprehension washed over him. "Christ."

"And then sometimes—" Her voice broke, became a whisper. "Sometimes the music's playing . . . and the whiskey smell . . . and those hands."

"Oh, baby . . ."

"It's like a terrible dream, except sometimes when those hands feel good." She shattered before him, her voice almost inaudible. "And that's the worst thing of all." With a cry, she slid down the wall and crumpled like a broken toy on the floor.

He rushed toward her, wanting to hold her, to help her. She screamed and grabbed for her purse.

"No!" she shrieked. *"No more!"*

He gasped as a sharp pain pierced his side. Jerking back, he saw the blade in her hand and realized she had stabbed him. She moaned in horror and dropped the knife, staring at the blood welling from his side. Through his pain he saw her face grow ashen and knew the exact moment when the past and present clicked together in her mind.

"Dear God," she whispered. "Oh, God, no . . . What have I done?"

Eric pressed one hand to his side against the welling blood. He thought it was only a flesh wound, but there was no time to make certain. For now he could think only of his daughter.

"Is Rachel with your father now?" he demanded. "Is that where she is?"

Lilly's eyes were terror-stricken but lucid. "Oh, God, Eric," she whispered. "It was never you. It was him all along. He did those things to me, but I blocked them out. And now I've let him take the girls."

He pulled her to her feet. "Let's go."

Her eyes were dark with horror. "You're bleeding. I cut you."

"I'll worry about it later." He snatched up the T-shirt he'd thrown over the bottom of his bed earlier and wadded it against his side.

"Oh, Eric. I'm sorry. What have I done? Oh, God, I'm sorry."

"We don't have time. We have to get to them right away." But as he pulled her from the bedroom, he wondered if it was already too late.

The keys were still in the ignition of her car. He pushed her into the passenger seat and jumped behind the wheel. The tires squealed as he backed down the narrow drive. The digital clock on the dashboard read 11:48. Almost midnight. The perfect time for a monster to molest a little girl.

Lilly sobbed next to him, her arms wrapped around her chest as she rocked back and forward. "Not Becca . . . He won't hurt Becca. It's Rachel." Her sobs intensified. "How could he do it? I loved him so much. Please, Eric. Don't let him hurt her. You don't know what it's like. Please."

He gritted his teeth and shut out the heart-wrenching sounds of her pleas. Over the years he'd driven in a dozen movie car chases, but now it was for real, and as he floored the accelerator, he blotted everything from his mind except the dangerous, twisting canyon road and the little girls whose life would never be the same if their father didn't reach them in time.

30

A funny, bad smell woke Rachel. She couldn't remember what it was and then she knew it was booze like Mommy's parties. She huddled more deeply into the covers and rolled over onto her side. Her long nightgown was twisted around her waist.

The mattress moved and she started to poke Becca and tell her not to be such a wiggly worm, but then she remembered that she was at her Grandpa Guy's house and Becca wasn't in bed with her. She heard music playing and forced her eyes open. A red light glowed from the radio on her bedside table.

The mattress moved again. There was someone sitting on the other side of the bed. She felt scared. Maybe a wild thing had slithered out of the closet and was coming to get her. She wanted to call for her daddy, but she was too scared to make a sound, and then the bed moved again and she twisted around and saw that it was only her Grandpa Guy sitting on the other side.

"I was scared," she said.

He didn't speak. He just looked at her.

She rubbed her eyes. "Did my daddy call on the phone?"

"No."

"You smell bad, Grandpa. Like booze."

"A little good whiskey. It's just a little good whiskey, that's all." His words sounded funny, not like the way he usually talked, but slower, and he was saying each word carefully, like Becca's speech therapist. His hair was messed up, too. Grandpa Guy was always neat, and she was surprised to see him with messy hair.

"I'm thirsty. I want a drink of water."

"Let me . . . Let me rub your back."

"Now!" she insisted. "I'm very thirsty."

He swallowed the rest of the whiskey in his glass, then rose slowly from the side of the bed and left the room.

Wide awake now, Rachel waited until he had disappeared before she pushed back the covers and climbed out. Her bare feet padded across the carpet as she made her way into the hallway. It was long and as dark as a castle's, with a heavy wooden chest, big, ugly vases, and a wooden chair like a throne. Some swords that Grandpa Guy had used in one of his movies hung on the wall, and yellow lights that looked like candles were set into the dark red wallpaper. They glowed dimly, making her shadow huge.

Her tummy felt scared—Grandpa Guy's house was so big and dark—but she moved cautiously down the hallway until she got to her sister's room. She turned the knob carefully and pushed with both hands on the heavy door until it opened far enough for her to slip inside.

Becca was curled up in the middle of the bed making a funny *ptt-ptt-ptt* sound with her mouth like she did when she was sleeping. Sometimes the sound woke Rachel up and she'd give her sister a little kick, but now the familiar *ptt-ptt-ptt* made Rachel feel better. Rachel liked knowing that her sister wasn't scared or crying or something. Being Becca's sister was a big responsibility. Daddy used to tell her that she was sometimes too much of a fussbudget with Becca, but Daddy wasn't around now and Mommy was sort of scared of Becca, so Rachel felt responsible.

Her brow furrowed as she gazed at the bed. Becca was starting to forget Daddy, but Rachel couldn't forget. Mommy said Daddy was too busy to see them, but Rachel thought maybe he didn't want to see them anymore because she did so many bad things. Maybe if she was a goody-goody like Becca he would come get them. Her lips set stubbornly. And when he did come, she was going to hit him hard right in the middle of his heart because he shouldn't have made them stay with Mommy so long.

Becca moaned in her sleep and her mouth moved like she was getting ready to cry. Rachel crept over to the side of the bed and patted her. "Don't be scared, Becca," she whispered. "I'll take care of you."

Her sister quieted. Rachel was turning to leave when she saw a dark figure standing in the doorway. Her legs went all Jell-O, and then she knew she was just being a big scaredy cat because it was only Grandpa Guy.

She crept quietly over to meet him. He stepped back from the doorway to let her out of the room and closed the door. She looked up at him. He held her glass of water in his hand and another glass of booze in the other.

"Go back into your bedroom," he said, still talking in that funny, slow way.

She was getting sleepy again and she followed him. He was walking a little crooked, and he spilled some of her water on the carpet near her bed. When she spilled, she was supposed to clean up her mess, but Grandpa Guy didn't seem to notice.

He pulled back the covers on her bed. She got under them and took the glass from him. Holding it with both hands, she took a sip before she handed it back.

"Is that all you wanted?" He sounded like he might be mad at her.

She nodded.

"All right, then. Lie down and go to sleep." He had started to whisper, and she wondered if he was afraid he might wake Becca, but Becca was far away.

"I'll just rub your back," he said. "I'll rub your back for a little bit."

She didn't like the funny way he was talking, and she didn't like the way he smelled, but she liked getting her back rubbed, and she rolled obediently over onto her stomach and shut her eyes.

Grandpa Guy's hands reached under her nightgown. She lifted her hips so he could push it up far enough to reach her back. He began to rub. His hands felt nice, and she yawned. The music on the radio was soft and pretty. Her eyelids drifted shut. She thought about Max and the wild things in her favorite book. Maybe tomorrow Grandpa would read it to her. Maybe tomorrow . . .

She drifted on her bed like Max in his private boat.

And then something terrible jerked her awake.

The gold and black wrought-iron gates, some of the most elaborate in Bel Air, came into view. Eric jammed on the brakes, and the car fishtailed as it skidded to a stop. The clock on the dashboard read 12:07. It had taken him nineteen minutes to get here. What if he was too late?

He knew Guy didn't have live-in help. Everyone arrived in the morning and left after dinner. At night, Guy slept in the big mausoleum of a house alone. Alone except for two little girls.

Lilly's eyes were glued to the gates. "I forgot about the gates. Oh, God, Eric, they're locked. We can't get inside."

"I'll get in." He jumped from the car, ignoring t[...] his side where Lilly had stabbed him. He could do [...] told himself. Drive fast cars at supersonic speeds, [...] impenetrable barriers, break into locked houses, save the innocents. He'd done it a dozen times. He'd done it with his bare fists and with an Uzi in his arms. He'd done it bleeding from his gut and blind in one eye. But when he'd done it before, it had been make-believe, and this time it was all too real.

He found a toehold in the ironwork. The fence wasn't difficult to climb, but the pain in his side encumbered him. His shirt was blood soaked, and he hoped Lilly hadn't hit anything important when she'd cut him.

The house and grounds were protected with a series of photoelectric eyes. As he reached the top of the gate and threw his leg over the curling grillwork, he hoped he was setting off alarms everywhere—inside the house, at the security agency, right in God's ears. He dropped to the ground and sucked in his breath at the bolt of pain that shot through him. As he ran toward the house, he kept his hand shoved against his side where the blood was wet and slick. He sprinted to the front door and leaned on the bell with one hand while he pounded with the other on the carved panels.

"Open up! Open up, you son of a bitch!" As he slammed his fist against the door, he prayed that his daughters were safely tucked in bed, alone and untouched, but he wasn't enough of an optimist to believe it.

Seconds ticked by, each one lasting forever. Guy didn't appear, and Eric knew he couldn't wait any longer. He ran toward the thick growth of trees at the side of the house then along the east wing. As he reached the gardens at the back, the memory of the first time he had been here passed through his mind, the night Lilly had taken him to the playhouse and the twins had been conceived. The attraction he had once felt for her was so different from the meeting of the souls he experienced with Honey that it seemed to have happened to another person. He pushed away thoughts of Honey. They were an indulgence he couldn't afford.

Over the sound of his breathing, he heard water running in the hexagonal Mediterranean fountain. He ran toward the door that led into the kitchen. With one hand clasped to his side, he lifted his foot and smashed the lock.

The door splintered as he crashed through. For the space of a few seconds the pain in his side numbed him. He steadied himself as he became aware of the persistent beep of the security alarm. And above that beep, he heard a sound that froze his blood. Rachel's shrieks for help.

Rachel had wedged herself into the corner of her mommy's old bedroom. She was wearing only her underpants and she was screaming because the wild thing wasn't a friendly monster anymore but her own Grandpa Guy.

"Stop that screaming!" he yelled as he came toward her. "Stop it!"

The whole house was beeping, but Grandpa Guy didn't seem to hear it. He shoved a chair out of the way as he came nearer. He wasn't talking in that careful way anymore. His words were running together like too much food in his mouth, and he kept bumping into things, and his pants were open. She'd seen what was in there, and it was ugly.

"No!" she screamed. "No! I'm scared!"

She was crying and her nose was running. Everything had been nice at first when he was rubbing her back, but then he'd put his hand in her underpants. She knew about good touches and bad touches, and it woke her up. She had started yelling, but he had done another bad touch, so she had kicked him and jumped out of bed. But now he was coming after her.

"Come here, Rachel!" Grandpa Guy commanded. His teeth showed, and they were big and fierce. "Stop screaming and come here! I'm going to punish you if you don't come here."

He lurched forward and she screamed again. She ducked to run past him, but he caught her.

"No!" she screamed as his fingers dug into her arms. "No! I'm scared!"

"Be quiet!" His breath was stinky as he picked her up,

squeezing her so tightly that he hurt her. "Be quiet! I won't hurt you. Shh. I'm just going to rub you."

"I'll tell!" she screamed, trying to kick him. "I'll tell my daddy you touched me bad!"

"You won't tell." He carried her toward the bed and dropped her there. "If you tell, you won't see your mother again."

She started to sob.

He pulled away the covers that she had grabbed and reached for her underpants.

"No! No, don't do that!" Rachel kicked as hard as she could.

Grandpa Guy gave a grunt as one of her kicks landed. But then he pressed down on her and reached for her underpants again. Her arms and legs were so tired and shaky that she couldn't fight hard, but she didn't stop. She remembered her daddy and Patches and the pirate raids where girls could fight just as good as anybody else. She kicked again and screamed again and said the same words over and over.

"Daddy! Daddy!"

Eric took the front stairs two at a time, hauling himself up by the banister so he could move even faster until his feet barely seemed to be hitting the carpeted treads. His blood was pounding, his heart racing. Rachel's screams were coming from behind a closed door at the end of the hallway, and from the opposite direction he could hear the softer, more muted sound of Becca crying. He threw himself down the hallway and exploded into the room.

Guy was on the bed pressed over his daughter. He lifted his head and looked at Eric through alcohol-deadened eyes. There was nothing handsome about him now. His hair was disheveled, his face slack, every wrinkle visible. The room reeked of liquor.

Eric hurled himself across the room and hauled Guy from his daughter's small body.

"You bastard!"

"No . . ." Guy whimpered.

"I'm going to *kill* you, you son of a bitch!" Eric threw him against the wall, then went after him. Grabbing his shirtfront, he wrenched him up from the floor where he'd fallen and began to punch him. Blood lust roared in his ears and only the crunch of bone could make it stop. He struck again and again, shattering his face. Guy slumped into unconsciousness, but Eric didn't stop. Two innocent children had to be avenged, Rachel and her mother. Guy's head snapped back under the force of Eric's next blow.

"Daddy!"

Gradually the roaring in his ears subsided, and the world around him began to steady. As he came back into himself, he saw the ruin of the man before him. His cheekbone was shattered, and blood streamed from the mouth and nose of a face that would never again be called handsome. He released Guy's shirtfront, and Lilly's father crumpled to the floor.

Eric heard a sob and saw that Rachel was running toward him. With one long stride, he caught her to him and swung her up into his arms.

"Daddy! Daddy!"

She cried out his name and buried her face in his neck. The tiny bumps of her spine pressed against his fingers. His eyes squeezed shut from the strength of the love he felt for her while his heart slammed against his ribs. One of her knees dug into his wounded side, but he barely noticed the pain. He felt the soft fabric of her underpants against his arms and allowed himself to hope that he had arrived in time.

"It's all right, sweetheart," he crooned, gasping for breath. "Everything's all right. Daddy's here. Daddy's right here."

"Grandpa Guy . . . He tried to . . . He wanted to . . . hurt me."

"I know, sweetheart. I know." He kissed her cheeks and tasted the salt of her tears. In the distance he heard the sound of a police siren, but his only concern was the child in his arms.

"He wanted to hurt me," she sobbed.

"Daddy won't ever let him hurt you again."

Becca's crying had grown louder in the other room, and with Rachel still in his arms, he turned to go to her.

"I don't—I don't want . . . " Rachel's words got lost in a sob and her stranglehold on his neck tightened.

He stopped walking and stroked her back. "What, sweetheart? What don't you want?"

Her small ribcage heaved.

"Tell me," he whispered, his lips pressed to her cheek, his eyes full of tears.

"I don't want you . . ."

"What, baby?"

"I don't want you to—" She hiccupped. ". . . to see my underpants."

His heart melted in his chest and he slowly lowered her to the floor. "Of course you don't, sweetheart," he whispered. "Of course you don't."

Still holding her close, he reached for the soft yellow cotton robe with the border of dancing bears that had fallen to the carpet. Gently, he wrapped it around her and gave her back the privacy that was hers by right.

With Rachel clasped tightly in his arms, he carried her from the room and made his way down the hallway to reclaim his other daughter.

31

Honey had just finished making a phone call to one of the food vendors when she heard a banging on the back door of the Bullpen. "Come on in."

The door swung open and Arthur Lockwood entered. Even in the middle of a South Carolina amusement park, he managed to look like a Hollywood agent. Maybe because he always seemed to be waving papers.

"The people who are renting the rides are here," he said, "and you have to sign off on the carousel."

"The carousel wasn't supposed to be delivered until

tomorrow." She took the papers and scrawled her name across the bottom of them.

Arthur shrugged as she handed them back. "I don't work here. I'm just the messenger boy. When you get back to L.A., promise me that you won't tell anybody that I've been running around negotiating with hot dog vendors and Good Humor men. It spoils my image as a shark."

"I promise. And thanks, Arthur."

Arthur had shown up at the park two days ago to go over her contract for the television movie Eric had chosen as her comeback vehicle, the project he had discussed with her last Christmas about the Japanese internment camp. Filming would begin in a month. It was a wonderful script, but the part of the North Dakota farm wife seemed so far beyond her abilities she was glad that she was too exhausted to worry about it.

Arthur could have discussed the details of the contract with her by phone, and the fact that he had decided to put in a personal appearance told her that he hadn't been certain she would sign the contract in the end. But a deal was a deal, and no matter how painful the consequences, she wouldn't welsh.

Incredibly, Arthur hadn't uttered a single word of rebuke about the agreement she had made with Eric. He'd even approved the paperwork that made it official. Apparently the men talked frequently, but Arthur hadn't discussed the details of their conversations with her, and she hadn't asked. She tried to feel relieved that Arthur would be dealing with Eric instead of herself.

She wished she could ask him about Eric directly, but she couldn't seem to find the right words. Three months ago, at the end of January, Lilly had held a widely publicized press conference in which she had revealed the sexual abuse she had suffered as a child. According to reports, both Eric and her mother had been at her side during the press conference. There was no mention of the accusations Lilly had made against Eric, so Honey could only assume that those accusations had been the result of Lilly's own childhood trauma and that Eric had his children back.

She felt the sting of tears and busied herself with the clipboard that held a stack of grimy papers. "I hope Eric doesn't have any more projects lined up for me."

"Uh—we're talking." Arthur grew extremely interested in his Rolex. "It's getting late, and I have a plane to catch."

"Is he— You said he'd been injured."

"I told you, Honey. He's fine. It wasn't serious." He waved the carousel papers and kissed her cheek. "I'll hand these over on my way out. You take care now. Don't wear yourself out with the festivities this weekend."

He frowned at her, and she knew he was unhappy with the way she looked. Once again, she was finding herself unable to sleep. She was always on edge, and only the trips she continued to make to the hospital offered her any pleasure. She alternated between exhaustion and an almost manic aggressiveness that left her feeling as if she were about to jump out of her skin. But only by working hard could she drive away thoughts of Eric.

"I'll be fine." She saw Arthur off and then, after making another phone call, left the Bullpen herself.

She had decided to make an event of the reopening of Black Thunder on Saturday, three days from now. Since she was already deeply in debt, a few thousand more wouldn't make any difference. The county office of family services had given her a list of seventy-five needy families, and she had invited them all to enjoy an afternoon at the park. The event wouldn't be elaborate, but everything would be free: the food, a few rented rides for the younger children, some game booths, and, of course, Black Thunder.

As she walked back to the coaster, every part of her ached with a weariness brought about as much by tension as physical labor. Today was Wednesday. If all went well, Black Thunder would have its first test run that afternoon. That would give them another few days to work out any problems before the families arrived on Saturday for the coaster's official reopening. Two weeks later she would leave for California.

A crew was putting the final touches of paint on the shiny black station house as she approached. Inside under protective plastic sheeting sat the refurbished train with its seven purple and black cars. The electricians had been wiring up the control board, while the engineers and project foreman were engaged in a series of checks and cross-checks. Today the new lift chain would be rotated for the first time by Black Thunder's original flywheel, using power fed through the hundred-horsepower motor. The brake inspection was in progress, and by late afternoon they hoped to send the train out, its cars loaded with sandbags for its first run.

Only a fraction of the work crew remained, and without the shrill whine of power saws and the pounding of hammers, the construction site was abnormally quiet. She stopped next to a pile of scrap waiting to be hauled away and gazed at the enormous piece of artwork that hung over the entrance to the station house.

It was wonderful, even better than the artwork over the old House of Horror. The coaster stretched the length of the painting, rearing and bucking like a wild mustang against a terrifying sky of boiling clouds and runaway lightning bolts. Executed in violent purples, blacks, and stormy grays, the painting had the same uncontrollable energy as the ride. It had arrived from Winston-Salem, North Carolina, in the back of a construction truck. The bottom right hand corner held the signature of the artist—Gordon T. Delaweese. Gordon's talents were just one more thing she had been wrong about.

She remembered her last conversation with Chantal, a nonstop monologue in which her cousin had described all the wonders of the beauty school she was attending to learn how to do hair. Honey wearily rubbed her eyes. How many times had Dash told her that she should stop trying to run other people's lives?

Sandy Compton, the project foreman, came toward her. "Honey, we're about ready to load the cars with sandbags and send out the train."

She felt a combination of anticipation and anxiousness. It was finally going to happen.

"Don't be surprised if the train can't make the entire run

the first time," Sandy said. "Remember that the track's stiff, and we have to make adjustments. We're expecting trouble on the lift hill, and the spiral may give us problems."

She nodded. "I understand."

For the next three hours she watched as Black Thunder slowly came to life. The sandbag-laden train struggled to climb the lift hill. It stopped, then moved, then stopped again until a problem in the motor was corrected. When the train finally cleared the crest and plunged into the first drop, she felt as if she had been lifted off the ground herself. It managed the rest of the course, including the spiral, and by the time it had coasted into the station, everyone was cheering.

Black Thunder was rolling again.

The rest of the week flew by for Honey. The coaster was ready for human occupants by Thursday and the engineers were euphoric after their first test run. Although sections of the track still needed to be smoothed to take out some of the brutality, it was exactly what they wanted—a fast, dangerous ride, barely in control.

Late Thursday afternoon, the foreman approached Honey to tell her they had passed the safety inspection. And then he asked her if she wanted to go out on the next test ride.

She shook her head. "Not quite yet."

She didn't ride it on Friday either. Although she spent the day rushing to get ready for Saturday afternoon's celebration, it wasn't her work load that made her refuse, but the fact that there were too many people around. The board operator who would be running the ride had agreed to come to the park early Saturday morning before anyone else arrived. Only then, when she could be alone, would she take her ride.

She gazed around her. More than half the park was fenced off for safety reasons, but this section had sprung to life before her eyes. The equipment for the food vendors sat in place not far from Black Thunder's station house, and a rented carousel stood where the old one had once run. They had installed an inflated Moonwalk for the smaller children, and a variety of game booths, which were going to be run by members of a local church. But the real attraction was Black Thunder.

The coaster had cost her a million dollars to rebuild. She was broke and in debt, but she didn't regret anything. At dawn tomorrow she would climb into that first car and see if she could touch the eternal that would finally let her make peace with Dash's death.

She saw a little girl, one of the workmen's children, gazing up at the coaster. The child had craned her neck at such a sharp angle that the ends of her straight dark hair brushed the waistband of her jeans. Her expression was so intense with concentration that Honey smiled as she approached her.

"Hi. Are you looking for someone?"

"I'm waiting for my daddy."

The child's hair was held back from her face with a set of barrettes that didn't match. Along with her jeans, she wore a T-shirt appliquéd with a red and yellow satin tugboat, a pair of battered Nikes, and a neon-pink plastic bracelet flecked with silver glitter.

"This roller coaster's really big," she said.

"Yes, it is."

She turned to study Honey. "Is it scary?"

"It's pretty fierce."

"I wouldn't be scared," the child scoffed. "I'm not scared of anything." And then her face fell. "Except that I have nightmares."

"Did you ever ride a roller coaster?" Honey inquired.

"Only baby ones."

"That's too bad."

The child gave an indignant snort. "I was going to ride Space Mountain when we went to Disneyland, but my daddy wouldn't let me 'cause of the nightmares. He was *so* mean. And then he made us leave early just 'cause he said I was crabby."

Honey concealed her amusement. "Were you?"

"I sort of throwed my ice cream cone, but I didn't mean to hit his shirt, and he shouldn't of made us leave."

416

Honey couldn't help but smile, especially since she wasn't the one responsible for raising this cute little hellion. Something about her made Honey remember another little girl who had also plunged dauntlessly into life.

The child regarded her reproachfully. "It wasn't one bit funny."

Honey immediately sobered. "I'm sorry. You're right. It definitely wasn't funny to leave Disneyland early."

"Daddy already said I can't ride Black Thunder. I even cried, but he wouldn't change his mind. He's *really* mean."

No sooner were the words out of her mouth than her face splintered into a wide grin as she caught sight of someone behind Honey's back.

"Daddy!" she shrieked. Arms and legs pumping, she took off.

Honey smiled as she heard an oof of expelled breath. Which one of her workmen had fathered this little stinker? Just as she was about to turn and see, she heard that unforgettable voice.

"Jeeze, it's only been five minutes, Rach. Watch that elbow. And I asked you to wait while I took Becca to the bathroom."

Honey's entire world tilted. Her emotions leaped between a piercing sense of joy and a suffocating fear. She was abruptly conscious of her dirty jeans and untidy hair. What was he doing here? Why hadn't he stayed away so she would be safe from him? Slowly, she turned to confront him.

"Hello, Honey."

The man who stood before her was no one she knew. He was an expensive stranger, an icon with a gilded Oscar on his mantel and the world's power brokers at his feet. The eye patch was gone. The long hair that she remembered so well had been civilized in a two-hundred-dollar haircut that didn't quite reach his collar. His clothes screamed money and European style: a designer shirt instead of soft flannel, loosely fitting slacks in a subtle gray-on-gray windowpane rather than faded jeans. He pulled off his costly sunglasses and slipped them into his shirt pocket. His turquoise movie-star eyes revealed nothing of what he was feeling.

She tried to get the pieces to click together so that she could connect the movie star with the clown, the construction worker, and, most of all, with the man who had let her see his private demons, but she couldn't make the link.

Not until he gazed down at his daughters. At that moment, his false identities faded away and she knew that the man who stood before her was the same one who had laid bare his soul that night four months ago while they sat on top of Black Thunder.

"It looks like you've already met Rachel," he said. "And this is her sister, Becca."

She dropped her eyes to the child whose hand was completely enveloped in his, but before she could say anything, Rachel broke away from his side and ran to her.

"Becca's got Down syndrome," she said in a fierce whisper that was loud enough to be heard by the world. "Don't say anything mean to her. Just 'cause she doesn't look like everybody else doesn't mean she isn't smart."

Honey found her tongue with difficulty. There was no use trying to explain to Rachel that her silence hadn't been caused by her sister's handicap, but by her father.

"Hello, Becca," she managed, her voice shaky. "I'm glad to meet you."

"Hi," Becca said shyly.

Apparently Honey had met Rachel's standard for behavior because she nodded her approval and returned to her father's side.

Honey slipped her fingertips into the pockets of her jeans and addressed Eric for the first time. "I—I thought you were working on a film."

"Just finished up. I decided I couldn't miss the great event." His eyes were expressionless as he looked up at Black Thunder.

"I didn't expect you," she said inanely.

"No, I don't imagine you did." His bad boy's mouth gave that cynical twist he hid behind when he was hurting. "How was your magical mystery ride?"

"I—I haven't taken it yet."

He lifted his eyebrow. "Waiting for a full moon?"

"Don't, Eric."

Rachel's voice interrupted, and her tone was decidedly condemning. "I thought you said Honey was a grown-up. She's *little.*"

"That's enough, Rach."

"I bet I'll be taller than her by the time I'm in third grade. She's a shrimp for a grown-up."

"Rachel . . ." Eric's voice held a note of warning.

"It's all right, Eric." There was something decidedly calculating about Rachel's comments, and through her own distress Honey felt a spark of admiration, not to mention a strange kinship. She knew all about this sort of challenge.

"I may be short, kiddo," she said. "But I'm tough."

"I'm tough, too," Rachel retorted.

"I can see that, but you have a way to go before you'll be as tough as I am." Honey stuck the tips of her fingers in the back pockets of her jeans. "I was running this place when I wasn't much older than you. It's what's inside a person that counts, not what's outside. Nobody who's got any sense *ever* messes with me."

"Oh, Lord," Eric muttered. "I knew this would happen."

Rachel regarded her with the first hint of respect. "Are you strong enough to fight a man?"

"A dozen of them," Honey replied without hesitation.

"I had to fight my Grandpa Guy. He was giving me bad touches."

Honey felt a jolt of outrage as she realized there was more to Lilly's story than had been made public. She concealed her dismay, and the only emotion she permitted herself to display was respect. "I'll bet he was sorry he tangled with you."

Rachel nodded vigorously. "I screamed and yelled real loud, and then Daddy beat him up. Grandpa Guy had to go to a special hospital for—" She looked uncertainly at her father.

"Alcoholics," he said, supplying the word.

"A hospital for alcoholics," Rachel continued. "And me

and Becca don't ever have to be alone with him again. And Daddy said I don't ever have to let anybody see my underpants."

"That's good," Honey replied. "Some things are private, aren't they?"

But Rachel was no longer interested in talking about the past. Her eyes returned to Black Thunder. "I'm not a baby. I don't see why I can't ride the roller coaster, Daddy."

"It's not negotiable," Eric said flatly.

Honey interrupted the argument she could see brewing. "Where are you staying?"

"The hotel in town."

"I don't see why we can't stay here like you did, Daddy." Rachel turned to Honey. "Daddy told us how he helped build Black Thunder, didn't you, Daddy? And he lived right here in the middle of the 'musement park."

"It's not much of a park, Rachel," Honey warned. "If you're expecting Disneyland, you're going to be disappointed. There's just what you see. Black Thunder and a few rented attractions that get sent back on Monday morning."

"I don't care. Why can't we stay in the park where you stayed, Daddy? Becca wants to, don't you, Becca?"

Becca nodded obediently. "Becca wants to stay here."

"Sorry, girls."

Rachel tugged on her father's arm. "If we stay at the hotel everybody'll bother you for autographs just like they did on the airplane. I want to stay here. And so does Becca. And she doesn't wet the bed anymore, Honey, so you don't have to worry."

Becca regarded Honey so sheepishly that she couldn't help but smile. "I wasn't worried at all."

Eric didn't look at Honey. Instead, he kept his eyes on his daughter. "I'm sorry, Rachel, but I don't think it's a good idea."

"Remember last time we stayed at the hotel, and I had a nightmare, and I couldn't stop screaming. That man came and pounded on the door and said he was calling the police."

Honey saw Eric's hesitation, and although she wasn't

privy to the details, she could guess his dilemma. "I don't mind, Eric," she said stiffly. "It's up to you."

"Please, Daddy! Pretty please!"

Eric shrugged. "I guess I don't have much choice, do I?"

Rachel squealed and began to hop up and down. Becca squealed, too, and also started jumping.

"Let's go look around." Rachel snatched Becca's hand and began running toward the rented carousel, which was just visible through the trees.

"Stay in sight," Eric called after them.

"We will," Rachel shouted back.

"They won't," Eric sighed.

He turned back to Honey. "You could have said no."

"And be forced into another shoot-out with your daughter? No, thank you."

He smiled. "She's pretty awful, isn't she?"

"She's wonderful, and you know it."

An awkward silence fell between them. He stuffed his hands into the pockets of his slacks. "I planned to come here alone, but Rachel went into a tailspin when I talked to her about it."

"I imagine she was afraid you wouldn't come back."

His face darkened. "As you may have gathered, Lilly's father attacked her, and she's had terrible nightmares almost every night since."

Honey felt sickened as he filled her in on the details.

"Just getting her to separate from me during the day has been difficult enough. The child psychologist who's working with us doesn't think I should push it, and I agree. Rachel needs to feel safe again."

"Of course she does."

"No child should have to endure what she has," he said bitterly.

Honey wanted to reach out to him, but instead she looked toward the roller coaster. "She's going to give you a hard time tomorrow about riding Black Thunder."

"I know. It's one of the reasons I shouldn't have brought her here, but I was too self-absorbed to think it through."

Why had he come? She was afraid to ask, and he didn't seem ready to volunteer the information.

"I think I need to go on a scouting mission," he said.

She glanced over toward the carousel. Just as he had predicted, the girls had disappeared. "Why are you here, Eric?"

His movie-star eyes caught her up. "I need to get on with my life, Honey. I want to find out if there's any future for the two of us, or if I'm just kidding myself."

His frankness both surprised and dismayed her. She realized the real Eric was something of a stranger to her, and she wasn't certain how to protect herself against him.

"Eric, I—"

Rachel's voice interrupted, calling from the other side of the trees. "Daddy! Come see what we found."

"I have to go. We'll pick you up for dinner at six."

"I don't think that's—"

"Wear something pretty."

She opened her mouth to argue, but he was already walking away.

Honey wore the only dress she had brought with her, a simple jade-green sheath that stopped well short of her knees. She accessorized it with matching opaque stockings and jade-green pumps. A heavy gold Egyptian necklace complemented the plain round neckline. Her only other piece of jewelry was her wedding ring.

"Neat!" Rachel spun in a circle in the middle of the living area of Honey's trailer. "This is so neat, Daddy! Why can't we live in a trailer like this?"

"I'll sell the house tomorrow."

"He's being sar-cat-sick, Becca."

"Sar*cas*tic." He corrected her automatically while his eyes drank in the sight of Honey Jane Moon Coogan. She had bent forward so Becca could touch her necklace, and as he watched his daughter slip her hand into Honey's long hair, he tried not to think about how much he wanted to do the same thing.

"I get to sit next to Honey," Rachel announced as they left the trailer and walked toward the lot where his rental car was parked. "You sit in the front seat with Daddy, Becca."

To his surprise, Becca stamped her foot. "Me want to sit with Honey."

"No, dummy. I saw Honey first."

Honey stepped between the girls and took their hands. "All three of us will sit in the back. We'll let your daddy chauffeur us."

"Great," he muttered, beginning to wish that he'd brought the girls' nanny with him so he could have Honey to himself for a little while.

By the time dessert arrived, he was definitely wishing he'd brought the nanny along. His daughters had completely monopolized Honey's attention. Not that he could have had a lengthy conversation with her anyway. Every time he lifted his fork, someone else appeared at the table asking for his autograph.

Across from him Honey gave a soft whistle of admiration as Becca counted out their four water glasses. "That's terrific, Becca. You sure are a good counter."

Becca had blossomed since Eric had gotten her back. The bed-wetting had stopped, and her language skills had taken a giant leap forward. Normally shy around strangers, she was chattering like a magpie to Honey.

His gaze moved to her sister. Honey and Rachel had had several clashes of will during dinner, but Honey had won every one. He kept expecting Rachel to throw a tantrum in retaliation, but there seemed to be some kind of unspoken understanding between them. Not that he was entirely surprised. In every way except physical appearance, Rachel could have been Honey's child instead of Lilly's. Both these females he loved had crusty, aggressive exteriors and marshmallow interiors. They were affectionate, loyal, and fiercely protective. They also shared an entire truckload of negative traits that he didn't want to think about with pigheaded stubbornness leading the pack.

Across the table, Rachel was unhappy with the fact that

her sister had claimed Honey's attention, so she licked her spoon and stuck it on her nose. Honey ignored her until the spoon dropped off, then she complimented her on her dress.

He shifted his thoughts to Lilly. Just last week, they had talked. She was working with an excellent therapist—the same one who was helping him deal with Rachel's trauma—and she was more at peace than he could remember. To ease the guilt she felt over what she had put them all through, she had given him full custody of their daughters, believing he could help them heal in a way that she couldn't.

After one of her early sessions with the therapist, the two of them had talked.

"I love the girls so much," she had confessed, "but I've realized that the only times I'm really comfortable with them is when you're around to supervise. I wish I could be Auntie Mame."

"What do you mean by that?"

"You know. Fly into town. Shower them with presents. Kiss them like crazy. And then disappear, leaving you with the business of raising them. Do you think I'm horrible?"

He had shaken his head. "I don't think you're horrible at all."

He knew Lilly was coping with the events in her past in the best way she could, and so far the girls had been accepting of their mother's appearances and disappearances in their lives. His disappearances were another matter, however, which was why he'd been forced to bring them to South Carolina.

"Do you ever have nightmares?" Rachel asked Honey.

"Sometimes," Honey replied.

"Scary ones?"

Honey's eyes flickered toward Eric. She quickly looked away. "Pretty scary."

Rachel regarded her thoughtfully. "Are you going to marry my daddy?"

"Enough questions, Rach." Eric signaled for the bill.

As the waiter walked toward them, the knot in his gut confirmed that he didn't want to hear Honey's answer.

32

Honey kissed first Rachel and then Becca on their fore-
heads. "Night, girls."

"Sleep tight," Becca murmured, before snuggling down
into the covers.

"Night, Honey." Rachel blew three loud kisses.

Honey slipped out of the bedroom while Eric said his
good nights. She had been flattered when the girls had
insisted she participate in their bedtime ritual, but now that
it was over, she felt empty and alone. Dash had been wrong
not to let her have a child.

Eric addressed his daughters from the doorway behind
her. "Honey and I are going to take a little walk outside. We
won't go far. The window's open, so I can hear if you call."

"Make sure you come back, Daddy," Rachel said.

"I will, Rach. I promise. I'll always come back." The
emphatic quality of Eric's response indicated that this was a
frequently repeated ritual between the two of them.

Honey didn't want to take a walk with him, but he was
already at her side lightly clasping her elbow and leading her
to the door. It was the first time that he had touched her.

The night was warm and the moon hung so low in the sky
it looked as if it had been stolen from the backdrop of a high
school prom. Eric had left his jacket and tie inside, and his
shirt gleamed blue-white in the light.

"You were great with the girls. Rachel's so demanding
that most adults tend to overlook Becca."

"It was my pleasure. You've done a good job with them,
Eric."

"These past few months have been tough, but I think
we're on more solid ground now. Lilly's given me full
custody."

"That's wonderful, although a lot of men would regard that as more of a burden than a pleasure."

"I love being a father."

"I know you do." Once again she thought of how much she had always wanted to have a family of her own and to create for someone else the childhood she wished she'd had. The desire to be part of a group of people who loved each other had been the driving force behind her life for as long as she could remember, and she was no closer to obtaining it than she had ever been. Only during her marriage to Dash had she known what it was to be part of someone else, and the gift of love he had given her had been so precious that her life had ended when she lost it.

They walked for a few moments in silence until they reached the clearing that bordered the lake. Eric glanced back at the Bullpen. His actor's voice, usually so much under his command, sounded ragged. "Don't take that coaster ride tomorrow, Honey."

The prom-night moon hung behind him, outlining his head and shoulders in silver and making him look larger than life, just as he did on the screen. But this was no movie star who stood before her, only a man. An awful war began inside her—the irresistible urge to slide into his arms battling against the despair that even considering such an act of betrayal produced.

"Eric, I've given up everything to do this. I don't have anything left."

"You have a career waiting for you."

"You know more than anyone how much that frightens me."

"But you made your deal with me anyway," he said bitterly. "You sold your soul to the devil so you could take your magical mystery ride."

I sold my soul to an angel, she thought, but she couldn't risk saying any soft words to him, so she kept silent.

He gave a snort of disgust. "I can't even come close to filling Dash's shadow, can I?"

"It's not a competition. I don't make comparisons like that."

"Lucky for me, because it's not hard to figure out who'd be the loser." He spoke in a voice that held no trace of self-pity; he was merely reciting facts. "Dash will always wear the white hat, with a shiny tin star pinned to his vest. He stands for everything good, everything noble and heroic. But I've always walked too close to the dark side."

"Those are movie parts. They don't have anything to do with real life."

"Who are you trying to convince, Mrs. Coogan? Me or yourself? It comes down to one simple, inescapable fact. You've already had the best man, and you're not going to settle for second best."

"Don't even think that about yourself," she said miserably. "You don't have to take second place to anyone."

"If that's true, why is it so important for you to ride that coaster tomorrow morning?"

She had lost the vocabulary to explain. In the light of his relentless hostility, her belief in the power of a roller coaster ride seemed ridiculous. She had tried and failed to make him understand that she wanted back the faith in God she had lost, the belief that love was a more powerful force in the universe than evil. She could never make him understand her certainty that she could once again find hope in the eternal on that ride, and, in the process, say her good-byes to Dash. In frustration, she spoke words that were damaging instead of healing.

"I have to find him! Just one more time."

His eyes darkened with pain, and his voice was a hoarse murmur. "I can't compete with that."

"You don't understand."

"I understand that I love you and I want to marry you. And I understand that you don't feel the same way about me."

A rush of emotion so intense that it left her weak coursed through her. Eric was a man who had erected a million defenses against the hurts of the world, and all of them had come tumbling down. It made her love him more—this beautiful, tortured man who had been born with too much sensitivity to walk unscathed through the evils he saw around him. Except she wasn't free to love him. Her heart was still shackled by another love, one that she couldn't let go.

She turned her face up to his. "Eric, I'm sorry. Maybe after tomorrow morning I can think about the future, but—"

"No!" he exclaimed. "I'm not going to compete with a ghost any longer. I want something better than that."

"Please, Eric. This doesn't have anything to do with you."

"It has everything to do with me," he said fiercely. "I can't build my life with someone who's looking backwards." He shoved his fists into his pockets. "Bringing the girls here was a terrible mistake. They've had enough instability in their lives. I knew how much they'd like you, and I shouldn't have taken this risk with them. If it were just me, maybe I'd stand around and hold your hand for the next ten or twenty years while you decide whether or not you're going to climb out of the grave. But they've been cheated too many times, and I can't let anyone in their lives who doesn't have something better to give all of us than leftover love."

She wanted to shut out his pain. If only she didn't understand so well what he was feeling. "Don't you realize I want to give you something better than that?" she cried. "Don't you realize how much I want to love you back!"

Again, the bitter twist to his mouth. "Tough job, isn't it?"

"Eric—"

"Don't take that ride tomorrow morning," he said quietly. "Choose me, Honey. This time choose me instead of him."

She saw what it had cost him in pride to ask, and she hated herself for the pain she was giving him. "I'll do anything else you ask me," she said desperately. "Anything but that. It's the one thing I can't give up."

"And it's the only thing I want."

"I need that ride to set me free."

"I don't think you want to be set free. I think you want to hold on to Dash forever."

"He was the center of my life."

The beautiful planes of his face were bleak, bereft of hope.

"When you take your ride tomorrow morning, I hope you have your epiphany—or whatever it is you're expecting to happen—because otherwise you'll have paid an expensive price for nothing."

"Eric, please—"

"I don't want your pity. And I don't want your leftovers. Love has to be freely given, and if I can't have that, I don't want anything." His eyes held a sad dignity. "I'm tired of walking on the dark side, Honey. I want to walk in the light for a while."

He turned away from her. Her skin felt as cold as the grave as he walked back to his children and left her standing alone in the still, silent heart of her dead amusement park.

That night when she couldn't sleep, she pulled on her work clothes and made her way to Black Thunder. Fog had rolled in during the night, and the coaster was an eerie sight. The geometric lacework of the bottom half had an unearthly sulfurous glow from the yellow security lights that hung inside the frame. But the upper half had disappeared into the swirling fog, so that the tops of the great hills looked as if they had been snapped off.

She hesitated for only a moment before she began to climb to the top. Streamers of fog enclosed her, and before long, she could no longer see the ground. She was alone in the universe with the coaster she had given up everything to build.

When she reached the top, she sat on the track and drew up her knees. The night was as silent as death. She let herself drift far above the earth in a world of wood and fog. She found herself remembering the little girl she had been, the child who had once ridden the great wooden roller coaster straight through the valley of death. But she was no longer a child. Now she was a woman, and she couldn't hide the fact that she loved him.

Just Eric. Not the dangerous stranger with the black eye patch, not the pirate clown she had convinced herself it was safe to love, and not the millionaire movie star. His identities had been stripped away. There were none left for him to hide behind. Nothing left behind which she could hide her own feelings about him.

She pressed her cheek against her bent knee, huddling miserably into herself as tears leaked from the corners of her eyelids. He was right. Her love for him wasn't a free and joyous offering, as love should be. Instead, it was shadowed by the past, by the love she couldn't forget, the man she couldn't give up. Eric deserved something better than the leftover love she was offering. But the only way she could hope to free herself from the past was to ride the coaster, and if she did that, she would lose him forever.

Dash, I need your wisdom. I can't go on if I can't put you to rest. Tell me how I do that without betraying everything we meant to each other.

But the barrier of death remained impenetrable, and once again, he refused to speak to her.

She stayed at the top of the lift hill throughout the night. In the inky blackness before dawn, the silence was broken by the shrill screams of a child. The sound was distant—it came from the other side of the park—but that didn't make it any less chilling as over and over again Rachel Dillon screamed out the terror of lost innocence.

The sky was pearly gray, poised at that precise moment just before the full break of morning. Tony Wyatt, the board operator who would be running Black Thunder that day, walked toward Honey through the wet grass. The fog from the night before had lifted, and steam rose from the Styrofoam coffee cup he held. As he nodded, he looked as if he were barely awake.

"Mornin', Miz Coogan."

She stepped down off the bottom rungs of the ladder and greeted him. Her body ached from weariness. She was chilled, and her eyes were scratchy from lack of sleep. "I already walked the track," she said. "Everything looks fine."

"That's good. Heard a weather report driving over. It's going to be a nice day." He headed off to the station house.

Honey stared up at the coaster. If she took her ride, she would lose Eric, but if she didn't take it, she would never be able to come to terms with her past.

"Honey!"

Startled, she spun around and saw Rachel flying through the trees toward her. She was dressed in jeans and a pink sweatshirt that was turned wrong side out. Her hair hadn't been brushed and her expression was fierce with anger.

"I hate him!" she cried, coming to a stop in front of Honey. Her eyes were bright with unshed tears, her mouth trembling, but mulish. "I'm not going home! I'm going to run away! Maybe I'll die and then he'll be sorry."

"Don't say that, Rachel."

"We were supposed to stay for the celebration, but Daddy woke us up this morning and said we're going to the airport. We just got here yesterday! That means I won't get to ride Black Thunder."

Honey tried to blunt her pain at the news that Eric truly was leaving by concentrating on Rachel. "He wasn't going to let you ride it anyway," she reminded her gently.

"I would have made him let me!" Rachel exclaimed. Her eyes slid along the length of the coaster. "I have to ride it, Honey. I just have to."

Honey felt as if Rachel's need were her own. She didn't try to understand the kinship she experienced with this child; she simply accepted it. As she stroked her between her shoulder blades, she felt like crying herself. "I'm sorry, sweetheart. I really am."

Rachel shook off her sympathy. "It's because of you, isn't it? The two of you had a fight."

"Not a fight. It's hard to explain."

"I'm not going! He said he'd give us a special treat to make up for leaving, but I don't want a special treat. I want to ride Black Thunder."

"Rachel, he's your father, and you have to do what he tells you."

"You're damn right she does!" Eric's voice rang out from behind them. "Get over here right now, young lady."

He strode angrily through the trees with Becca in his arms. When he reached the clearing, he set her on the ground and then straightened to glare at his other daughter.

Rachel glared right back, her small body unconsciously

431

arranging itself in imitation of his, legs splayed, arms tense at her sides.

"No!" she shouted. "I'm not going to the airport with you! I don't like you!"

"That's tough. Get over here."

Honey's heart constricted in her chest. She saw by the exhaustion in his face that he had reached his limit. She wanted to plead with him not to leave, but she had no right. Why did he have to be so stubborn? Why did he insist on putting her to the test? But even as she asked herself the questions, she knew he had every right to expect all those things that she wasn't yet able to give.

"Now!" Eric bellowed.

Rachel began to cry, but she didn't move.

Honey took a half step forward, gripped by a sudden and unshakable certainty that Eric was wrong not to let Rachel ride Black Thunder. She forgot that she had no real connection to this child. She felt as if Rachel had come from her own body.

And at that moment, she knew what she had to do.

She grasped Rachel's hand and gazed over at Eric. "She has to ride Black Thunder first."

"The hell she does!"

"Don't stop her, Eric." Her voice dropped to a whisper, pleading. "Let her ride it for me. For herself."

All the angry tension seeped from his body, leaving him looking old and exhausted, a man who had fought one too many battles. "She's too young, Honey. She's only a baby."

Rachel's mouth snapped open to voice an indignant protest, but Honey squeezed her hand in a warning to be silent.

"She has to do this, Eric."

"I don't want her frightened."

"She's already been frightened. Her grandfather took care of that."

Turning her back to him, she knelt in front of Rachel. "I was just your age when I rode Black Thunder for the first time, and I was more frightened than I've ever been in my life. This ride is fierce. It wasn't designed for young children, sweetheart. The first drop is worse than any horror movie. You're so small that you'll come right off the seat, and the tops of your legs will slam against the lap bar. When you hit the spiral, you'll feel as if you're going to be sucked straight down to the bottom of the lake. It's going to scare you to death."

"Not me," Rachel scoffed. "I wouldn't be scared."

Honey gently cupped her cheek. "Yes, you will."

"You rode it."

"My uncle made me."

"Was he bad like my Grandpa Guy?"

"No, not like that. He just didn't like little kids very much."

"Did you cry?"

"I was too scared to cry. The train took me to the top of the lift hill, and when I saw how far it was down, I thought I was going to die."

"Like when Grandpa Guy squished on top of me."

Honey nodded. "Just like that."

"I want to ride," Rachel said stubbornly.

"Are you absolutely sure?"

Rachel nodded, and then her eyes began devouring the coaster with an intensity that Honey understood all too well. Both she and Rachel knew what it was to feel defenseless in the world. They knew that women had to find courage in different places from men. Without looking at Honey or her father, Rachel broke away and ran to the station house.

"Rachel!" Eric rushed forward, but Honey threw herself at him.

"Please, Eric! This is something she has to do."

He looked at her, his eyes defeated, full of pain. "I don't understand any of this."

"I know you don't," she whispered, finally allowing the full force of her love for him to rush over her. "You're big and you're strong, and you see life differently."

"I'm going with her."

"No, Eric. You can't. She has to do this alone." She looked up into his eyes, straight through into his soul, begging him to trust her. "Please."

Finally he nodded, the movement so full of reluctance that she knew what it had cost him and loved him all the more for it. "All right," he said. "All right."

She drew him toward the station house, and they passed beneath Gordon Delaweese's painting. Rachel had climbed into the first car, and her face was animated with a combination of excitement and apprehension. At the same time, she looked incredibly small and defenseless in the empty train.

Honey's hand trembled as she checked to make certain Rachel was secure under the lap bar. "It's not too late to get out."

Rachel shook her head.

Leaning down, Honey kissed her forehead. "When you're done," she whispered, "the nightmares will be gone forever."

Honey wasn't even certain if Rachel had heard. Her small fingers were white as they gripped the bar, and Honey saw that her excitement had been replaced with fear. Which was exactly as it should be.

She stepped back from the train to stand at Eric's side. Tension radiated from him, and she could sense the force of will he was exerting to hold himself back. Rachel was his most precious possession. She knew he didn't understand, and she was humbled at his trust in her.

She turned toward Tony, who was waiting at the control board, oblivious to the drama that was being played out before him. Then she nodded.

She and Eric rushed out from under the roof of the station house in time to watch the train begin its climb up the great lift hill. Behind them, Becca sat cross-legged in the grass watching her sister. Rachel's bright pink sweatshirt made her highly visible at the front of the long train of empty cars.

Ride it for me, sweetheart, she thought. *Set me free, too.*

Eric slipped his hand into hers. His fingers were cold, and she gripped them tightly. She could feel Rachel's terror in her own body as the car ground relentlessly toward the top of the hill. Her heart began to race, and she was perspiring. When Rachel reached the top and saw the drop, she would once again be forced to face her grandfather.

434

The car hung suspended at the apex of the hill, and Honey went rigid with fear, a fear that she knew was her own as much as Rachel's. And then as the train plunged down the drop and swooped into the second hill, she understood it all. She saw that she was Rachel and that Dash was her. That people who loved were always part of each other. She saw that her love for Dash didn't prevent her from loving Eric. Instead, it made it possible.

A joyous sunburst opened inside her. She turned to Eric. His face was tense with concern as his eyes followed the racing pink blur that was his daughter, fearing that she would try to stand, that she would fall out, that the coaster he had helped build would not carry her safely back to him. But Black Thunder did not desert those it sheltered anymore than God did, not even in the darkest of hours.

Honey's own fear had left her, and she understood how simple her love for Eric was. It held no dark corners, no psychological complexities. He was not a father to her. He wasn't her superior or her teacher. He didn't possess a lifetime of experiences of which she knew nothing. Eric was simply Eric. A man who had come into the world with too much feeling. A man who was as vulnerable as she, as needful of love.

She wanted to laugh and sing and enfold him in the universe of her love. He began to run, and she realized the train had cleared the spiral over the lake and was speeding back to the station. She followed him beneath the roof, her heart dancing.

The train screeched into the station. Rachel's face was stark white, her hands frozen around the bar, all her defiance gone.

Eric ran to her, and as the train braked to a stop, he reached out. "Baby . . ."

"Again," Rachel whispered.

"Yes!" Honey shouted out the word. Laughing, she threw herself at Eric. "Oh, yes, my love. Yes!"

The train left the station with Rachel Dillon in its front seat while Eric held Honey in his arms and felt those soft, full lips claiming his own.

At that moment he gave up trying to understand the drama these females he loved were playing out. Maybe women were even more different from men than he had assumed. Maybe they had to find the courage to face life in a different way.

Honey had smeared herself against him almost as if she were trying to inject herself into his body. Her mouth opened under his, and he knew that she was offering him all of her love, her loyalty, all the passion with which she attacked life. This woman who occupied his soul was giving him everything. And at that moment the jealousy he felt toward Dash Coogan slipped away forever.

"I love you!" Honey said against his lips. "Oh, Eric, I love you so much."

He groaned her name and lost himself in her mouth. They kissed while Rachel left her nightmares behind on the hills of Black Thunder.

"I think I've been waiting for you forever," he murmured.

"Do you still want to marry me?" she asked.

"Oh, yes."

"I want a baby."

"Do you? I'm glad."

"Oh, Eric . . . This is right. I finally know this is right."

He couldn't get enough of her mouth. It was sweet and rich, promising him love and abundance. It carried him through space, through time, into a place where only good existed. And as he settled into that miraculous place he heard a rough, weary voice, so deep it could have come from God's belly.

It's about time you took what was yours, pretty boy. I was just about ready to lose patience with you.

Startled, he drew back from her. Her eyes, still drugged from their kiss, opened and she looked at him quizzically. Feeling foolish, he reclaimed that sweet, soft mouth.

The train raced by and, for a few moments, all of them touched eternity.

Epilogue

1993

Honey located Eric and the girls through the glare of lights and the flash of strobes. As the applause finally quieted, she stepped to the Plexiglass podium and gazed down at the gold Emmy that had been placed in her hands.

"Thank you so much." Her voice cracked and the audience laughed. She laughed with them and leaned closer to the microphone.

"If anybody had ever told me that a puny little redneck girl from South Carolina could end up with one of these, I would have told them they'd been out in the sun too long."

More laughter.

"I've got a lot of people to thank, so I hope all of you will be patient with me for a minute." She began her list with Arthur Lockwood and then went on to name the people associated with *Emily,* the Hallmark Hall of Fame presentation on the life of Emily Dickinson that had earned her the award.

The gold lace skirt of her evening gown rustled as it brushed against the podium. "But most of all I have to thank my family. Families are funny things. People who have them don't always appreciate them. But if you've grown up without one, it's sometimes hard to find your place in the world.

"Tonight I want to acknowledge my family. It took me a long time to find them, but now that I have, I'm not letting a single one of them go. My stepdaughters Rachel and Rebecca Dillon, and their beautiful mother Lilly who shares them with me. Zachary Jason Dashwell Dillon who'll be two years old tomorrow and is the cutest toddler in the world. His baby brother Andrew, who's waiting in the greenroom right now for me to stop talking and bring him his next meal."

Everyone laughed.

"Two people I love in Winston-Salem, North Carolina, Chantal and Gordon Delaweese. A person I'm proud to call my friend, although it took us a while to get there— Meredith Coogan Blackman. And Liz Castleberry, the stubbornest lady I ever met in my life."

Liz smiled from her seat directly behind Eric.

"One person I love isn't here tonight, at least not physically." She paused, and a stillness fell over the crowd. "Dash Coogan was the last of America's cowboy heroes, and he was my hero, too. He taught me a lot of things. Sometimes I listened to him, sometimes I didn't. When I didn't, I was usually sorry."

She saw several people in the audience dab at their eyes, but she had made peace with Dash's death that day three years ago when Rachel had ridden Black Thunder, and she didn't feel like crying. Instead, she smiled. "I loved that cowboy, and I'll be grateful to him for the rest of my life."

She cleared her throat. "This last one's hard. Marriage is always a balancing act, and it's never a good idea for one partner to get too big a head, but I'm afraid that's what's going to happen here. People write a lot of things about Eric Dillon's talent, and most of it's true. But nobody writes about the important things. The fact that he's a wonderful father and the best husband a woman could have. The fact that he cares about other people so much that he sometimes scares me. That doesn't mean he's perfect, of course. It's hard living with a man who's prettier than all of your girlfriends put together."

Eric groaned good-naturedly as everyone laughed.

Honey gazed through the lights straight into his heart. "But if it weren't for Eric Dillon, I wouldn't be here tonight. He loved me when I wasn't lovable, and I guess when it comes right down to it, that's pretty much what family is all about. Thank you, sweetheart."

Eric watched from the second row, his chest so filled with love and pride he felt as if he would burst. It amazed him that Honey could thank him when she was the one who had given him everything.

She finished to wild applause and was escorted off into the wings. He knew that she would head first for the greenroom and their two-month-old son. Only after she had gathered up Andrew would she go to the reporters waiting to interview her.

In addition to questioning her about her career, he suspected the press would also ask her about the special camp for abused children the two of them had built on the site of the former Silver Lake Amusement Park. Honey had a theory that Black Thunder might help just a few of the children heal. Although he'd ridden Black Thunder dozens of times over the past three years, he had never found it to be anything more than a thrilling ride. However, when he'd been foolish enough to offer this opinion to Honey and Rachel, they had both been so outraged that he'd vowed to keep his mouth shut in the future.

The ceremony was drawing to a close when an all-too-familiar voice echoed in his head. *You've done all right by her, son. I'm proud of you.*

Eric suppressed a groan. Not now. Ever since Rachel had taken that damned roller-coaster ride . . .

His rational mind knew that he wasn't really hearing Dash Coogan's voice. After all, Honey never heard him, so why should he? But his irrational mind—That was another story entirely.

Rachel leaned across her sister and whispered, "Honey did good, didn't she, Daddy?"

He swallowed a lump in his throat and gazed at both of his daughters. "She did real good, sweetheart. Real good."

Damned right she did, the voice said.

He shifted in his seat, not altogether displeased with the idea that his family just might have a cowboy guardian angel looking out for them.

* * *

Three hours later, after the celebrations and congratulations were behind them, Eric and Honey moved through the bedrooms of their quiet house hand in hand, Honey in her golden gown, shoes kicked off, hair tousled; Eric with his bow tie undone and collar open. They went from one child to the next, straightening the covers, rescuing a teddy bear, removing a thumb from a small mouth. They stepped over toys and books, adjusted night-lights, and removed a leaking squirt gun from beneath a pink-and-lavender pillow.

Only when they were reassured that each child was safe for the night did they go to their own room and turn to each other.

They were finally home.

Author's Note

I am deeply indebted to the following people and organizations:

Tim Cole, who designed Black Thunder and served as my patient and enthusiastic technical adviser.

Randy Geisler and The American Coaster Enthusiasts.

The National Down Syndrome Congress.

My friends and fellow authors, who answered all the questions I couldn't: Joan Johnston, Jayne Ann Krentz, Kathleen Gilles Seidel. And Meryl Sawyer, for help above and beyond the call of duty.

Linda Barlow for her thoughtful critique and unflagging friendship.

Steve Axelrod for his continued wise counsel, and Claire Zion for her insights and support.

The members of my family who give me so much.

And my readers, who continue to enrich my life with their warmth and enthusiasm.

Susan Elizabeth Phillips
c/o Pocket Books
1230 Avenue of the Americas
New York, NY 10020